FRACTURED

BOOK 5 OF THE CAGED SERIES

AMBER LYNN NATUSCH

FRACTURED

Editing by Jennifer Ryan
Design by Jamie Rosen
Layout by Incandescent Phoenix Books

An Amber Lynn Natusch Book

www.amberlynnnatusch.com

ISBN-13: 978-0-9891023-0-8

First Edition: 2013

To my husband, who mends all that is broken, rights all that is wrong, and loves all that is unlovable.

ACKNOWLEDGEMENTS

As always, there are so many people to thank for the completion of this novel. Rather than gushing, I'm just going to list them off in no particular order. They're all pretty awesome; no need to rank them.

A huge thanks to Jennifer Ryan (editor), Jamie Rosen (cover designer), Jen Krom, Kristy Bronner, Eryn Bagley, Virginia Nicholas, Jena Gregoire, Ginny Lurcock, and Kristy Atkinson. My husband and all around amazing guy, Bryan, gets a shout out for doing the work I just can't be bothered to do. Without you, these books would literally never make it to Amazon. And last but not least, Shannon Morton gets a particularly large thank you for being the voice of reason when I can't see anything clearly and call babbling about story lines that aren't making sense and characters that won't behave. You never laugh at me or doubt my ability to get past the hurdle in front of me. I'm not sure I would have made it through this book without you.

PROLOGUE

S ilence...
It surrounded me, permeating the air while it clung
to the trees. I felt hemmed in by it, claustrophobic. The
sun was falling just below the canopy of autumn leaves
far above my head, creating an eerie glow of fiery
crimson and gold. I sat confused as I stared up at the
ceiling of foliage. The trees hadn't started to change,
not that I remembered.

A flash of memory jarred me to my feet: my fear,
Scarlet's passion, Sean's anger, Matty's death. I was
suffocated by it, reliving the moment when Scarlet
shoved me down, down so deep inside myself that I
drowned in the darkness of my soul, tucked away.
Never to be let out. Never to be found again. She told
me this herself, told me I would pay.

I had lived in a state of black suspension from that
moment on. No sense of time or place or existence, lost
in a perpetual tunnel of night. There was no escape.
Scarlet had warned me several times that she wasn't to

be trifled with, that her retribution would be epic. A liar she was not.

So why had she suddenly let me out? Why leave me stranded in the woods, naked, left to the elements, helpless? Because she knew it would bring back the personal hell I'd once lived through, when my parents were murdered and I Changed, my werewolf side emerging. Out of all my nightmares, it was the only one that I had on a recurring basis. She wanted me to live it again.

As if on cue, three darkened figures slowly wound their way towards me, weaving through the trees so fluidly that they nearly lulled me into a trance.

Nearly.

My fight or flight response kicked in when I heard the screams that were ripped from my parents' throats that fateful night echo through my brain. I took off in a flat-out sprint in the opposite direction of their approach. My skin stung as the thick underbrush bit me repeatedly, but the pain motivated me.

I heard the rhythmic cadence of their running getting louder and louder behind me, but I didn't dare look. I recognized the sound. They weren't human. I was.

Knowing that my attempt to escape was futile, I panicked, hoping that Scarlet, angry though she was, would come to my aid as she always had in the past. If not for me, then at least to save herself. She had a reliable sense of self- interest and an undying commitment to staying alive. I screamed at her, both inside and aloud, searching through my mind for her, desperately seeking my other half.

The hit from behind me drove me face first into a fallen tree. The pain was immediate and fierce. As my vision narrowed and darkened, I had a very sobering realization.

Scarlet was gone.

CHAPTER 1

I stared blankly at the intercom in front of me, afraid to ring it. I should have wanted to run straight into my home and resume my life, but I didn't. Instead, I wandered the streets of Portsmouth, New Hampshire aimlessly, soaking in the final few rays of sunlight that dusk was willing to afford me until I found myself standing outside Sean's building. It seemed I couldn't bring myself to ring that buzzer either.

I still wasn't sure how long I'd been gone, and I was even less sure about how warm the reception was going to be from those who were hurt by my absence, especially Sean. He'd nearly died because of me—or at least I *thought* he had nearly died. The jury was still out on his whole invincibility schtick. Cooper would have only been informed about what had really happened if Sean felt it was necessary in order to find me, and that was a big "if" considering he may not have *wanted* to find me at all. That left Cooper completely in the dark as to my disappearance, and I knew how mad that would drive him.

Deep down, I didn't want to believe that Sean would have withheld that information, but I just wasn't certain. I also wasn't convinced that Sean didn't want to find me; it was what he'd do to me when he did that had me worried. My gut said he wouldn't harm me, but my gut had been proven wrong before. I hoped I wasn't having a relapse of that behavior.

With a sigh, I focused my attention back on the buzzer beside the front entrance to the building. In my mind, I repeated the phrase *just lift your finger and press it* over and over again. But I couldn't. I wasn't ready for whatever dramatic scene that was sure to follow.

Instead, I walked away as the darkness of night began to settle in, and cut back through town to my place. All I wanted to do was slink into my apartment unannounced, crawl into my bed, and sleep for days, without having to explain myself to anyone. Not that I could, even if I had wanted to.

After a chilly walk home in the crisp fall air, I arrived home and reached my arm out for the door handle. I knew it would be locked, but I just had to check. Much to my surprise and extreme delight, it wasn't locked at all. Cooper had apparently picked up the same absentminded habit that I'd had of forgetting to lock the door once it closed. Or maybe he'd just left it open in the hope that I'd wander into the apartment one day. Either way, I was going to find out.

I crept up the stairs slowly, trying to detect whether he was home. I saw no lights from the street, but that didn't tell me a whole lot since only my bedroom faced out onto the road. If my door was closed, no light from the rest of the house would be seen. Once I reached the landing, I put my ear to the door, looking down at the floor. Still no light, and definitely no sound.

Anxiously, I tried the knob, which too was unlocked. I froze for a moment, wondering if something was wrong. It was such a knee-jerk reflex to assume the worst, though my history warranted that behavior. With a deep, cleansing breath, I quickly talked myself down off of that ledge, reminding myself that all known threats had been eliminated before Scarlet had run off. Feeling more at ease about any pressing danger, I pushed the door open into a darkened living room and made my way quietly to the kitchen.

The fridge was full of leftovers; Cooper had clearly been home. He always cooked as if he was feeding twelve, but he usually ate two-thirds of it himself. I grabbed a bowl of noodles covered in sauce and started to inhale it, shoving fistfuls at a time into my mouth with my bare—and questionably clean—hands. It wasn't until I saw the contents of the fridge that I'd realized how hungry I actually was.

When did I eat last? Was she trying to starve me to death?

I stood up, closing the door as I stepped back out of the way. When I turned around, I slammed into a very muscled and extremely tense Cooper. The container of noodles crashed to the floor.

My eyes slowly worked their way up to meet his. His hands were balled into fists at his sides. His chest pumped, rising and falling at breakneck speed. His eyes glowed a dangerous yellow. He was close to Changing, his wolf trying to take over. My tears welled and spilled over, but I made no attempt to wipe them away. I kept my gaze fixed on his.

"Cooper, I—"

"Three weeks," he growled, eyes still blazing.

"What?" I blurted involuntarily, totally confused.

"You've been gone for three weeks and you just waltz in here like everything is normal?" He inched towards me and I backed away from his anger.

"Three weeks!" I exclaimed. "How is that possible?"

"I searched night and day for you," he continued, completely ignoring me. "I didn't sleep. I found your car, your phone, your clothes..."

"I'm sorry, Coop—"

"But not you," he said, sounding suddenly mournful. "Never you."

I reached forward to touch him, but dropped my hand immediately. His rage was palpable, and I didn't want to stoke that fire any further.

"I didn't know," I protested softly. "I *still* don't know what happened."

"That makes two of us then, doesn't it?" he snarled. "Sean wasn't very forthcoming about what had occurred that night when he showed up here, encrusted in dried blood, and dragged me back to his place. All I pieced together was that you were gone and he was livid. I've been looking for you ever since."

I dropped my eyes to the floor. Sean hadn't told him about the attack or Scarlet's involvement in it. It seemed cruel, even for Sean, to leave Cooper so far out of the loop.

I racked my brain for anything I could possibly say to smooth things over a bit with Cooper. Had it been up to me, I never would have left without filling him in, but it hadn't been my choice. Scarlet did what she did against my will, leaving me with a mess to clean up. I hated knowing how distraught I had made Cooper with my disappearance. Nothing felt right when he was angry with me.

And he was pissed.

Just as I opened my mouth to offer some placating remark, he snatched me into his arms and hugged me violently. A rush of emotions emanated from him, relief being the primary—anger and love were right behind. As happy as I was to know that my empath abilities from childhood still remained intact even though Scarlet was missing, I would have preferred a much more pleasant way to test the waters.

As quickly as he'd taken me in, he let me loose, turning on his heels to walk away and grab his phone off the kitchen island. He rounded the corner to the hall, dialing as he went. Once my head stopped spinning and my vision sorted itself out, I followed behind, mute, still unable to formulate a defense of any kind. I didn't think claiming head trauma was going to help my case for very long.

"She's back," he said gruffly. "Nope. About ten minutes ago." He paused for a moment. I tried to hear the words that were being shouted at Cooper, but I couldn't make them out. The owner of the voice, however, I could.

"She says she has no clue...well, I think it's very interesting too," he said, drumming his fingers along the wall, his back still to me. "She's skin and bones, but she doesn't look injured, if that's what you mean. She's right here if you want to—"

He pulled the phone from his ear and hung up. The line had gone dead before he'd even finished his sentence. A knot immediately formed in my stomach, twisting tighter and tighter with every passing second.

"Sean doesn't want to talk to me, does he?" I asked sheepishly. Cooper turned to face me slowly.

"No, he doesn't," he said with a pause. "And I'm not entirely sure that I'm ready to either."

He at least had the decency to look remotely pained while sharing his sentiment, his eyes returning to their human, hazel color. A moment later, the door to his room slammed shut, announcing the official end to my homecoming. I hadn't thought that much about how I'd be received upon my arrival, but I would never have guessed that hostility and the cold shoulder would be the options of choice.

Embarrassed, I schlepped my way to my room and quietly closed the door. I turned on the small lamp just inside, shying away from brightness it emanated; my eyes were having a hard time adapting to the light. Three weeks of virtual darkness seemed to have real-life lasting effects.

I made my way over to the bay window that faced the downtown streets of Portsmouth and looked out over them. Since it also faced the apartment of the one I wanted to talk to most, I quickly located the grand windows on the top floor of Sean's building. It was only two streets over from mine, and though dimly lit, there was just enough light to outline a figure hovering. A figure that immediately turned and walked away. Darkness fell on his apartment only moments after. He had refused to speak to me only moments earlier. I guess he didn't want to see me either.

My stomach lurched at his actions, but I couldn't analyze the situation any further. I was thoroughly exhausted, and all I wanted to do was climb into my bed and sleep until the sun woke me. Stripping off the clothes given to me by my rescuers, I threw them in the trash. I scanned the floor for something to wear to bed, but found nothing. Someone had tidied my room in my absence, preparing it for my return. Too tired to rifle through my drawers, I threw back the covers on my bed before I plopped my naked, weary body onto it and wrapped the duvet up tight around me. I liked the feeling it gave me—warm and secure. I hadn't felt that way for a while.

I plummeted into a deep sleep instantly, but regretted it almost as quickly. An auditory montage of screams plagued my dreams. I saw nothing, but felt everything. The horror enveloped me, coming to a crashing crescendo of fear and pain that I could not escape.

When I finally broke free, I shot up out of bed, only to be greeted with more darkness. Frightened beyond measure, I launched myself to the wall switch, squinting tightly when the deluge of light assaulted my still-sensitive eyes. My breath came shaky and rapid while sweat poured down my face and back. I ran to my closet, pulled out a white robe and threw it on, fastening it snugly around me before heading out of the room.

I tiptoed up to Cooper's door, leaning my ear against it as soundlessly as I could. He'd told me once that I had the grace of an elephant, and he could hear me coming from miles away. I didn't want to wake him. What I did selfishly want was the feeling of safety he could offer in times of distress. Just being close to him helped, and that was exactly what I needed.

The door was shut tightly, so I carefully turned the knob, creating as little sound as possible, and pushed slowly inward. Cooper's back was to me, lit only by the moonlight penetrating the gap in the curtains. I really needed to get him some that fit the window better. He never stirred, so I continued my way in, stopping at the edge of the bed. I eased my way on as gingerly as I could, thankful that foam mattresses didn't transfer much motion.

Once on top of the comforter, I inelegantly scooted my way backward towards him an inch at a time. He'd have laughed if he'd been watching me; I'm sure I looked utterly ridiculous. Stopping just before I made contact with him, I balled myself up into the fetal position and tried to go back to sleep.

"Did you get lost on your way to the bathroom?" Cooper asked over his shoulder. His tone was cold, but his humor was back.

"Sorry," I said, sitting up. "I'll go. I just—" I cut my explanation off at the start. He didn't want to hear my excuses. In fact, he'd been pretty clear that he didn't want to hear anything from me. Not for a while.

I moved to push off of the bed when his hand caught my wrist, turning me to face him as he rolled towards me. We shared a long moment eyeing each other in that lone sliver of light that shone across his bed.

"You 'just' what?" he asked, his voice noticeably softer.

"I can't sleep. The sounds in my head...," I said, trailing off.

"Sounds of what, Ruby? What happened when you were gone?"

I wanted to offer him something concrete, something to help end the agony he'd clearly felt during my absence, but there was nothing to give. Whatever horrors Scarlet had inflicted on the world while she'd held me hostage were unknown. All I had were occasional soundbites and audio snippets, none of which were encouraging.

"I don't know, Coop. Honest," I said, tears again rolling off my face. "All I know is that two days ago I was sitting in the woods, naked, freezing, and scared shitless. It was like—" I choked on the words that I couldn't bring myself to say. Cooper, seeing my distress, finished them for me.

"When your parents were killed?" he said softly, wiping the tears from my face.

"Yes," I whispered.

"And you don't remember *anything* before that?"

"*No.*"

His face scrunched up in confused frustration.

"What happened with Sean? Why did you leave in the first place?"

"She tried to kill him," I said quietly, staring at my hands resting in my lap. "Scarlet nearly let Matty stab him to death. He tried to get her to kill Sean, which she, of course, didn't do in the end. She killed Matty instead. The pain she felt...Cooper...it was unbearable," I whispered. "Angry...she was so, so angry. She told Sean he would pay and ran off. Right before her escape, she shut me out. After that, I didn't see a thing."

He stared at me in utter disbelief. I couldn't blame him; it was a lot to take in.

"I thought Sean was...? How did Scarlet...? Wait...how did you get back?" he stammered, barely able to finish his thoughts. I hesitated, not knowing what exactly to say to any of his questions. I really only knew the answer to one.

Sensing my anxiety, he pulled me down to lie next to him, and I nestled in close, still resting on top of the bedding. He wrapped his long, muscular arms around me, tucking me into the crook of his neck. My apprehension left me instantly. That was the

12

homecoming I had wanted.

"Do you not want to talk about this tonight?" he asked, stroking my hair slowly.

"It's just that I don't have the answers, Coop. I can tell you a bit about the men who found me, but that's it."

"Then start there."

"Like I said before, Scarlet left me deep in the woods. When I came to, I saw them through the trees, walking towards me. It was like they knew I'd come to my senses, like they'd been following me for a while, waiting for me to snap out of it. Of course, I panicked and took off running, but as soon as I heard them behind me, I knew what they were."

"Werewolves...," Cooper said, his grip on me tightening ever so slightly. I wondered if he noticed.

"Exactly. One of them tackled me from behind. I cracked my head on a log and knocked myself out. I woke up a day later. They'd brought me back to the cabin where they lived. They patched me up, treating what they could, and then they helped me get home," I said, hedging slightly. "To my *mate*."

"Your mate? But—"

"I don't know what they sensed, Coop, but that's what they said. They treated me with the utmost respect. They never laid an unwanted finger on me the whole time I was around them—barring the tackling incident, of course," I explained. "There was something about the way they said mate...it made me wonder if I might have been in trouble if they hadn't sensed what they did."

"You might have," Cooper growled. "And who exactly were these wolves?"

"I don't know. They must have mentioned their

13

names, but I don't remember."

"You don't remember?"

"Hello, I had a head injury. Wasn't thinking clearly."

"You're a walking head injury," he mocked, giving me a playful nudge in an effort to calm his growing rage. "So do you know *where* you were?"

"Somewhere up in Maine, they said. Near the Canadian border. They said they had been trying to track me for a while, but they couldn't catch me. As far as they knew, I had only been in northern Maine for a few days. They never saw me before that."

"So Scarlet was on the move?"

"I guess."

"That would explain why it was so hard to find you."

"I'm sorry, Coop. I know you tried. If I could have stopped her—"

"Make me a deal, okay?" he asked. "No more apologizing tonight. I think it actually makes me angrier."

"Fine. Consider it retracted then," I said, yawning. "I'm going to try and sleep now."

"Okay, Rubes, but I gotta say that something isn't adding up with all of this," he said, adjusting his arm under my head. "I mean...where's Scarlet? She didn't come out when you were in the woods; she didn't come out when I was ready to attack you. She *lives* for moments like that. Why didn't she come out to help you?"

"Because she's gone, Cooper," I whispered in reply.

"Gone?" he asked, his disbelief apparent.

"Yep. Gone, as in left the building."

"But *you're* the building. She's part of *you*."

"Exactly."

"I'm not trying to be thick here, Ruby, but I don't get it."

"I don't either, Coop, but my guess is that whatever darkened space she shoved me down into is exactly where she's gone. I don't hear her. I can't feel her. And no amount of fear or anxiety even coaxes her," I informed him. "Something went wrong, Cooper. Really, really wrong."

"You need to tell—"

"Don't say it. *Please* don't say it," I said, propping myself up on my arms. "It's pretty plain that he wants nothing to do with me, and I certainly can't blame him for that. Telling him won't change anything. Not right now, anyway." I lay back down, cutting off the conversation before my true emotions spilled out. Sean's dismissal had been a knife through my heart.

Cooper kissed me on my forehead and pulled me in closer.

"If that's what you want. I'll leave it alone for now."

I said nothing, but snuggled into him tightly. I was done talking about things I couldn't understand. Couldn't change. Couldn't fix. I wanted to press into the comfort that Cooper provided and dream the pleasant dreams that always came when I was in his net of safety.

Cooper was *home*.

And I was glad to be there.

CHAPTER 2

"I know you're exhausted, Rubes, but you need to call Peyta," Cooper said as he expertly scrambled eggs. "I can't even begin to describe the stress she's been feeling. First the whole thing with her dad, then you..." He paused mid-stir, staring at the pan in his hand.

"Why do I feel like there's something else you're leaving off that list?" I asked while gingerly sipping my orange juice. After scarfing down the noodles the night before, I felt terrible—my stomach wasn't adjusting well to food.

He sighed heavily before turning to look at me.

"It's Jay."

My heart instantly sank. My attention was immediately brought back to the screams I'd heard coming from the hallway outside Sean's apartment the night that Scarlet took over. Jay had been out there, guarding the door.

"Nooo...," I whispered, eyes searching Cooper's

for any shred of evidence that what I feared wasn't true. All I found in his expression was pain.

"It was bad, Ruby," he said soberly.

I couldn't listen. I sprang from my seat and headed straight for my room. I needed to find my keys.

"Ruby!" Cooper called to me as he pursued me to my room. "Would you wait a second?"

He caught my arm and whirled me around to face him.

"This is my fault," I said, sniffling softly.

"It's not what you think, Rubes. He's not dead," he said, still gripping my arm. "Sean got to him just in time, apparently, and then took him to Peyta. From what I've managed to surmise, Sean was in pretty rough shape himself when they arrived at Ronnie's."

"Peyta healed them," I muttered under my breath.

I felt sick. I fell to my knees, and what little food I'd been able to keep down came up violently all over the hardwood floor. I knew what it was like to look down at someone you loved and watch while their life slipped away. Luckily for Jay, Peyta wasn't a helpless bystander in that situation.

"You need to sit down," Cooper ordered, placing me on the edge of my bed. "I'll take care of this." While he walked out of my room to find whatever materials were necessary to clean up the mess I'd made, I wondered if there were enough in existence to address the metaphorical one I was in.

I looked up to see my phone taunting me from my nightstand. "Go ahead...call her," it seemed to say. "One call will fix everything." Then it laughed at me— an evil, all-knowing laugh.

"Fuck you," I muttered, staring it down.

"Fuck *me*?" Cooper thundered. I hadn't even

realized he'd returned. "Is that the thanks I get for cleaning up your breakfast?"

"I'm sorry, Coop," I said, hedging slightly. "I wasn't talking to you..."

Before I could process why, he shot up quickly, grabbing my shoulders to pull me closer to his face. He glared deep into my eyes, searching them for something.

"*Scarlet?*" he growled. "You and I need to chat."

Suddenly, his actions made sense. It had been a while since Scarlet and I had had one of our little back and forth banters. I didn't realize when I answered him what my outburst would imply.

"No, Cooper. It's not her," I said softly, trying to calm him. His hazel eyes started to glow with a hint of gold. He was pissed off. Big time. "The phone...I was talking to the *phone*."

A look of concern quickly bled through the anger in his expression. It was apparent that he was unsure of how mentally sound I was in that moment. In fairness, I had been talking to an inanimate object.

"I don't know how I can face Peyta, Coop," I explained as I tried to coax him into sitting next to me. "How do you say sorry for being a party to the near death of the man she loves?"

"Ruby," he said, the warmth returning to his eyes, "she loves *you*, too. She's never given me even the slightest indication that she blames you for any of this. She's missed you." He finally came to sit next to me, taking my hand in his. "She's *mourned* you."

"But I'm not dead," I whispered.

"I know. In truth, I don't think she ever believed you were," he said, tucking a stray piece of hair behind my ear. "You would have been so proud of her, Ruby.

She was so brave. When she learned that you had disappeared that night, she called me right away. She asked what we needed to do to find you. She has been the driving force behind the store, keeping it going. All she talked about was how we needed to have it running smoothly so you wouldn't have to worry about anything when you got back."

I felt a tear escape my eye, rolling slowly down my cheek while he continued.

"She eventually went on as though you were just out of town, about to return at any time. That's when I started to worry about her—we all did." His face grew hard, trying to mask the pain he felt, but it didn't matter; I felt every ounce of it. "She tried so hard to keep up the act, but when she thought she was alone, her true emotions came through—she was in a dark place inside. She didn't think you were coming back, Ruby...she just needed to *believe* you were."

"I don't know what to say to her, Cooper. How do I explain something that I don't understand myself?"

"You think your return needs any explanation?" he asked, looking utterly perplexed. "Ruby, all that kid wants to do is wrap her arms around you and squeeze until they go numb and somebody has to pry her off of you."

I wanted desperately to believe him, but so often I found myself on the wrong side of expectations. If that trend proved true in the Peyta situation, I needed to be mentally prepared for it.

"What day is it?" I asked, mulling something over in my mind.

"It's Sunday. Why?"

"Will you come with me?" I asked, giving his hand a squeeze. "To Ronnie's...will you go?"

He squeezed my hand in return.

"Go get cleaned up. I'll address your regurgitated breakfast while you do. We can leave as soon as you're ready."

"Thanks, Cooper," I replied, wanting to say more than I could bring myself to. We had so easily fallen back into our friendship, and I wanted to acknowledge it, but I knew my sentiments would somehow botch the moment.

I hoped that Peyta and I would be able to mend just as quickly.

*   *   *

The drive proved unbearably long, yet painfully short. Cooper guided the car along the familiar route while I fretted away in the passenger seat. As much as I was dying to see Peyta, a small part of me was terrified by the potential complications of the encounter and wanted to avoid them at all costs. I knew Cooper was speaking to me, trying to calm me, but I heard nothing. The voices of doubt in my mind drowned out all other sound.

When we turned into Ronnie's driveway, I felt as though someone was sitting on my chest. The pressure was intense, nearly piercing my heart.

"Did you call before we left?" Cooper asked, parking in front of the garage.

"No," I whispered. "I thought it wouldn't matter. Besides...I didn't know what to say."

"Well, I guess it's a moot point now. Let's get this over with, shall we?" He popped open his door and got out of the car. I stayed where I was.

He paused partway up the path to the house,

looking back to see if I was coming. He sighed heavily when he realized I wasn't following.

"Ruby," he called, making his way back to the car. "You need to get out and—"

The front door opened abruptly, snapping our collective attention back to the house. Out stepped Peyta with an expression I'd never seen her wear—disbelief. Not once, in all that she'd been through, had I seen 'does not compute' register on her face. That day, I did.

I sprang from the car with an immediate need to hold her, but by the time I made my way to Cooper, she wore a very different face entirely. I didn't like it one bit. I'd seen that face too many times to count, but never on her. Stoic indifference looked all sorts of wrong on her, but she wore it like a veteran—her mother's daughter for sure.

"Peyta?" I called to her as Cooper grabbed my arm. I tried to pull away from him, but he held me firmly where I was. He felt what I couldn't feel because of my own fear—*anger*.

"When did you get back?" she asked. Her voice was eerily controlled. That's when I first felt the hostility rolling off of her in waves so large I thought they would have washed me away if Cooper hadn't held me steady.

"Yesterday," Cooper offered.

"How did you get back?" she asked, folding her arms.

"P," I started, trying yet again to move toward her. Cooper's hold was unyielding.

"Why didn't you call?"

"There was so much to sort out when I got back," I said, hesitating. She was right; I should have called. A friend would have called—so would a sister.

"I see," she replied, her voice colder than ice.

"You're angry," I said, trying to placate her.

"I would have called," she said quietly.

"I'm sorry, Peyta. I really am," I pleaded. "Please let me explain."

"I don't need an explanation," she said, turning back to the door. "I'm glad you're back."

She walked inside and closed the door, leaving Cooper and me dumbfounded in the driveway.

"What just happened?" I asked him, looking up for a sign in his expression. I found none.

"I have no idea."

"I can't leave it like this, Coop," I said, feeling helpless.

"Then fix it," he replied without any words of wisdom. "You're the only one who can."

I thought about the girl I knew—the happy, loving sprite, whose powers of sarcasm rivaled my own. I thought about what she meant to me and I to her. Then I thought about how I would have felt if she'd left without a trace, without any reasonable explanation. How would I have dealt with her absence? How exhausting would it have been to keep up a façade of optimism while inside I felt part of my soul eroding slowly?

Peyta had an uncanny ability to make sense out of the insensible because her view of life was black and white. Shades of gray didn't matter to her at all. When she had learned what Cooper and I were, she accepted it without a second thought because she knew us and loved us. That was what mattered to her; what we were did not. So why did the 'why' matter so much to her in that moment? I was home and that was what she wanted. The details were just shades of gray—or were they? Something was holding her back, and until I figured out the why behind it, nothing would be right between us. I needed an epiphany in the worst way.

Instead, I got Ronnie.

"She took your disappearance really hard, Ruby. You can't expect her to shed that armor at the drop of a hat, can you?" she asked, making her way to the edge of the porch. "I've never seen her this bad before, though. She won't talk to any of us about it."

Her face looked more grim than ever, which spoke volumes given Ronnie's history. She was worried about Peyta too.

"What should I do?" I asked, walking up the path toward her. Cooper stayed behind, which was fine with me. I needed to solve the problem without exploiting his relationship with Peyta.

"Explain why you did it."

"She said she didn't want to hear it," I lamented.

"And you believe her?"

"I don't know what to believe anymore, Ronnie," I sighed. "I feel like everything has flipped on its ass since I've been back. Nothing is the same. Nothing *feels* right."

"That's because it isn't. You of all people should know what it feels like to lose someone. It changes you. She didn't just lose *you*," she started, choking ever so slightly on her words. "She lost her father too. Her world has slowly been crumbling around her, Ruby. Her uncomplicated view on life has become significantly complicated."

"I can't fix that," I whispered, coming to stand before Ronnie at the base of the steps.

"No. You can't," she said softly. "But you can

23

teach her how to survive it better than anyone else I know."

I stood motionless, stunned by her words. Of all the things I expected to get from Ronnie when I returned, a nod of approval was not one of them. Once I collected myself, I started up the narrow stairs, trying not to get too close to her as I passed. She caught my arm when I stood beside her, halting my ascent up the final step.

"It's good to have you back," she said, staring away from me, across the street. Her words were soft and gentle as was her hold on my arm. However, her expression when she turned to me was not. "Don't ever pull a stunt like that again."

Always black and white.

CHAPTER 3

Swallowing hard, I pushed my way through the front door and quickly made my way upstairs to her bedroom. I knew she'd be there; it was her sanctuary.

Just tell her the truth. It's all you have to do...

I knocked lightly on the door, knowing that she wasn't going to answer me, so I turned the knob before she could object.

"Peyta," I called softly. "I've got to get this out..."

I quickly found myself standing alone in her room, talking to nothing but the TV that was still on. Knowing she was in the house, I started to storm the upstairs, throwing open doors in search of her. I wasn't certain as to why a feeling of distress took me over, but I just knew something was wrong. The more I focused on it, the more panicked I felt. Frustration, helplessness, and shame overtook me, inexplicably forcing me to understand her reaction to my homecoming.

Control... must get control.

I thought and felt those sentiments as if they were my own, and that's when I knew where I would find her. The bathroom door remained closed at the far end of the hall, and I charged it like a bull seeing red. I crashed through it with a thunderous sound, busting the door wide open to a scene that disturbed me more than any I'd ever seen before.

Peyta sat pantless on the edge of the tub, her back toward me, completely unfazed by my entrance. I watched as she drew her arm back fluidly, her hand gliding along the inside of her thigh. Only once that pass was complete did I see the razor she held delicately in her hand.

"No," I gasped, lunging for the silver blade before she could do any further damage. She didn't even fight me when I ripped it from her hand. One look at her face and I knew I why—her trance-like state nearly made my heart stop cold.

"It should hurt, shouldn't it?" she asked, staring eerily at the tile in front of her. The white tub below her bled slowly to pink. "But the deeper I cut, the better I feel."

"Why?" I asked, using the last ounce of breath my lungs possessed to force the word out.

She turned her face towards me so slowly that it was an almost inhuman action—unnatural.

"I was sinking," she said as I stared into dull, empty eyes. "This kept me from drowning."

"Peyta," I whispered, crushing her in my arms before the guilt could overtake me. "I never left you. I would never leave you...I need you to understand that. Do you understand that?"

"You all left," she said matter of factly. "But it's okay. This makes it okay."

"This," I said, indicating her bloodstained and scarred thighs, "is *not* okay. Peyta...this isn't like you. What's going on in your head right now? Please tell me. I'm begging you. You're *scaring* me."

"I told you—I was sinking. This made me feel like I had some control over things," she explained. Her focus came back slowly, removing the frightening appearance of someone who'd been temporarily possessed. "There's just so much...so much I can't control," she continued, grabbing a towel from the bar beside her and pressing it to her leg. "First my father, then Jay, then you. It was too much. Don't you ever feel like it's too much?" she asked in a tone far too casual for the discussion at hand. "I felt like my body was going to explode, like every cell in it was fighting with the one next to it. I didn't know how to let that emotion out. Everyone expects so much from me. I couldn't very well fall apart, could I?"

I said nothing, only stared in disbelief at her words. How could someone answer a question so riddled with disturbing subtext?

"Everyone needed me to be strong," she said, the faintest of smiles painting her face. "And I was. I was there for everyone. My mom, Cooper..."

"But why was nobody there for you, P?" I asked, taking the towel from her hand so I could investigate the damage. "Why couldn't you lean on anyone?"

"That's not my role, Ruby." She said it as though that fact was painfully obvious. It wasn't to me. "People have always expected a certain level of maturity from me, and this situation was no different. In fact, it called for me to be the best I'd ever been."

"What changed, Peyta? At what point did this all go so wrong?" I asked, begging for any shred of light she could shed on when things got so bad that she had resorted to mutilating herself. "Is this the first time you've done this?"

Judging by the faded silvery-white lines on her other thigh, it wasn't.

She saw where my eyes were locked and tried weakly to obscure my view of them, but the damage was done—I knew. It was the first time that night that the shame of her actions seeped through to the surface.

"I don't do it often," she defended, wrapping the towel around her waist. "Maybe a handful of times total."

"Does your mother know?" I asked, shuddering at the thought of having to tell her.

"NO!" she screamed, grabbing my wrists so tightly that my hands started to turn purple. "You can't tell her either."

"Peyta," I sighed, sitting down beside her. "You can't keep this from her. She's worried about you. She knows something is wrong."

"It's fine, Ruby," she snapped, moving away from me. Her anger had returned, and I knew that wasn't a good sign. I needed to find a way to dissipate some of her emotion so she wouldn't find herself in the tub, only hours later, dancing with a blade again.

"You want to get mad?" I asked, my voice rising slightly. "Fine! Get mad at me. Take everything out on me. I deserve it. I left you, remember? Make *me* hurt."

"I'm not mad at you," she said, forcing a composed front.

"Bullshit!" I yelled before leaning in closer to her. "You may think you're fooling everyone, but you're not. Especially not me. You're *furious* at me for leaving—for what happened to Jay—because you know that *is* my

28

fault too, right? I'm the reason Matty attacked him. Hell, I'm practically the reason your father was killed too. Why don't you take that out on me? Go ahead, Peyta," I challenged, still up in her face. "Take that out on me."

"Why are you doing this?" she asked, her bottom lip quivering slightly.

"Because I want you to channel your fucking emotions at someone other than yourself," I prodded, desperately wanting her to let something out—*anything*. "You want to cut someone? Why not cut me? Why don't you inflict some pain on a deserving party for once?"

"But you don't deserve it," she started, stepping away from me. She looked frightened.

"I do deserve it," I shouted, picking up the razor and handing it to her. "Do it! DO IT!"

"I don't want to cut you!" she screamed, throwing her vice against the tiled wall of the shower. It ricocheted wildly back at us, causing me to flinch slightly as it fell to the floor at my feet. "I want to cut *her!* I want Scarlet to pay! I want that bitch to bleed. She nearly killed Jay," she screamed before crashing to her knees on the floor. "He...I...I couldn't help him. He just laid there. Sean brought me a corpse—*my* corpse, and I froze, just like I froze when my mom was dying. When you were dying. I nearly let him bleed to death in front of me."

Her sobs came heavy between her words. Her emotional levy had broken, and this time tears, not blood, flowed freely through its cracks.

"For once in my life I didn't feel alone, like my past was finally going to stop haunting me, and then BOOM," she yelled, slamming her fist into the wall, "everything crashes down around me. I can't take this!"

I couldn't take it either.

The overwhelming surge crashed over me and took my breath away. If those were the emotions she'd struggled with while I was gone, then I was thankful that the cuts on her legs were all she'd done in my absence. The reality that I might not have had Peyta to come back to at all did nothing to normalize my breathing.

Before I could make myself useful to her, Cooper knocked on the door, and without awaiting the go-ahead, opened it immediately. Peyta scrambled to cover herself fully with the towel while I did a quick assessment of what he was about to see. It looked grim. The tub was still streaked with trails of crimson, the blade lying innocuously on the floor next to it.

"Everything okay in here ladies? I heard some shouting and—"

He froze once the door fully unveiled the macabre secret it had only just moments before contained. I watched as the tenuous nature of what he beheld unmasked his expression, disbelief setting in. He stared down at Peyta, who scurried more tightly behind my legs for shelter, before looking up to meet my gaze.

In a rare moment, we shared no words at all. With a single and deliberate shake of my head, I silently ordered him out of the room. He complied without question. I would explain everything to him later, as I always did, but he didn't need the full impact. Seeing Peyta in that state for a second more would have given him that, and Cooper would never have forgiven himself for not seeing her strength for what it was at the time—a façade of bravery to mask her dark secret.

With a sigh, I moved quickly to lock the bathroom

door before any more unwanted visitors could arrive, then I came to sit by Peyta, who had again perched herself on the side of the tub. She shook violently while she let out years' worth of emotions in the tiny bathroom. All I could do was hold her and ride out the storm.

I cried with her, desperately needing to let out some emotions myself. Different personality types dealt with grief and trauma in different ways. Some needed to talk their feelings through, some stuffed them down deep enough that on most days they could function as though the feelings never existed. Others, like Peyta, held a certain volatility at bay with only the weakest of supports—add too many stressors to the pile and everything collapsed.

"She's gone," I whispered, leaning my head against her as we rocked together on the edge of the tub. "I don't know where Scarlet went, but she's gone. I can't find her. I wish I had more answers for you, P, I honestly do, but I just don't. When Scarlet killed Matty, something snapped inside her. She took me hostage and ran wild for three weeks, only to let me out at the most inopportune moment," I explained, wishing I could tell her more. "I didn't know how to break it all to you, but you have to know that I wanted to call you right away. I love you, Peyta. You're my family."

"I kept the store going for you," she sniffled, gripping me tighter.

"I know you did, P. Cooper told me all about it. He was so proud of you. *I'm* so proud of you, but I'm worried too," I said, pulling away from her enough to see her face. "I've seen plenty in this past year that scared me, but nothing has scared me more than what I just saw you doing here today. I can't let you continue

31

this, and whether that means telling your mother or dragging you to some program somewhere, I'll do it. Nothing about this is okay, Peyta. You need help."

"I know," she whispered. "I don't want to feel this way anymore."

"We'll fix it," I said softly before kissing her head. "Together, we'll fix it."

CHAPTER 4

It took forever to get home.

After I helped clean Peyta up and made it abundantly clear to her that she needed to confront her mother about her issue or I was going to do it for her, I left her to it. I prayed that she would. That was a conversation I would *so* not look forward to having with Ronnie.

When I emerged from the house, I saw Cooper sitting in the car, doors closed, engine off. His hands gripped the wheel as though he was driving while his gaze was off somewhere in the distance, unfocused and unsettled. He was rattled to the core by what he'd seen, just as I had been. It appeared that I was dealing with it far better.

Nothing changed as I approached the TT or when I walked in front of it. He just sat and stared blankly out the windshield at nothing. When I popped open the passenger door, I got in with absolutely no response from him. He was clearly in shock. I didn't know what to do, so I sat there in silence, staring out the front window with him while I waited for him to come back to the present. To come back from whatever dark place he'd found in his mind.

As the minutes passed, I worried about what was going on inside the house. I wondered how Ronnie was taking the news. Eventually, I looked over at Cooper and gently placed my hand on his, which still gripped the wheel tightly.

"Cooper?" I whispered, trying to coax him back from wherever he was.

"She was...," he started, unable to force the words out.

"Yes. She was," I replied softly, giving his hand a light squeeze.

"Because you..."

"Yes."

"But why? Why *that*?"

"Because it's what she knows, Cooper," I explained delicately. "She's done it before. I saw the scars."

The leather under his hand groaned as he strangled the wheel. He hung his head down to his chest and slammed his eyes shut. After a minute, he pulled himself together enough to sit back up and release his grip ever so slightly, but he wouldn't face me. His gaze drifted straight ahead yet again.

"I thought she was taking everything so well at first," he whispered in a confessional way. "I knew she would break down when she thought she was alone, but it seemed understandable. I had no idea..."

"You couldn't have known, Coop. It's not your fault."

His expression was pained. He was fighting to keep his emotions in check.

"How many?" he asked out of nowhere.

"How many what?"

"Marks...on her legs. How many?" I frowned, not wanting to answer him. The answer I had to give was not going to help. "Ruby, please. How. Many?"

"More than I could count in the short time I could see them. Some were fresh. Others were long healed," I said, wishing I'd had better news for him. "She told me she's only done it on a few occasions in the past, but I'm not sure I believe her."

He squeezed his eyes hard, wincing away from the information he'd requested. When he opened them again, a single tear escaped and slowly rolled down his face. Reflexively, I wiped it away.

"What do we do, Ruby?" His expression was pitiful when he finally turned to face me. It was plain on his face that he felt helpless, and it was a feeling he was beyond uncomfortable with.

"She needs help, and not the kind that we can give her, Coop. She needs counseling. I told her that she has to tell Ronnie or I'm going to do it for her. This can't be blown over."

"Will she do it?"

"I don't know, but I'm checking with her tomorrow. I'm not letting this go. God knows I don't want to, but I'll tell her mom if she forces my hand. Peyta needs all the support she can get right now. From *all* of us."

He breathed out forcibly with one large gust, then fired up the Audi.

"Okay," he said curtly. "Whatever it takes."

"Agreed," I added, forcing a smile.

He forced a grim one in return.

"I guess we should head home before any more enlightening facts can pop up."

"It's still early, Coop. Haven't I taught you not to say things like that out loud? Don't taunt the Universe. It doesn't like it," I sighed. "I know these things. It seems to have it out for me more often than not."

He put the car in reverse and rolled it gently down the driveway.

"Glad to see that you're on your best driving behavior in the new car," I mocked, trying to lighten the mood a tad. "Don't think you played me with the whole 'I don't think you should drive when you're this upset' thing. You just wanted to drive the new car."

Once he hit the road he threw it in first gear and peeled out, literally burning rubber in Ronnie's neighborhood. He glanced over at me with a slightly haunted smile.

"What do you think I've been doing while you were gone? I spent a lot of time in this car trying to find you."

"Cooper, I think you should slow down a bit," I said calmly as I watched the speedometer steadily increase.

"I spent a lot of miles running up and down the Eastern Seaboard too," he mumbled, begrudgingly obliging my request.

"I'm sorry, Cooper," I whispered.

He gave his head a shake then turned and smiled at me. Truly smiled.

"I didn't mean to sound that way, Rubes. I just..." He paused for a moment to choose his words carefully. "I've got a lot built up too that needs to come out. I need to find an outlet for it."

Filled with concern, my eyes darted toward him, searching his profile for explanation. I didn't like the subtext of his statement. Clearly seeing my distress, he elaborated.

"Not drugs, Ruby. A *healthy* outlet."

"Okay," I sighed, sinking lower in the passenger seat. "I think we all need one of those all-inclusive vacations in Aruba or something. We're all wound *way* too tightly at the moment."

"Aruba," he scoffed. "Your pale ass would practically go up in flames there."

I wanted to argue, but he was right. Not wanting to admit that directly, I conceded the point.

"You know what I mean."

"I think you have a little too much on your plate to be planning any trips," he said with a chill to his tone. "You just got back from one."

"How's that list of healthy outlets coming?" I asked curtly.

"Poorly. It's coming along poorly, apparently."

"So it seems."

Our conversation stalled momentarily as we rolled into downtown Portsmouth, neither one of us wanting to say the wrong thing and potentially start a fight. There were entirely too many emotions packed far too tightly in my little sports car. We needed to decompress.

Cooper suddenly chuckled to himself at some thought he hadn't gotten around to sharing with me. It was a nervous laugh that held a hint of instability. I was used to hearing that from myself—never him.

"Well, at least you won't have to go to jail for Matty's murder."

"What?" I exclaimed, wheeling around to face him. "I was a suspect? Holy shit, Cooper!"

"Of course you were," he said flatly.

"Wow," I muttered to myself as I sank in my seat. "I just never thought about the authorities, but I guess it makes perfect sense. I was the last one to see him alive." I tried to process what he had said. The last thing on my mind had been the human authorities, but it was an oversight of epic proportions. Why wouldn't I have been a suspect? I was the last known person he had seen that night.

That reality brought about an entirely new revelation.

"Wait! Why am I *not* a suspect, Cooper? I should be. There is no good reason why I wouldn't still be considered one. In fact, my absence should only strengthen their case," I rambled as my mind started to pull the pieces together. "Double holy shit, Coop! I *could* go to jail for murder! Why would you joke about this?"

He gave me his 'don't be such a dramatic blonde' face, forcing me to sink down further into the seat.

"I'm not going to go to jail for murder?" I asked. He shook his head no, once.

"Why am I not going to jail?"

He graced me with that same condescending expression.

"*Sean...*" I whispered. I should have factored him into the equation long before then.

"Yet another mess he had to clean up for you."

"Seriously, Coop. I know I deserve the attitude, but I'm going to need you to take the hostility down a notch or two. Just for today. Please," I pleaded, not able to deal with any more digs even though they were well deserved. "I'll make you a list of healthy outlets myself. Jogging, Tai Chi...*ooooh*, how about pottery."

"Okay, okay, I get it. Point made. I'm sorry," he replied, throwing both hands up in surrender.

"Hands on the wheel! Hands. On. The. Wheel!"

He looked over at me in all my craziness, giving me his most annoyed face. All I could do was snicker in response. Apparently, we were both a wee bit jumpy and prone to overreacting that morning.

Before I could make a flippant remark, a sobering reality slammed its way into my mind.

"Cooper," I started, my tone questioning. "If I'm not a suspect, then what am I?"

"Technically," he started with a sigh, "you're a missing person."

Missing person...

"Oh my God. Are there people out looking for me still?"

He gave me a grim look.

"Not anymore. Your case is still considered open, but Boston PD and Portsmouth PD both assume that you were murdered too, and your body never washed ashore like Matty's."

"Boston? Why are they involved? And what do you mean 'washed ashore'? Matty was never in the—"

"Sean makes things go away, Ruby. He wanted to get the heat away from town. My guess is that he dumped the body in the Charles River somewhere and it got dragged out to sea with the current. He washed up along the coastline."

"So why is Portsmouth still involved then?"

"Because that's where you were last seen," he replied somberly. "Alan questioned me. I told him the truth, that you walked out of our apartment that night and never came back." He paused for a moment and took a deep breath. "I also told him that I had no idea where you were going or who you were meeting up with, which was partially true. They made me take a polygraph. Guess I was a suspect for a little while too."

"I'm so sorry, Cooper. I had no idea."

"Don't sweat it. Alan never believed I had anything to do with it from the get-go. He got me cleared ASAP so that they would focus their attention elsewhere," he said, blowing off his near-murderer status. "He's a good guy."

"He's a *great* guy," I corrected. "Maybe you should take me to the precinct. I need to see him."

Cooper immediately turned the car around illegally in a one-way, then pulled up moments later in front of the police station.

"Do you want me to come in with you?" he asked, searching my face for his answer. Though my nerves were high, my resolve was strong. Like with Peyta, it was something I needed to do on my own.

"No thanks, Coop," I replied with a tight smile. "I'm going to fly solo on this one too."

He gave a nod. "I'll wait for you out here. And don't even start to argue with me. You're not walking home by yourself. Not today," he added. "Not for a while..."

I leaned over and kissed him softly on the cheek, lingering by his face for just a moment or two longer than necessary. I'd missed his smell. Cooper always smelled amazing.

"I'll be right back."

I hopped out of the TT and made my way up the stairs to the precinct, my stomach knotting tighter with every step. I didn't know what I was going to do or say once I was inside; I prayed for some divine intervention.

Once through the heavy double doors, I approached the presumably bulletproof glass that encased the front desk. A woman at the tail end of her fifties looked up at me, not unkindly, and spoke into the intercom.

"Can I help you?" she asked.

"Yes," I replied, taking a deep breath. "I'm here about a missing person case."

"I'll get one of the detectives down here right away," she said as she picked up the receiver to page someone. "Can I please get your name, miss?"

"Ruby," I said softly. "Ruby Dee. *I'm* the missing person."

CHAPTER 5

Her blank and disbelieving expression quickly gave way to realization, and she buzzed me through the locked entrance to the main offices behind her. She whisked me down the hall, jabbering on about news reports and knowing that miracles did happen; I stopped listening to her. My stomach was in my throat, and even though Cooper was certain I'd been removed from the suspect list, it did little for my confidence once I found myself in the lion's den.

I followed her down the winding corridors and up a flight of stairs to the second floor where the detectives' offices were located. Rounding the final turn, I heard a door squeak as an officer emerged from the bathroom a half step in front of me. In true Ruby fashion, I slammed right into him, not having had time to react.

"Sorry!" I exclaimed, spinning off his body with the momentum he created. "I'm so, so—"

I stopped cold once our eyes met. Alan stood

before me only feet away, staring down at my frazzled self as though he'd seen a ghost. I guess, in all fairness, it wasn't such an irrational response; for all intents and purposes, I had been considered dead. My case still being open seemed a formality at best.

Not knowing what to do, I stood paralyzed, just staring back at him. The reactions I'd received since I returned had been far from what I'd expected. Cooper had yelled and pushed me away. Peyta had feigned indifference then imploded. I wasn't certain I wanted to know what Alan would do. He was a no- bullshit kind of guy who always cut to the quick. He wouldn't sugarcoat anything for me, and in that moment, I could have used a little powdery dusting.

The moment seemed to go on forever until, thankfully, the receptionist returned to retrieve me, not realizing that she'd lost me in the first place.

"Ruby, I need you to—"

"I've got it, Alice. Thank you," Alan said, cutting her off mid-sentence. His eyes never left mine.

"Of course, Detective Beauchamp," she replied, scurrying around him to return to her post.

"It's really you," he mumbled. I'm not sure he meant to actually say it aloud. Before I could even respond, he advanced on me, scooping me up in his long arms and crushing me against his chest. "They thought you were gone, but...I never believed it. I knew this little kitten had a few lives left." He pushed me out to arm's length to look me over, and I squirmed under the intensity of his gaze.

"I missed you guys," I whispered uncomfortably.

"Come on," he said, his voice taking on a more serious tone as he surveyed the hallway. "Let's have this conversation somewhere more private."

He ushered me into an interrogation room to ensure we wouldn't be interrupted or overheard. I wasn't clear on whether our 'conversation' was to be on or off the record, but I went obligingly regardless. I knew I had some serious explaining to do.

Pulling out one of the clichéd metal-legged chairs, he motioned for me to have a seat and situated himself on the far side of the table.

"You want some water or something?" he offered.

"No. I'm fine, thanks," I replied, avoiding his gaze. "How are Kristy and the baby?"

"Good. They're down at her mom's right now, taking care of her. She finally got her knees done."

"Oh, that's great. She really needed that surgery. I'm glad Kristy could be down there to help..."

When I looked up at Alan, he merely nodded in response.Our ridiculous attempt at casual conversation quickly died, leaving an awkward silence that hung in the room as we stared at each other across the table. While we did, I watched a visible shift in him occur. He went from concerned friend to hardened-beyond-his-years detective in an eerie switch of personalities. It seemed I wasn't the only one capable of those.

"So, let's start from the beginning, Ruby," he said, tenting his fingers against his mouth. "I think that would be easiest."

"Okay...," I replied, not certain as to where "the beginning" was.

"You were at your place with Cooper, then suddenly left. Were you alone?"

I lied.

"Yes."

"Where were you going?"

"To meet Matty."

"Where?"

I lied again.

"Just in town...down by the docks. We hung out there sometimes," I added for credibility. "There's an older couple that lives down there. They've seen us there together before. You can ask them."

"No need," he said flatly. His cop persona was in high gear. "Did you see Matty?"

"Yes. I saw him."

"And what happened then?"

"I don't know...," I whispered, trying to conjure up something to tell him that would go along with what he already knew.

"Were you attacked?"

"I'm not sure. I—"

"Was there more than one of them?" he pressed, leaning forward on the desk.

"I can't say...I don't know."

"You don't know?"

"I don't really remember."

"You don't remember? What *do* you remember, Ruby?"

"Not much," I mumbled weakly.

"Where have you been for the past three weeks?"

"I don't know."

"You don't know?" he echoed disbelievingly.

"No. Alan, I—"

"Because I'm having a hard time understanding how your friend ended up outside of Boston when you said you met him here in town."

"I—"

"And I'm also having a hard time swallowing that you don't know anything about how he died or who did it."

"Why are you doing this?" I asked, a tear escaping the corner of my eye. He'd been so happy to see me only moments earlier. It appeared the honeymoon period was over.

"Because you're lying to me, Ruby. It's not the first time either, and it's getting under my fucking skin at the moment because I don't believe that you would lie to me unless *someone* was putting you up to it or you were trying to protect someone," he yelled, slamming his hand against the table. "And I have a pretty fucking good idea who that someone is too. What has he gotten you into, Ruby? What did he do? And don't think for a second that I don't know about what happened down at Langley. Your buddy was down there when McGurney was executed. That isn't coincidence in my mind."

I stared at him, totally flabbergasted. He thought Sean killed Matty—killed both him and McGurney, for that matter. And worst of all, he thought I knew.

"Alan," I said softly, tears still staining my face, "Sean did not kill Matty. He didn't kill McGurney either."

"Really?" he asked, his tone dripping with disdain. "You weren't there when some fucker shot my friend in the back of the head, were you?"

I offered nothing in response.

"I didn't think so."

"But Sean called me from Langley...when he was flying back. He *found* McGurney dead, Alan. Sean needed his help—information on a CIA cover-up that only he could provide. Why would Sean kill the one person willing to help him?" I asked, thinking my points were both true and valid.

"Because I have the sneaking suspicion that your friend *Sean* is a 'clean up your messes' kind of guy. I have no doubt that, once he got what he was looking for, he tidied up," he rumbled, his tone low and menacing. What was frightening about his accusation was that, as far as the supernatural world went, he was pretty much spot-on. "Is that what happened to the Carmilo kid? Was he a mess that needed to be cleaned up?"

I once again found myself meeting his question with silence.

"You'd be surprised at what I can dig up when the mood strikes me, Ruby," he retorted. "I've been looking into your buddy, Sean. What's most interesting about him is the information I *can't* find. I can't seem to locate so much as an address for your little friend. I'm not even sure he has a last name."

"Alan, please...it's been a rough day already and it's barely kicked into gear yet. It wasn't Sean. You have to believe me."

"Then who?" he yelled, pushing his chair back quickly to jump to his feet. "Who was it?" He loomed over me like I was a criminal he was trying to break. Too bad he wasn't aware of the irony the situation held.

"I don't know," I whispered, crumbling weakly under his frustrated energy.

"Tell me, Ruby," he said in a warning tone. "Tell me or this changes things between us. I've given you a lot of latitude in the time I've known you because I haven't wanted to believe that you were complicit in that man's actions. But if you want to sit here and lie to my face like I'm some rookie that you don't know—whose family you haven't become a part of—then you're going to find out what it's like to be on my wrong side."

"Stop it!" I screamed, bursting under the growing

pressure in the room. "It wasn't Sean. I didn't see who did it. All I *do* know is that I don't remember a thing. Nothing! The last three weeks of my life are gone, Alan. Gone! I woke up in the woods somewhere in Maine. Some people found me and brought me home. I didn't even know I'd been gone that long. And from the second I got back, I've had nothing but animosity and aggression thrown my way with a healthy dose of accusation to boot. I can't answer your questions when I don't remember anything from the time I saw Matty until the time I woke up naked in some random forest."

I could barely manage, but I brought my gaze up to meet Alan's as he slowly withdrew his position, sitting back down in his chair. The look on his face was empty. I could practically see his mind trying to process everything I'd said after the fact, but I decided to continue anyway.

"Sean was on a plane when Matty died, Alan. I talked to him earlier that night. That's when he told me about McGurney...just like I told you."

He looked distant, like he was trying to put the pieces of a mental puzzle together but couldn't quite do it.

"That's what he claimed when he came to me about—"

"Wait a minute...what do you mean he came to you? What are you talking about?"

"It means that he came to my house to report you missing himself. I'm guessing, given whatever *occupation* it is that he's in, he wanted to take more creative avenues to find you," he said, eyeing me tightly again. "I didn't know about your friend Matty until long after Sean had come to me. Had I known at the time, I wouldn't have let him leave so easily."

"And now?" I asked, thinking Alan still wasn't going to believe my story. In fairness, it wasn't exactly true.

"There's nothing to do. The homicide is a closed case," he said with a certain distaste. "A body was found just outside of Boston in the victim's car. He was identified as the Portsmouth murderer based on some evidence that was never released to the public. Carmilo's blood was found on his clothes and in the vehicle. The best the Boston PD could determine was that the perp had driven down to Hopkinton to dump the body in the river and let it wash downstream. What was left of it had wounds that indicated a fight had gone down. All we could assume was that the perp had been badly wounded and slowly bled out." Alan leaned forward, elbows resting on the table, his head in his hands. "Convenient—don't you think—that a murderer, who was already 'eliminated' by your own account, came back to life to kill your friend? I think it's *highly* convenient, and I also think it's bullshit. I have no idea how Sean did what he did, but he manufactured this whole cover-up, and I want to know how and why."

So did I. Knowing that Keith James had been long since been burned to ash in Ronnie's backyard, I was acutely aware that it couldn't have been his body in that car that the BPD found. It made me wonder just whose body it was and exactly what lengths Sean had gone to to clean up my mess.

I had no explanation to offer Alan. He wasn't stupid; he knew that I knew more than I was letting on. As far as he knew, I was being evasive, but I knew that he couldn't prove his little theory. Sean and the boys had done exactly what Alan had accused them of, and consequently, done what they do best—make problems disappear.

"I don't know what more I can do here, Alan. I'm telling you what I remember, which is nothing. I have fucking amnesia or some stress-induced whatever that's blocking my thoughts. Hell, I could have been roofied for all I know. Hook me up to a polygraph if you don't believe me. Ask me anything you want about the last three weeks. I guarantee you I'll sail through it because I don't remember," I postured, gaining a little composure. "If you want to talk to Sean, have at it. You'll have to find him first, and believe me, he's the type that can't be found if he doesn't want to be. He's a ghost."

"You don't know how to find him? Get a hold of him?" he asked disbelievingly.

"Not if he doesn't want me to," I replied with a twinge of sorrow in my voice. "He and I aren't what you think, Alan. I'm nothing to him now. I can't help you."

I stood slowly, awkwardly picking at the hem of my tee. Alan told me that my refusal to explain would change things. I knew with one hundred percent certainty that he wasn't bluffing. The frustration and resentment that rolled off of him told me so.

"I'm sorry, Alan. I really am. I know you hate cover-ups and conspiracies more than anything, and finding the truth is a fundamental need for you, but I can't help you. I have a whole lot of things to figure out for myself right now, mainly what in God's name happened to me for the last three weeks," I said softly, hating myself for having to lie. "Do me one favor, please..."

"What?" he asked, trying unsuccessfully to quash

the hostility in his voice.

"Tell Kristy I'm sorry. I didn't do this to hurt any of you. I know you seem to have forgotten that in your quest for truth, but I'm a victim in all of this, Alan. Matty was my friend. I loved him, and I know for damn sure that he loved me too. Try not to forget that when you're painting horrible scenarios in your head of what you think went down that night."

Without another word, I walked around the table and straight out the door. I didn't wait for a response from him. I didn't want one.

Nearly in an all-out run by the time I got downstairs, I quickly made my way past Alice at the front desk before she buzzed me out. Through the double doors and down the flight of concrete steps outside, I fled to the TT that sat idling, waiting for my arrival. I practically tore the passenger door off before I jumped in and slammed it behind me.

"Sounds like that went well," Cooper observed with his typical sarcasm.

"Drive," I barked, not wanting to get into it.

"Another cheery homecoming?"

"Exactly."

"Do you want some more good news or should I save it for later?" he asked, losing some of his mocking tone.

"*Fuck*. What now?"

"I was reading the paper while you were in there," he started, shifting uncomfortably in his seat before pulling into traffic. "Matty was in there—in the obituaries. Do you want to—"

"No!" I shouted, putting my arm up defensively as he reached between the seats for the paper. "I don't want to see it." I took a moment to catch my breath before continuing. "I'm sorry. I didn't mean to yell at you. Is that the good news you spoke of?"

"No," he said plainly.

"Just lay it on me, Cooper. Please."

"It said that his funeral is tomorrow. In Boston." *Fuck me.* "What are you going to do?" he asked, eyeing me out of his periphery.

"I don't know..."

"I could go down with you, if you want to go."

"No," I said abruptly. "That's something I need to do on my own."

He pressed his lips together firmly in a half frown.

"There's a freak storm coming up the coast. It's going to be brutal."

"I've driven in snow before, Cooper. I'll be fine," I replied, staring off towards my apartment as we rounded the final corner on the way home. "I'm not sure what I want to do yet. I'm going to sleep on it first."

"Whatever you think is best." Cooper parked the car in front of the shop and we simultaneously got out. "Go upstairs," he ordered, throwing me the keys. "I've gotta do something in town. Go have a nap. I'll be home in a few."

I nodded silently and did as I was told.

Once inside the main door, I schlepped my weary body up the stairs to the apartment. Exhausted didn't even begin to describe how drained I felt. I closed the door behind me and shuffled down the hall to my bedroom, flopping down onto the bed the second I reached it. Cooper wanted me to get some rest, and that was exactly what I was going to do.

* * *

Hours later I awoke to darkness surrounding me and a shrill beeping sound somewhere in my room. Disoriented and startled, I fumbled my way out of my bed in a panic only to crash into the night-stand by my bed. In my half-awake state, I had no idea where I was.

"Cooper!" I yelled, trying to control my rising unease.

As always, he was by my side in a flash.

"What's wrong?" he asked as he flipped on the bedside lamp. It illuminated the concern on his face.

"There was a sound, and I jumped out of bed to see what it was, but then I ran into the furniture...and it was so dark, and I...I...," I rambled, feeling increasingly ridiculous. "I didn't know where I was."

He scooped me up in his arms and hugged me tight to his chest.

"You're *home*," he whispered softly. "That's where you are. For good."

And I was. Good or bad, drama or not, I was finally back where I belonged. I welcomed the feeling.

"Sounds perfect to me," I said, smiling.

"Good. Now what the hell was this sound that woke you up in such a tizzy anyway?"

I pulled away from him to search the room for the most likely suspect. I found it lying on the table that had taken a chunk out of my leg only moments earlier. My innocent-looking cell phone looked at my laughingly. A text had been the cause of my near meltdown.

"My phone must have gone off," I replied, walking over to retrieve it. I was surprised by what I saw—a message from Alan.

Filled out the proper paperwork regarding your reappearance. BPD has been notified as well. It'll be on the news this evening. Be prepared for the backlash. I'm sorry about today. Talk later.

So much for my quiet reentry to life.

"I guess I won't have to call the Carmilos to tell them I'm alive and coming," I said dryly.

"Why's that?"

"Because I'm about to be breaking news. Alan spread the word about my return."

"Well," he said, scratching his head. "He didn't really have a choice, and in fairness, that cat had to be let out of the bag at some point. Guess now is as good a time as any."

"I guess so," I muttered to myself, getting up to go into the living room and hunker down for the rest of the evening. I wanted to crawl into a cave and hide, but I'd already done that for three weeks, metaphorically speaking.

"Where are you going?" he asked, following behind me.

"I don't want to miss the big story," I replied sarcastically. "I think I'll make a stiff drink for the show."

"Better make two, then. Can't have you drinking alone..."

I scoffed as I entered the kitchen, Alan's words running rampant through my mind.

Be prepared for the backlash...

The story of my life.

CHAPTER 6

There hadn't been a Nor'easter like that in New England for decades. Twenty inches of snow was forecast to pummel the coastline from the Providence area up, but only after an inch of freezing rain laid the foundation for treacherous road conditions. Just as the weatherman had predicted, it was the perfect storm.

While I drove to Boston, signs of that storm were already visible, the weather steadily deteriorating. Along with it went my resolve. I had dreaded that day, fiercely.

During the time the commute provided, I reflected on things that only deepened my sadness—my sense of loss. Thoughts of the hours Matty and I had spent together in dance class, joking around instead of paying attention, clowning our way through choreography, and stopping for food afterward. His twenty-second birthday party at his parents' house was one of my favorites. I loved his family, and they took me in like I was one of their own.

Carmen...Dominic...

The pain in my chest was excruciating when I thought of them. They'd already lost one son by the time I had met Matty, and, because of me, they would bury another. I didn't know how I could face them.

I flew past exits on the interstate while I drove, and, before I realized what I was doing, I took one of them, turning off the highway in an attempt to loop back onto it to retreat north. I pulled into a gas station before my cowardice fully took over and tried to pull myself together. My hands shook uncontrollably, and no matter how hard I gripped the wheel, it did nothing to quash the quaking.

Laying Matty to rest was not something I wanted to be a part of. The three weeks I'd spent tucked away in Scarlet's mind had offered me a certain escape from reality. Though the events that had occurred on the night of Matty's murder played through my mind repeatedly, I could detach from them because I hadn't faced the aftermath. The final vision of Matty's decapitated body should have clearly illustrated that he was gone, but it didn't.

Burying what remained of him would.

I took multiple deep breaths before putting the car back in gear, driving off towards the entrance ramp for I-93 South. The rain was falling harder and the temperature plummeted as I drove. Funeral or not, the worst of the storm wouldn't hold off for long. My emotions couldn't be held back forever either, and I was suddenly in a hurry to get the whole ordeal over with.

I thought about watching from afar, hidden by trees or headstones nearby, so I could avoid the onslaught of grief I was sure to be bombarded with. It was cowardly, but I was certain that, when faced with the totality of my own grief, I would crumble under the weight of anything else. Matty was always so strong, both physically and emotionally. I selfishly wished for his strength in that moment. If I couldn't be strong, then I would at least be honorable and bear my pain publicly, for all who loved him to see. It was by my actions that he was about to be put six feet under, and I owed it to him to be there.

Cars thickly lined the street on both sides, forcing me to park nearly a block away. I had dressed for the unseasonable cold, but not the freezing rain. My black stilettos offered little stability on the icy walkways, and I teetered my way across the street to the main entrance of the cemetery.

"He always said you had impeccable fashion sense," a voice called to me from inside the wrought iron gates. A man around thirty rounded the corner, headed in my direction. He was difficult to make out at first through the assaulting rain, but once I was closer, I saw that it was one of Matty's brothers-in-law.

"I guess I didn't review the weather as thoroughly as I should have before I left," I said, walking towards his extended hand.

"Let me help you," he said, placing my hand in the crook of his folded arm. "I had to run back to the car for another umbrella. Rosa's didn't hold up well with the wind." I looked up at the flimsy, travel-sized one I held and prayed it would manage the weather. "I saw you on the news last night," he said softly, uncertain as to where to take his observation after that.

"I was going to call Carmen..."

"She was elated, Ruby. She'll be so glad to see you alive and well...even if she can't see Matty." His tone was somber, and I fought against the growing sorrow he felt. We were awkwardly quiet after that as we made our way through the cemetery. I eventually lost my battle and his energy penetrated me, adding to my cloud of growing sadness. He had loved Matty like a little brother. That was plain.

As we neared the plot, I noticed the sea of black encircling it. My heart skipped, realizing what was in the center of that sea, and the end of my denial was official—tears spilled onto my cheeks effortlessly. Without skipping a beat, my escort offered me a tissue, which I gladly took. I had left my purse in the car, not wanting to carry that and an umbrella in the likely event that I would fall and have no free hands to catch myself with. It also left me without my stockpile of Kleenex.

"Thanks," I said, sniffling.

"I've gotten really good at having those on me," he said soberly. "There haven't been a lot of dry eyes in my house lately."

Just then, he was called away by his wife, leaving me to deal with the metaphorical knife he'd just plunged into my side. I caused those tears. I brought that sorrow on his wife. His children.

I wanted to run back to the car and hide, but instead, I found a station near the rear of the massive crowd. Matty always joked about how expensive his wedding would be one day because his family was so enormous. Based on what I saw, he wasn't kidding; there were easily two hundred people in attendance. I did my best to blend into the background, but I made a pointed effort to be sure I could see his casket. For some reason, seeing it eased my pain rather than intensified it.

The sermon was done entirely in Italian, leaving me unable to follow, but the beauty of the priest's words was apparent, regardless. The priest sang as Matty was lowered into his final resting place, his words traveling so clearly through the air. I felt carried away by them, then realized that I was actually walking forward toward the grave on guided feet. I swore I could actually feel Matty's arm around my shoulders, guiding me towards him—his resting place. When I finally stopped, I was standing right next to his mother, whose cries snapped me back to reality.

For years I had been influenced by the emotions of others, but nothing before had ever come close to the rawness that she felt in that moment. My knees buckled, and I fell upon them beside her, taking her hand in mine. Physical contact only intensified our connection, but it was what she needed and the punishment I deserved, so I stayed where I was, weathering her storm.

I looked up at the faces around me, red and tear-stained, and reached out for their energies—all of them. Taking it all on at once was masochistic, but pain had a tipping point for me, allowing it to become welcome and warming. In that moment, I was *so* there.

The rest of the funeral was a blur. Someone helped me to my feet at the end, and I was engulfed by the swarm of people trying to pay their respects to Matty's parents. Emotionally exhausted from the ordeal, I tried to make my way out of the mob and back to my car. I had dropped my umbrella somewhere in my journey to join Matty's mom by the grave, so I was left exposed to the freezing rain that viciously pelted me with the gusting wind.

I wrapped my arms tightly around my stomach and tried to escape as quickly as I possibly could. My heels repeatedly sunk into the wet sod, eventually leaving me with no choice but to take them off or suffer a sprained ankle. My black-stockinged feet were frozen instantly, causing me to break into a jog through the centuries-old headstones, barely able to see through the veil of precipitation around me.

Once I located the entrance gates, I started to run full out, but I was no longer just running from the elements. I was running from Matty and the emptiness I felt without him.

In a flash, I was no longer running at all. Instead, I was sprawled out on the concrete walkway, hosiery torn, coat ripped, knees and hands bleeding. In my haste, I had overlooked a small grave marker, snagging my toe on it. It was a classic Ruby move. I hoped that somewhere Matty was having a chuckle at my expense.

I managed to pry myself off the ground and locate my shoes that had flown through the air during my fall. Soaking wet and completely disheveled, I decided to walk the rest of the way to the car. It seemed the safest game plan.

As I approached the gates, I heard a voice calling my name behind me. I turned to see Matty's mother, Carmen, hurrying carefully towards me. My heart sank instantly. Offering her support was one thing, having to face her directly was another. Even in my frozen condition, I could feel the sweat bead along my neck, rolling slowly into the back of my black cashmere sweater-dress.

"Ruby!" she called one last time before I acknowledged her.

"Carmen...," I started, unsure of what to say. "I'm...I'm so sorry." That was all it took. I choked on the last word, unable to speak further.

"I know, Ruby," she said, pulling me into a

crushing hug. "My baby's gone. He's *gone*. But you're still here...Matty would be so happy to know you're all right." Her sobs came violently, body convulsing with the purging emotions. "My girls are all I have left now," she eventually added after gaining some amount of composure. "How did this happen? How could somebody take my Matty from me? From you?" she asked, her eyes searching mine wildly for answers.

I felt faint, thinking that I was going to pass out for certain, right there in front of her. *I* had the answers she sought.

"He loved you, Ruby. More than you probably even knew," she said softly. "You were all he talked about from the moment you walked into that first class with the company. He marveled at everything about you for the longest time. We joked that he had a crush on you, which seemed to be exactly what it was in the beginning, but then something changed. It became more than a fascination with somebody who was more together than the girls he'd dated in the past; he knew you two were right for each other. After your first performance together, he came home and told us all that he had found the girl he was going to marry one day. She just didn't know it yet..."

She took my bleeding hands in hers, her expression becoming far more serious again.

"The news report said that you couldn't remember anything about that night, Ruby, about what happened to Matty," she said, moving in dangerously close to my face. I couldn't breathe. I was so afraid of what she was going to say next that I stood frozen. "Regardless of what occurred, I am certain that he would be glad to know that his last moments were spent defending you."

My knees weakened, but thanks to my grip on

Carmen, I managed to stay upright. I saw the rest of her family off in the distance, headed our direction, and I panicked. Having all of them engulf me was more than I could bear.

"Carmen, I...I have to go," I said, choking back a sob.

"He *loved* you, Ruby," she repeated. "Please don't ever forget that. He wanted you to be part of our family one day."

I tried to pull my hands free, but the middle-aged woman's grip was like a vise. I started to back away, but she resisted, pulling me closer.

"You *are* family, Ruby. You have been from the first time we met you," she said, hugging me one last time. "That's what Matty would want. We love you too, Ruby."

I tried to return her sentiment, but it came out so strained and strangled that I'm not sure she understood. I didn't stick around long enough to find out, turning to flee the instant she let me go. It took only seconds to break through the entrance gates out onto the sidewalk in my stockinged feet. Momentarily forgetting where I had parked, I scanned the street for the TT, which was virtually useless given the density of the sleet falling rapidly around me.

Once I determined where I needed to go, I continued running down the street to my car. I needed to get out of the cold, out of the elements, and away from Matty's family before they could unknowingly inflict any more pain.

There were few cars on the road given the conditions, so I ran along the parked cars, hoping to make it easier to spot my own. As I neared the TT, I saw a man leaning against a car just across the street from me. He stood stoically, staring at me. I thought my day couldn't have gotten any worse, but, once again, the Universe had my number.

Sean moved to cross the street, and I screamed a sound so desperate and pained that the loud, shrill noise rang out through the neighborhood. He froze in place, just staring at me, his face expressionless from what little I could see. My outburst hadn't been for him; it was for me—a cleansing of everything I'd pent up that day. Whatever fate Sean held for me, I couldn't face it. Not then.

He said nothing, just stood by his car, motionless. As more tears ran down my face, camouflaged by the falling sleet, I shook my head 'no' at him slowly, then turned and ran the rest of the way to my car. I got in without looking back and drove off as quickly as the weather would permit.

My body was numb, either from the cold or the fear and emotion that overwhelmed me. I fought hard against my growing rigidity to keep the car on the road. But regardless of what caused the icy feeling coursing through my veins and the paralyzing sensation overtaking me, I was very clear on one thing.

That was not the homecoming with Sean I'd hoped for.

CHAPTER 7

I t took me three hours to drive back to Portsmouth in the deteriorating weather. During that time, New England had amassed eight inches of snow and counting. The TT may have had appropriate tires, but thanks to the layer of ice already on the road, she didn't fare as well as I would have liked. Just outside of Seabrook, NH, on I-95 North, I found myself doing donuts in the center of the road, praying that I wouldn't hit any of the cars around me. Making it through that ordeal unharmed was a blessing, but I still had several miles to go, and I found myself white-knuckling the wheel the rest of the way. My distress over the funeral, as well as seeing Sean, had to take a back seat to the driving crisis at hand.

I heard my phone vibrating in my purse beside me, but didn't dare reach for it. Whoever it was could wait until I was safely home, in one piece. It was most likely Cooper checking to make sure I hadn't caused a twenty car pile-up on the freeway; the irony was that I almost did.

I was relieved when I pulled up to my home, wanting to just leave the TT out front and make my way inside as quickly as possible, but parking on the street was not an option, so I managed my way down the side alleyway and left my car in the secluded parking lot that was hidden between two other buildings. I knew I would be plowed in, but where to leave your car in a New England storm was always the million dollar question for those who lived in town, and I made do with what I could. I wasn't exactly in a hurry to go anywhere.

After cramming my battered feet back into my stilettos, I wobbled my way to the main entrance of my building, using the brick façade for stability. Once inside, I took a deep breath, leaning against the door for support. It had been a long, trying day, and I was so thankful it was over. All I wanted to do was clean myself up, climb into some warm jammies, and curl up on the couch. With that plan in mind, I worked my way up the stairs to my apartment.

The sound of my clicking heels alerted Cooper to my arrival, and he swung the door open abruptly, looking the slightest bit frazzled.

"Jesus, Ruby. What happened to you? Are you okay?" he asked, eyeing my unkempt appearance.

"Long story, Coop. It's been a rough day," I said, dragging my weary body into the house.

He flashed a look of acknowledgment, remembering why I'd been gone in the first place. He ushered me to the couch, his arm around my shoulders, and helped me sit down.

"How was it?" he asked softly, taking my hands in his. I winced slightly when he brushed a cut that was barely scabbing over. He frowned when he looked down and saw them, immediately getting up to go retrieve something from the bathroom and returning with a warm washcloth. Without another word, he started to clean them up.

"It was awful, Cooper," I whispered. "He's *really* gone, and his family—the pain—I couldn't take it." I watched while he delicately wiped the dried blood from my hand, turning the washcloth over and over in an attempt to find a clean area. "He loved me, Coop," I admitted, my voice laden with guilt.

"Of course he did," he said, finally meeting my gaze. "It's impossible not to." He smiled weakly as he brushed a cluster of drying curls off my face, tucking them gently behind my ear. I leaned in and kissed him on the cheek with the same tenderness that he'd just shown me.

"That's not exactly what I meant," I said, suddenly feeling awkward. "I meant he *loved* me, and not just after his Change, but before. Long before, apparently."

Cooper stopped cleaning my hands and looked at me intently.

"How long before?"

"Months," I said, before hesitating; I wasn't sure I wanted to open my emotional can of worms. "His mother said he wanted to marry me. He told her I was the girl for him, and I killed him, Cooper. I can't take this! The guilt is unbearable..." I launched off of the couch and paced frantically through the living room. Something had to give, and it needed to do it soon. The scream I'd let out in front of Sean was only a momentary release of pressure. If I didn't find an outlet for the rest of it, the lid was going to officially blow.

"Ruby, just calm down for a second," Cooper said,

following me on my wandering path through the apartment. "You *have* to know that you didn't have a choice. He wasn't their son anymore—"

"But that's my fault too, Cooper! Don't you see? Everyone around me—close to me—pays a price for that! You, Peyta, Matty...even *Sean*. The Beauchamps would have, if we hadn't caught the Rev when we did. Christ, Cooper, their *baby* would have been killed. What kind of fucking person endangers everyone around them? Everyone they love?" He had no answer for me, though the pain in his expression indicated that he wished he did. "You see? Even *you* can't deny it."

"Ruby—"

"No, Cooper! No placating statements from you, please. You *know* that I'm right. I've struggled with this for months now, and every time I think the matter is resolved, a new casualty hits and I'm right back where I started again."

"And where is that?" he asked, looking saddened.

"I'm cursed, plain and simple. Sean said that RBs were an aberration, but maybe it's not that. Maybe *abomination* is a better word, because precious little seems to be positively influenced by my presence, Cooper. Maybe I'm some force of darkness, meant to plague the world with tragedy and sadness. Maybe the PC was right to put us all down."

"Listen, you're tired, you're emotionally exhausted. You need to eat something and rest. You're not thinking clearly right now," he argued, making his way over to me.

"A good night's sleep isn't going to make this go away, Coop. I'm a fucking calamity," I said, dodging him as he reached for my arm. "Maybe you should go...move out, before something else happens to you."

"I'm a big boy, Ruby, and I don't know how many times we're going to have this very discussion before it sinks into that thick head of yours," he said, lunging for my arm again, successfully that time. "I'm. Not. Leaving. Whatever chaos may come, you and I will face it together. Fate has bonded us, Rubes. For better or worse, we're a team."

My eyes snapped to his face as soon as the words left his mouth. I'd been bitch-slapped by a realization.

"A *pack*," I whispered softly, my mind scanning back to a conversation I'd had with Sean on the night of our first official date. We were rehashing an argument that Cooper and I had just had before I went to see him. I couldn't figure out something that Cooper had said to me; something regarding his feelings for me and how they'd changed. How he couldn't explain them.

I'm connected to you in a way that's beyond my comprehension...

It all started to make sense: Cooper's shift in power, his need to keep me safe, our bond; he had become an *alpha*. Something in him had emerged the night he'd killed Gregory in the forest. Gregory himself had admitted that he'd underestimated Cooper's strength and power, and taking Gregory out only furthered those qualities. It explained how deeply he loved me and I loved him, but even more so, it made sense of why we could never quite get past being friends. We weren't meant to be *mates*; we were *pack,* and he was my alpha.

"What did you say?" he asked, his look of disbelief slowly melting into one of understanding.

"We're a pack, Cooper, you and I," I said, standing my ground. "Think about it. It explains *everything,* especially why you go so nuts when you think I'm in danger. Your job is to protect me. *You* are my alpha."

For once in his life, Cooper was speechless.

I started to go into further explanation of my theory, but was rudely interrupted by a banging on the apartment door. My adrenaline spiked instantly—people pounding on my door in the past never boded well for me. Cooper shot me a look of irritation, most likely because I had once again forgotten to lock the outside door.

"I'm sorry," I cried. "It's been a bad fucking day, Cooper."

He muttered something while he made his way down the hall, frustrated by my ineptitude.

"It's as if you *want* someone to just walk in and kill you," he bitched, walking in front of me.

"Hey! At least they'd still have to get through the apartment door," I protested as I hurried up beside him. I flashed him a grin that I hoped would soften him slightly. It did, but only minutely.

"You're going to give me an ulcer if you're right about this alpha thing," he said, reaching for the doorknob. "Now would you mind stepping behind me, please? You're harder to defend when you put yourself first in the line of fire."

"Yes, master," I conceded, sidestepping into a spot directly behind him, just as he'd asked. A small part of me was put off by his domineering remark, but the reality was that he was right. He would die trying to protect me in any and all situations that I managed to get myself into, most of which could likely be avoided if I took a second to think before acting. Food for thought.

Perhaps we were both getting paranoid, given that

we didn't even know who was at the door, but paranoia had served us well in the past. The other reality I still had to face was that I was essentially human and more fragile than ever. Scarlet was gone, and I couldn't depend on her to heal me if I got shot up, stabbed, or nearly clubbed to death; yet another inconvenience of her absence.

Something in his eyes flashed at my submission, and it cemented everything for me. He really was an alpha, through and through. The question that stirred in my mind was: what *kind* of alpha would he be?

"Shall we see what's behind door number one?" he tossed over his shoulder at me as he turned the knob.

What he revealed nearly stopped my heart.

CHAPTER 8

"I see that you're still alive and doing well," a voice said from the stairwell. Cooper growled at the man who looked past him at me. "I was worried about you."

"*We* were worried about you," another male voice added.

In front of Cooper and me stood the three men who had found me in Maine. One stood slightly in front of the others, so I took him to be the alpha. He was taller than Cooper and thinner too. His hair was a washed-out blond that he kept short, and his gray-blue eyes were large but dull, like he was in a constant state of exhaustion.

The two behind him were similar in size and shape, both of them with brown hair, but that's where the similarities ended. Where one was muscular and scholarly looking, the other was a tad leaner with hardcore tats and steel decorating what I could see of his body, leading me to believe that there were many others just out of view.

"Ruby...," Cooper prodded, wanting my explanation ASAP.

"Should I assume that this is the one you spoke of at the cabin?" the tall one asked, still ignoring Cooper to stare at me.

"Who the fuck are you?" Cooper growled, clearly unhappy with the situation.

"Coop," I said, cozying up beside him. "These are the men I told you about. The ones who found me in Maine."

"They're not *men*," he replied, still staring them down.

"Okay, fine, poor choice of words." I looked over at the males on the landing and tried to figure out what exactly was important enough to make them drive through one of the worst storms New England had seen in years. "Why are you here?" I asked bluntly, not feeling up to idle chat when there was clearly none to be had.

"We need a favor, and since you owe us one, I figured that perhaps we could make an arrangement of sorts," he said, folding his arms across his chest.

"Like what?" Cooper asked, cutting me off before I had the chance to ask the same question.

"Refuge."

"Like you want to *stay* here?" I asked, thoroughly confused. "I'm not a fucking hotel!"

The professorial-looking brunet stepped up to the side of the lanky blond. He looked wicked pissed off.

"We could have left you to fend for yourself in the woods where we found you," he said, his British accent dripping with disdain. He didn't seem big on asking for help. "You didn't look too capable at that moment, so we intervened. I'd think that would buy us at least a chance to plead our case."

Cooper's look was murderous. I had to physically grab his shirt to let him know he needed to tone it down a notch. They weren't looking for a fight, but they weren't winning any points either. Sensing Cooper's growing rage, the leader of their trio attempted to mediate.

"Alistair," he said, his tone laced with warning. "Maybe you should step outside and cool off a bit. I don't think you're helping our situation at all."

"Good idea," Cooper growled in agreement. "Maybe you should *all* head outside."

I grabbed his arm and tried to calm him slightly because I knew he was dangerously close to letting his wolf out, and that was the last thing our little impromptu party needed.

"Okay, boys, I think we need to take this down a notch," I said, moving to get in between the men. Cooper was not having it and pushed me behind him. "If you plan to accomplish anything here tonight, I suggest you guys tread very lightly around my boy Coop. He's got a *really* short fuse, especially when it comes to me."

"Duly noted," the blond replied, nodding once. "So how do you want to do this?" he asked, looking nervous that I was about to boot him out of my place.

"Why don't you start by reminding me who you are," I told him, trying to slide past Cooper again.

"My name is Janner. This is Alistair, and the quiet one is Beckett," he said, motioning to the other two men.

"Janner? Like *yawner*?" I asked, trying not to giggle. "How did I manage to forget that?" He had a strange accent that I couldn't even begin to place, so I shouldn't have been surprised that he had a crazy name to accompany it.

"Yes," he said, his jaw clenching slightly. "It's a common name where I'm from."

"So, *Janner,* what exactly is it that you need refuge from?" I said, eyeing him tightly.

"We're in a bit of a pickle...," Janner started, choosing his words carefully. "We're in the market for a new pack. We thought maybe you would be able to help with that."

"No," Cooper barked, moving to slam the door in their faces. I lunged in front of him, stiff-arming the century-old door back open.

"Maybe we should hear them out, Cooper," I said, looking up at him. "They did help me."

"They did, though I'm sure that served their purpose more in the long run," he snarled. "And had you not been mated, I don't think I would have liked how they went about helping you."

"Probably not, but that didn't happen," I argued. I looked back at Janner and company and tried to feel their energies. Something about them was guarded—I'd never felt that kind of shielding before and wasn't certain what to make of it. "Come in," I offered, moving back out of the doorway. Cooper shot me a scathing look, which I ignored. "This should only take a minute."

After they entered, Cooper pulled me aside and proceeded to bicker with me in front of them about me being crazy and irresponsible. I countered about him being rude and overprotective. We would have gone on forever, but a single statement jarred us both out of tirades.

"You are not her mate," a gravelly voice called out softly. Cooper and I did an about-face to stare at Beckett, the quiet one. He may have been short on words in general, but he chose to use them when they counted. I wasn't sure I liked where he was going with that statement.

"Your bond," he continued, moving towards me cautiously, "I don't sense it like I did before. It should strengthen around your mate, not weaken."

I looked at Cooper with panicked eyes and saw that his feelings were very different than mine. His eyes glowed yellow, and I knew it was all about to go down because Beckett had to make that single observation known.

The other two men eyed me strangely then followed Beckett's lead, moving towards me slowly, their expressions curious. I didn't feel a menacing energy from them—I couldn't get a read on them at all.

"She isn't his," Janner said, clearly coming to his own realization.

Cooper's growling was more menacing than I'd ever heard it, and I feared that, on the same day that I learned I had an alpha, I would lose him.

The trio kept approaching with little trepidation visible while I continued to retreat silently out the door after Cooper shoved me toward it. I quickly met resistance where I shouldn't have. Before I could turn to see what I'd bumped into, his energy slammed through me like a bull through a crowd.

Calm.

"No. She isn't his," Sean rumbled over top of me. "She is *mine*."

CHAPTER 9

When I finally turned to see Sean's face, he was already leaning down, his lips at my ears.

"You didn't think you could get rid of me *that* easily, did you?" he purred, making every hair on my body stand up. Part of me wanted to cling to him violently; the rest wanted to run like hell. His comment was far too laced with double meaning for my liking.

When he pulled away slowly, I nervously waited to see the expression on his face. I was met with a middle ground of sorts. His curious smirk said "Are we still playing cat and mouse...I thought we were past that," but his eyes told a different tale. Their forest green hue did not help to settle my need to flee.

"I am her mate," Sean barked at the trio, who had ceased to move the second he appeared. "Anyone here care to challenge that?" He stood solidly, staring them down across the narrow divide.

Janner and Beckett slowly and deliberately shook their heads 'no' while Alistair stared him down.

"Who the fuck—"

"Alistair!" Janner cried, shutting the other man up. "For once will you please keep your foot out of your mouth? He is not to be questioned, understood?" Alistair glared at the side of Janner's face, but said nothing else. He apparently followed directions better than I did. "I'm sorry...Alistair is *young*. He has a lot to learn yet."

I looked Alistair over again, thinking he didn't look all that young to me, maybe a little older than myself. Then it dawned on me that he wasn't talking chronological age—he meant werewolf years.

"I think these clowns were just about to leave, Sean," Cooper said, turning his attention away from the men for the first time. "Perhaps *you* would like the pleasure of showing them out? If not, I'm happy to do it. Whichever you prefer."

"No," I said, instantly regretting my insubordination. I knew it would take a while for me to get the hang of not contradicting Cooper in front of others; our whole relationship had been built on bickering. "Sorry," I said, bowing my head slightly. "It's just...I'm kind of curious as to why they drove through one of the worst storms in New England's history to come here."

"I think I'd enjoy hearing that myself, Ruby," Sean said from behind me. My hairs stood on end at the sound of his voice. It was calm and collected, but the undertone I felt was murderous. I had a sneaking suspicion that if he didn't like what they had to say, I'd be having a PC clean-up crew taking care of my living room—again.

"Of course," Janner said with an incline of his head to Sean. "We were all members of the South

London pack. I'm sure you heard that there was some...*dissonance* amongst the family."

"I had," Sean replied shortly, implying that Janner had better start telling him something he *didn't* know, and fast.

Janner acknowledged the situation with a nod and continued.

"Then I won't bother to go into detail about the murder and unrest within the pack as I'm sure you're well apprised. I'll also assume you already know about the change in leadership that took place recently." He paused long enough for Sean to shoot him a curious look. Sean had no idea what he was getting at. "Oh, I see," Janner said flatly. "Well, there were those of us who felt the alpha was getting into things he shouldn't and sought to counsel him on the matter. Needless to say, the meeting did not go so well. He was killed."

"And am I to assume then that you three were responsible for that?"

Janner nodded once.

"So you didn't mean to take his place?" Sean asked, moving forward.

"No. Only to stop the violence."

"So you fled?"

"Yes," Janner replied, dropping his gaze to Sean's chin. "He had many supporters within the family, and one of them was all too happy to take his place, ruling as he had. It was banishment or death. We chose the former."

I looked over to see Cooper's expression soften slightly. He had been a member of a similar pack once, so he understood the quandary they were in.

"But why are you *here*?" Cooper asked.

"We were allowed to leave with what we could

carry and what money we could gather before our accounts were shut down. We escaped to the airport and got the first flight to the USA that we could. Once we landed in Boston, we asked where the best and most secluded camping area in the region would be, which led us to northern Maine. We've been hiding out ever since."

"I don't understand," I said, trying to work through the logistics of what he'd just said. "Why are you hiding out? They *let* you leave...why not just go somewhere you want to be and start a new life?"

"Because, Ruby, they have no honor. They'll come for us when they think we've dropped our guards—become complacent. It's their nature."

"Okay, but I still don't get why you're *here*," I argued.

"We saw you in the woods," he said, hesitating slightly. "There are stories—rumors—of a wolf so powerful that she can't be stopped by anyone or anything. A Rouge et Blanc," he said cautiously, looking directly at Sean. "When I first saw you, I knew it was true. You are that wolf. We want to join *you*."

"Are you saying I have a worldwide reputation?" I asked, dumbfounded.

"Jesus, Ruby," Cooper sighed. "This is hardly a time to worry about your international street cred."

"That's not what I was saying!" I snapped at him. "I'm just trying to clarify that there are people that know about me. That know what I am."

"Yes, Ruby," Beckett said gruffly, still flanking Janner like a good little soldier. "When you tore past us in the woods one night, red eyes blazing, we all knew. We just never imagined you'd show up on our doorstep. It's a sign."

"I liked you more when you were quiet," Cooper snarled. "She didn't show up on your doorstep. The way I heard it, you stalked her through the woods and then attacked her."

Sean growled, lunging at the trio. He had Janner pinned to the ground before I even saw him move. Beckett knew enough to stand aside, but he looked pissed about it to say the least. Not knowing any better, Alistair attempted to aid his brother wolf and got tackled by Cooper for his efforts.

"Ruby," Sean grumbled, still holding Janner tightly by the throat. "*Explain.*"

"Nothing happened, Sean," I said, finally grasping the severity of the situation. He was going to kill Janner if he didn't find my explanation satisfactory. "They found me. They fed me, clothed me, and brought me home. I wouldn't be here if it weren't for them." His grip lightened a miniscule amount. I realized I wasn't answering the right question.

I knelt beside him, wrapping my hand around his wrist, trying to lower my face into his line of sight.

"Sean," I said softly, "they didn't *touch* me...okay? Nothing like that happened, I promise."

His eyes were black as night, but when they finally met mine, a flash of emerald broke through, if only for a second. He released Janner and stood, hovering above him. I leaned forward to see if Janner was all right, but Sean snatched me by the shoulder and stood me up before I could even get near him.

"Don't touch him," he ordered, still holding tightly onto my arm. "I think it's time for your company to go, Ruby."

"Sean," I started, choosing my words and tone very carefully. "They came to me because they need help. They did as much for me. I want to hear them out. *Please*."

His chest rumbled violently, but his hostility never fully made it to his face— that he kept as expressionless as possible.

"Cooper, maybe you should take these mutts out of here for a while. Can you handle that?"

"I'm not wild about your plan, Rubes," Cooper said, addressing me before he answered Sean's question. Always a pissing contest with those two. "But yes, I can take them out of here for a bit. Maybe we'll go somewhere really nice and private so I can get some real answers out of these accent-wielding chuckleheads."

"Cooper...," I sighed, hating his attitude.

"I know, I know. Be nice to the strays, I get it," he moaned. "You're such a buzzkill sometimes." He looked over to the homeless trio and motioned for them to follow him out. Much to my surprise, they followed without so much as a word—not even from Alistair.

I caught Cooper's eye before he shut the door. *Be careful,* my gaze told him. His eyes drifted to Sean briefly then back to me saying, *be careful yourself.*

The door closed heavily, leaving Sean and me shut in with our growing silence. I could feel his penetrating stare willing me to look at him, but I couldn't. I was emotionally wasted and physically exhausted, and not up for the talk that I knew we had to have. How do you apologize for nearly killing the one you love?

Without explanation, I slowly started down the hallway to my room, knowing that he would likely follow my lead. He wasn't going to let me walk away; he'd said as much when he showed up at my apartment.

What I wasn't sure about was how that conversation was going to go once it started.

My room was dark and chaotic as usual. I'd left for Matty's funeral in a frenzy, and the clothes strewn all through my room were evidence of that. It wasn't surprising—"vintage disaster" seemed to be the theme for it at all times unless someone else cleaned it for me. I didn't even bother making excuses for it; Sean was used to my affinity for messiness.

Since I'd arrived home, I'd never had the chance to change my clothes, or even take my coat off for that matter, and I found myself desperately wanting to get out of my somber, tattered attire and into something far more appealing, like a ratty T-shirt and sweats. Instead, I schlepped myself over to the window seat, which was dimly lit from the street lights outside. I plopped my butt onto the upholstered cushion, then pulled my knees up to my right side, leaning my left shoulder against the wall for support, and stared out the large glass pane.

My eyes suddenly felt heavy and began to close, shutting out everything around me—even Sean. My exhaustion knew no bounds.

"Ruby," he said calmly, prompting me to acknowledge him. I couldn't read his tone though; he seemed reserved, like he was purposely holding back from me. I wondered if that was for his benefit or my own.

"Sean, I'm sorry about—"

"I'm here to talk, not listen," he said, cutting me off. It was probably for the best, given my track record of digging holes deeper than they were to start with. "What happened that night...I know it wasn't *you*. You were not behind those actions." I turned to see his face, all his features beautifully highlighted by the tiny strands of light that permeated far enough into the room. I wished he'd worn an expression to match. "But we still have a problem, you and I," he continued. "Your inability to trust me has once again caused a rift between us."

"Seems like a little more than a rift," I muttered to myself.

"Quiet!" he snapped, and I jumped at the harshness in his voice. He slowly advanced toward me, and I wanted to mold my body against the wall, frightened by his behavior. "After *everything* we've been through—all the drama...the death," he growled, still closing the distance between us. "When you came to me that night in the rain—the night you said you chose me—I thought things changed, and yet, only days later, I found myself nailed to the floor with knives, courtesy of Scarlet's lover and *mate*." He wasn't shouting at me, but his voice was loud and menacing, and I'd have given anything to have been anywhere but in that room with him in that moment. I'd seen that rage before, but never directed at me. He'd been angry, even fearsome when the whole incident in question took place, but he'd never had the energy to back it up. Cornering me in my room that evening, he did.

"You're scaring me," I said, trying not to sound like the sniveling weakling I was.

"Good," he said, leaning in close. "I want you *terrified*." His black eyes told me everything I needed to know. Whatever proclamation he had made earlier in the night about being my mate was a ruse; he wanted to con everyone out of the apartment so he could punish me. I'd seen the justice he was capable of handing out and heard tales of worse. My day was *not* looking up.

The tremors started low, coursing through my body, especially my hands, growing until they hit critical mass. At that point, there was no concealing the sheer horror I felt as my body knocked against the wall in a spastic, uncontrollable seizure. I felt like it was trying to purge something by literally shaking it out of me. Did my nervous system want to eject Scarlet to neutralize the threat? If so, I definitely preferred my blackouts to the new alternative.

It was hard to read Sean's expression because I couldn't get his face to stay still enough, but something in him shifted slightly. The rage was dying out.

"Where is she?" he growled, pinning my face against the wall in an effort to look me in the eyes. My jaw was spasming so badly that it made it too hard to talk. "Tell that bitch to get out here, now," he seethed, his grip tightening.

I felt the tears roll in a jerky pattern down my face.

"She's gone," I stammered, trying my best to be coherent.

"Where. Is. She?" he asked one last time, his irises and pupils bleeding into one large black orb of warning.

"Sean...please," I begged. "She's gone.... I...I don't know how. Please, *please* let me go." His grip eased and he backed away a foot or two, leaving me some breathing room.

"What do you mean 'gone'?"

"I thought Cooper told you," I said, scrambling further away from him until I was pressed against the cold panes of glass. "When Janner and the other two found me in Maine a couple of days ago, that was the first time that *I* had been let out in what I later found out was three weeks' time. Scarlet totally flipped out over Matty's death. I don't know what she did, or how she did it, but she stuffed me away somewhere in my mind, locked the door, and threw away the key."

He eyed me dubiously.

"So for three weeks you had no idea what was going on around you? What she was doing?" he asked, folding his hands over his chest. He thought I was lying.

"No! I had no idea, that's what I'm trying to tell you," I yelled, my voice getting tight with emotion. "I'm not sure she planned on ever letting me out initially, but for whatever reason, she left me in the woods, cold and naked. She *knew* those three were tracking her. I'd bet my life on it. I think she left me there to relive my past—the night my parents died," I whispered, picking at the tattered hem of my coat. "She wanted me to pay, Sean. For both of us to pay."

I rubbed my eyes, trying to clear my vision, but it was no use. The fatigue and excessive amounts of crying throughout the day had left them blurry and tired. Reading Sean's face was growing increasingly difficult, and I once again couldn't get a feel on his energy. He, like the boys from Maine, was shielding me from something.

"You can't sense her?"

"No."

"You can't hear her?"

"No."

"So she would have left you to face my wrath alone?" he asked incredulously.

"Yes, she would. She left me to face the refugee trio in Maine alone, and she was a total no-show when Cooper flipped out upon my return."

My body still shook, but the convulsive nature of the movements had simmered down to a much duller roar, and my heart rate was finally slowing. I wanted to stand, to face his anger head-on, but I couldn't. After everything that had happened, that anger was warranted. It was hard to blame him for his hostility, especially with Scarlet. Though my fear demanded I run, I did something else entirely. I submitted.

Understanding my actions, his demeanor softened ever so slightly.

"I don't see how this is possible," he said matter of factly, though there seemed the slightest hint of questioning in his tone. "She's a part of you. She can't just disappear."

"She's a genetic expression, Sean. You told me that. Maybe the environment that first allowed her to come forward has now sent her back. You said RB's Changed because of trauma. Maybe trauma can Change them back..."

"Something is off about you. I sensed it at the funeral," he said to himself. "So you think she's truly gone?" he asked, stepping cautiously towards me.

I shrugged, biting my lip to fight back the tears welling in my eyes.

He turned away from me, pacing the room as he ran his hand through his hair slowly.

Then he put it through my wall.

"Fuck!" he yelled, slamming his other arm against my bedroom door. His anger startled me, and I once again found myself shaking uncontrollably. The rage that had simmered was bubbling over again. Whatever shield he had in place wasn't capable of retaining that.

"This is not what I wanted," he grumbled, his words coming from deep within his chest. "Not what I planned." I said nothing in response, thinking that playing possum on the window seat was the best game plan. He seemed to be talking more to himself anyway. "*She's* the one who needs to pay," he said aloud as he paced alongside my bed. "Not you. This is all *her* fault, and now she's conveniently gone."

"Sean?" I asked, moving towards the edge of the seat. I'd never seen him so unraveled, uncomposed—unhinged.

"Do you have any idea how *maddening* losing you has been?"

He jumped the bed in a single, effortless leap to land right at my feet. "All this time," he said, staring out the window above me with vengeful eyes that seemed to fluctuate in color by the second. "All this time I thought you *chose* to leave me...wanted to escape me, and yet here you are."

In that moment, I did want to escape him.

"Why would I choose to leave you when I only just got you, Sean? That makes no sense," I protested gently, reaching for him before dropping my arm to my side.

"And you're the queen of rational thought?" he asked in a mocking tone, his dark eyes overtaking him.

"Hey! You have no idea what I did to keep you safe. I *begged* Scarlet. Threatened her. Did everything I could think of to make her stop Matty. In the end, she did it to avoid her own destiny. She knew Matty was becoming what made him and she would not be suffocated by his love," I said, standing to face him finally. Apparently, submission wasn't what Sean wanted after all. He appeared to want to know that I had some skin in the game and that I didn't just walk out on him at the most convenient opportunity. I could give him that in spades. "All I thought about when I was locked away in my own body was how I could get out and get to *you*," I told him, steeling myself against his glare. "*You* consumed my every thought. I didn't even know if you'd survived, Sean!"

He gave me nothing in response but a steady stare.

"You want to know the first thing I said when I woke up in Janner's cabin?"

Again, he gave me nothing.

"Is he alive?" I shouted, ramming my palm into his chest, his heart. "I asked them if *you* were alive! So don't you get all fucking pity party on me, like this whole thing has been a vacation for me. Do you know how maddening losing *you* has been? How crazy I made myself in my darkened prison, wondering if I was ever going to come home to you at all, and if I did, and you were still alive, wondering if you'd ever want to have me again? You wouldn't even talk to me when Cooper called you! I thought we were over, Sean, over...and that you hated me so much you couldn't muster the decency to tell me. Not even over the phone."

With my face so near him, I could finally see a flinch of emotion, however fleeting it was. All it left behind was the tiniest trace of green in the blackened pools of his eyes.

"I'm sorry, Sean. I'm so sorry that I couldn't trust you with what I thought I'd done to Matty. But you have to understand that you don't make it easy for me," I said, collapsing back down to the seat behind me. "When reactions like this," I said, waving my hand at him, "are what I can expect, I tend to choose a different course."

"What I did tonight...," he said, pausing slightly. "It had a purpose."

"Scaring the shit out of me is one helluva way to make your point."

"I didn't do it to scare *you*," he said, eyes blazing. "I did it to get to *her*. *She* was going to pay for her actions, not you."

A flash of nerves ignited down my spine at his words.

"But Scarlet doesn't feel pain, Sean," I admitted softly. "All you would have done was hurt *me*..."

He looked stunned for a moment, then I realized that maybe that was yet another little detail I hadn't bothered to share with him over time.

"I didn't know," he said quietly. "I just...there's so much anger. I needed to get it out. Needed someone else to share my burden."

Fear washed over him quickly, overriding whatever emotional barrier he had erected earlier, and he pulled me to my feet, yanking my coat open to access the neckline of my dress. He drew it down gently, then ran his hand delicately over my collarbones and across my sternum, examining any damage I'd sustained when he'd pinned me to the wall.

"It's hard loving something so fragile..."

"I know," I whispered, turning away from him. His statement was an observation of my physical fragility. Mine was of his emotional one.

With that realization, his reactions made far more sense. His rage wasn't driven by fear at all, and, as that anger waned, all I could sense was guilt. Guilt and need.

"I want nothing more than to be the man you need right now...the man you had hoped to come back to," he said, walking away from me, distancing himself from the moment we'd just had. "But I can't. I don't know how to explain it to you. No matter how much my mind knows that you are not at fault—that you are not to blame—a part of me still wants someone to pay."

His eyes wouldn't meet mine when he expressed something about himself that he clearly detested—a dichotomous nature that I, of all people, could easily wrap my mind around. "I *need* someone to pay. The beast will not rest until then..."

"Beast?" I asked hesitantly.

"My rage, bloodlust, black void of hatred— whatever you wish to call it. It cannot be quieted. I'm fighting for control every second I'm here with you now. Can't you feel it?"

And boy, could I.

"Yes, but there has to be a way to fix it...isn't there?" I asked beseechingly. "If Scarlet never returns, it can't be like this forever. You can't feel this way every time you see me, can you?"

He looked up at my pleading eyes. All I saw was a sadness so deep that it threatened to engulf me. Then it disappeared entirely, leaving only the menacing blackness that had dominated just moments before. With the return of that pigment came the return of his rage.

"And if there was a way?" he asked, stalking toward me slowly.

"I would take it." The confidence in my words was directly contradicted by the knocking of my knees. Dark-eyed Sean was not easy to get used to having around, especially when I was the subject of his undivided attention.

"Do you trust me enough?"

"To do what?"

"To take that option?" he asked, meticulously assessing my every response. "To not harm you..."

"What are you going to do?"

"There are only two ways to release what I feel

right now," he told me, his voice cold as ice. "Killing you is clearly not an option..." His words trailed off as though, whatever option number two was, it may not have been favorable either. It made me glad that I hadn't directly answered his question about trusting him, given that my personal jury was still out on that matter at the moment.

"And the other option...?"

He spun me around and pulled my back firmly against his chest in a flash, holding onto my arms in an effort to keep me there. He exhaled heavily in my hair while he struggled to keep his breathing controlled.

"Tell me you *need* me," he said, rubbing his face slowly through my curls.

A jolt of fear shot through me, and I fought hard to overcome it.

"I need you," I told him, my voice so quiet the words were barely audible.

A small rumble of satisfaction vibrated through his chest and into my back.

"Tell me you *love* me," he demanded, his nose gently stroking the lobe of my ear.

"I love you," I replied as my pulse quickened.

The rumble became stronger as he nipped my neck with his teeth.

Suddenly, I felt the raw sense of need coursing through him, and, as a result, through me. It quickly started to make more sense to me why he was so concerned about my trust in him. He knew he was about to tread on unstable ground for me—ground that I had only begun to reinforce before Scarlet abducted me. Even in all his menacing wonder, he still did not wish to harm me, physically or otherwise. Not even to meet his most inborn instincts.

"Tell me you *want* me," he growled in my ear, his hold on me tightening.

"I want you," I said, finding it hard to breathe, my mouth too dry to even swallow.

When his hands found their way to the hem of my dress, one thrust it up above my waist, the other plummeting down my pantyhose and underwear, settling on its clandestine destination.

"Say it again," he ordered, body motionless, as if awaiting my permission to continue. My breath caught in my throat while I tried to respond.

"Sean—"

The second his name passed my lips, his hand instantly worked against the restrictive spandex surrounding it, furiously rubbing my body into a frenzy. My mind was overwhelmed, and I could barely process his words.

When his hand stopped and I caught my breath, I was able to comprehend.

"Say. It. Again."

To reassure him that I understood, I pressed my body back into him as firmly as I could—as much as the weakness in my knees would allow.

"I want you," I sighed, reaching my arm back over my head to touch his face. "Now."

He intercepted my hand, pulling my arm back down to my side.

"No, no, no, little one. I'll be giving the orders tonight," he whispered in my ear before violently pulling my underwear and tights down around my ankles. "I hope Cooper and the boys are out for a while. I plan on taking my time."

When his hand found me again, I gasped, trying to remain upright, but luckily for me, that wasn't part of his plan. Before I knew it my chest was pressed tightly to the window seat, arms splayed out beside me. I felt him press against me, the rumbling sound in his chest returning.

"I need you to know that I love you, Ruby," he told me, sounding business-like. "Now tell me to fuck you..."

CHAPTER 10

I startled awake in the middle of the night, shooting up in bed, still tangled in the covers. Beside me was nothing but empty mattress. He was gone.

I sighed heavily, slumping against my vintage wooden headboard. I'd been naïve to think that everything would be fine after our encounter, which made me feel ridiculous for letting it happen in the first place. My head collapsed into my knees, which were tucked tightly against my chest, while I groaned in frustration with the situation as well as my stupidity.

"I'm over here," a voice called from the shadows. My head snapped to attention, searching the darkness for Sean's location. It took me a moment to make him out, but sure enough, he sat motionless in my armchair tucked in the far corner of the room. "I was concerned that the *enthusiasm* you showed earlier might have worn off by the time you woke up. I thought it best to leave you some space," he explained, moving into the scant light the moon provided. "I didn't leave you..." His voice was tender and soft—my heart nearly melted. Such a stark contrast to the brute who only hours early had demanded my love. Now, the man left behind was scared he may have lost it.

"So, you've just been sitting here, watching me sleep?" I asked curiously, trying to lighten his mood slightly.

"You'd be surprised," he said with a subtle curl of his mouth. "It's highly entertaining at times."

I forced a smile in return, but he saw right through me as always.

"Do you want me to go?" he asked, his words again carrying a rare softness.

I didn't know what I wanted. Only hours earlier I'd gone through a roller coaster ride of emotional highs and lows that still had my head reeling. It's what woke me up in the first place. When Sean came into my apartment, my heart skipped a beat—granted that was partly fear driven—but his effect on me was still as intact as mine was on him. Regardless, his anger remained, and given how the whole thing went down, he was completely ill-equipped to deal with that anger.

As for the sex, that was the most complicated event of the evening. I couldn't explain it, but somehow I knew he *needed* that, not only for a release, but also for something deeper, darker—a punishment of sorts, meant to prove that he still had some level of control over me. As barbaric as that sounded, I understood it. It wasn't sex with the Sean I'd been with before, the green-eyed god who had saved me more times than I could remember. I'd had sex with his other half, his inner Scarlet, the black-eyed mercenary I'd grown to know and fear, and although he was intense, dominating, even brutal at times, I learned a very important fact from all of that. *He* loved me too. Both sides of Sean loved me equally, though they had decidedly different ways of expressing it. Submitting to him was exactly what he'd needed to move past his rage.

"I'll go," he said, making his way to the door.

"No!" I blurted out as I stumbled out of the bed, wrapped in my comforter. I crashed to the ground before scrambling inelegantly to my feet. "I'm sorry. I was thinking about something."

"And?" he said, pausing by the door.

"I think I get it...what happened last night—" I started before Sean cut me off, looking moderately embarrassed.

"Ruby, I—"

"You forgive me now," I said, taking my turn to interrupt him. "You *both* do."

I hesitated with my last statement, unsure that he would follow what I was attempting to say. Instead, he looked at me with wide eyes that clearly got my message.

"That's why you had to...why we..." I fumbled, trying to find a delicate way to describe the raw, angry sex that had occurred in my room that night. "It's like you have two sides too, but not literally, and yours isn't a wolf. It's something else, but oddly similar. *He* needed that from me—for me to *let* him have that, didn't he...er, uh, you? Am I making any sense here, or—"

"*Yes,*" he said, cupping my face softly. "You are, though the details are a little off as usual." He smiled at his jab, but it quickly faded. "Of course I forgive you, Ruby. There was never any question that I would. The question now is whether or not *you* can forgive *me?*"

"Do I get breakfast out of the deal if I say yes?" I

asked, smiling up at him while my stomach rumbled. It was one thirty in the morning, but our bedroom escapades had left me famished.

He leaned in slowly to kiss me, and I found myself with eyes closed, rising up on my toes to meet him. My heart beat faster and the electricity that flowed between us was in full force. Time stood still, the seconds drawing out painfully while I awaited his contact. When his breath tickled my lips, I parted them with an inhale of anticipation.

Instead of a kiss, I got interrupted by an unwanted banging on my door.

"Are you up?" Cooper shouted, knowing damn well I was since he could usually hear me from the living room. Without any acknowledgment, he slammed open the bedroom door.

"Seriously, Coop?" I snapped, scooping the blankets up around me tighter.

"Oh, please, Ruby. Like I haven't seen it before," he sighed, flipping on the light. Sean growled. "I think we need a family huddle. These guys are making me crazy already. I think it's time for them to go."

"I think it's time for *you* to go," Sean said calmly, staring Cooper down.

"Oh," Cooper said, looking back and forth between Sean and me. "I wasn't interrupting, was I? So sorry. Please continue. I'll entertain your squatters while you two carry on with whatever it was you were doing. No problem."

He turned off the light and threw the door closed behind him, punctuating his sentence with a slam.

"You two are really going to have to try and find a way to get along," I told Sean, making my way to my walk-in closet. "It doesn't make things easier on me to have you two constantly at odds. And frankly, I don't even know why you are."

"It's a male thing," Sean offered for explanation.

I stuck my head out and gave him my best hairy eyeball.

"I still haven't officially forgiven you, you know," I said haughtily. "I could drag that out for months, if you'd prefer. It's kind of a *girl* thing."

"Point taken," he said, walking towards me. I pulled on my pants just before he cornered me in the closet. I kept my back to him while I fumbled with my tank top, trying to figure out which end was which in the dark.

"Does your offer still stand?" he asked, turning me around as I pulled the hem of my top down past my navel.

"It does, but now I'm tacking on good behavior. You have to promise to try," I pleaded. "Cooper will be getting the same speech, if that makes you feel any better."

"And what of the trio of foreigners in your living room? Must I be well-mannered to them too?"

"I'm undecided on that," I said, pulling myself up to kiss him quickly. "I'll keep you posted."

"Do that," he said intensely. "I think Cooper's right about one thing; it's time for your unwanted houseguests to leave."

"Sean," I breathed, preparing for a battle. "I really want to hear them out."

"And I want to *see* them out," he countered, positioning his body only inches away from mine.

"And they came here to see me, not you, so I'm going to entertain their plea and then decide what to do," I told him firmly. "This is still my home, and I'm still in charge of what goes on in it. I know that fact pains both you and Cooper greatly, but it's the truth and your reality." His expression cooled ever so slightly. "Please, Sean. You ask me to trust you. Please trust me enough to do the right thing here."

His face contorted in such a familiar way that it startled me momentarily. He was giving me Cooper's famed 'are you fucking kidding me?' face. I knew that good judgment wasn't my strong suit, but there was something about the boys that seemed honest, despite their reserved energy. They saved me from my hell; I owed them one. If I could help them escape from theirs, then I would.

"Please?" I asked, pressing against his fortress of a body. "I'm *asking* you to let me lead on this one." His chest rumbled beneath me. "I promise, the second bodies need to drop, it's all you and Cooper."

"Well," he started, pulling me up off the floor to wrap my legs about his waist. "Since you asked so nicely..." He pulled me in forcefully for a kiss. It was good that he was holding me up because my body went weak the instant he started.

He put me down moments later and straightened my disheveled clothes while I came to my senses.

"I like it when you ask for my permission," he purred in my ear.

"I'll do it more often if that's the reward I get," I replied, sounding mildly winded.

His eyes were darker than normal, but that wasn't entirely surprising. I was getting a crash course in how to navigate Sean's split personality. Why he had it in the first place was becoming clearer, though it was still a bit of a mystery. Exactly how it worked was too.

"Are you two fucking finished in there yet?"

Cooper hollered from the living room.

"Coming," I sighed, not looking forward to our family meeting.

Sean looked at me with a controlled harshness that told me he was having a hard time letting me take the lead. I placed my hand in his and gave a little squeeze.

"I guess we should get this over with," I lamented.

"The second one of them screws up..." Sean started, eyeing me tightly.

"Agreed," I nodded. "You can get medieval on them."

He choked out a harsh and hearty laugh.

"I've never understood that saying," he declared, pulling me towards the bedroom door. "There were periods in time far more torturous than that one. I actually found the medieval methods to be rather civilized."

"Of course you did," I groaned, following him out to the living room.

The four men stared when we entered. Nervousness coursed from the Maine trio, and hostility rolled off of Cooper at an alarming rate. He really wasn't pleased with his babysitting role. Funny how he survived keeping an eye on me just fine.

"So what did you guys figure out during your little outing?" I asked, needing to break the silence in the room.

"Nothing," Cooper said with great annoyance. "They only want to talk to you."

"Seriously? They didn't say anything?"

"Not a word."

Cooper was hanging on by a thin thread. His distrust was apparent to all parties present, and unfortunately for me, Sean was completely on his wavelength.

"And if I ask for answers?" Sean asked, his voice calm and menacing.

Janner shrugged slightly. "That is an entirely different matter."

Cooper growled. I don't think he enjoyed being one-upped by Sean.

I decided to try and sort the mess out, seeing that it was still either that option or a bloodbath in my living room. The little cooling-off period Sean had mandated the boys take hadn't done anything to help. There was too much testosterone in too confined a space.

"You said you need refuge," I started, trying to recall what Janner had said earlier. "But why here? Why do you think you're better off here with me? With *us*?"

"Because of what you are," Janner stated like that point was painfully obvious. "I have to admit that we were surprised that it was so easy to *collect* you in the woods that day. We thought we were possibly going on a suicide mission even attempting to approach you. But once we saw you sitting against the tree, you seemed so frightened—fragile even. We were far more concerned with your well-being at that point. More so than our own.

"So we took you in and helped you, which afforded us an opportunity to see how the real you stacked up against your reputation. Pleasantly, we found you to be far more rational than we had been led to believe. Had we not seen you in action prior to that, I don't know that we would be here now, asking for your help. You seem as though somehow, unlike other werewolves, you and your wolf are polar opposites."

"Yes, well, I do seem to be a bit of an enigma," I replied with a smile, trying to make light of his observation. He had hit the nail on the head and it made me uncomfortable. It seemed to have the same effect on Cooper and Sean.

"So what you're basically saying is that you want to hide behind Ruby's skirt just in case your big bad alpha comes looking for you?" Cooper sneered. "You made your fucking bed. Figure out a way to sleep in it."

"I don't hide from anyone, you fucking prick," Alistair barked.

Cooper laughed."I wouldn't even break a sweat killing you."

"Well, I guess it's good that nobody will be killing anyone tonight, so we won't have to test the veracity of that statement," I interjected.

"Not yet," Cooper and Sean chimed together. The two slowly turned to look at one another with the most unsettled expressions.

"Anyway," I said, trying to bring the focus back to the issue at hand. "You think that I'm going to take you in so that I can just invite trouble to my doorstep?"

"My hope, Ruby, was that you would consider our situation and think about it before readily dismissing us. The stories that I've heard never spoke of your dual nature. You seem so very human to me. I wonder if our plight could possibly appeal to that inflated sense of humanity. If Tobias were to find out about our location...," he said, letting his lack of completion speak for itself.

"You think he'd be dissuaded from coming after you because this seemingly too-human werewolf is actually a ruthless assassin."

"If you're comfortable putting it that way, then yes."

"So I'm the 'just in case' plan?"

"In a sense." His expression was surprisingly unapologetic.

The irony of the situation was too much for me. They wanted to be near me for protection, and I couldn't even take care of myself because Scarlet had taken a leave of absence.

"I don't really know how to tell you this, guys, but I'm not really going to be able to help much because—"

"Ruby!" Sean and Cooper yelled simultaneously. It was truly bizarre.

"I think what Ruby is trying to say," Cooper started, "is that she's on a tight leash these days. She can't just go and take care of your problems without consequence." Cooper shot a glance at Sean and then back to the boys. "He may be her mate, but her survival is dependent on keeping her nose clean. All you three seem to want to do is dirty it for her."

"I don't think it'll be an issue," Janner countered. "If Tobias knows that we're aligned with you, I don't think even he would be dumb enough—or suicidal enough—to come after us. He enjoys breathing far too much for that."

"That's quite a gamble," Sean added. "And one that none of us are willing to make."

"Agreed," growled Cooper.

Flanked by the two men in my life, I looked over at the somber threesome. Beckett's face was impassive, but Janner and Alistair had looks of uncertainty and the energy to go along with it. Their shields had been dropped the instant the conversation started, and whatever they had hoped to accomplish by coming to my house during the storm of the century wasn't panning out. It looked as though they were running out of hope as well as options.

"Now that we've heard what you came here to say...," Sean began, motioning toward the door.

I watched as Janner took a deep, cleansing breath before giving Sean and Cooper both a curt nod and leading his men to the door. Beckett followed without argument or acknowledgment of any of us. I looked on, feeling as though something just wasn't quite right. It didn't feel good sending them away. When I brought my attention back to Alistair, he stood steadfast, staring at me with a pained expression. He looked desperate to say something.

"Ali," Janner called from the doorway. "We'll find another way..."

Alistair's eyes remained fixed on mine with a pleading gaze. He opened his mouth to speak, then closed it and started to go to his packmates, a slightly defeated posture overtaking him.

"Alistair," I called, lunging toward him. He startled at my approach, but halted all the same. "Is there something you want to tell me? Something other than what I've heard?"

He looked to Janner, seeking permission with his eyes. Janner pressed his lips tightly and sighed before giving him a nod of approval. Without skipping a beat, Alistair dropped a bomb on us.

"They've been going missing for a while now," he told me, jumping right to the meat of his story. It left me completely bewildered.

"Who? Who's been going missing?"

"Pack members," he said flatly. "At first, we thought it was coincidence. One or two had disappeared, but there always seemed to be a reason to explain away any doubt. Most were lower ranking members who weren't really in love with being a part of the pack. They would rather have been loners. Initially, we thought they'd all just buggered off."

Again, he looked to Janner with an air of uncertainty clouding everything around him. It was apparent that this was a card he'd hoped to not have to play.

"But later...," I prodded, trying to drag it out of him.

"Later, it was random members of the pack. And the last one to be taken, she was my mate. Someone took my Jemma."

My shoulders sagged with compassion. The pain he felt was staggering, and part of me knew all too well what that felt like. The other part of me that also knew exactly what that felt like was still too AWOL to care.

"When?" Sean asked, his booming voice startling me.

"A few months ago," Alistair said, trying desperately to compose himself. "She left to run some errands one day and never came back."

"I'm so sorry, Alistair," I whispered.

"What does this have to do with you staying here?" Cooper blurted out from behind me.

"Cooper!"

"Well?" he snarled. "It's a sad story and all, and I feel bad for him, but that doesn't have anything to do with us. Maybe you should send Sean over there to figure out what's happening."

"Have a little compassion, Coop! How would you feel if your mate were taken?"

He looked at me angrily, but I could see him processing that thought. It eased the harshness in his face ever so slightly.

"Please go on," I urged.

"The reason we killed the last alpha isn't quite what we let on before," he said with hesitation. "The truth is that we acquired evidence indicating that he had been selling his own to someone for testing, but testing for what and by whom we never found out. I overheard him on the phone one night. He was talking to whoever had Jemma. He told them to kill the bitch if it wasn't working. He had her murdered." He paused for a moment, squeezing his eyes shut tightly. "The rage I felt was unlike anything I've ever experienced. I tore him to pieces with my bare hands before I even realized what I was doing."

"And that's why you left," I uttered as my heart fell into my stomach.

"We had no choice," Janner offered from his place in the doorway. "Had we stayed, the repercussions would have been immense. The next alpha couldn't have allowed that kind of mutinous behavior, so he gave us one chance to escape with our lives. We took it. It was only later that we learned that he might have orchestrated the entire event. I'm quite certain he used us."

"If you have served your purpose to him, why are you so convinced that he will come for you?" Sean asked frankly.

"Like I said before, he has no honor. And, to be honest, I think he was a little frightened by Ali's display that night," Janner explained. "Many of the pack saw how easily he tore through our late leader. I was there. I've never seen anything like it in all my years, though I don't think it could be reproduced on demand. He was beyond lethal. Tobias will have that weighing on the back of his mind at all times, wondering if we'll come back for him. He was Deacon's right-hand man. He's known all along what was going on and decided to play both sides of the fence while it suited his purposes. I'm afraid he's still carrying out whatever had been started. From what we've heard through the grapevine, pack members are still going missing..."

"Interesting theory, but I'm not buying it," Cooper said, moving closer to me.

"Would you not avenge Ruby if something were to ever happen to her?" Ali asked, his voice uncharacteristically soft and distant.

Cooper growled.

"I would stop at nothing to take down anyone or anything that harmed a single hair on her head," he rumbled threateningly. "A point that you would be wise to remember—*very* wise."

"Then you understand how I feel, and you know it gives validity to Tobias' fear," Alistair added. "My revenge isn't complete until all who hurt Jemma are cold and dead. *All* of them."

Sean stirred behind me and I jumped; I'd nearly forgotten he was there.

"This Tobias," he said, walking toward Alistair. "Do you have proof that he knew what was going on or that he's still doing it now?"

Alistair's expression went grim. "No, not directly. Everything we had obtained about Deacon's involvement was through Tobias. Even the phone call I overheard; Tobias had tipped me off to it. When we left, all that evidence was left behind, and I'm sure has been long since destroyed. We were hoping that maybe the PC could assist us in locating some new information." Sean's eyes narrowed accusingly. "When we heard about Ruby, we also heard that she may have had some...*influence* with the PC. We were hoping that she would help us with that as well."

"Sean," I said quietly, "I know you're uneasy about this, but Alistair is right. You both would go to any length to hurt someone that tried to harm me or anyone else you love. Can't you empathize with his situation? And, really, if there's some psycho selling off pack members to God only knows what fate, can you tell me you're okay with that?" He stared at me without responding, so I pulled out the big guns. "I was sold off...," I whispered, moving closer to him. "Please, I want to help them. You have to understand why."

I reached up onto my toes, not caring that everyone in the room was staring, and kissed him softly. His forest green eyes penetrated mine, telling me that he was willing to concede, but less than thrilled with the idea.

"I will have one of the brothers go to London to check on matters there," he said, speaking over top of me to Janner. "And I'll alert those already there to be on watch for anything suspicious. Perhaps a mild crackdown will strike a little fear into this Tobias' heart, if he has one."

"That would be much appreciated," Janner replied with great sincerity.

"Thank you," Alistair added. He looked so vulnerable standing in the middle of my living room— young and grief-stricken.

"Cooper," I called as I turned to face him. "Can you accept this?"

He audibly sighed.

"I can. For now. But we're going to have to set some serious ground rules first. If it comes to a choice between our safety and theirs, those bitches are going down any day of the week."

"Cooper," Janner said, lowering his head slightly to avert his gaze. An act of submission. "We do not wish to bring harm to you or yours. If it becomes a situation where that is the bottom line, we will happily give ourselves up so as to divert any violence away from you both. Will that appease you?"

"It's a start..."

"Okay then," I said, walking down the hall to the linen closet. "Looks like we're going to have a good old-fashioned sleepover."

"No," Cooper and Sean barked just seconds apart.

"They are not staying here," Sean informed me. It was clear by his tone that there was no negotiating that point.

"Well, they could stay upstairs," I offered in compromise. He looked at me dubiously. "Sean, it's late. Just for tonight. It should be fine. It won't even be comfortable; they'll be miserable, doesn't that make you feel better?"

"Immensely."

I loaded up my arms with every extra sheet, blanket, and comforter I could find. I didn't have extra pillows, so I stopped by the couch to swipe all the toss cushions I could find off of it. Cooper and Sean watched me intently as I did, neither one of them lifting a hand to help. It was their silent declaration that, though they had conceded to my desire to help our little stray wolves, they weren't happy about it. They were growing more and more alike every day.

"Here," I said, loading up Alistair's arms with the bedding. "Follow me."

I made my way out onto the landing and led the trio up to the third floor with Sean and Cooper pulling up the rear. I opened the studio up and flipped on the light. With a grand sweeping gesture, I showed my guests their accommodations.

"It's the best I can offer."

"We're happy to take it," Janner said, looking around the room. "I'll get everything else set up here. It's been a long night. You should get some rest."

"She doesn't need your advice," Sean threatened.

"Of course," Janner replied with a small bow.

With that, I was ushered down the stairs and back into my apartment, which was fine by me. The testosterone cocktail I'd been swimming in all night was starting to drown me, and I was thankful to find myself in my house with only half as much of it to deal with.

Cooper made a show of locking the door behind us before making his way over to me to give me a huge hug goodnight. Sean seemed to take it well until Cooper planted a long and gentle kiss on my cheek. It wasn't sexual at all—his energy told me as much—but he knew it would rattle Sean's cage so he did it for one last jolly before he went into his bedroom and shut his door for the night.

Sean's eyes were glued to the hallway that Cooper had just disappeared down.

"You know he just does it to rile you up, and you take the bait every time," I informed him as I headed to the bathroom. He didn't follow. "Are you staying?" I asked while my stomach did a little flip.

He eyed me strangely in response.

"Of course, I'm staying," he replied as though my question had been utterly ridiculous. Perhaps it was. "But I think I'll be staying out here tonight. Wouldn't want one of the boys to wander in while we all are sleeping."

"Through the locked door?" I asked incredulously.

"Exactly," he replied with a mischievous grin. I loved that grin.

"Suit yourself." I shrugged and continued on my path to the washroom. "It's really too bad though. I wasn't quite ready to go to sleep." I flashed him a mischievous grin of my own.

"Jesus Christ, you two." Cooper's muffled voice groaned from his bedroom. "If I have to put up with this from now on, I'm moving out."

"No, you're not," I quipped. "Who would you have to boss around all day? You know that's your favorite activity."

"Ugggh," he lamented. "I hate it when you're right."

"Love you too, Coop."

I looked back to see Sean smiling at me.

"I see you two have straightened a few things out. I'm glad to see that," he said, with an impish grin that implied he knew Cooper was my alpha. I don't know why it surprised me.

"Yep. We sure did, though it probably would have been easier had you just told me you knew."

"I tried," he said, suddenly right in front of me. I could never get used to how quickly he could move. "I was rudely interrupted by the Rev at the time. After that, there was always a crisis to attend to. That seems to be your gold standard, does it not?" The wattage on his playful grin turned up even further.

"It certainly is, so I'll let you off the hook this time," I said, leaning in to kiss him gently before catching his bottom lip between my teeth and giving it a light, punishing tug.

"How gracious of you," he replied with a whisper. "Now...how about we go and try to remedy that little sleep issue of yours."

CHAPTER 11

With precious little sleep, I awoke the next morning only to have to drag my ass down to the shop and work. It would be my first official day back since Scarlet went AWOL with me weeks earlier; I was nervous, but excited all the same. It meant spending time with Peyta, which promised to be a double-edged sword, but she needed my help. I wanted to be there to support her like she'd always supported me.

As I made a move to slip out of bed, a large and muscular arm wound its way around my waist, pinning me down so its owner could gingerly nibble on my ear. My pulse raced instantly.

"Sean, I have to get ready to open the shop."

"And you will," he replied, working his way down my neck. "In a minute."

"Nope," I retorted, wiggling my way free. "I have a business to run, and you still have a mystery to solve, don't you? What are you going to do about what Alistair told us last night?"

He tensed slightly before answering.

"I've got someone on a plane there today."

"Who?"

"Jay," he replied after a slight hesitation.

"Oh..." It was all I could muster in response.

"He'll be fine, Ruby. He's a far better soldier than you—or even he—would ever give him credit for."

"It's not that," I hedged, not wanting to spill beans that weren't mine to spill. "It's just...well, it's Peyta. She's not doing well right now, and I don't think it'll be good for her to know that Jay is in harm's way again."

He sighed.

"This is the world she lives in now, Ruby. I can't change that."

"I know, but she isn't dealing well with it," I added. "Putting Jay in danger isn't going to help that."

"Ruby, they will have to work through these things as we have. He loves her more than I can put into words," he said, getting up out of the bed. I stared at the sweatpants hanging dangerously low on his hips. "He loves her nearly as much as I love you. They'll sort it out, I'm certain of it. And he *can* handle this mission. He hid his abilities to lead for eons because of Jer. He's not hiding them anymore. You should feel sorry for whoever is across the pond selling those wolves off. They're about to be in a world of hurt, not Jay."

"Okay," I said, forcing a smile. He hugged me in response and kissed the top of my head firmly, letting me know it was going to be all right.

"He'll only be gone for a while, which means I'll finally have my place to myself again."

"What? What do you mean?"

"Jay's been staying in town while I was gone— while I was out searching for you and trying to find who killed McGurney."

"So, the other night when you hung up on Cooper...?"

"I was in Virginia."

"That wasn't you in your apartment?"

"No. Why?"

I felt a rush of blood flood my cheeks.

"I...I thought it was you. You walked away from the window when I looked up at you. I thought you didn't want to see me."

"Jay was there, Ruby. Not me," he replied softly. "I wanted to see you."

"But you hung up on Cooper—"

"Because he called at a very bad time. I didn't have time to talk."

"Why didn't you call back? I thought you hated me," I whispered, averting my gaze.

"Do you still think that now?" he asked, pulling me tightly against him.

"Well, no, but—"

"I did not want to talk to you on the phone because I wanted to do it in person," he said with a strain in his voice. "I knew that you would be at Matty's funeral. Please understand that as furious as I was with Scarlet, I never meant you harm. Watching her disappear through that door, knowing that she held you prisoner—it nearly drove me mad. I spent day and night searching for her to no avail. I can assure you, Ruby, if she had been anywhere on the face of this earth, I would have found her. Eventually, I thought that perhaps you both did not wish to be found, and there were things that I had neglected that I could not any longer. Duty called. Duty always seems to call." His voice was sad as he uttered his final thought.

"I would never have chosen to leave you," I said, squeezing him tightly. "But I can't tell you how happy it makes me to know that you never held what happened against me."

"Never."

I smiled.

"Well, I'm *super* glad we just cleared that mess up," I joked, pulling away from him.

"Agreed," he replied dryly with a devilish grin on his face. "Now, as much as I would love to show you just how happy it makes me, I can't. You should go clean up for work. I've got matters to attend to. I'm assuming that Cooper will be keeping an eye on your new roommates to ensure their good behavior." His tone was soft but warning. He still didn't trust the newbies. "I think I'll have one of the boys stick around to keep an eye on you and Peyta...for good measure."

"Sounds like a plan to me. I'm sure I can talk Cooper into it, but I'm going to owe him big time," I informed him, tossing an off-the-shoulder long-sleeve top on. "I'm going to have to give him the car if I keep it up."

"He can have the car, just not you."

"Oh, I'm his and he knows it," I said in mocking tone. "Now that we've straightened out that he's my alpha, I'll never hear the end of it! He *loves* a chance to boss me around."

"Don't we all," Sean said, looking at me through hooded eyes. Those eyes were dangerous and destined to make me late.

"Okay, well, I'm gonna jet," I told him as I wiggled into my skinny jeans. "When am I going to see you?"

"Soon," he murmured. "Very soon."

I walked over to him to give him a quick kiss

before running down the hall to the kitchen.

"That's super helpful, thanks," I yelled over my shoulder.

"I aim to please," he called after me, following me out of the room.

I grabbed a water bottle and banana off the counter then made my way to the front door.

"Call me," I ordered, turning to face the mysterious man in my life.

"And how will you answer?" he asked, flipping my phone over and over in his hand.

"Please. Like you couldn't figure out a way."

"Where you're concerned, Ruby, I'll *always* find a way."

*   *   *

The bells jingled when Peyta walked through the store entrance. They were music to my ears. I was busy in the back workroom when she came in, trying to see if anything needed my attention while admiring Peyta's truly award-winning organizational skills. Like Pavlov's dog, I quickly made my way out front to greet her.

"Hey P," I called out when I walked through the open door.

"I brought you a coffee from the place down the street that you love," she said, walking toward me. "And I got you one of those pastry things too. You look skinny. They were out of chocolate but—" Her words cut off suddenly, as though some outside force had pressed pause, freezing her in place. Her eyes glazed while they widened, staring just beyond me.

"Peyta? Peyta, what's wrong?" I asked, my concern ever-growing. "Did something happen? You look like you've seen a…"

CHAPTER 12

"*Ghost.*"

My spine chilled as that single word narrowly made its way out of my mouth. A familiar but unwelcome sensation washed over me. I had hoped to never feel it again.

"Ruby," Peyta called, still unable to pull her eyes away from whatever stalked me from behind. I, however, seemed unable to force myself to turn around and face it at all.

My abdominal scar burned as if the memory of Gregory's attack was physiologically etched into it, and I prayed that I wasn't in for a repeat performance. By the look on Peyta's face, she wasn't up for a round two either. When her eyes finally met mine, they were filled with fear. Before I could do anything to calm her, I felt the faintest brush of something against my hair.

I had no intention of staying around to see what else he could touch.

"*Run,*" I mouthed to Peyta, barely making a sound.

She didn't hesitate, and neither did I. Darting for the entrance, she had the door ripped open only moments after I rounded the counter to join her. So much for no more running, though I felt that instance warranted an exception to the rule.

I turned to slam the door behind me, but what I saw looking back at me halted my progress. His body faded minutely with every stride Peyta took down the street, but his face was unmistakable. The expression it wore was too—the perfect mix of sadness and confusion. I'd seen it once before through Scarlet's eyes.

"PEYTA!" I screamed at her just before she could round the corner at the end of the block. "Come back! *Now!*"

With hesitation, the tiny brunette jogged back toward me. I frantically looked from her to the ghost in my store, watching as his form solidified little by little with her approach. When she was only yards away, I cautiously reentered the shop. My hands shook—tremors growing—as I approached him. His expression remained unchanged.

I was surprised he wore one at all, given that the last time I'd seen him he didn't have a head.

"*Matty?*" I called, my voice cracking as my throat tightened violently. Tears rolled freely down my face; I barely felt them. Disbelief coursed too strongly through my body and off of his to feel anything else.

"You can see me," he whispered, slowly bringing his hands before his face to investigate their solidity.

"Yes," Peyta replied from behind me. "We both can."

His attention drifted to her as she came to stand beside me. Her demeanor had done a complete one-eighty from what it had just been. Her energy was calm like it had always been when the subject of the ghosts came up, though it was tinged with a hint of sorrow when she looked at me.

When she looked at Matty, that sorrow turned to rage.

"Ruby—" he started before Peyta cut him off.

"You shouldn't be here," she fumed, her rage building rapidly. "You need to leave."

"Peyta!" I snapped, grabbing her arm.

"He nearly killed Jay," she yelled, turning hateful eyes on me. "It's time for him to go...somewhere far away and *very* warm."

Matty and I both visibly cringed at her words. Peyta had clearly found an outlet for her emotions far sooner than I'd expected, though I wasn't certain it was going to be an especially healthy one.

"What?" he asked, trying to make sense of what she had said. He seemed disoriented and confused, with no obvious recollection of the event Peyta spoke of. I broke out in a cold sweat. Would he remember what Scarlet did?

"You," Peyta growled as she stalked closer to him, "you ruined *everything*. This is all your fault."

"Ruby?" he asked, his wide eyes pleading for understanding.

I clasped a hand around Peyta's thin arm to keep her from advancing any further. She was too enraged to see what I did. Matty was frightened.

"It's okay, Matty," I said softly, walking past Peyta. "You don't remember. That's all right. I don't remember everything either."

"Are you...? You're not...?" he started, unable to finish his thoughts.

"No, Matty," I said as another rogue tear worked its way loose. "I'm not dead."

He closed his eyes, and I watched as the tension left his body with one large exhale. Of all the things he had to be concerned about, my well-being was first and foremost on his mind. Instead of making me feel better, I felt infinitely worse. I thought I was going to be potentially dealing with the mindless, bloodthirsty rogue who had nearly killed Sean, but, much to the contrary, I found myself face to face with the man I thought I'd lost months ago. My Boy Scout.

"Thank God," he whispered to himself.

"You leave God out of this," Peyta snipped, picking up where she left off. "You won't be seeing him where you're going."

"Peyta, please," I begged, turning my bleary eyes on her. "I know you're angry, but—"

"But what, Ruby? He mowed Jay down without a thought and wounded Sean pretty badly too. You think I give a shit about how he feels right now? I don't, and neither should you."

"Peyta, it's not that simple."

"Yes, Ruby, it really is." It was her turn to grab me by the arm and squeeze for dear life. Her bony fingers dug painfully into my flesh while her eyes bore holes into my head. "He nearly took from me everyone that has helped to keep me grounded in this supernatural life. I don't give a *fuck* about him. You shouldn't either."

"Jay is alive, Peyta, and so am I."

"*Jay* won't see me anymore. He may as well not be alive for all it counts now. I'll never see him again, and it's all thanks to him," she said, flinging an accusatory arm in Matty's direction.

"What are you talking about?" I asked, suddenly feeling the same confusion Matty was.

"He wants nothing to do with me," she replied with eyes as cold and hardened as her mother's. "He never even bothered to tell me why, though I'm sure it has a lot to do with me nearly failing him—my complete inability to do the job I was born to do."

"That can't be right," I argued, thinking that Jay had always been the sole voice of reason and perspective when all others were lost. "Did you ask him?"

"What about 'he wants nothing to do with me' wasn't clear, Ruby? He hasn't spoken to me since I healed him. He won't answer my texts, my calls, and I have no idea where he is, not that it would matter much. I highly doubt he'd be willing to see me either."

"Peyta, I don't know what to say."

"There's nothing to say," she said, her voice still cold. "I guess things make a lot more sense to you now though." She sent me a knowing glance then pinned her eyes back on Matty. She was right; her cutting made even more sense after knowing that she and Jay were done.

"Matty, do you remember what happened that night at Sean's?" I asked in an attempt to ascertain exactly what he remembered from that fateful night.

"I can't...I don't know. My head starts to pound whenever I try to put the pieces together."

"Let me give you the Cliff's Notes version," Peyta sneered. "Your crazy fucking wolf charged Jay and nearly tore his throat out before you went on a rampage with Sean, driving knives the size of machetes into each of his major joints and organs."

He pressed his eyes closed as if he was trying to

hide from her words, but he couldn't, and eventually it was apparent that the fuzzy spots in his memory became crystal clear.

"You killed me," he whispered, bringing his eyes up to meet mine.

"Matty, I—"

"You don't need to explain shit to him," Peyta spat. "In fact, I'm pretty over this whole situation. I'll see you tomorrow, Ruby. I'm out."

She snatched up her belongings and stormed through the door without another word. I was hot on her heels.

"Peyta, wait. Please," I called at her as she made her way to the corner and down the alley. She moved fast for someone with legs far shorter than mine. Pausing to let me catch up, I slammed into a wall of hostile energy as soon as I did.

"No. Not this time, Ruby. This is too much."

"I'm worried about you, P. Why didn't you tell me about Jay earlier?"

"Why? It wouldn't change anything. He's not going to listen to you if you try to smooth things over, which, by the way, you're not going to do, understand me?"

"Of course I won't, but we need to talk about this."

"I'm all set with talking today. It doesn't help anyway."

"Oh, and your solution does? Have you even told your mother about that yet?"Her glare told me she hadn't. "I'm not letting this go, Peyta. I love you too much for that. I swear that I'll call her right now unless you promise me that you're going to go to her shop right now and tell her. I'll be checking in with her tonight to be sure you did."

She sighed heavily, fighting back her tears.

"Fine."

"Peyta, please understand that regardless of what happened, the Matty that's standing in my shop right now, he's not the one that hurt Jay. He never would have done something like that until your father infected him. Matty didn't stand a chance—he was destined to become what made him. Please don't hold that against him." I choked on my tears that I could no longer withhold. "I never got to say goodbye to him properly. Please let me have that. *Please.*"

She tried to remain angry at me, but she was above projecting her hostility, and soon her rage petered out to sadness. Sadness for her, for me, and maybe even the slightest bit for Matty. The calm after the storm always afforded the perspective that couldn't be found in the moment.

"Okay," she sighed, starting back down the alley to the main road. "But I'm not staying. I'll hang out just long enough for you to say goodbye. That's it."

My tears rolled off my cheeks freely. I was elated and horrified by what was about to happen. I'd never wanted something more and less at the same time.

As we walked down the street, I took her hand in mine and gave a squeeze. The minute tightening I felt in return made me smile through the pain. We entered the store together, expecting to find Matty where we'd left him, but he wasn't. We searched high and low, but the reality was plain. Matty was gone and I'd missed my chance to tell him how sorry I was.

I'd missed my chance to say goodbye.

CHAPTER 13

"**N**O!" I screamed, slamming the workroom door shut. "I have to tell him, P. I just have to."

"Don't panic yet," she said in an unsuccessful attempt to calm me down. "It doesn't mean he's *gone*, gone. He may have just gone somewhere else for a while."

"Do you think so?" I asked, my desperation plain.

"I don't know. I wasn't very focused on what state he was in. I didn't get a read on how long he had before he'll fade."

"*Fade?*"

"You know," she said, trying to urge me to see the obvious. "Cross over."

"Oh."

"Listen, I'm sorry about this. I know he was your friend, but I can't help blaming him for what happened," she said apologetically. "I never knew the person you claim he was before he tried to kill Jay and Sean and then drove Scarlet away."

I didn't know what to say. Her points were valid, her feelings warranted. I couldn't help but think how I would have reacted if the shoe had been on the other foot. My guess was not nearly as well as she did. She may have gone off on him, but she'd still held some measure of composure. I wouldn't have.

"So, I'm going to head out," she informed me, rocking back on her feet slightly. "But I'll be back tomorrow. Maybe he'll stop by then...and maybe I'll have calmed down about it by then too."

"Sounds like a plan." I forced a smile, hoping that she was right about Matty. "Go see your mom. I believe you still have things to tell her."

She smiled tightly and nodded once.

"Come here," I ordered before scooping her up into a big hug. "Tell her everything too. She needs to know that you and Jay are having issues. This isn't time to skimp on the details." She shot me a dubious look. "Well, yes, skimp on *that* detail. We still don't need her knowing about the PC."

"I'll manage to leave that one out," she joked weakly. "I'll see you tomorrow." She turned away from me, heading toward the door before stopping just short of it. "And, Ruby? I really am sorry about my meltdown. If I can help you say goodbye to the Matty you claim he is, I'll do it."

"Peyta, I am hardly one to talk when it comes to epic meltdowns. If you need to, melt away, my dear. I'm totally good for it."

She giggled as she walked through the door, tossing a parting goodbye over her shoulder. Those shoulders were carrying a lot of weight. I hoped she was on her way over to her mother's to unburden them.

*   *   *

Hours later, I found myself mindlessly playing with a trio of silver hammered beads on the front desk. I couldn't manage to do anything that required focus on any level. My mind was a million miles away in Clusterfuck Land, trying to sort through all the craziness in my life. I had been working under the impression that the CF list and I had finally broken up. Perhaps I jumped the gun on that assumption.

By the time I was entirely too frustrated to stay at the shop any longer, I put a note up on the door saying that we were closing early and locked up behind me. The unseasonably cold weather was still going strong, but I'd planned ahead for once and brought my down vest and mittens with me to work. I slipped them on outside the door and took off to walk through town. It always brought me clarity when I needed it, and I hoped that trend would continue as I made my way down to the docks.

There was one more person I needed to see since my return.

The wind whipped down the winding streets of Portsmouth, stinging my cheeks to a rosy pink. It felt refreshing and was exactly what I needed to bolster my resolve. When I rounded the final turn by the waterfront, I looked down at the boats in the marina—and my heart sank instantly. The houseboat was gone.

Sighing heavily, I proceeded down to the dock anyway. It brought forth a wave of bittersweet emotions. I had nearly died there thanks to the keen and sociopathic efforts of the Rev. Gavin had been the one to save me, but in the aftermath of his efforts, he caused a whole new dilemma for me. For whatever reason, he seemed hellbent on warning me off of Sean, and it almost worked for a fleeting moment. Almost.

I had come back to get those answers he promised me and to find out once and for all why he had it in for Sean so badly. It was clear that Gavin wasn't telling me something, but the *what* was a gnawing question mark in my mind that needed to be erased. For good.

Unfortunately for me, I wasn't going to get much of anything out of someone that wasn't there. Frustrated, I plopped myself down at the edge of the dock, making sure to keep my feet well above the water line. Not only was it way too cold to dip my feet into, but it was also just a little too soon after my near drowning with the Rev to tempt fate.

I knew how much fate adored me.

As I stared off into the harbor, searching for answers that weren't there, a familiar voice nearly scared me right out of my pants—and into the water.

"I don't think that went so well for ya last time, missy. I don't suggest ya be trying it yet again."

Gavin.

I turned to find the aged version of him, cocking his head at me in mocking. He had poured the accent on pretty thick, making me a little concerned that he and I were going to be starting off on the wrong foot, just as I had with nearly everyone else upon my return. As far as I knew, Gavin only spoke with that accent when he was good and riled up.

I seemed to have that effect on him.

"Wasn't planning on it," I smiled, pulling myself up carefully so as not to repeat the impromptu swim he was implying. I didn't think it was likely that Scarlet had decided to take swim lessons during the three weeks she took off and held me captive in my mind.

"I haven't seen you around here for a while..." He trailed off at the end, leading me to offer up an explanation.

"Yeah, well, it seems that I took an unplanned vacation of sorts."

"Indeed. The kind that requires teams of police and volunteers to dredge up Portsmouth Harbor and the greater portion of the lower Charles River," he said, narrowing his eyes slyly. "I think you need a better travel agent. The one you have did a shit job."

"No arguments on my end."

I wondered just how much he knew about my little three week disappearance, but I didn't want to offer up anything more than I needed to. I was there to get answers, not give them. Instead, we stared at each other silently for a moment, neither seeming to want to budge on their agenda.

Finally, I caved.

"I got your note..."

"Did you now?" he mocked, dialing the accent back to his normal American one. I hoped it was a good sign. "Did you actually *read* it? Seems it might have saved you some grief."

"How do you figure that?"

He smiled wide.

"The dark-eyed one has a bit of a temper, doesn't he? Even with *you*." My mouth hung agape in response to his words. *How could he know that?* "I warned you about him. I'm wondering how long it will take for you to decide that I'm telling the truth."

"Probably about as long as it takes you to give me something solid to go off of as far as evidence is concerned. Or maybe once you stop talking in riddles and actually explain in detail why you think he's bad news for me," I quipped, irritation tainting my tone. "Either would be fine."

"And that's exactly what I'd planned before your little escapade, or should I say, *Scarlet's* little escapade?"

My irritation started to bleed to anger. Even when he shouldn't, Gavin seemed to have all the answers about everything, and I had none. It felt like the early days of Sean and me, minus the animal attraction and occasional flirting.

"I came here to talk to you. If all you're going to do is be an all-knowing prick about everything, I'll leave," I said, starting to make my way past him. "I don't suppose it really matters anyway. You'll know where to find me."

He caught my arm just before I was out of reach.

"You may not like my methods, Ruby, but I can assure you that everything I do for you is in your best interest."

"Hmm, that sounds oddly familiar. I think I've heard it before," I mocked, rolling my eyes up and to the right as though contemplating something. "Oh, that's right. I believe the '*dark-eyed one*' has used that line on me a time or two, and, correct me if I'm wrong, he is the one that you're warning me against, no?" My observation was met with a sour look. "Interesting. Shall I hold that against you too?"

"I don't care for your tone."

"And I don't care for your double standards."

"You seem to be awfully fond of his," he purred, his voice and energy laced with disdain. "And I don't recall ever threatening to kill you. Would that be helpful? Would you be more likely to listen to me then?"

"No," I replied flatly, "I wouldn't. Sean can pull

that off. You can't."

"Yes, it's actually quite amazing the feats that Sean can '*pull off*' when he's motivated. I think I'll tell you some of those stories about him soon, but not today," he said condescendingly. "You're not ready to hear them just yet."

"Well then, why are we still here talking? You're not going to tell me anything helpful and I'm over it, so...?"

"Tell me something, Ruby. Did you sleep with Sean the night I warned you about him just to spite me, or had that been on the agenda from the get-go?"

My skin crawled as every hair on my body stood at attention. Apparently, the list of things he knew about was far longer than I had bargained for.

"Like it's any of your fucking business. How could you possibly even—"

"You're easy to follow. You don't pay any attention to your surroundings, and, for your information, I was trailing you to be sure that the Rev didn't come back and finish you off," he snarled as the sparkle died out of his eyes. "You went to *his* place and didn't come out for an hour or two. When you did, it was clear that something was wrong, given the speed with which the dark-eyed one peeled out onto the street."

"And from that you determined I slept with him?"

"Are you denying it?"

"What does it matter?"

"Because this is how he works, Ruby. I've seen it time and time again. He destroys those closest to him," he said, willing me to read between the lines. When I didn't, he did it for me. "I believe you've had the pleasure of meeting Sophie."

"Yeah, though a 'pleasure' is hardly what I would

call it, and just what are you getting at there?" I growled, not liking the direction our conversation was taking. "Sophie was a damn headcase as far as I'm concerned. She was a well-contained sociopath, and I would know. I've met more than my fair share of them over the past year or so."

"Yes, she certainly was," he chimed, scratching the side of his face where his five o'clock shadow lurked. "I wonder how she got to be like that."

"Are you trying to tell me that Sean is the reason for her bat-shit crazy status?" I asked, nearly choking on the words. "No way. Noooo way is that true. There are a million reasons why that girl could have melted down over the centuries, and that's assuming that she resembled a human being at some point, which I *highly* doubt is true."

He shrugged ambivalently while he stared me down.

"Are you willing to bet your sanity on that? Your *life*?"

"I've bet my life on less," I replied, feigning indifference—but I was full of it. Both his words and energy were penetrating me, chewing away at my bravado and eating through my defensive façade. I was starting to doubt Sean, and perhaps rightfully so. He would never talk about his past. Maybe there was a really good reason for that avoidant behavior. Maybe I really didn't want to know who he was. Or who he had once been.

"Well, if you keep heading down the path you are on, I can assure you that it'll only end one way, Ruby—with heartache, destruction, and death," he warned, his voice as soft and chilling as a haunting tune. "Secrets kill, Ruby, and not just people—relationships too, especially when those secrets can't stay hidden away forever. Light eventually falls on even the darkest of corners."

And with his words, I felt the last of my resolve to defend Sean slip away. Gavin was right, or at least he sure made me feel that way. My life wasn't headed in a positive direction, and it was likely that Sean's involvement wasn't improving that fact.

"I have to go," I whispered, needing space and air and a way to escape the sinking feeling in my chest. I turned away from him, heading back into town, when he called after me one last time.

"Ruby? There's one more thing," he said, sounding oddly satisfied with himself. "Your new house-guests...I'd keep my eyes on those three. Something about them just doesn't *feel* right to me. I'm sure you can sense it as well."

All I could sense was impending doom and an overall uneasiness that I wanted desperately to escape. I took off running through town, headed home to find Cooper. I needed to figure out what all this enigmatic double-talk meant and what the hell I should do with it. Unfortunately for me, Cooper wasn't the most objective wall to bounce things off of when it came to certain topics of conversation. He was not a fan of the UK threesome, a fact he had made abundantly clear, nor was he a big Sean supporter. If I'd gone running in there flipping out about both, he would have been all too happy to get on board with Gavin's observations, and, though a part of me seemed to crave that, another fought fervently against it. I did not want to believe his words, truth or not.

Even if my denial meant my demise.

*   *   *

"Ruby," Cooper growled as I walked in the apartment door. "So good of you to actually join us. We need a family huddle. *Now*."

Before I'd even made it two feet in the door, I was whisked away to my bedroom by my elbow and plopped down on my bed. Cooper was pissed.

"What the fuck are you doing leaving these ass clowns with me all day? I'm not a goddamn babysitter, Ruby. You wanted to keep them. You're going to help me deal with them. They can't just hang out all day doing God knows what in town. I still don't trust them and neither should you. I'm going to have to keep tabs on them, and I am so not doing that alone."

"We can hear you, you bloody wanker," Alistair shouted from the living room.

"I know you can fucking hear me, dickhead. That's the point. And this is America—try insulting me in a way that doesn't require translation."

"A wanker is kinda like a douche—" I volunteered before I was cut off for my efforts.

"I *know* what a fucking wanker is, Ruby, thank you very much."

"Right. Sorry," I replied, wincing slightly. He was wicked angry. "I didn't mean to be gone forever or stick you with them, but..."

"But what, Ruby?"

"I had to go to work, and then something else came up, and I had to deal with that."

"What came up?" he pressed, leaning toward me.

"Nothing crazy," I said hesitantly, trying to stall. "I ran into that old guy, Gavin, in town. You know, the one that left me that note? I couldn't seem to duck out of our conversation politely. I'm sorry. What do you want me to do with the boys from now on? Take them to the shop with me? Have them say ridiculous things to Peyta to cheer her up?"

"No!" he roared. "I don't want them anywhere near her."

"I was joking, Cooper. Of course I'm not going to bring them around her."

"Good," he barked, staring me down. I half expected his eyes to turn that familiar shade of black that belonged to Sean when he was in similar humor. "They need to move out, Ruby. There's just no way around that. Even if I thought they were on the up and up, there's no room here, and there are too many people that would be endangered if something goes awry. I know you know I'm right about this."

I sighed, not wanting to discuss the matter.

"Okay, but I don't want you running them out of town. Not yet. I know you don't believe their intentions are pure, but you also know that I have a way of knowing those kinds of things. I don't get anything from them that leads me to believe that they're going to do anything other than annoy the shit out of you and take over my third floor," I argued. "The bathroom situation might get sketchy here soon, but I've dealt with you. I can deal with them too."

Fine," he said, turning on his heels to stalk out of my room. "But we are still going apartment hunting tomorrow. I hope these assholes have money. And, yes, Alice, I know you can still hear me."

He had already conjured up insulting pet names for them. I couldn't tell if that was good or bad.

"But then how will we keep an eye on them if they move out?" I asked, feeling like we were going in circles.

"I guess I will have to go with them," he mumbled, clearly unhappy with that reality. "You, however, will be staying here. Far away from them."

"Um...didn't you just tell me that you weren't going to babysit them on your own? I may be blonde, Cooper, but this is getting confusing even by brunette standards."

"I know," he snarled, his eyes flaring gold. "You are going to stay here because that is what's best." He shot me a glance that nearly seared my flesh. "I don't want you around them. Am I understood?"

And then it hit me. Cooper was pissed because he had no choice but to babysit the boys. I couldn't do the job because of my lack-of-Scarlet status. He was torn between wanting to punish me and wanting to keep me alive.

"Do you want me to send them away?" I asked sheepishly.

"Yes," he snapped, "but I know that, for whatever reason, you're convinced they need to stay. I'll play along with that plan for now, but I swear on all that's holy, one screw-up and they're dead. Not sent away. Just dead."

"I wish I could explain it to you, Cooper..."

"I'm in no mood to hear it even if you could, Ruby."

Ruby—not Rubes. Things were worse than I had thought.

"Okay. Not tonight," I said softly, thinking of something else I needed to talk to him about that he wasn't going to be happy to hear. "Coop? There's something else," I admitted quietly, not wanting to get into the whole Matty deal.

"Does it involve anything life-threatening?" he asked, rubbing his forehead.

"Um...no."

"Is it about P?"

"No."

"Great. It can wait then. These guys are sucking away my will to live at an obscene rate. I can't deal with any other issues today."

Without another word to me, he stalked into the living room and ordered the boys upstairs, threatening them with bodily harm and death if he heard them rouse at all before morning. Alistair started to complain about being hungry but seemed to think better of it when Cooper began growling at him. I watched the three of them disappear from my home before Cooper slammed the door behind them, waiting to hear their footsteps ascend to the loft above. Once he seemed satisfied that they were where they should be, he walked down the hall to his room and closed the door. He didn't even toss me another glance.

I was too wired to go to bed, my mind reeling with all the newly gained half-truths and warnings from Gavin, and the new reality that Cooper would be moving out. Instead of trying to sleep, I went to the living room and plopped down on the couch in silence. The quiet was sobering and isolating.

Who knew living with so many others could make me feel so alone

CHAPTER 14

I didn't want to open the shop the next day. I'd slept terribly, leaving me with sunken eyes that just couldn't quite focus on anything no matter how hard I squinted. Eventually, I just stopped trying.

Cooper was milling about the apartment, and as much as I wanted to talk to him to figure out a solution to our family crisis, I just couldn't deal with any more hostility from him. Instead, I studiously avoided him, sneaking into the bathroom as best I could while he banged around in the kitchen cabinets. Unfortunately for me, I wasn't nearly as stealthy as I thought I was.

"I know you're up," he called from the adjacent room. "And you pee louder than anyone I've ever met. If you're trying to avoid me, it's not going to work. Besides...I owe you an apology. You might want to come out here so you don't miss anything."

I finished up in the bathroom before joining him in the kitchen. He was leaning his hip against the edge of the stove, arms crossed, face stern. He didn't look like he was feeling overly remorseful.

"I'm sorry I snapped about you leaving me with the *girls* yesterday. I don't like them being here—that hasn't changed—but as much as I may dislike it, they did help you, and if you feel that they're legit, I'm going to trust you. You know...trust? That thing that you and Sean don't have? Yes, that trust. We're a pack, Ruby. We are going to start acting like one. And, as my first official order as your alpha, I want to reiterate the casually-made comment from last night that I don't want you alone with them. Period. End of story."

I was dumbfounded. I hadn't expected an apology, no matter how creatively it was wrapped.

"I can't explain why I want to help them, Coop; I just do. But you were right to be mad at me. I can't just dump them here and then go along like everything is fine and dandy, business as usual," I replied, moving in to wrap my arms around his waist. It was easier than having to look him in the eye. I sucked at apologizing. "*I'm* sorry, Coop. I'm just not quite sure how to fix this until we find them somewhere to go." I hedged slightly before amending my statement. "Somewhere for all of you to go."

"Well," he started, squeezing me a little tighter, "you could start by getting that boy toy of yours to lend me his Navigator so I can cart them around in style while we look for apartments."

I laughed, thinking that Cooper was far more desperate to get his hands on his own car than I'd thought.

"Why don't you take their car?"

"Apparently, it wasn't so much *their* car as it was an *acquired* vehicle. They ditched it outside of town when they came here. That's where it's going to stay. We don't need the cops finding a stolen vehicle here, nor do I need them driving around town unsupervised."

"Agreed," I said with a smile. "And, yes, I'm pretty sure I can sweet-talk Sean out of the SUV."

"Oh, I have no doubt that you can get just about anything you want out of that one at this point, except maybe the truth, though I'd really rather not think about your methods for trying," he said, pushing away from me slightly. "I'm going to go wake the ladies up for our long day of house-hunting. Wish me luck."

"You won't need it," I called to him as he reached for the door. "Just wiggle that ass of yours at the realtors and you'll get whatever you want."

"Ha! Too bad it doesn't work on the trio upstairs."

"Maybe it does," I said with a wink. I was met with one in return.

"Perhaps I'll go test out your theory..."

"Don't be upset when it works!"

A harsh laugh rang out through the hallway as he closed the door behind him. And with that, he was gone.

$$*\qquad*\qquad*$$

Having firmly decided to be an irresponsible business owner and keep the store closed for the day, I posted some lame excuse on the shop's door before deciding to head over to Ronnie's. I was grateful that my inheritance had left me enough money to be mildly aloof regarding REWORKED when situations arose, but it wasn't a luxury I would have forever, a fact I needed to keep tucked away in the back of my mind.

The reality was that I was far more concerned with Peyta and whether or not she had let her mother in on her little secret than I was about working that morning. If she had told her, I wanted to be sure that Ronnie was handling it well. Nothing was more important to Ronnie than Peyta, but when blindsided, her reactions weren't always the most well thought out or sensitive.

I entered *Better With Age* to find nobody awaiting my arrival; it appeared deserted. Just as I was about to call out for her, my panic rising, I heard a laugh from the back room.

A *giggle*.

Then I heard the low rumblings of a man's voice.

More laughter.

"Ronnie? It's me," I said tentatively. I wasn't entirely sure what I was interrupting.

"Ruby!" she yelled before an outbreak of scurrying and whispering broke out in the back storeroom. "I'll be right out."

"Don't worry," I mumbled under my breath. "I'm not coming in."

A minute later, Ronnie stumbled through the beaded curtain, smoothing her vintage blouse out and fussing with her hair. A moment after that, a familiar man followed.

"Ruby, you remember Malcolm," she said, trying her best to not look like she'd just gotten caught making out under the bleachers in high school.

"Yes," I replied with a tight smile. "It's nice to see you again."

He looked a tiny bit sheepish as he ran a hand through his disheveled hair.

"Always a pleasure to see one of Ronnie's friends."

The three of us stood awkwardly for a moment, ignoring the neon pink elephant—or herd of them—in the room. I felt like they were multiplying while I stood there. Eventually unable to smile uncomfortably any longer, I cracked.

"Is this a bad time, Ronnie? I could come back later..."

"No, no, it's fine. We were just," she started, taking a pause to grin at Malcolm, "*looking* for something in the back."

Like a condom...

"Right, well, I just came over to ask about Peyta," I said, shooting her a glance that said 'read between the lines, please'. She got me loud and clear.

"You can ask whatever you need to," she informed me, taking a step closer to Malcolm. "He knows. He knows everything."

"Oh, okay." I stumbled on the words. Was I missing something more than I thought? The two had history, that was plain from the first time I'd met Malcolm Reed. He was a *friend* from a long time back. A friend of her husband's. A friend from the *Underground*. The piece of the puzzle that I seemed to be lacking was when he'd become someone present enough in Ronnie's life to warrant knowing the most intimate details of her daughter's mental well-being. Perhaps I had missed more in those three weeks than I bargained for. "So Peyta told you? Told you *everything?*"

"She came to me about it yesterday," she replied, regaining some of the sharpness of feature that I was accustomed to seeing on her face. "She said you were going to tell me if she didn't." I nodded. "I'm so glad you pushed her about this, Ruby. I had no idea."

Her guilt wove around me, wrapping me in an energetic blanket that nearly suffocated me. Ronnie was not likely to forgive herself for her oversight anytime soon. Maybe never.

"So you're getting her help? I looked up some really great places that deal with this specific disorder. Did you find somewhere for her to go or do you want the list?"

"Malcolm was able to help get her into a therapist in Boston. The doctor is an old grad school buddy of his. We never would have gotten in without his help. There's a one-year waiting list, and it's a cash-only practice. Even if I could have secured an appointment there, I wouldn't have been able to pay for it." Her gaze dropped as she fidgeted slightly, picking at her nails. It was apparent that Ronnie thought she'd not only failed her daughter in emotional support, she also thought she'd failed to provide for her too.

"Hans was a housemate of mine," Malcolm started, allowing Ronnie to get a hold of herself. "We've kept in touch over the years. I called in a favor to him and he agreed to take Peyta on as a courtesy to me." He smiled warmly and took Ronnie's hand in his. "Veronica, there's no need to feel badly about it; besides," he said, a tiny glint of mischief flickering in his eyes, "it gave me a chance to bring up some interesting photos of him that I found in my attic not too long ago. He'd have done anything to keep those off of the internet."

"You didn't!" Ronnie gasped.

"No," he roared with laughter. "But that snapped you out of your self-loathing for the moment, didn't it?"

I had to laugh too; his move was well played. I could see why Ronnie liked him. I was starting to like him more as well.

"So she's in good hands then?" I asked, trying to compose myself.

"The best," Ronnie replied. "And I have you to

thank for that too, Ruby. I'm not sure I would have ever figured out what she was doing without you."

"If I hadn't caught her in the act, I wouldn't have either, Ronnie. None of us would. You should have seen Cooper after he walked in on the aftermath. He was in bad shape about it. He blamed himself for not being more of a help to her."

"He was busy doing his job, Ruby. He was out looking for *you*," she said, her voice taking on that familiar seriousness that I'd come to find comforting from Ronnie. From anyone else it would have seemed threatening, and on occasion, it still was. "Peyta isn't Cooper's responsibility. She's mine. Tell him it's not his fault, please."

As if just putting it together, she narrowed her eyes and cocked her head slightly to the side.

"Is that why he left the house the other day looking pale as a ghost? He walked right past me without so much as a word. I figured he'd overheard something he didn't mean to and that had freaked him out a little. Now it's starting to make more sense."

"Yeah, poor guy. He might need a therapist now too," I joked, trying to lighten the mood slightly. "Got any other friends you can call favors into, Malcolm?"

The room boomed with his low and hearty laughter.

"I'm afraid not, Ruby. But I have some senators I can blackmail if that ever comes in handy."

"You never know," I cautioned. "I'm pretty adept at getting myself into trouble."

Ronnie's sly smile lit up her face.

"Like no one I've ever met."

*   *   *

I stuck around and chatted with Ronnie and Malcolm, or *Reed,* as she referred to him in a more casual atmosphere, then excused myself, sensing that they still had some unfinished storeroom business to finish. It still floored me that Ronnie, or *Veronica,* as he called her, was acting like a carefree teenager, but it made me oddly happy for her—envious too. What I would have given to have had a midday sexual encounter in the back of my shop. Instead, I usually filled that time with one crisis or another. Carefree was an approach to life that I couldn't afford to indulge.

With that in mind, I made my way back to the shop to open for at least part of the day. Peyta had asked for the day off and would have been disappointed to know that I shucked all my responsibility at the first sign of her not being around. There were only a few hours left in the business day, so I decided to work on some pieces out in the showroom so I could do double duty. I hoped my tired eyes would allow me to accomplish that.

I found that customers always enjoyed seeing me fiddle with the jewelry. They seemed to love knowing how something came to be—the steps taken to create a particular outcome—as if seeing and understanding how a piece was molded and shaped gave it greater appeal. Maybe it did.

Perhaps that same concept applied to people as well. Did we love them more when we knew their full story? How they came to be who and what they were? Or was the mystery what kept us coming back for more, slowly enticing us, knowing that once the truth was out, the appeal would be lost?

I wasn't sure I wanted answers to those questions.

CHAPTER 15

After close, I stuck around for a little longer, knowing that Coop and the boys weren't back yet. Not wanting to give the illusion that I was open, I dimmed the front lights and locked the front door, flipping the sign to closed. I then made my way to the back to finish the earring I had nearly completed.

Focusing hard on twisting the tiny wires of the intricate piece together, I didn't expect to hear the jingle of the door bells, and almost didn't hear them at all. Almost. My heart surged as I shot up from my chair; I knew I had locked the door that time. Panicked and unarmed, I bolted into the showroom, unsure of what fate awaited me. Fearing the worst, I never imagined who I would find waiting for me.

Sean donning a Cheshire cat smile was pretty low on my list of possibilities.

"Did I startle you?" he asked, knowing damn well he'd scared the shit out of me. "I was hoping to find you alone. Looks like I accomplished that for once."

"You almost found me *dead*," I retorted, breathing hard. "You won't be smiling when you give me a damn heart attack."

I should have known it would be him. He had a key for everything.

"How are your refugees?" he asked with a certain cheeriness to his voice. I didn't buy it for a second.

"They're great. They're making Cooper insane, so that should make you happy."

His smile widened, taking on a genuine quality.

"It does. Very much so."

I shot him my angry parent face.

"You promised, Sean. You swore you would try to get along with him!"

"Old habits," he replied, trailing off as he shrugged ambivalently.

"...are going to be the death of me," I murmured in response, leaning against the counter while my heart rate tried to normalize.

"Nothing is going to be the death of you, Ruby. *Nothing*." I looked up to see all the humor wiped from his face. Forest green eyes met mine, telling me that playtime was over. There was no mocking in his statement.

"You said you were trying to get me alone," I prompted, hoping to easily transition to what it was he had come for. When my heart started to race a little with his approach, I realized that my body was hoping it was *me*.

"Was I?" He fluidly made his way toward me, closing the distance between us. Only the front counter separated our bodies, and he swallowed up that space quickly, leaning forward over it to prop himself up on his elbows. It put him at eye level, pinning his once again emerald irises on me. "I did want to see you alone, Ruby. I wish it was for a more *entertaining* reason." While his eyes raked me over, his energy surged through me, and my body reacted as it always did. "Jay is over in London, looking into the pack. It seems that the boys' story checks out thus far. Their previous alpha is gone and the new one is dirty, that's for sure, but he's smart. Whatever he's up to, he's keeping it well under wraps. Nobody is talking, especially not his pack."

"Somehow I find it hard to believe that your brothers weren't able to coerce answers out of them."

Another noncommittal shrug.

"They know how to interrogate effectively, if that's what you're getting at. So I'm left with two potential implications. Either these pack members truly don't know anything, or they fear Tobias more than they fear us," he said, his expression hardening slightly. "And *that* would be a fatal error in judgment on their part."

No shit.

"How is Jay doing?" I asked casually, hoping to gain a little insight into that situation.

"He's well," he replied curiously, eyebrow in full force. "How's Peyta?"

"Just dandy," I quipped, still trying to play it cool. As we stared at each other, I couldn't help but wonder if there was more to the disappearance of Jay from Peyta's life, and, if there was, if Sean knew more than he was letting on. Before I could let my imagination run away with me, I changed the subject. "So how's the stuff with McGurney coming? Anything new to go off of?"

He smiled a cunning smile, knowing that I'd just changed the subject intentionally.

"Professional hits are not easy to trace, Ruby. Someone very powerful, with a vested interest in keeping things quiet, called in that hit on McGurney. I've got as many PC brothers as I can spare on the case, but nothing has turned up as of yet. Whatever McGurney had intended to show me that night must have exposed someone enough for them to go to great lengths to shut him up for good. Unfortunately for me, I got there too late. His house was wiped clean. Everything was gone."

"There has to be some way to get into Keith's file without CIA clearance or somebody on the inside."

"Maybe, but it doesn't matter now. Keith James no longer exists in their database. He's a ghost—a specter. Whoever knew we were onto them wiped out his entire existence as if he never once set foot in Langley."

"Holy shit..."

"Indeed."

"So you just walk away from it?" I asked disbelievingly.

"Not a chance," he growled, eyes narrowing. "Now we pour on the heat like there's no tomorrow, because for someone there won't be. I want to know exactly who's behind this. If the government has somehow stumbled upon the werewolf population, I need to flesh out exactly who knows what and how deeply that knowledge permeates."

He stopped himself before continuing. I had a pretty good idea what he'd do to those in on it. He didn't want to confirm my suspicions.

"So until then?"

"Until then, we dig, interrogate, and dig some more."

"Alan isn't going to give up on McGurney, Sean.

He's certainly not going to let you off the hook for it either."

The third shrug of the evening.

"Alan doesn't concern me."

"He's my friend, Sean. And currently he thinks you had something to do with it. That concerns me."

"Absurd. Why would I kill my own contact?"

"I don't know, but he doesn't trust you at all, and I can't blame him for that. Everything that he knows about you revolves around lies, cover-ups, and murders. He thinks you're a criminal—a high-end one. The kind that doesn't get caught," I informed him, my voice taking a stern tone. "He knows you had something to do with Matty's body dump and the corpse posed as the Portsmouth killer in a car in Mass somewhere. He has you pegged, Sean. He's not going to let up on you. He's going to dig and dig until he finds something, or, in your case, doesn't find *anything,* which will only incriminate you further in his eyes."

"Why are you so concerned about this? He can't do anything to me."

"I know that, but he's my friend. I'm close to his family, and I can feel that slipping away because he doesn't trust me now. He thinks you're blackmailing me, or using me—I don't know exactly what he thinks is going on, but it's not good. He thought that maybe I killed Matty and that's why you covered it up, for fuck's sake! He wants answers, Sean. Badly."

"And he'll have them when I find out who killed McGurney. The ones he needs to hear, anyway."

I didn't want argue. I had other issues that needed attention, and I knew that starting a fight over Alan was not going to be the best way to segue into them.

"Fine," I whispered, pushing away from the

counter.

"Ruby," he said with caution in his tone. "I don't wish for this to be difficult on you, but I must do my job. If I find out that the government knows about your kind, I can't begin to tell you the shitstorm that will follow." He came around the counter to join me in the tight area behind it. His presence always seemed to take up more space than it needed, like the intensity of his energy demanded it. I eased against the wall to make room for it. "I've told you more than I should have already," he said, reaching for my face. My eyes closed instinctively, awaiting the contact.

"Sean," I said softly, the words catching in my throat when his hand grazed my cheek. "I need to tell you something."

I opened my eyes to find him staring at me from only inches away, his expression holding a hint of amusement.

"Offering up information to me?" he mocked, leaning his body against mine ever so slightly. "Who are you and what have you done with my Ruby?"

My Ruby...

"I'm being serious," I grouched, though it came out as more of a breathless protestation than anything else. That was Sean's effect on me.

"I can see that," he purred as my hands drifted up into his hair of their own volition. *Traitors.*

His lips were on mine, soft and coaxing as if they were trying to con me out of my attempts at a serious conversation. They were painfully close to succeeding. I was falling into his scheme beautifully when I felt a strange buzzing against my hip. Once. Twice. The third brought a growl from deep within Sean's chest.

"I have to take this," he said, abruptly pulling away

from me to head for the door. "I'll be right back."

Suddenly, I felt like I needed a cold shower. *What had I been just about to tell him? Oh...Matty!* I knew that it was going to open up a can of worms, but I'd learned from my past, and keeping secrets from Sean never panned out well. I was taking a new approach.

I watched him through the front window, standing stoically, his back toward me. Whatever his conversation was about, it wasn't good. The more still Sean was, the deeper the crisis.

Minutes later, he returned, looking reserved. Things were worse than I thought.

"I have to leave tonight, Ruby," he said like it was an admission of guilt. "I had wanted to take you somewhere. I had it all planned, but—"

"It's okay, Sean. I understand."

He smiled weakly.

"I know you do. It's one of the best things about you. You understand me."

Within seconds he was back behind the counter, pressing me against the wall that I'd only moments earlier managed to peel myself off of. His arms caged me in as his body hovered just far enough away to not be touching me. The distance seemed painful.

His breath tickled my ear, his mouth playing dangerously close to it.

"You wanted to tell me something. Can it wait until I return, or should you tell me now? You decide."

My brain was scrambling in a severe case of sensory overload. Too many things to process at once were threatening to blow a circuit. I wanted to kiss him, tell him, then throw him out the door as quickly as possible so I could avoid the fallout. It was cowardly but honest—a step in the right direction as far as I was concerned.

"It can keep until later," I whispered, my air coming in and out in sharp gusts.

"Very well," he said slyly. "I'll look forward to later then."

He slid out the front door seconds later, and I was left clutching my chest, feeling like I had the first time he'd come to my store—confused and frustrated. My frustration was of the sexual variety.

With a sigh, I headed toward the front door to lock it—*again*—when a familiar face popped up in the window. Waving a paper bag that undoubtedly contained baked goods of some sort, Ginger smiled warmly as she waited for me to let her in.

"Hi," I said, stepping back to allow her entrance to the shop. "It's good to see you!"

"No, Ruby," she said with sad eyes, "it's good to see *you*. I wasn't entirely sure that I would ever again, but not Gavin. He knew you'd be back. I wish I had his confidence in things sometimes." She gave me a hug, wrapping her old and weathered arms around my waist. She was frail in appearance, but those arms held a strength that far surpassed expectation, and I started to ache slightly from the tenacity of her grip. She really had worried for my safety, which was ironic given that her husband seemed to know so damn much. Apparently, he wasn't very forthcoming with her either.

But for all that Gavin appeared to lack, his taste in spouses was top-notch. Ginger had always been nothing but motherly, caring, and quick to rein in her husband when the situation warranted. She'd come to check up on me after my near drowning by the Rev and was once again on my doorstep to see how I was.

And she brought tasty treats to boot.

She smiled as she caught me looking at her brown paper bag of deliciousness and laughed.

"I believe you said these were your favorites last time," she said, handing me the bag. I opened it to find her killer chocolate chip cookies. Mysteriously, two were in my hand a second later on a mission to my mouth.

"You're the best," I told her, motioning toward the front counter. I stepped around back and grabbed the stool I kept there, offering it to Ginger.

"Thank you, dear, but I don't want to stay long. I'm sure you have more pressing things to do than indulge my need to be sure that you're indeed safe and intact."

"If it means you're bringing goodies, you can check up on me anytime," I replied with a wink as I bit into my second cookie. She beamed with approval. Her intense gaze and parental vibe made me wonder something that hadn't occurred to me before. "Ginger," I started, putting my cookie down, "I hope you don't mind me asking, but...do you have any kids?" She looked at me longingly, and I instantly regretted asking. I'd hit a nerve of sorts, her sadness pouring out freely. "I'm sorry. I don't know why—"

"Don't fret, Ruby," she said, patting my hand in the most comforting gesture. "No, I do not have any children. Neither does Gavin." I looked at her sympathetically, not knowing what to say. "He had none before me, and it seems that our *incompatibility* would not allow for us to bear any."

Silence hung heavy between us for a moment, forcing me to address the thought running rampant in my mind. Could Sean and I have children? With all his daddy issues and my not-so-stellar parental models, would we even want them? I found it funny that something I'd never given any previous thought to suddenly seemed like a life-changing revelation.

"Whatever made you ask that?"

I shrugged, embarrassed.

"There was something about the way you were looking at me—I've seen my friend Kristy watch her little boy that way. I'm sorry if I offended you."

"Of course not, dear. You'll have to try harder than that if you wish to."

"That's not a challenge you should carelessly throw out," I replied with a laugh. "I seem unbelievably gifted at saying the wrong thing at the worst possible time."

She smiled wryly.

"I wouldn't beat myself up about that, if I were you. Perhaps you come by that honestly."

"I'm not sure," I said, grabbing my half-eaten cookie off of the counter. "But I guess you're probably pretty used to dealing with it. Gavin seems to have a knack for pissing people off, pardon my language."

"That he does," she said, chuckling. She grabbed a cookie and lifted it as though giving a toast. We clinked our treats together like glasses of champagne, bonding over her enigmatic spouse.

"Ginger, can I ask you something else?"

"Certainly, Ruby. Anything." Her composure was instantly regained.

"Does Gavin always speak around things? You know, talk in riddles, or is that just something he enjoys doing to me for his entertainment? I know he's old. Maybe he just needs to get his kicks in new and irritating ways."

She pressed her lips tightly, taking a sharp breath before slowly letting it out. Laying her cookie down, she took my hand in hers and clasped it firmly.

"Ruby, Gavin has faults—many of them—but believe me when I tell you that he has nothing but your best interest at heart," she said earnestly. "We *both* do."

"But why?" I prodded, desperate for some level of understanding. "He holes himself up in that boat, hidden away from everyone and everything supernatural, and then suddenly gets involved when the Rev comes to town, but only to help me? It makes no sense."

"I know it seems that way, Ruby, but Gavin knows you're special. He wants to see you safe without risking exposure. He's survived this long by being smart and cunning. If it weren't for him, they all would have been extinct by—" She cut herself off abruptly, unwilling to finish her defense of Gavin. "I'm sorry. I shouldn't have said that."

The woman I'd known to always be so formal and poised was suddenly flustered and very much in a hurry to get out of my shop. In a hurry to get away from *me*.

"Who?" I asked, not wanting to let her leave without clarification. I needed to know what she wouldn't tell me. "*Who* would have been extinct?"

"I'm sorry, Ruby. I have to go," she told me curtly, collecting her handbag to leave. "You'll have to talk to Gavin. I shouldn't have said that." She stopped just shy of the exit before turning to face me. Her expression was pained, her energy dissonant. "Please forgive my evasiveness. It is not my story to tell."

I started to badger her further, but she sped surprisingly fast down the sidewalk, and I just couldn't bring myself to chase her down and demand answers. She wasn't in a position to give them and even I was above threatening a little old lady. For the first time since I'd returned, I was glad Scarlet wasn't around.

*　　*　　*

I was not pleased to know that Gavin's much better half was equally capable of being mysterious, and as I contemplated the newest CF in my life, four more pulled up in front of the building. To be fair, it was more like three and a half. Cooper wasn't a full-blown issue since his morning apology, but, judging by the look on his face, he was headed in that direction.

I stepped out to greet them, thinking that sucking up was the best plan of action.

"You look pretty hot driving that gargantuan vehicle, Coop," I told him, grinning ear to ear.

He totally took the bait.

"I look hot in everything, Ruby. You should know that by now," he replied with a sly smile.

"What about us?" Ali asked, stepping out of the SUV. "We don't look hot?"

"You look twelve, Alice," Cooper spat over his shoulder. "Ruby isn't a pedophile."

I laughed, even though I tried not to. It was just too good.

"You look pretty sexy too, Alistair, but it's hard to look badass crawling out of the backseat."

He looked at me with a deflated expression, then shrugged.

"Fair enough," he said, pulling bags of food out from the back of the car. "But do I look better as a delivery boy?" He wiggled his eyebrows at me playfully.

"Yes. That suits you."

"Come on, Alice," Cooper called from the doorway to the residential part of my building. "All of you, upstairs. *Now*."

Without complaint, they all filed in while Cooper held the door open for them, watching their every move.

"I'll be right up," I told him, opening the shop door. "I just need to grab my stuff and lock up."

I ran back inside and did just that, then made my way upstairs. When I opened the apartment door, I was surprised to see the foreigners sitting on the couch, eating their takeout. Cooper hadn't relegated them to their floor above. I smiled slightly. Maybe they were growing on him?

"Your dinner is on the counter," Janner called to me as I threw my purse on the sofa table by the door. "Pad Thai. Cooper said you'd like it."

"Sweet! Sounds awesome. I'm going to go clean up a bit first, then I'll be right out."

"Hurry up," Alistair called out as I disappeared down the hall. "You don't want to miss out on all the family fun!"

"You're not family," a voice grumbled from the kitchen.

"But you're always saying we need to have family huddles..."

"Right, but you're never actually *in* the huddle, therefore you're not family," Cooper argued. "Being the topic of conversation doesn't mean you're in."

"You boys are going to be the death of me," I shouted from my bedroom before shutting the door.

Cooper was suddenly very silent, as were the others. Then it dawned on me. My choice of words was exactly the outcome that Cooper feared most.

If I was honest, deep down, there was a small part of me that feared it too.

CHAPTER 16

Our night was surprisingly drama-free—*enjoyable* even. Cooper looked relatively miserable for the better part of it, but even he cracked a few times when Beckett, with his incredibly dry sense of humor, ragged on Alistair for the various infractions he hadn't realized he'd committed. Alistair was the most entertaining when he was trying to be serious, a trait I'm sure was equal parts annoying and endearing to those who knew him best.

It made me wonder what his mate was like.

On occasion, throughout the night, I got that strange guarded feeling from one or all of the boys. I just couldn't wrap my head around it. There was nothing negative or malicious about it: more of an interruption of sorts. At least that's what I felt. It reminded me of how Sean's face could go completely impassive at the drop of a hat, masking whatever was going on inside his mind. The neutral but impenetrable tone to their energy made them impossible to read.

What I had trouble understanding was the timing of it. It never occurred when any awkwardness plagued the conversation (and that was often), but just seemed randomly interspersed throughout the night. Was it a coping mechanism of sorts, born of necessity in a pack that seemed as riddled with evil as Cooper's? If so, I wondered just how much they weren't telling us about the atrocities they'd faced under the rule of the alpha they had destroyed and how horrific their deaths would be should they ever be discovered. It made even more sense as to why they wanted to align with the baddest wolf on the block.

Too bad she was on an untimely leave.

I wanted to ask them more about their pasts, but Cooper was always around, and they just didn't seem willing to open up much around him. I couldn't really blame them. He wasn't really warm and fuzzy when it came to the boys.

I went to bed with a rare sense of calm, though my body was completely exhausted. In my amassing fatigue, I managed to walk squarely into a wall that hadn't exactly moved since the day before. It was a blonde moment of epic proportion, and I was thrilled that nobody had witnessed it. I wouldn't have lived it down anytime soon.

The next day started out without a hitch. Peyta was back at work. The boys had two promising homes to check out and had planned to spend the rest of the day better organizing their temporary abode. Cooper would be supervising that activity. Sean sent me a message in the morning saying that he would be back in town that evening. He had plans for us and made a point to put "plans" in all caps. Whatever they were, they sounded promising. Lastly, I got a call from Kristy, who was still down south with her mother, who was recovering from surgery. I heard Louie jibber-jabbering in the background, and my heart nearly melted. In the few weeks it had been since I'd seen him, I could already hear the changes in him. The cliché was true: kids really did grow up too fast.

It took me a while to get off the phone with Kristy. She wasn't going to be convinced that I was okay until she got to physically see me and hug me to death. I promised to call her soon and made her give my little buddy a squish for me with a big, sloppy smooch for good measure. I heard him squeal in the background while she did it before yelling, "Aunty Booby! Booby smooch me. Booby smooches." He was just too cute for words.

Since the call ran longer than expected, I was late to work as usual. If I didn't know better, I'd have thought Peyta was the responsible business owner and I the slacker employee. Graciously, she didn't taunt me too much when I crashed through the front door with a coffee carafe in hand.

"Nice to see you this morning," she mocked, lifting a quizzical brow. "Did you get dressed in the dark or something?"

I looked down quickly to see what she was getting at. When I was greeted by the tag of my shirt, which was not only facing out but also turned in the wrong direction, I got her point.

"No," I lamented, "but I was in a hurry." Embarrassed, I scurried past her, leaving my coffee on the counter as I made my way to the back to rectify my wardrobe mishap. She followed me back.

"Long night?"

"Kind of." I didn't want to go into great detail

because she didn't know about the UK trio, and Cooper wanted to keep her in the dark as much as possible. Sean agreed. We knew she was as well protected as she was going to be with PC boys surveying the shop while she and I were there. Given the tenuous nature of her mental status, we didn't want to add to her stress level any more than necessary. Once the boys were out of the house and we knew what we were going to do with them, we would let her in on our little secret, or secrets, as the case may have been.

"Are you being evasive on purpose or are you just tired and grouchy?" she asked, leaning a shoulder against the wall.

"I'll go with the latter."

"Path of least resistance?"

"Always."

"I'll allow it this time," she sighed, feigning annoyance. "Next time, I expect all the sordid details."

"Deal." Conceding was far easier than arguing with her and was clearly the best option given Peyta's genetic predisposition to get to the bottom of things when you least wanted her to. She was just like her mother.

"So Mom said you stopped by yesterday," she said, changing the subject.

"Yep..."

"Was Malcolm there?" she asked curiously, her face impassive.

"He was." I did my best to be as neutral as Peyta. I couldn't tell if she was trying to get a read on how I felt about him, or to hide her sentiments.

"So, what did you think?"

"He seemed fine. Better than fine, actually. He made a horribly off-color remark that made me laugh. How bad can he be?"

She said nothing, only eyed me from the other side of the room.

"Anything else?"

I sighed.

"Your mom seems happy with him—like a different person almost. I saw glimmers of her hardened edges, but it was as though he filed them off with a single glance," I explained with a shrug. "And what he did for you, P..."

"I know," she whispered, looking away. "I met with the therapist yesterday. Mom let me go by myself. I need to do this for me."

"How was it?" I asked softly, moving slowly toward her. "Did you like this über specialist?"

She looked at me thoughtfully for a moment.

"I did. I really did. It's like he understood me. He knew where I was coming from."

"Well, that's great, P!"

"I know. It really is. I'm not sure how to thank Malcolm for his help though. We never could have afforded it without him."

"Peyta," I said firmly, "I would have made sure you got what you needed. I don't like to talk about it much, but my inheritance was substantial. I would have paid for it myself, if it had come to that."

She smiled up at me with watery eyes.

"Well...thanks, Ruby," she said, giving me a hug around my waist, "but it looks like Daddy Warbucks beat you to the task. I could use a car though."

"Get in line," I joked. "Cooper's been singing that tune for a while now, though I did manage to snag him a car from Sean. It seems to have placated him for the time being."

"Fine," she grumbled in true teenager fashion. "I

had to try."

"Of course you did. Now how about you go out front and earn your keep around here. I have trinkets to make."

*   *   *

The store was remarkably busy, so I got little done in the back. I'd forgotten that the holiday season was approaching and people would be getting a head start so as to avoid the Thanksgiving through Christmas shopping melee. I wasn't about to complain; business was business, and *always* welcome.

We worked straight through our normal lunch break, and, as the town courthouse's bell chimed three o'clock, I realized just how hungry I was. Judging by the lack of animation in Peyta's face, she was dragging too.

"Do you want to shut down for thirty minutes? We could go grab something upstairs."

"Yes, but we need to do it quickly or you'll be carrying me up there. I'm starving."

Not wanting to have to piggyback her up the stairs fireman-style, I shut down the shop and left a note on the door stating we'd be back by 3:30. We hurried upstairs, making our way into the apartment and directly to the kitchen where Peyta quickly found a bag of chips to nibble on while I ransacked the fridge for anything edible. The boys had a showing just outside of town at a little after three, so I knew the coast would be clear long enough for us to eat and run.

"Okay," I started, knowing our food situation was looking grim, "we have pickles, cheese, cranberry juice, and something in a Tupperware container towards the back. I think we might wanna leave that one alone actually. It looks fuzzy."

"How about soup?" Peyta suggested, pulling two family-sized cans from the pantry.

"Fabulous!" I cried, starting to rummage through the drawers for the can opener. It was nowhere to be found, and I quickly remembered why. "Um...P, I have to run upstairs for a sec. I'll be right back."

"Why?" she asked, looking at me strangely. It was a look I got fairly often.

"I need to go grab something to open those things. Just sit tight and eat your chips. I'll be right down."

"You left your can opener upstairs?"

"Yeah," I replied weakly. "I get hungry when I dance sometimes. I must have forgotten it. I just need to run up and grab it."

"Why are you acting so weird?" she continued, hot on my heels.

"I'm not."

"You are."

"Peyta, seriously. I'll be right back."

"Why don't you want me to come?" she asked with her mother's seasoned detective glint in her eyes.

"Because I just about had to carry you up the stairs, remember? Sit. Eat chips. The longer you keep badgering me about this, the longer it's going to take to actually have lunch. We have customers to serve, don't we...?"

"Fine," she grumbled in response. We were two skinny girls who really needed our blood sugar to stay above a certain level to maintain civility.

Without any further protestations from Peyta, I sped up the stairs to the third floor, praying curiosity wouldn't get the best of her. I didn't have an excuse prepared for why it looked like I had people squatting in my studio. Actually, I did, but I wasn't going to tell her that.

Once I entered the space, I took in the mess. Thankfully, it was relatively well-corralled at the far end of the room, but it was still a bit of a disaster. Clothes were strewn about, twisted up in the sheets, blankets, and pillows that they were using for their temporary beds. Topping it all off was a large green trash bag, stuffed to nearly overflowing. Those boys liked to eat, and one in particular. Alistair had a canned pineapple infatuation. Maybe they didn't have it across the pond, or maybe he was just odd, but he was definitely the reason why I found myself on the hunt for a can opener.

With my pressing need to hurry, I attacked the chaotic pile, throwing things around at will, doing my best to track down the missing kitchen utensil. It became abundantly clear in my search that it was time for those runaways to do some laundry. Even if I had found the opener in that pile, I wouldn't have used it.

Coming up empty-handed, I sighed aloud, pressing my hands on my hips as I scanned the rest of the relatively vacant room for my missing item. Then I spotted it, sitting benignly on top of the stereo that I adored—the one that had been dormant for weeks. I ran over and snatched it up, turning quickly to head downstairs.

I slammed right into Peyta. That girl was sneaky—for an almost-human.

"Jesus!" I screamed, clutching my chest. "You scared the crap out of me, P!"

"Um, Ruby?" she asked, looking at the mess I'd scattered about. "Do we need to have an intervention or something? Leaving your room a complete disaster is one thing, but when it spills over onto an entirely different floor of your home, I think it's time to get some help." She pried her eyes from the boys' stuff to meet mine. "Should I see if my therapist has any buddies who specialize in some kind of hoarding-like disorder?"

I laughed nervously, trying to usher her out of the room.

"Nope. I just need to hire a cleaner, that's all. Let's go eat."

"Wait a minute," she said, grinding to a halt when she saw a pair of stray boxers that had landed near the exit. "Why do you have *men's* underwear up here? This isn't your stuff, is it?"

"Well, no. Not exactly." I cringed as she went over to investigate further, praying for a distraction of any kind to derail her from her mission. She was like a dog on a trail; she wasn't going to let up easily.

In a rare act of kindness from heaven above, I got what I asked for.

"Ruby?" a male voice called from behind Peyta and me.

Matty...

CHAPTER 17

When I turned to see him, he grinned shyly, making him look younger than the last time I saw him. His expression tightened slightly when he saw Peyta come up behind me, but she soon put him at ease. She was all apologies.

"Matty...the other day," she started as she nervously avoided eye contact. "I may have overreacted. I didn't realize that you weren't *yourself* when everything happened."His face was blank while he stood still, staring at Peyta as she muddled her way through her explanation. "I know who made you; you didn't stand a chance. Ruby told me that you—the *old* you—would never have done those things. I was so upset about Jay...about Ruby too. I took it out on you, and that may not have been entirely fair."

She was beyond uncomfortable; I could feel the erratic vibrations humming around her body.

"I'm sorry too, Peyta," he said softly in response. "I wish you could have known me before."

I felt the tears start to sting the back of my eyes. In that moment I wanted nothing more than to have him back—for Peyta to have the chance to get to know him. But it would never be. Matty couldn't stay.

I walked away as the first tear fell. Bracing myself against the cabinet that held the stereo, I hunched forward, doing my best to contain everything that threatened to escape me. Then he was right behind me.

"Don't cry, blue eyes." His hand brushed my cheek lightly, and I lifted it up toward him. "You'll force me to do something embarrassing to cheer you up."

He reached around me to turn the stereo on. I watched, completely infatuated, as he pressed the power button on and cued up one of the many playlists. Peyta's powers allowed Matty, like Gregory, to make contact with objects and people around him. It implied that Matty was a pretty powerful wolf as well, but I was already more than aware of that.

He expertly scrolled through it until he found what he was looking for. When he did, he laughed. Drake's "Take Care" came blaring through the speakers at an uncomfortable volume, the bass violently shaking the floor. It felt amazing.

Just as he had on so many occasions in dance class, Matty started clowning around in a grand effort to cheer me up. It always worked. He'd picked a hip-hop piece that was done by a guest choreographer for our company. Hip-hop was *not* my forte, and he knew it. He'd shown me up that class, but I never let him know it. He was mocking me in true Matty fashion, and I totally took the bait.

Hook, line, and sinker.

"Remember this?" he goaded, easily breaking out the choreography we'd learned months earlier. "I believe the term 'hot mess' was thrown around during that class. It was aimed at you, was it not?"

"I got better at it while you were in LA," I retorted.

"Well, let's see it then, white girl."

"Who are you calling white, Italian boy?" I snipped, taking a long and dramatic slide in his direction before I busted out the steps to that section of the song. He was in total sync with me in seconds.

I saw Peyta snicker in the mirror while she watched us go head to head in a dance-off of epic proportion. Dancing with a ghost easily qualified as epic, regardless of how ridiculous we appeared doing it.

"Looking better this time around, Ruby," he mocked, sliding in behind me as we both watched the other in the mirror.

"Ha! I look good all the time," I retorted. "You just haven't noticed."

He stopped suddenly, catching my arm. His touch felt strange the longer he held on, like it was leaching me, draining me slightly.

"I always noticed, Ruby," he said, leaning into my ear. "You just didn't notice me noticing."

My heart sank.

I pulled away to look at him and assess the expression on his face. Unfortunately, I never got the chance.

I felt them enter the room before a word was said. Before their bodies were visible to me. Anger crashed into my back as I spared one glance over at Peyta's blank expression. I knew the jig was up—big time.

I wanted to hide, but knew that was an impossibility, so instead I turned to face the music—or the alphas, as the case seemed to be. Facing an angry Cooper would have been bad enough, but with Sean at

171

his side, forming a wall of hostility, it was just about more than I could take. Before I could even get a word out in my defense, Cooper started in.

"What. The. Fuck." It wasn't really a question, more an acknowledgment of how, once again, I'd managed to not let him in on crucial information.

"Cooper," I protested. "I can explain."

When I started to move toward their collective boiling rage, Matty stepped between us. He thought *I* was the one that needed protecting.

I looked at them beseechingly, but when my hopeless stare turned to Sean, all I saw was a wild, fearsome look in his pitch black eyes. His energy crashed with violent waves in our direction, and I feared we were seconds away from his war cry that would threaten to shatter the windows as well as any hope that I could salvage the situation.

Cooper started in on me again, but Sean silenced him with the slightest of hand gestures. His eyes never left Matty, glaring at him with emotions bubbling under the surface that I couldn't even place. He wouldn't look at me as I slinked around from behind Matty. He didn't speak to me either.

I watched his hateful stare pierce Matty and wished that I'd just told him that his ghost had returned when I had the chance. My body was failing me, hovering between the two of them as though somehow I alone could keep the shitstorm that was brewing at bay. The one thing I knew about Sean was that there was no stopping him. Ever. He would have some form of revenge, and I wondered just how big the cost would be for him to get it.

Suddenly, his arm drifted up slowly, extended toward me. His eyes wouldn't meet mine, but his body would. Knowing that he was affording me the choice to go to him, I did my best not to falter, and I laid my hand in his softly, half expecting to be yanked toward him before a brawl broke out. Instead, he led me gently over to him and Cooper.

"Sean," I whispered, knowing he'd hear me anyway. "This is what I was trying to tell you about the other day. I wanted you to know that Matty was back; I just didn't know *how*. And then you had to go..."

"I don't want to see you ever again," he rumbled, and my heart plummeted. My pleading eyes shot up to his face to find that, once again, his were pinned to Matty. "This ends *now*," he threatened. "If it doesn't, you won't enjoy the outcome."

Matty scoffed.

"I'm already dead," he replied, splaying his arms wide, displaying his ever so slightly translucent form. "What exactly do you think you're going to do that trumps that?"

Sean's face gave nothing away, but I felt a surge from him, a rush of some sort, and I knew that he was barely keeping himself composed. He'd secretly prayed that Matty would come around again so he could show him just what was worse than death.

"A wise man wouldn't ask such a question for fear of finding out the answer."

Every hair on my body stood at attention while he purred those words.

"Cooper," he growled, his voice so low it was hard to hear over top of the music that raged on around us. "Take Peyta somewhere far away and safe. *Now*."

I watched as Cooper hesitated. I wasn't sure if he didn't want to appear weak, or if he didn't want to leave me alone with Sean. Eventually, he walked over to her, wrapping his long arm around her petite frame and ushered her to the door. That's when I first noticed that the boys were there. The three of them were crammed together in the doorway, watching curiously as everything unfolded. Cooper snarled at them slightly when he approached, signaling for them to make way.

Peyta was asking questions before they even left the room. The one she repeated the most was, "Who are they?" Cooper was going to have some serious explaining to do on the drive to her house.

The farther away Peyta got, the more Matty faded, but his bravado never wavered. He stood his ground against Sean in their silent battle until he was almost gone.

"I'll see you around, blue eyes," he said before his silhouette vanished entirely. My heart seized a tiny bit.

"But I won't see you..."

Saddened, I walked through where Matty had just stood and shut off the stereo. The silence was deafening.

Sean's eyes finally fell upon me, but I couldn't read them at all. The deep pools of black gave nothing away.

"What in the bloody hell was *that*?" Alistair asked, slowly making his way into the room.

"Long story," I replied with a shaky voice. "You guys stay up here, please. Cooper will be home shortly, and I don't want to get shit for something else when he gets back."

Alistair looked as though he wanted to argue then thought better of it. Janner eyed me as sympathetically as his unexpressive face would allow. Surprisingly, it was Beckett who had something to say.

"You loved him," he said softly, his face impassive as always.

I nodded.

He gave a nod in return and took a step back away from the door, clearing a path for me. Sean placed his hand on my lower back and guided me forward to the landing then down to the second floor. His hand never left me as we entered the apartment or while we made our way down to my bedroom. When he closed the door behind him, a tiny jolt of fear shot through me.

"How long have you known?" he asked quietly.

"The day before yesterday. Sean, I had every intention of telling you when you stopped by the store, but—"

"I didn't let you," he replied, cutting me off. "I know you sensed my anger upstairs, Ruby, but it was not for you. I didn't let you tell me the other day. I cannot hold that against you."

I was floored. That was not the speech I was expecting to get at all. It was almost impossible to process.

"So you're not mad at me? At all?"

"No."

A nervous laugh escaped me.

"Do you think I'll get off this easily with Cooper?"

He shot me a look that said, "You'll get away with whatever I tell him you can get away with." Point taken.

I slumped down onto the bed and propped my elbows on my knees, dropping my head in my hands. Sean moved towards me silently, but I felt his approach as I always could, his body calling to mine in the most inexplicable way. His tall frame blocked the light above as he loomed over me like a dark-eyed angel. In a sense, he kind of was. When I finally lifted my head to see him, his eyes displayed a much lighter shade of green when they met mine.

"I missed you," he said softly, cupping my face in his hand. I pressed my face into his touch, soaking up every bit of it.

"I missed you too."

"I had an evening planned for us the other night before I was so rudely pulled away. Can I make it up to you?"

"Well, since I hadn't known we were going to be doing anything at all until after you told me we couldn't go, I'm not sure you need to, but I'll take it, if you're offering."

I slowly stood up before him, leaving our bodies inches from one another, still connected by that single hand to my face. Then his lips were on mine, light and sweet as if he hadn't been ready to do murderous things only minutes earlier. He truly was a two-sided coin—a product of two diametrically opposed parents.

"Then I should go," he mumbled over my mouth, not wanting to break our kiss to explain. "I have to get a few things..."

My heart cartwheeled around in my chest.

"Okay," I replied breathily.

"I'll be ready for you in an hour."

I'm ready for you now...

He looked down at me and laughed, undoubtedly knowing what I was thinking because, true to form, it was plastered all over my face.

"I'll be there," I replied, trying to play it cool.

He laughed a little more.

"I'll be back to get you," he said as he headed toward the door.

"I think I'll walk, if that's okay. I've got some things of my own to do, you know. *Important* things," I told him with the slightest hint of mocking. I may not have been as smooth as he was, but I could do sarcasm like nobody's business. It was the next best thing as far as I was concerned. "I'll meet you at your place in an hour. Maybe. Maybe I'll be fashionably late just to keep you guessing."

Again with the laughter.

"Ruby," he said with a voice smoother than silk. "You won't want to be late."

CHAPTER 18

He was right; I didn't. But, as luck would have it, I inevitably was.

Even after the shenanigans upstairs, I returned to work without Peyta to finish out the day. Cooper stormed into the store about ten minutes after I returned, none too happy about what he had just witnessed. He calmed down uncharacteristically fast when I pointed out that he was the one who shut me down when I tried to tell him about Matty. He wasn't happy about it, but he admitted it was his fault. I'd gotten two of those in one week, and I wondered when the third would drop. Things *always* happened in threes.

By the time I kicked him out, I only had half an hour left to clean up and close down the store, run upstairs, and get myself ready. It took an hour and a half. *Thirty minutes late and counting.* A frantic text on my way out of the house to Sean was the best I could do to remedy the situation.

The air was brisk with an edge of humidity to it. If

the temperature had dropped any further, snow would have inevitably fallen. I pulled my coat tighter around me and buried my face deep in my pink hand-knit cowl while I ran through the downtown streets in an effort to make up for my tardiness. I was making great time until I hit Sean's block.

That's when everything got derailed.

I rounded the corner right into Gavin, who stood waiting—waiting for *me*.

"Ruby," he said, looking down at me. He was parading around as his younger self, the one who'd pulled me from the bay where the Rev had attempted to plant me deep below the water's edge. I still wasn't used to seeing Gavin that way, so it took me a moment to realize who he was, and I stifled a scream just in time.

In retrospect, maybe I shouldn't have.

"Ginger mentioned she saw you with the dark-eyed one. 'Canoodling' was the word she used, I believe." His eyes were hard and shrewd, attempting to pry my head open and search for the answers himself, knowing it was likely easier than confronting me for them.

"So she's spying on me too? Awesome. I would have thought she was above being your lackey," I snapped, trying to step around him. Quick as lightning, his arm was out, blocking my way.

"Ginger adores you, and, if I were you, I'd watch how you speak about her."

"Sweet! We're going to skip right to threats then, are we?"

"If need be," he growled. He lowered his arm in an attempt to lessen the tension between us, but as far as I was concerned, we were way beyond that. "Ginger told me that she said something she shouldn't have. She's very protective of me, Ruby. You mustn't rile her up like that."

"She did. Something about extinction and how you apparently saved the day. Funny that she clammed up as soon as the words left her mouth. I couldn't get a thing out of her after that."

"It's not her story to tell," he said, leaning in closer. "And I'll tell it when and if I choose to."

"Well, unless you plan to do it right now, I'm late," I informed him, shooting a glance up at Sean's building.

"You're not making this easy for me, Ruby," he said, closing the distance between us to an intimate gap, our bodies nearly touching. "I'll have to try harder to convince you."His hand grasped my elbow. It wasn't an uncomfortable pressure, but what coursed through me as a result was. "He is your enemy—*our* enemy. Do you understand me?"

I shook my head, trying to clear the fuzzy sensation that was wrapping around it, suffocating my rational thought. My heart warred with my brain, each telling the other that it was right. Love versus truth.

"No," I said, snatching my arm away, "I don't understand. If you want me to believe your creepy ramblings, then give me *answers*, not more questions for once. And don't talk around shit either. I *hate* that. You want me to stay away from Sean then give me something solid. Tell me *who* would have been extinct without you."

"No," he replied, low and menacing, "but I'll tell you who did the eradicating. I believe he's upstairs waiting for you right now."

He reached into his pocket and pulled out a photo. It was old and weathered. He handed it to me without explanation.

The picture was of a stunning raven-haired woman who would have been around thirty at the time. Beside her was a towheaded toddler with wild, untamed curls. It was hard to make out under the street lamp, but around them was a pale, hazy glow.

"What is this?" I asked, trying to make sense of his offering.

"A good faith token."

"And how is it that? I don't even know who this is."

"That's you," he explained with an irritated tone, indicating the child. "And *that*," he said, pointing to the young woman, "is someone that I could not keep safe when the time came." His energy fell heavily around me. There was true sadness behind his words. "Keep this for now," he continued, his voice slipping back from the distant tone it had just held. "You have so few mementos of the happier times."

With that, he started to walk away.

"But *who* is she?" I pleaded, begging to know. My childhood had always been a blacked-out blur, and I was desperate to know just who the mysterious woman of my "happier times" was.

"When you're ready to believe the worst of the dark-eyed one, ask him. He knows."

"He's not *all* dark, Gavin," I argued defensively. "He's equal parts dark and light."

Gavin whipped his head around to stare me down, further emphasizing the importance of the point he was about to impress upon me.

"He *is* part angel, Ruby," he agreed, his eyes menacing and mocking, "but does that imply he's *good*? You seem quick to base your favorable opinion on the illusion that angels are all creatures of the light. But what happens when that light has been snuffed out?" He paused to assess my reaction, searching for a sign that he was getting through to me. "I wonder just how convincing your illusion will be when your faulty logic crumbles from beneath it."

"So you're saying there are *bad* angels?" I asked incredulously.

"Yes. The Dark Ones. They are the things that nightmares are made of."

A nervous scoff escaped me.

"Isn't that what you say about Sean? That he's what nightmares are made of?"

A broad and satisfied smile crossed Gavin's face.

"One and the same, Ruby," he called over his shoulder as he walked away. "They are one and the same..."

CHAPTER 19

I stood alone in the street, staring in the direction where he had disappeared into the night. With the innocuous photograph still in my hand and visions of an evil Sean etched into my brain, the barrage of questions started to race through my mind, none of which were going to be answered anytime soon. Gavin was scheming, but I didn't know why. Apparently I knew the woman in the picture but had no clue how. Worst of all, Sean allegedly could tell me who she was, but, somewhere deep down inside me, a seed of doubt had been planted. Was he as dichotomous as I thought he was? A product of both good and evil? Did I really want to know the truth if it meant collapsing the house of cards that Sean and I had so precariously built? Was that all Gavin was trying to do, and, if so, why? To what end?

I needed to figure out his end game and fast.

As I looked down at the picture one last time before tucking it into my coat pocket, I wondered about the stunning woman who looked so happy to be staring down at me. I'd never remembered feeling overly loved as a child, and judging by the pure joy in her face, she loved me more than anything. She looked at me the way Kristy looked at Louie.

Forcing those thoughts aside, I made my way across the road and over to Sean's building. Instead of a growing sense of anticipation with every step, all I felt was doubt overtaking me. It pissed me off that I was letting Gavin's mind games get to me, and I wondered why I let him play them at all. *Answers. He has answers,* I reminded myself. Supply and demand was a bitch when the supplier had a warped sense of how to distribute the information.

With leaden feet, I climbed the stairs to Sean's apartment. Hesitating before the door, I swallowed my lingering insecurities as best I could, hoping that I could overcome them. Love could conquer all, couldn't it?

Before I could knock, he was there, smiling down at me with the face of an angel. *Light or dark,* I found myself wondering as the happiness slowly bled from his expression.

"What's wrong?" he asked, stepping out to meet me on the landing.

I took a step back.

I needed to get a hold of myself before irreparable damage was done. Letting Gavin's curious riddles plague my mind was not a way to live, nor was it fair to Sean. He had no way to defend himself against Gavin's ambiguous accusations, and I had no intention of going to Sean with anything until I had more solid evidence. All that would prove was that I didn't trust him. After everything we'd been through, I owed him more than that. And yet, one single photograph threatened to undo it all—a photograph and an unsettling feeling that Gavin attached to it. Something wasn't right about the situation, and come hell or high water, I was going to figure out exactly what before it swallowed me whole.

"I'm sorry," I said, shaking my head a little for clarity. "It's been a long day. Can I come in?"

"Of course," he replied, stepping back into the apartment. He watched me acutely, no doubt trying to read me like the open book he always found me to be. For once, it looked as though my novel was closed.

"I'm sorry I'm so late," I told him as I slipped out of my coat.

"I expected you to be here about ten minutes ago. I was getting mildly concerned."

You should have been...

"I got hung up after I texted you. I'm living in a bit of a madhouse at the moment, if you hadn't noticed," I explained. "It's a hindrance of sorts."

"You're welcome to stay here," he offered, heading to the kitchen. "You know that, right?"

I smiled inside.

"I do now." I moved to join him at the stove. He turned quickly to intercept me as I passed. I gasped, momentarily startled by the speed of his movement. It wasn't because I was still thinking about what Gavin had said—not at all.

"Something is bothering you," he said matter of factly. "Tell me what it is. *Please.*"

"I just have a lot on my mind."

"I can see that, Ruby. What I want to know is *what* is on your mind."

No you don't.

"I have a feeling that you of all people won't be able to relate to what I'm about to say, but here it goes," I said, taking a deep breath. "I always feel like I have more questions than answers, Sean. I'm not quite sure how to settle the constantly-running state of my mind. It's wearing on me. I'm not sleeping well. It's starting to affect my mood, my vision, my weight..."

He eyed me tightly, assessing both me and my statement.

"Change of plans," he announced unexpectedly. "You're eating then going to bed. And no arguing, though I'm sure it will pain you greatly."

I stared at him in total disbelief.

"You're not going to interrogate me about what's running through my mind? Demand to know what questions I so desperately want answers to? Nothing?"

"No, Ruby. I'm not." He looked down at me with genuine confusion. "You've been honest with me since you've been back. You offered me information without hesitation the other day and it was I who dropped the ball," he said, pressing his lips gently against my forehead. "I love you. I trust you too. Now, let's eat before you get any thinner and put you to bed. It may not have been my original game plan for the evening, but I'm sure I can make it interesting nonetheless."

Without awaiting my response, he took my hand and led me to the barstool by the kitchen island. A plate of gourmet something or other was in front of me before I could lift a utensil to eat it with, and then he was beside me, eating his dinner as though we were an ordinary couple, staying in on a Friday night.

I stared at him for a moment in silence while he ate with the grace of royalty. The normalcy of our evening was unsettling, and instead of putting my mind at ease, it only seemed to disturb me further. Did he know what I was thinking and want to throw me off by doing the opposite of what I expected? Was his calm façade all an act? I reached down deep to feel for any undercurrent to his energy, but found none. All I got from him was ease and contentment.

"You're staring," he muttered before taking the final bite of his food.

"I'm a mannerless heathen," I said sarcastically, snapping my gaze back to my plate. "You should know that by now."

"I know a lot about you, Ruby. Almost everything there is to know, but you still surprise me on occasion," he replied, turning to look at me. I kept my gaze firmly affixed to my plate.

"I thought it was a good thing to keep a man guessing. Is it not?" I asked nervously, pushing my food around with my fork.

"With you, one can't be too certain," he whispered in my ear. "But I'm more than willing to take my chances." My breath caught in my throat as I turned to look at him. His bright green eyes were playful as ever. "If you're done with your food, I think it's time to get you off to bed."

He scooped me up out of my chair and carried me to his bedroom where he laid me down delicately on the bed and started to arrange the covers around me, tucking me in.

"I'm flying solo?" I asked, surprise tainting my voice. "I doubt that was part of your grand scheme for the evening.

His brow furrowed slightly.

"No. It wasn't," he replied, "but you're exhausted, and I want you well."

"Thanks," I whispered, thinking his gesture was surprisingly nurturing.

"Don't thank me yet. I might have to wake you up early to make up for fallen-through plans."

"Deal," I agreed, pushing up out of the bed.

"And where do you think you're going?"

"The bathroom, unless you'd prefer I take my chances tonight."

He laughed.

"Go," he ordered, pointing to the bathroom door. "I have to make a phone call anyway. I'll be just outside the apartment if you need anything."

He started to make his way to the living room, and I watched as his casual posture morphed into a more businesslike one with every step. I knew that I didn't want to know what that call was about, and, for once, I didn't bother to ask. For one night, I was happy to pretend that everything was okay.

But it wasn't.

The nightmares I endured that evening about the unknown woman in the picture made sure that I remembered that fact.

CHAPTER 20

A nd the nightmares kept coming. Every night for the next eight days, to be exact. While everything else seemed to be looking up around me, I couldn't get the image of her face scraped off the back of my mind.

I wanted to talk to Cooper about it, but we never seemed to be alone enough for that to happen. He avoided private conversation even when the boys were upstairs; with superhuman hearing, they would be privy to what was said anyway. And if it wasn't the boys getting in the way, it was Sean; I still had no intention of bringing anything up with him until I had some answers from Gavin. I didn't want to play the card that Gavin had so graciously placed in my hand. Something about that seemed too easy—like he was counting on me to do that. I had no intention of being a pawn in his game.

By day nine, I'd stopped fighting it and just went with the flow, though exhausted and mentally fatigued. I hadn't realized just how out of it I really was until I slammed my shoulder into the kitchen doorway late that afternoon while carrying popcorn to the living room for the guys. It flew everywhere, creating a ruckus when the stainless bowl crashed to the hardwood. The four of them snapped their attention to me instantaneously, looking for danger. The only danger to be found was me—a danger to myself.

"What the hell was that, Ruby?" Cooper asked with a look of confusion. "We didn't just throw that wall up today."

"I'm so tired," I whined, trying to pick up the mess. Beckett moved to join me until one look from Cooper sat him back down quick. Cooper may have been warming up to the boys enough to not want to kill them on a daily basis, and he even let them come down and join us in the living room from time to time, but they were still on tight leashes, and those leashes had no give wherever I was concerned.

Instead, Cooper came to join me while the others looked on, bewildered expressions on all four faces.

"Rubes, this can't be good. You're walking into walls, for Christ's sake. You're like a zombie most days. Mind telling me what's going on?"

"I've tried to," I snapped under my breath, "but I can't find an appropriate time."

He looked over his shoulder at the others then nodded at me in acknowledgment.

"Maybe Sean can send over a couple more boys to babysit one day so you and I can get out of here and talk?" he offered up as a solution.

"We need to do it sooner rather than later, Coop. I feel like I'm falling apart."

"Telling you that you look like it too isn't likely to help, is it?" he asked with a tiny smirk.

I chucked whatever popcorn I'd picked off the floor at his head.

"No. It's not, thank you very much. Is it weird that I don't love hearing that I look like shit?" I mocked, getting up to leave him with the mess. "I think I need to just rest for a bit. De-stress or something like that."

"You go do that then. I'm taking these guys out in a bit to follow up on a house for rent out of town. Near the woods. Away from people. I think it's going to work out beautifully."

"Have fun," I yelled, giving a wave in the general direction of the living room.

"I will," he replied playfully. A little *too* playfully. "I'm taking your car. I need to see that these idiots can drive on the right side of the road without killing anyone."

"Get so much as a scratch on her and you die."

"Mhmm."

The door closing behind him signaled just how not frightened he was by my threat. What was I going to do, chastise him to death? I had nothing and he knew it. His lack of response called my bluff. Even though he had the upper hand with the car, he was still getting the short end of the stick. He had to babysit once again, and I was happy to be missing out on that.

But I wasn't happy for long.

Not five minutes after they disappeared down the street, my phone started to ring. When I answered it, I immediately wished I hadn't. It wasn't a conversation I was ready to have just yet.

"Ruby," Gavin drawled. "I haven't heard from you since our last meeting. I assume that means you have not yet shown the dark-eyed one the photo."

"Hello, Gavin," I lamented in return. "You assume

correctly, though you probably knew that for a fact given your penchant for following me around and knowing every intimate detail of my life."

"Fair enough," he replied, denying nothing. "But I'm not calling about that specifically. I think you and I need to meet."

I couldn't help but roll my eyes.

"Because those tend to go oh-so well..."

"Your sarcasm is both noted and unappreciated, young lady. I was trying to be civil and request a get-together, but I'm sure I could just ambush you instead, if that's more to your liking."

"It's not. Thanks."

"Just as I thought." His condescending tone seeped through the receiver, irritating me to no end. I didn't like that he presumed to know me so well—even if he did. "I'm going to be out of town for about a week or so. We'll have to schedule something for when I return."

"Taking Ginger on vacation?" I quipped, smiling at myself for my efforts.

"As if one would possibly have time for that while trying to keep you from being a menace to yourself," he sneered, sounding every bit as put-upon as he believed himself to be. "I have some business to attend to. Ginger will be in town during my absence. I returned the houseboat to its usual dock a few days ago, in case you might need to find refuge there."

"And why would I need that?" I asked nervously.

"Because your life is a boiling pot that incessantly threatens to bubble over. Even you can't deny that you need to escape it on occasion."

He was right. I couldn't.

"So what's this pressing business you have to

attend to?" I asked in an attempt to change the subject.

"I need to gather some information..."

"On what? What could possibly pull you away from tormenting me for an entire week?"

He was quiet for a moment, though I could hear him breathing hard on the other end. I was getting under his skin, and I relished the thought of being able to get even the slightest bit even with him on that front.

Then he blindsided me.

"Something wicked this way comes, Ruby. And it comes for you." His voice was as dark and foreboding as his message. A chill shot down my spine in response. "I am going to see how this evil can be avoided."

"What?" I whispered, barely able to force the words out. "What evil? What's coming?"

"All in good time, my dear," he replied, sounding the teensiest bit pleased with himself. "It is not upon you yet. I will call you when I return and we will pick a time to meet. Until then..." He hung up the phone, leaving me utterly shell-shocked.

Although he had made a point to say that the evil was not yet upon me, I found precious little comfort in that. Gavin was calculating, manipulative, and terribly smart. He would not have left his wife alone in a danger zone, so I knew that I was in less danger than my imagination was leading me to believe. But still, he'd dropped one hell of a bomb on me before buggering off to go play supernatural spy. I didn't appreciate the jolt to my nervous system.

He seemed unimpressed by the text I sent him telling him so.

His response was poetic, yet not especially helpful:
The danger I speak of will not befall you before my return. Find

peace in that for now.

More riddles.

Without much choice, I tried to do as he ordered and find comfort in the fact that death wouldn't be on my doorstep for at least a week.

So much for my de-stressing plan.

*   *   *

"Coming!" I yelled at Cooper, who was banging on the apartment door. "Why you can't just use your friggin' key is beyond me."

I unlatched the deadbolt and swung the door wide open to see all the boys, sans Cooper.

"Sorry," Janner said softly, looking a touch sheepish about thumping on the door. "I wasn't sure you heard the knock the first time. Can we come in?"

"Uh, yeah...sure," I hesitated. "Where's Coop? I thought he was with you guys."

"He was," Beckett said with a shrug. "He isn't now."

"Maybe you should check your phone," Ali added helpfully. "Perhaps he's left you a message?"

I looked at them with trepidation. They felt normal and at ease, but I didn't like that Cooper was missing. *That* didn't sit well at all.

With a smile and my best attempt to appear normal, I swallowed my growing discomfort and excused myself to get my phone out of my room. No sense in letting on that a full-blown panic was threatening to overtake me. If something had happened to Cooper, it would have been entirely my fault. I brought those three into our lives.

I closed the door lightly behind me and snatched

my cell up off the nightstand, my palms sweating making the task harder than it should have been. Sure enough, there was a text from Cooper.

    Fucking cops. Fender bender. Be home
    in a few. Do NOT let them in until
    then. I MEAN IT!

I was beyond elated to see his message. It was classic overprotective Cooper. Knowing that he wasn't dead, my first thought was that I'd already fucked up his orders. He wasn't going to be thrilled about that upon his return, but I saw no point in kicking them out. I was going to be in shit anyway.

My second thought was that his 'fender bender' had taken place in my car. Two TTs and two car accidents—a perfect score.

I sighed and tossed the phone down before proceeding to the living room. The three still stood, not making themselves comfortable. They looked stiff and awkward.

"Ruby," Alistair started. "Is everything okay with Cooper?"

"Yes. He's fine."

"Brilliant," he replied with a boyish smile. "Do you think there is any chance you'd be willing to let us watch a little football on the telly? At least until he returns?"

"Sure. Whatever you want," I agreed, heading back to my room to retrieve my phone. I thought it best to have it near me just in case Cooper was going to announce his arrival. It would give me time to clear out the troops.

He smiled at me as he plopped on the couch with Janner not far behind. Beckett, on the other hand, made his way to the kitchen, opening the fridge for a peek.

His frown spoke volumes.

"You've got nothing in here. How in the bloody hell are you supposed to keep your strength up with pickles and ketchup?"

I chuckled to myself. They didn't know about my magical drawer of takeout menus. I hadn't had to use it for quite a while because of Cooper's culinary prowess, but in light of all the changes to our living arrangements, he hadn't been to the store. I never bothered going.

"Watch and learn, my British friend," I smiled as I dramatically pulled the handle and unveiled the piles of folded paper. "I may be the sole reason that takeout was invented. What are you guys up for?"

"Pizza!" the two on the couch shouted out in unison over top of the ruckus on the television. I poked my head around the corner to see what kind they wanted.

"I don't know how it works in England, but on this side of the Atlantic, you have to be a wee bit more specific about what you'd like *on* your pie." They didn't take their eyes off the screen to answer. With a sigh, I trudged in there, hoping that if I stood in front of it I would actually get an answer. "So, should I just pick something, or—" I cut myself off when I saw what they were too engrossed in to answer me. "Wait, I thought you said you were watching *football?* This is *soccer.*"

"No, love, it's football. Fucking Americans," he muttered under his breath.

"Well, this fucking American is trying to feed your superior British ass, so if you would be so kind as to direct your attention this way for two seconds to tell me exactly what it is you'd like, it would be super, or *brilliant*, if you prefer."

He gave me an impish grin before he rattled off what he wanted. Janner followed suit. Beckett had the good sense to write it down as orders were being barked out over the roaring television.

"Do we need anything else?" I asked, grabbing the phone to dial.

"Beers!" the couch-dwelling duo yelled in perfect synchrony yet again. I looked to Beckett, and he gave me an impassive shrug. Apparently he was on board with their plan.

"Well, I can't exactly order those. Somebody's going to have to walk down to the market and get them."

I wasn't sure what the best plan of action would be. Should I go get them myself and leave the trio unattended, or should I send one of them with the explicit instructions that death would rain down upon them all if there was even the slightest deviation from my orders? They did still think that I was a killing machine. I wouldn't have pissed me off if I were them.

With Beckett nominated for the task, I shelled out some money to him for brews, surprised by how much he said would be necessary. Apparently, they planned to get a little rowdy. Cooper really wasn't going to be pleased when he got home.

After lecturing Beckett ad nauseam and ordering the multiple pizzas to feed four werewolves—Cooper would want some too, once he calmed down—I plopped myself down in the armchair and pretended to know what was going on. The announcers were virtually impossible to understand with their thick Scottish accents, and I had no clue who I was supposed to be rooting for or how the game was even played. When the blue team scored a goal, I cheered, wanting to seem enthusiastic about watching. I was met with death glares from the couch commandos.

"You never, ever, *ever* cheer for Chelsea, Ruby. It's bloody blasphemy," Ali scolded. "You should be thankful that Becks wasn't here for that slip-up. He'd have gone mad."

"Right. Sorry," I replied, shrinking into my seat. "Red guys. I'll cheer for the red guys."

"Bloody right you will," he muttered under his breath.

Ten minutes later, Beckett returned with the entire imported beer selection from the liquor store. Box upon box was unloaded into the fridge, making it serendipitous that there hadn't been any food in there to occupy the necessary space for their beverages. Beckett popped the caps off of four bottles using some fancy countertop trick, then made his way into the living room to distribute the first round. When he thrust one toward me, I smiled and accepted. I felt like one of the boys.

"Ruby cheered for Chelsea," Alistair baited from the far end of the couch before turning a mischievous grin my way.

"Turncoat!" I yelled at him, chucking a pillow at his head that he easily ducked.

"She didn't...," Beckett whispered, turning disbelieving eyes my way.

"It's true," Janner concurred. "Shall we vote her off the island?"

Beckett slowly shook his head in negation.

"We'll have to teach her a lesson later." The closest thing to a smile that I'd ever seen on Beckett flashed across his face. "A few more beers first though, eh?"

At that second, a goal was scored on a 'breakaway'

of some sort, and they all shot to their feet cheering, then chugged their beers in a contest to see who could slam their bottle down first. Janner won that round and quickly ran to grab fresh ones before the game kicked off again. When he returned, he'd brought an open one for me too.

Much to my dismay, it was only minutes before the red team—Manchester United—scored again after some man bounced the ball off of his head into the goal. *I thought they were supposed to use their feet?*

Again, they all shot up and downed their drinks, only this time they insisted that I join in the race. I'd never tried to guzzle a beer before, and it wasn't an especially successful effort, but with minor spilling, I choked it down, dragging my mouth across my sleeve to clean my face afterward. I was met with a wall of stares as I slammed my bottle down. Apparently I needed to work on my chugging skills.

"You'll get the hang of it," Alistair called, heading to the kitchen for yet another round. As he did, the doorbell rang, signaling the arrival of the pizza. I sighed in relief; I was going to need it if we were going to keep up drinking at that pace.

"Hurry, Ruby. They're back on the pitch!"

"What?" I asked, fumbling with the pile of boxes stacked precariously in my arms. "What does that even mean?"

"He means they're on the field and ready to go," Janner called from the sofa.

"Why do you guys have to call things such weird names?" I lamented as I laid out the food on the island.

"So much to learn...," Beckett patronized, shaking his head disapprovingly. His dry sense of humor was oddly refreshing. The whole scenario was.

By the time the second half began, I was five beers in and feeling it. Janner had graciously offered to explain the basics of the game to me, so I joined him on the couch with the others so I could hear over the general volume of the shenanigans. The four of us were cozily crammed on the sofa, drinking, eating, swearing, and shouting like crazy people. *'Hooligans,'* Beckett had called us with a look of pride.

They taught me chants and even random little dances that they did after every favorable call or goal, and I soaked them up like a sponge, enjoying every second of our tomfoolery. It was the most fun I'd had since I returned.

I'd forgotten all about Cooper in his absence, but we all snapped to attention when he stormed through the door, his look murderous. In fairness, we were quite a sight to behold. Our team had scored in the final minute and we were dutifully celebrating, me propped up on Alistair's shoulders, beer in hand as the boys all jumped up and down chanting between swigs of beer. The merriment quickly died as Cooper's anger permeated the air.

"What the *fuck* do you think you're doing?" he growled, standing in the doorway.

I tried to scramble down off of Alistair, but only managed to fall back onto the couch in a heap, spilling my beer all over myself. The UK trio was suddenly silent, which was a stunning contrast to moments earlier. Beckett reached for me to help me up, and Cooper growled. *Truly* growled. I looked up to see my golden-eyed alpha desperately close to Changing. Explanations were needed and fast.

"Everything's fine," I offered, tripping over my own feet as I walked toward him. I was beyond drunk, and my vision seemed to suffer because of it. "We were just watching some soccer. *Football!* I mean football," I slurred, stumbling over the empties piled on the floor. They scattered like bowling pins after a strike, and I triumphantly threw my arms up and cheered as if I'd just bowled one. Cooper was not amused.

"You're drunk," he rumbled, flexing his hands.

"Yes. Yes, I am, but it's cool. Everything's cool, Cooper. Look! We have food! Why don't you c'mon in and have some," I said, grabbing his arm to usher him in. He didn't budge. "There's beer too."

"It doesn't look like there could possibly be any left."

"It's in the fridge. I'll go get you—"

"Don't. Move," he snarled, his eyes pinned on the boys. "Why are you three in here? I'm certain I told you that you were never to be in here without me present. Was I not clear? Shall I make myself clear?"

"We arrived and waited for you upstairs, but when you didn't return, we decided to come down and see if we could watch the game. Maybe eat dinner," Janner replied weakly, hoping to diffuse my tightly wound alpha.

"And is that what I *told* you to do? No. It isn't. I told you to wait for me if you arrived here first. It wasn't a request."

Alistair stirred uncomfortably, clearly wanting to say something and knowing it might be more to his advantage to keep quiet instead. Cooper eyed him wildly.

"Something you'd like to add, Alice?"

"I was hungry. I thought it might be nice to have dinner with Ruby. To get to know her more."

Cooper snapped.

"I'll decide when you eat, shit, and socialize, is that clear?" He'd closed the distance between himself and them in a blur, and it made my head dizzy. "She is not yours to get to know, understood?" "She's not yours either," Alistair muttered under his breath.

Fuel to the fire.

"She is mine, make no mistake about that. She is my family, my friend—my pack. Any harm that befalls her will be avenged so ruthlessly that Satan himself will turn away from the brutality." He pulled Alistair closer, so that their noses were nearly touching, his eyes burning through the young wolf. "Do. Not. Touch. Her. *Ever.*"

Alistair didn't struggle. His boys looked on, clearly debating their next move. I don't think they wanted to challenge Cooper, but I could feel that they didn't want to stand idly by and watch their friend—their brother— be killed. I didn't want to watch that either.

"Cooper," I called, emanating whatever calming vibes I could given how worked up I was. I'd never seen him so vicious. His ever-evolving persona was taking on even more of Sean's qualities. As was often the case, that was not the time to point them out. "I got your message after I'd let them in. It's my fault really. I shouldn't have ignored it, but they were already watching the game and we were ordering food. It was...*fun*. I haven't had that in a long time."

He wouldn't turn to face me, still boring holes through Alistair's face with his gaze. I did feel his hostility waver ever so slightly though, so I kept talking.

"Please, Coop. Let him go. He didn't mean anything by it. I know what it's like to have a mouth that gets you into trouble."

His yellow eyes finally turned to burn through me. He dropped Alistair onto the couch like a ragdoll before stalking towards me.

"You may trust them, Ruby, but I'm far less convinced."

"Then why did you take so long to get home if you were so worried?" I asked, trying to find fault in his logic.

"I was detained by Portsmouth's finest," he grumbled. "Apparently, they don't enjoy being ignored or challenged."

"What did you do, Cooper?"

"I was trying to reach you while the reports were being filed by the officer on the scene. He didn't like my lack of focus and tried to take my phone away," he said, clenching his jaw. "...I protested."

I cringed.

"Bad call, Coop. What were you thinking?"

He looked around the room theatrically then gave me his 'I could ask you the same thing' face.

"I was thinking that I needed to protect you, that's what I was thinking."

"So you've been in *jail* this whole time?" I asked incredulously.

"Not the whole time."

"Well, how did you manage to talk your way out of charges?"

"I didn't," he replied flatly. "I'm going to have to send Alan a fruit basket or something."

I exhaled heavily.

"Thank God he was there. Cooper, you could have been in real trouble!"

"And you could have been in worse," he shouted, snapping a look over at the boys. "You three. Out!

Now!"

Without skipping a beat, they filed out like good little soldiers, making their way upstairs. My heart sank as Ali gave me a sad glance over his shoulder before closing the door behind him. The air was full of tension, sadness, and longing. Those three had been displaced, forced from the only family they'd known. Cooper had every right not to trust them, and I knew he was going out on a limb for me in letting them stay temporarily, but I just couldn't write them off. They were growing on me. They just wanted to belong and I knew all too well what that felt like.

I was their ticket to a new life. It made no sense for them to squander it.

Cooper followed them out, hovering momentarily at the door.

"Go to the bathroom and make yourself throw up. I need you sober." His words were not a request, but an order. "I'm going to go have a chat with those three."

"Cooper…"

"I won't hurt them, Ruby, but we're not in a position to have a repeat performance of tonight anytime soon. Ground rules are going to be laid. So are the consequences for breaking them."

"Did you secure that rental?" I asked, wanting to change the subject.

"No, but I'm getting to the point that I don't care how suitable the conditions are. They need to go, Ruby. The sooner the better."

CHAPTER 21

The next day, I left early to head down to the shop. I was beyond out of touch with the books, and I needed to remedy the problem ASAP. Cooper walked me out on his way down to the college. Since he'd dropped his classes after my disappearance, he was going to see if there was any way for him to re-enter the next semester. Neither of us was overly hopeful, but it was worth a shot. He needed a positive distraction in his life, however small it might be.

"I'll be back in an hour or so," he told me with a somewhat stern look on his face. "Sean's got eyes on the foreigners, and those three are under direct orders to avoid you. Do I need to order you to stay away from them too?"

I shot him my best 'really?' face. When I was met with an all too familiar 'answer the fucking question' expression, I verbalized my response.

"No, Cooper. You don't need to go all Alpha McBossypants on me. I get it. They're personae non gratae."

He scrunched his face up at me like he'd just smelled something awful.

"That didn't sound right at all."

"It's correct. Don't hurt yourself over it."

"But isn't it persona non—"

"I made it plural, Coop," I snapped, irritated with his questions. "I took five years of Latin. It's right. Google it."

"Whatever, grump. Just do as I said, please. The boys are to remain upstairs until I return. I don't want to hear otherwise."

"Fine."

"Good."

We stared at each other silently for a moment before an impish smile broke across his face.

"I miss our talks," he said, turning to walk down to the campus. My car was inconveniently in the shop thanks to his mad driving skills, so he had feet-only transportation for the next few days. I made him leave the Navigator at home because I refused to be left without a car in case of emergencies. I wondered if I could bum yet another vehicle off of Sean.

"I miss my TT," I retorted. "Don't think that's water under the bridge, my friend."

"With you, Rubes, it never is."

He rounded the corner before I could reply, leaving me to stew and laugh. It was unnerving how he could get under my skin and still be charming. That trait clearly hadn't disappeared in our time together.

With a sigh, I unlocked the store and headed in. I shivered a bit, a gust of wind ushering me through the door, chilling me slightly. The weather continued to be unseasonably frigid, and I forgot to dress appropriately for it. A jacket would have been a welcome addition to my ensemble.

Seeking refuge from the blustery weather outside, I quickly found that the temperature inside my shop was not much of an improvement. An early winter was a highly inconvenient time to experience a furnace meltdown. Especially when the male most likely to fix the problem had just walked into town, leaving me to deal with it alone.

I let out an enormous breath of frustration, lips flapping loudly with the gesture. I knew nothing about furnaces or how to operate them, but I knew I had to at least check the situation out before I called Cooper or a professional to come out and service it. I didn't want to find out that only the pilot light was out—Cooper would never have let me hear the end of it. I'd also be left with a hefty bill and an even heftier blow to my self-esteem.

It took a while to hunt down a flashlight, but admittedly that had more to do with my growing discomfort over the task ahead rather than the flashlight's elusive nature. Basements had never affected me growing up as I'd heard they did others. Darkness was darkness to me—experiencing it below ground didn't change anything. Utah, however, had changed all that for me. Having to go down into the cramped, dirty crawlspace brought forth anxieties that I still struggled with one year after the fact. I wanted to tuck tail and run back to the apartment, but I just couldn't—for myriad reasons.

I'd spent months ignoring, avoiding, and denying that I had issues as a result of my confinement. I'd also spent thousands on therapy and frequented all kinds of support groups, none of which were especially helpful given my inability to truly share my experience. I really couldn't admit what had happened to me, given the supernatural components of the story. My attacks had been both brutal and scarring, and though those scars were starting to heal with the love and support of those around me, my kidnapping and incarceration still haunted me both day and night. I still hadn't admitted to myself or anyone else that I was a victim of sexual violence. If I didn't begin pushing myself to face my fears and move on with life, would I spend the rest of my life running from my past?

"No," I said aloud to myself. "No more."

With my Maglite clutched tightly in hand, I tried my best to ignore my shaking that was amplified by the rattling of the box of matches I held. I made my way into the workshop and quickly found the wall switch. I had high hopes that its light would carry down the narrow stairwell to the crawlspace-like basement below, but that proved wishful thinking. After I moved the boxes of whatnot that were blocking the way, I turned the knob and opened the door to a damp and musty smell. It sent shockwaves down my spine, and I broke out in a full-body sweat in the blink of an eye.

Staring down into the abyss below, I forced the air I needed into and out of my lungs while I strangled the flashlight in my hand. One step at a time, with a mantra of affirmation playing on a loop in my mind and my hand-held lifeline illuminating my path, I made my way to the basement. It was nearly impossible to stand fully upright with the ceiling so low and the dirt floor so uneven, so I hunched over and ducked my head as I made my way to my destination. Just before I reached the furnace, a mouse skittered across the floor in front of me. I screeched and jumped backward, cracking the back of my head on the floor joist behind me and spilling my matches everywhere.

"FUCK!" I screamed in frustration with myself as I rubbed the throbbing mass to be sure it wasn't bleeding. The anger was helpful, overriding my fear temporarily. I stormed the furnace, slapping the side of it with my open palm before attempting to procure a match or two just in case I did need to light the pilot. Once I had a handful of them and the box to strike them against, I crouched down in front of the mass of metal and looked around for any source of flame within it.

I found none.

"Well, at least this will be a cheap fix," I muttered under my breath, placing the flashlight down on the ground beside me, aimed precariously at the furnace.

Surprisingly, it was easier than I thought to find what needed to be lit. There were also convenient instructions adhered to the side of the box that detailed the process in full, alluding to the fact that any moron should be able to do it without issue. I was about to test the veracity of that claim.

I snatched up the matchbox and one of the five stray matches I'd collected and prepared to conquer not only my fears that day, but the furnace too. The sulfur smell assaulted my nose as the first match flared to life. I hoped the pilot light would follow suit.

As I leaned forward in an attempt to solve the heating crisis, the flashlight completely crapped out on me, leaving me with only the match as a light source. I scrambled to collect the others before the one I had burned out, not wanting to be alone in the dark for a second longer than necessary. Just as I corralled them next to my knee, the inevitable occurred and my match—directly after burning my fingers—fell to the ground and snuffed itself out.

"Dammit!" I snarled, slamming my hand into the ancient metal box beside me. I felt like it was taunting me while I fumbled with my shaking hands to get another match lit.

One.

Two.

Three.

One by one they sparked and fizzled as if they were a metaphor for my hopes at that moment.

Last one...

I calmed my breathing, knowing that my violent exhalation, with which I was attempting to stave off my panic, had blown out two of the last three matches. Whispering a prayer for help, I quickly drew the little wooden stick along the side of the box. I stifled a squeal when its flame stayed alight—but not for long. As I lifted the match up to illuminate the tiny place on the furnace I needed to put it, I was met with something else entirely—a face.

My screams snuffed out the flame.

CHAPTER 22

I scrambled backward, scurrying along the packed-dirt floor in hopes of getting some space between me and the owner of the stone gray eyes that were etched into my mind.

"Ruby," he called out to me. "Love, I've not come to hurt you...I heard a crash down here. I wanted to see that you were okay."

Right as I slammed into the stone foundation of the far wall, I heard the sizzle of a match lighting. Beckett knelt before the furnace, looking a cross between bewildered and amused. I was neither—scared shitless came to mind.

"Do all werewolves skulk about, or do any of you actually announce your presence before entering a room—or death-inspiring basement, as the case may be?" My tone was crisp and curt, but it was a mask for the absolute terror I felt rising up from where I'd long ago stuffed it.

And it wasn't going to come out pretty.

"I told you," he said, leaning in to coax the pilot light to life, "I heard you. I thought you might need my help."

"Aren't you just a knight in shining armor today? Where's your *steed?* Your *sword?*" I asked as condescendingly as possible while I attempted to strategically move around him. "I'm no damsel in distress, Beckett. I had this all sorted out until you just *poofed* yourself in here and gave me a heart attack." The path I chose had the widest berth possible. Everything about the situation made me uneasy, and I wanted to get out of there. Like *yesterday.*

The light was flickering wildly, and it was apparent that it was about to burn out. I didn't want to be anywhere below ground level when that happened. Not caring about the implications, I turned and bolted for the stairs, which was challenging given that I couldn't stand up straight.

I heard him bite out a few choice swears under his breath behind me as his footsteps approached. Knowing that he had been the one to sack me in Maine, it wasn't my fondest case of déjà vu. Just as I passed the halfway point up to freedom, I tripped on the stairs.

"What is wrong with you?" he asked, his accent thickening with his frustration. "It's like you've gone bloody mad all of a sudden! Are you all right?"

"Listen, you shouldn't be down here. You need to get upstairs," I bit out.

"Ruby—"

"I mean it!" I screamed, wheeling on him once I crested the top of the stairs. "You don't know anything about me, Beckett. What you just did..."

I cut off my words before letting them escape. He didn't deserve the tongue-lashing I was prepared to give him. He hadn't harmed me, touched me, or done anything untoward at all. With a little breathing room between us, I realized that all he'd actually done was help me. Before I had a chance to explain my reaction, a man who was only vaguely familiar to me came crashing through the workroom door, armed to the teeth and ready to throw down.

"Ruby," he called while eyeing Beckett tightly. "Go upstairs, please."

"No. I think there's a bit of a misunderstanding here," I replied, moving in front of Beckett.

"I was told that they were to go nowhere near you." His tone was flat and business-like; he was PC for sure. "He is where he shouldn't be. There is a price for that."

"That's my fault. I was trying to fix the furnace and couldn't get it to work. I called Beckett to come down and help me. He knew the rules—knew that he wasn't supposed to be around me alone—but I started to melt down so he placated me. I'm the reason he's here. He shouldn't have to pay for my ineptitude."

"I have orders," he said, moving toward us.

"From who? Sean?" I asked, seeing a potential out for our predicament. It was a card I really loathed playing, but desperate times called for desperate measures. Being the bitchy girlfriend was definitely a desperate move. "Let me explain something to you. Sean wants me happy, end of story. If you kill Beckett, I won't be happy, which will make Sean unhappy in the process. I've seen when Sean is unhappy; it's not especially pleasant. Do you want that rage raining down on you? I sure wouldn't. I've been there once. I don't recommend the experience. But, if you're hellbent on signing your own death warrant, please," I baited, sweeping my arms dramatically toward Beckett. "Be my guest."

The nameless brother eyed me in a way I wouldn't soon forget. It was how they all used to look at me back in the beginning—with utter hatred and resentment. My stomach did a sickening flip. I had only started to gain a little acceptance with the brothers. Once news of my theatrics spread, I knew that would be shot to shit.

"As you wish," he said with a mocking bow before walking out the way he had come. Beckett and I were silent for a moment, making sure the brother had left.

"You risked much to do that for me," he said softly.

"Well, I guess I could say the same for you with your handyman stunt downstairs. I lost a little clout with Sean's brothers. You almost died." He smiled lightly at me before leaning in to kiss me gently on the cheek. "Speaking of almost dying, might I suggest you get your ass upstairs before Cooper gets home? I may be able to keep the PC from annihilating your ass, but Cooper is another story entirely. After our shenanigans the other night, I think you guys are on thin ice."

"I believe you are correct, Ruby. If you are all set, I'll be on my way."

I nodded quickly, and, without a word, he was out the door.

For a moment, I had trouble wrapping my head around what had just happened. I knew that Sean and Cooper meant business with the new guys, but to see that business in action was sobering to say the least. Had I not been able to maneuver things the way I did, Beckett would have been dead at my feet and the PC working their clean-up magic to remove any trace of his existence. It made me wonder if the others would have been executed as a precautionary measure. Luckily, that wasn't a reality I had to face, but I worried that it wasn't far off in the future. We needed to get a handle on the Tobias situation in a hot hurry.

Shaking off the remnants of the near fatal clusterfuck, I headed for the paperwork pile of doom on my desk that awaited my attention. I still had time before the shop opened to put a small dent in it, and even with a growing headache that seemed to be affecting my visual acuity, I planned to take advantage of it. To my surprise, it was smaller than I expected it to be. Peyta truly had been running a tight ship in my absence.

I plopped down and started sorting through the bills while I fired up the computer. I had a solid hour before it was time to open the doors to the public, and I planned to use it to my advantage. Fortunately for me, it only took a few minutes to get back into the swing of Quickbooks, and before I knew it, three quarters of the stack was filed away.

Delighted with myself, I made my way out front to prep for opening. Peyta walked through the doors at that very moment, greeting me with a smug smile.

"Fancy meeting you here at this hour. I thought you left opening to your minion."

"Normally, yes, but today I'm feeling generous. Merry Christmas," I mocked with a condescending curtsy from behind the counter.

"If that's my Christmas present, it sucks," she replied, jabbing me playfully in the side while she went to put her things in the back. "Wow," she called from the workroom, "you have been busy, young lady."

"You're welcome."

She reappeared, an aura of snarkiness

accompanying her.

"Oh, yes...*thank you* for doing your job."

I swept my arms wide before taking a far more dramatic bow to irritate her further. She rolled her eyes as only teenagers could and made her way to the display cases, wiping everything down to a high shine.

"So," I started cautiously, "how are things with your mom?"

Her arm froze in mid-swipe.

"Okay." Her voice was cold and distant— unaffected.

"*Okay* how?" I probed, wanting to know more, but I was nervous to push her too hard.

"We're working on it," she said, a somber note tarnishing her tone. "Mom is a bit preoccupied these days, but she always makes time for me. I try to talk to her about my therapy, but I can see that it's hard for her to hear, so I keep it to brief descriptions about my progress." Her words were biting; a flash of memory assaulted me with pictures of her bleeding in the bathroom. Knowing where her life was likely headed, drama was only going to increase. She needed to learn how to compartmentalize her emotions in a way that didn't lead to her slicing herself for an outlet. One day those cuts would run too deep. That was a consequence I was unwilling to accept.

"Well, that's a great start, P," I said encouragingly, hesitating slightly before continuing. "I'm proud of you."

She finally turned to face me with a tight and mournful smile.

"Sometimes I'm not sure why."

"Peyta," I said calmly, as if speaking to a wounded animal, "please don't be so hard on yourself. I'm not exactly the poster child for healthy reactions to the curveballs life sends my way."

A flash of electricity shot through my body when I allowed myself to think of what had happened in Utah. Apparently, I jumped when I did.

"What are you getting at, Ruby?" she asked, her face full of concern.

"I'm just saying that I don't always deal with trauma in the healthiest fashion either. Denial, avoidance, and a sheer unwillingness to acknowledge the truth are gifts that I possess in abundance. I use them frequently to keep the memories at bay."

"Is this about what happened to you when you met Cooper?"

"Yes."

"The thing you said you didn't want to ever tell me about?"

"Yes."

"Ruby, I've seen a lot of what you've been through. None of it was good. How much worse could what happened there be?"

"Beyond unimaginable, Peyta."

It was plain to see that she was desperate to know what had had occurred when I was held captive. Not because she was being nosy, but in an effort to truly understand both me and how I could relate to her personal demons as well as I claimed to. After a moment of thought, I decided to tell her briefly. I had never said the word out loud to myself, or anyone else for that matter. Labeling what had happened to me in Utah always seemed like it would give that terror power over me. In retrospect, it did exactly the opposite.

"I was raped, Peyta. Not just once..."

I watched as her eyes slowly filled with tears that

spilled over freely.

"Ruby..."

"That's the first time I've ever really admitted that—using *that* word—to anyone."

"And how does that make you feel?" she asked, uncertain as to what to do.

I couldn't help but chuckle at her choice of response. The therapeutic process seemed to be rubbing off on her; a mini-psychologist in the making was the direct result. Regardless of the off-color humor I found in her words, I contemplated them heavily. How did it feel to declare that I had been a victim of unspeakable crimes? I had always talked around it before, a series of implications that were never fully explained. That day, I put the truth out there for both her ears and mine. I was immediately assaulted by emotions that I wasn't fully ready to process or deal with, but the one that bubbled up to the forefront was a strange sense of empowerment. Was I still traumatized? Yes. Was there damage that needed repairing still? Clearly. Was I going to choose to let that define me and control my life? No. No, I wasn't.

Victimization was just another cage.

"It feels good, Peyta. It hurts, but it feels right, you know?"

"I do, Ruby," she replied, coming over to hug me. "I really do."

We held each other silently for a moment, both shedding tears for various reasons, driven by various mitigating factors. But what mattered most in that moment was that we knew we were not alone, that we were there for one another no matter what. Only family could know your darkest secrets and still love you regardless, and that was exactly what we were. Family.

As much as I enjoyed our moment together, I was starting to feel slightly overwhelmed by it all the same. I needed to put a lid back on my emotions, if only temporarily, which were escaping their secured and locked location. I didn't need to try and make up for lost time as far as healing was concerned.

I looked at the clock on the wall, which indicated it was time to open the shop. With a tiny squeeze, I released Peyta, leaving a quick kiss atop her head as I did. She smiled in response, wiping the tears from her face. I did the same.

"Well, now that we're all set with the caring and sharing portion of the morning, let's get this show on the road, shall we?"

She laughed and nodded, walking toward the counter to put the glass cleaner away.

"Hey, speaking of the road, where's your car? I didn't see it when I came in. You're not actually letting Cooper drive it, are you? I mean, he drove it while you were gone, but...that was different."

"Ha!" I scoffed. "Not exactly. Cooper apparently got into an accident last night, so the TT is in the shop. I'm trying to ignore the whole thing and pretend she's on vacation."

She chuckled nervously.

"Guess he's glad Scarlet is gone. I think she loved that car as much as you do. She would have beaten his ass."

I could only laugh in response. She was spot-on, as usual.

"I'm going to go work on the rest of that paperwork, if you're good out here," I told her as a customer came in.

Peyta greeted her warmly before replying.

"Yep, I've got this. Go do your thing."

I took my leave and headed to my desk to complete my mission. Twenty minutes later, I was victorious; the desk was clean. I sat back and admired my work for a moment, all but patting myself on the back for my efforts. As I moved to get up, Peyta stuck her head in to tell me that there was someone on the phone for me. Intrigued, I made my way out front.

"Hello?"

"Ruby...I'm sorry to bother you, but I'm in need of your apartment for a moment," Janner said reluctantly.

"Okay, that's fine. Just go on in."

"It appears that you've locked it."

"Oh, shit! Sorry. I'll have to come up and let you in. I'll be right up."

"Thank you." The line went dead.

I looked at Peyta, whose expression read curiosity.

"I have to go upstairs for a sec. I'll be right back."

"Who was that?"

"How much did Cooper tell you the other night about the other guys who were there?"

"Not much," she said with the faintest of pouts. "He just said that they weren't going to be around for long and that I need to stay away from them. Why? Who are they?"

"Guests of sorts. They're in from out of town. Cooper's not a fan, but he's right about staying away from them," I explained. "Janner needs something from my place. I'm just going to go let him in. I'll be back in five."

"Should I be concerned if you don't return immediately?" she asked as her mental wheels spun. She was a smart kid. She was already planning for the "what if" scenarios.

"If I'm not back in five, I want you to lock up and leave, do you understand me?"

She nodded once.

Before she could say anything else, I fled the shop and unlocked the adjacent exterior door. Running up the stairs, I heard the door on the third floor creak as it slowly opened.

"You can come down," I called out, striding across the landing to unlock the apartment door.

Without a word, Janner's long frame lithely climbed down the stairs to meet me, stopping a few steps shy. He looked conflicted, as if he wanted to say something but thought better of it. I don't know what Cooper had said to them, but judging by his severely tense energy, it couldn't have been especially warm and fuzzy.

"Something wrong?" I asked softly, encouraging him to share his concerns.

"Beckett was not trying to get you into any trouble today, Ruby," he replied soberly. "Nor were we trying to the other night. It was just so nice to watch a little football. It felt so *normal*. We meant no harm by it, especially not to you."

"I'm sorry about yesterday too," I sighed, feeling incredibly guilty about the entire showdown. "Cooper is, well, you see, it's just that he's...," I rambled, trying to find an acceptable way to say that he was insanely protective because of my human status for the time being.

"He is your alpha," Janner said matter of factly. "It is his job to watch out for you. This is understandable. It's also very honorable—something we are not accustomed to seeing in a leader." His eyes were filled with pain and sadness. Whatever they had left behind in

London was not a family. "It is surprising though," he continued, daring to inch his way closer to me. "He acts as though you are incapable of protecting yourself. I find this so strange given your reputation."

I squirmed under his observation. He was right. Cooper's overly enthusiastic methods of keeping me safe were ironically more likely to expose me than anything else.

"He's a man with the values of an era past," I said in jest, hoping to sell my performance. "Cooper's had a rough go of things. When I took him in, I think he felt that he was my protector. It's been him and me ever since." I tried to keep all intensity out of my voice, but it inevitably leaked in with my last sentiment. "He would *never* let anything happen to me, regardless of my legendarily lethal werewolf reputation."

Janner's face softened slightly as he took his final step to close the distance between us.

"Completely understandable," he said with a light smile. "After your hospitality and kindness, I wouldn't want to see anything happen to you either."

There was an awkward pause, which I was desperate to break. Lingering silence made my skin crawl and my body itch to escape. Something about his energy was only heightening my response. The guarded nature from his arrival was leaking back into the air around him, and I just couldn't figure it out. It was too neutral, unreadable—*mechanical*.

"Okay, well, if that's all you need," I said, stepping toward the stairs.

"Yes, thank you," he replied, pushing the door ajar. "Oh, wait, Ruby. There is one more thing. The boys have been wondering when we might be able to go *out*."

"We can go out whenever. Where do you want to

go?"

He laughed to himself slightly before clarifying.

"I'm sorry. I should have been more clear," he explained. "They want to know when they can go out to *Change*. They're not accustomed to being so penned in all day. They want to run free for a while. Maybe hunt."

"And what exactly would they like to hunt?" I asked as my concern rose.

"Anything really. Deer. Rabbits. Coyotes. Whatever is available."

I breathed an audible sigh of relief.

"Yeah, that shouldn't be an issue. Ask Cooper about it. I'm sure he can arrange something."

Janner's eyes narrowed ever so slightly at me.

"Will you be joining us? We would love to see a Rouge et Blanc in all her glory—*hunting*. It must be a magnificent sight to behold."

I started down the stairs in a not-so-subtle attempt to flee my growing anxiety and hide my lack of game face.

"You've already seen me run through the woods in my were-human form. I doubt being furry would be all that different, except for the four-legged part. Besides, I'm really not that impressive, Janner," I called over my shoulder to him. "You shouldn't always believe the hype."

I tried unsuccessfully to slow my racing heart. We were flirting with disaster, Cooper and I. We agreed that it was best that the boys not know about Scarlet's AWOL status, but at some point, it was bound to come to light. I didn't know how much longer we could keep that cat in the bag.

As I reached the bottom, I heard Janner's phone

ring and him answer it through the open apartment door. Given the tone his voice held and the few choice words he used, something was up and it wasn't good. Whoever he was talking to was not an ally.

When a wave of fear washed through the stairway and over me, I knew who it was. *Alpha*...

Sprinting back up the stairs, I arrived just in time for Janner to greet me at the apartment door, his face slack and expressionless. He looked like he had seen a ghost.

"It's happening," he whispered, looking through me rather than at me.

"It was him, wasn't it?" I asked, my fear rising along with his.

"I'm so sorry, Ruby. We did not mean to bring trouble for you." He pushed past me and headed up the stairs, calling the others as he made his way.

"What did he say? What's coming?" I nattered, trying to keep up with the unending surge of questions that shot through my mind.

"I have to tell the others," he continued, ignoring my questions entirely.

"Tell them what, Janner?"

He turned his blank face toward me as the others met us in the hallway.

"*Death*, Ruby," he uttered with complete detachment from his ominous words. "Death is coming for us."

CHAPTER 23

The three of them started to argue back and forth about the best course of action as though they'd never once planned what they would do in such an event. Apparently, they'd put all their eggs in one basket—*my* basket. They were in for a rude awakening of epic proportions.

"Wait a minute!" I yelled over them. "Is that what he said?"

"In a sense," Janner replied.

"No, this is not time for paraphrasing. You're going to tell me exactly what he said," I informed him, heading down the stairs. "But I'm going to call Sean first. You're going to tell us both what he said so we can figure this clusterfuck out."

They eyed me tightly, not seeming too pleased by my bossy tone, but they were going to have to live with that. As far as I was concerned, I was next in line behind Cooper, so my word was law in his absence. They may not have liked it, but there wasn't time to bicker about who was in charge. When the universe threw you a curveball, it wasn't the time to discuss whether or not you should swing or stay. It was time to get the fuck out of the way, and that was exactly what Sean was going to figure out—how to dodge the pitch.

I stormed into the store, running past Peyta and a customer at top speed. Ungracefully, I slammed through the door to the back room and my purse, yanking my cell out before turning around to frantically exit. All Peyta got was a warning look from me. We'd learned to communicate without words during perilous times. I knew she got the message.

Dialing as I took the stairs two at a time, I had Sean on the line before I even heard it ring.

"I hope this is a social call."

"It's not. We've got a situation."

"Define 'we'," he demanded, his business tone in full bore.

I decided to cut to the chase. There was no point in trying to pretty it up.

"Tobias called..."

The name was met with a growl.

"And what did he say?"

"Well, that's what we're going to find out right now," I told him, cresting the final step to the third floor where Janner stood with the others. "Janner spoke to him. I didn't, but he's right here. I'm putting you on speaker."

I hit the appropriate button and adjusted the volume as loud as it would go for my benefit. I knew the boys would hear him regardless.

"Okay, Janner," I prompted. "Just spill it."

He sighed heavily, shooting me an uncomfortable glance. He clearly feared more than just Tobias. Sean was not going to take kindly to his suspicions of danger coming our way because of the boys. If they thought Cooper was overprotective, they were about to get schooled by Sean.

"He was his usual pompous self on the phone, making a game of threatening me. Threatening *us*."

"What. Did. He. Say?" Sean ground out. I could practically hear his jaw flexing, knowing how hard he was trying to compose himself. He wanted to find a solution to the problem first. He'd figure out how to make them pay later.

"He laughed when I answered and then quickly pointed out how irresponsible it was for me to not have gotten another phone, like I had made the game too easy for him."

"You have the same phone?" Sean roared.

"We left with next to nothing. We took whatever we could throw in a bag and the cash I had stashed away in a contingency fund. Our accounts were paid for the year. I had other more pressing things to deal with when we fled. It never dawned on me see if the numbers could be changed, not that changing the numbers would have been enough, really. Tobias is smart. Most likely, we would have had to dispose of them entirely," he said, trying to explain why they hadn't gotten rid of that connection to their past. It seemed that carelessness was the true reason. "As it stands now, I soon would have to have renewed the policy and would not be able to do it. Please understand, Sean, we left in chaos. We were not in Maine long before we happened upon Ruby. We haven't had much time to regroup. I had no idea that he would come for us this quickly."

"And now he's going to follow that phone right to

Ruby's doorstep." Sean was seething—I could sense it through the phone.

"Perhaps it hasn't come to that yet," Janner countered. "He said he was sending out a search party. He wouldn't have to search hard if he knew where we were."

"Sean," I interjected, thinking back to a conversation we'd had when he had offered to locate my phone for me. "Maybe not everyone has access to the technology you're used to working with. It's possible that they could know roughly where the boys are...maybe using the cell tower to trace their location, but they might not be able to do what Trey can. Maybe we still have a chance to fix this."

"Oh, it can be fixed." His voice was low and calm. Sean was at his scariest when devoid of emotion entirely.

"Sean..."

"I won't be back there in time to deal with this myself, so follow my instructions to the letter, understood?"

"Go ahead."

"You are going to drive down to Boston. You're going to find Trey, and he's going to make this go away, in a sense. Nobody is to get rid of those phones, is that clear?"

We all looked at each other with utter confusion. Knowing that the other three were too smart to ask questions, I served myself up and addressed the obvious.

"Why aren't we getting rid of them? I mean, if he's going to track them, why would we keep them?"

"He won't be able to track them once Trey is finished, but he'll *think* he can. Besides, he seems to have gone underground for the moment. Jay and the London boys seem to be having trouble tracking him. That's where I am now. I want Tobias to be able to reach them in the future. Trey will be able to locate him once he's worked his magic on the phones. We'll flip the situation on him and get the upper hand."

I liked Sean's plan immensely, but it all hinged upon Tobias not being able to directly trace Janner, or any of the boys' phones, and I wasn't overly optimistic about that. Luck rarely seemed to be on my side.

"Where is Cooper?" he asked, finally realizing that he hadn't heard him pipe up yet.

"He's not back yet."

"And he left you home alone with them?" Sean started with a low rumbling accenting his words. "Apparently he and I need to have a chat."

Sean didn't do chats. His euphemism fooled no one. Cooper was going to get his ass handed to him on a platter when Sean got back.

Damage control again...

"Sean, I'll explain later, but don't freak out on Cooper," I pleaded, knowing it was likely in vain. To distract him, I threw the more pressing CF back in his face. "So where are we going?"

"*You* aren't going anywhere until Cooper gets back."

"Sean—"

"I'm sending you directions now, but you are not to go *anywhere* without Cooper," he dictated, biting off his words for effect. "Nowhere. Understood?"

I sighed dramatically.

"Yes. We understand."

"No. I need *you* to understand," he countered. "I need *them* to get very comfortable with the reality that their lives will be short-lived if anything, and I mean *anything*, happens to you before I return."

They all looked to me and I shrugged. I had no control over Sean, and they knew that. Mate or not, I was *so* not in the driver's seat of our relationship.

"You are understood," Janner replied on behalf of the boys.

"Good. I'm on my way now," he said as the wind around him garbled his words slightly. "And Ruby, I love you. Don't make me live to regret your judgment."

He hung up before I could respond. I just smiled at the phone instead.

My smile dropped the second Cooper walked through the main door downstairs.

"Rubes?" he called. "Are you upstairs?"

"Yeah, I'm up here. Don't bother coming up. We've gotta go to Boston. Now."

We started down the stairs, meeting him on the landing by my apartment door. And he did not look pleased.

"I don't know how closely you three like to play with death, but I am telling you—"

"Seriously, Cooper. Now isn't the time. You can tear the trio a new set of assholes all the way down to where we're going, if you want to, but we have to go. Sean said to leave the second you got home."

"Hence his subtle text message: 'go home now'."

"Yep. That sounds about right."

"Boston? Christ, Ruby, I was gone for half an hour. How much shit did you manage to stir up in thirty minutes?" I gave him a sheepish look that told him everything he needed to know. Knowing my gifts, he scowled in return. "Worst case scenario?" he asked, leading the way down to the car.

"Tobias might be here." He stopped dead in his tracks on the stairs. "The car, remember?" I cried, shoving him onward to the door. "You can flip out in the car. Sean sent me directions to Trey's in Boston. We've got to get something done to their phones," I told him, hedging slightly. I'd hoped to not waste time explaining things until we were in the car.

"Why?" he asked, that time without stopping. "Do you want to give me the abridged version of what in the hell is going on?"

"Tobias called Janner. They still have their old phones...we think he traced them somehow." I flinched, stepping in front of the boys so Cooper couldn't kill them without harming me in the process—or at least to slow him down slightly.

"Mother. Fucker."

"He probably is," Alistair quipped from behind me.

"Sean thinks we can throw them off, but we have to get to Trey ASAP. Can we put a hold on the ass kickings until after we know we're on the right side of a war?"

Cooper stared the boys down over top of my head as we stood outside the building. He was breathing hard and furious, but for once, I didn't think he was going to kill them. Not yet anyway. I hoped for their sakes nothing eventful came of Tobias' threats.

"You three, in the Navigator. Now," he ordered. The boys complied without a word. "You," he said, golden eyes flaring, "you need to get Peyta home or send her to Ronnie's shop, but I don't want her anywhere near here until we have a better idea of just how pressing this danger is."

"I was going to do that," I replied, opening the

door to the shop. "Sean thinks we can use this to find Tobias. Jay hasn't been able to find him over there."

"Well, I sure as hell hope that doesn't mean he's already here," he snarled, before softening his tone. "This could be bad, Ruby. Really bad." His eyes held a sadness that was easily read. My questionably human status made me vulnerable, and if harm came looking for us, I was going to be a casualty for sure. There was no prettying up that reality.

"It won't be," I told him, forcing a wan smile. "I trust you, Cooper. I trust Sean too. It'll be okay."

I turned to push the door open and heard him mutter something under his breath as he walked to the car.

I have a bad feeling about this

, he'd said, shutting the car door behind him.

He wasn't the only one.

It took me a while to convince Peyta to listen to me and leave the store. She no longer had her constant guardian at her side to keep her safe, though I didn't bother to point that out. She was more than aware of his absence. I promised to fill her in later, when I knew we were all going to be safe. She accepted that for the time being and filed out of the store, leaving me behind to lock up.

I watched her walk to her mom's car while I turned off the lights and placed the 'CLOSED' sign in the window. She waved to Cooper, who yelled something at her from the SUV. Her face became serious, and she gave a brisk nod in response before jumping into the vehicle and speeding off down the street.

Apparently, I needed to have a chat with her about the dangers of having a lead foot.

I hoped to live long enough to have that talk.

CHAPTER 24

"Thanks for driving, Coop," I said as I buckled myself in. "My eyes are all whacked out today, and it's giving me a headache. I really need to get some quality sleep soon."

"Yeah," he grunted, having gone back to fuming about the situation. He was less than impressed by the boys' oversight. He and Sean both. "Please explain to me again why we aren't just destroying the phones and getting new ones?" His irritation was plain.

"Sean said he wanted them to be in contact with Tobias, if need be," I explained for the second time. "Sean has a purpose for everything he does, Cooper. You know that."

"Doesn't mean I have to agree with him."

"You never do. Why would I expect that to change?" I asked, looking out the passenger window. The boys quietly sat in the back, trying to keep themselves off of Cooper's hostile radar.

"So where exactly are we headed?"

"Sean gave me explicit instructions, but I'm not really familiar with the area. Don't worry—you drive, I'll navigate."

He shot me a dubious look from the driver's seat before firing up the vehicle. He was in a mood of grand proportions. The hour in the car was destined to be unbearable for all if something didn't lighten things up, and quickly.

"What? We got back from Utah just fine."

"Yeah, because you were unconscious for the better part of the trip!" he exclaimed, pulling onto the on ramp.

"I helped!" I retorted.

"Yes, Ruby, *technically* you did help. You got me from the highway to your house. It was a crucial part of the trip."

"One of these days I'm just going to punch you right in the face," I said as I folded my arms over my chest and sunk down into my seat like a petulant child. "You won't even see it coming. Just *BAM*, and you're out for the count."

He laughed. It was not the response I was looking for.

"I look forward to it, Rubes."

"Are you two always like this?" Alistair asked meekly from the backseat.

"*Yes*," we shouted in unison right before the car fell silent.

It stayed silent until we hit Boston.

"So where do I need to go?" Cooper asked, trying to sound less irritated than he actually was.

"Take a right up here, I think," I called out, pointing to the upcoming intersection as I squinted at the street sign above. "Does that say Massachusetts

Ave?"

"Jesus, Ruby," Cooper lamented. "No, that's not what it says at all. Not even close. Give the phone to Janner and let him navigate. Have a nap until we get there."

"Sorry," I whined, rubbing my eyes. "You try surviving on a couple hours of sleep a night and see how good your visual acuity is." Frustrated, I tossed the cell to Janner, who was seated directly behind me. "The directions are highlighted on the Google map. Sean assured me they'd get us there easily."

"Got it," he chirped before telling Cooper to take a right.

Fifteen minutes went by and we still weren't there. I turned to see Janner eyeing the map with a bewildered expression. It was clear that he'd goofed up somewhere along the way and was trying to find a solution before letting Cooper in on it. Not wanting to rat him out, I gave him a few minutes to sort things out before addressing the issue.

"Cooper," he said in his strange accent. "Pull in up here for a minute. The phone lost reception for a moment back there, and I think I've missed something in the process. I just need to get my bearings, and then we can proceed."

"I wondered if I should count on someone used to driving on the wrong side of the road for directions," Cooper sneered.

As Alistair launched into a rant about American arrogance, Cooper pulled into an abandoned warehouse parking lot. I hadn't been paying attention during the drive, taking Cooper's advice and trying to rest my sleep-deprived eyes, so I hadn't realized just how shady the neighborhood we were driving in was, until we stopped.

My dance studio was in an area that skirted the less refined areas of town, but it was nothing like where we had stopped. The area was destitute, ominous, and filled with a nefarious energy.

I soon found out why.

While the four of them bickered like spoiled housewives, I stared out of the front window to see five formidable men exiting a tank of a vehicle and heading our way. *Men* was a bit of a misnomer. *Werewolves* was far more accurate given the wall of violent, supernatural energy that slammed against me.

The sun shone through a crack in the clouds, casting a blinding golden-orange aura behind them as though they were encased in the fiery glow of hell. I had a feeling that, as far as we were concerned, that's exactly where they were from.

"Cooper," I called nervously, tugging on his sleeve. "I think we have a situation."

The four of them snapped to attention immediately, their collective gaze falling on the rapidly approaching group. Cooper turned the car on, preparing to escape, but it was already too late. The five descended on us in a flash, surrounding the SUV. Cooper hammered the gas, but we went nowhere thanks to one of them jacking up the rear bumper with one hand.

"Fucking rear wheel drive," Cooper muttered, his aggression rising.

The second I knew that there was no way to make a clean getaway, I knew that shit was about to get real.

"Janner," one of them called tauntingly in a pristine British accent while he tapped lightly on the rear passenger window. "Time to pay the piper."

"You know them?" Cooper asked, more to confirm his suspicions than anything.

"They are from our former pack," Janner spat through clenched teeth. "They are the *cleaning* crew."

A look of understanding flashed through Cooper's face. I did my best not to panic, but my fear polluted the air in the car, sending Cooper's protective instincts into high gear. The yellow of his eyes nearly fluoresced as the growl came low and warning from deep in his chest. The sound was matched by three others, rattling the interior of the vehicle.

The men outside backed up a step in response.

"Ruby," Cooper said, pinning his eyes on me. "I want you to get the fuck out of here right now. Do you understand me? As soon as we get out, I want you in this driver's seat and peeling out of here, tired eyes and all."

"But you're outnumbered—"

"Drive the fucking car, Ruby. It's not a goddamn request!"

"We need her," Alistair protested. I looked back at him to see a confused and disappointed look on his face. To him, the savior he had been counting on wasn't unavailable; she was deserting.

"Don't like it when the odds are unfavorable, Alice?" Cooper asked in a taunting voice. "Don't question my motives ever again...if you live to see tomorrow. Let's do this."

The boys turned their attention back to the assailants who awaited them patiently. I was surprised that they hadn't just ripped the doors off the car and started picking us off one by one, but instead, they had backed off slightly, allowing the boys space to exit as if there was a code of ethics to follow in a showdown of this type. An extermination mission with a rule book.

Without further warning, the four of them flew out of the car at inhuman speed, slamming the doors behind them to punctuate their attack. I punched the door lock and hopped over the console to the driver's seat, doing my best to follow Cooper's instructions. Whatever happened, he wanted me safe.

But I couldn't just throw the Navigator in reverse and leave.

I looked out to see a melee. Wolves, men, *blood*— so much blood. They moved so quickly that I could hardly keep tabs on what was happening and to whom. Cooper and a monster of a man were in a dead-even match. Janner seemed to be winning his battle, but it was hard to tell; the reddish wolf he fought just kept coming back for more. I couldn't see Beckett at all— Alistair either.

Whirling around in the seat, I tried to find them out the rear window, but a howl ripped my attention back to the events unfolding in front of me. Cooper had a grayish-blue mammoth wolf attached to his back, his fangs buried deep. In front of him stood the same man he'd been fighting with earlier, only this time, he held a gun. My mind raced with unwanted memories, and before I knew it, I was no longer thinking, only reacting.

"NO!" I screamed, flying out of the car. "Cooper!"

I sprinted towards him as the devilish man looked over at me and smiled, aiming the weapon at Cooper's head. He was at point-blank range. Cooper struggled against the hold of the gray wolf, but it was too much. I had to get there.

"An eye for an eye," the man said with a growl as I ran toward them. "And an alpha for an alpha."

Then the shot rang out.

I ground to a halt, feeling the blood as it spattered my face. I flinched away from it—I could barely breathe. My eyes eventually opened and drifted up from my bloodstained clothing to the grisly scene before me.

Bodies were everywhere, and I fought desperately against my welling tears to see exactly *whose* they were. The gray wolf lay dead, neck broken and severed behind Cooper, who was slouched over, looking down at something in front of him. Cooper hadn't been shot, which was cause for a combination of elation and fear, but if he hadn't been, who was?

"Ruby," Alistair whispered from right beside me. I'd never even heard him approach. "Love, we've got to get them out of here. *Now.*"

He was ushering me away from the carnage, but I shrugged him off, headed for whatever Cooper's body shrouded. Janner had joined him, stooping down low to reach the only person who was yet unaccounted for.

Beckett.

"No," I mumbled, stumbling toward them. "No, no, no!"

Cooper and Janner had been talking the whole time. In my shock, I hadn't heard them.

"All I can smell is burnt flesh. If it's not silver, he'll have a chance, but we've got to get him out of here," Cooper told him, scooping Beckett up in his arms gingerly. "Let's go." He stormed past me, shooting me a venomous look. My insubordination had not been appreciated.

I scampered along behind him, my limbs not fully obeying my commands. Cooper quickly loaded Beckett into the back of the SUV while Janner and Ali climbed in the backseat. I hadn't noticed that Alistair was naked until that moment. I hadn't been able to find him during the fight because he had turned furry. Cooper had once said that the younger wolves had trouble maintaining human form when their emotions ran too hot. Alistair was raw emotion incarnate.

"Ruby!" Cooper yelled, snapping my attention to him. "Call Sean now. Tell him to get someone down here to deal with this."

"Okay, but where is here?"

Cooper looked irritated, but realized I had a point. Then suddenly, in a light bulb moment, he snatched Janner's phone out of the car and tossed it on the ground. "Tell him to track Jan's cell. Seems like it worked great for these ass clowns." He marched me to the passenger seat of the car and stuffed me in, wincing slightly with the motion.

"Coop, your back—"

"I'm *fine*," he snapped, slamming the door behind him. I watched as he ran in front of the vehicle to the driver's side. Whatever wound he had was closing up at a shocking pace. I knew that the wolf had done some serious damage to have caused him to cry out at the time. He'd never healed like that before, even when I was helping. Something was fueling it and I knew I had nothing to do with it.

That thought brought my attention to the Brit in the back.

"I can help him!" I shouted, crawling towards the rear.

"You can sit the fuck down and do as you're told for once," Cooper snarled. "You have no self-preservation instincts whatsoever, you know that? You could have been killed. At least Scarlet—" He clipped off his sentence abruptly, remembering the company we were in.

"He saved you, Coop. Let me help him, please. Be mad at me all you want, but don't take it out on him."

"I'm not mad at you," he replied, trying to calm down as he tore out of the parking lot.

"Who's Scarlet?" Alistair asked from behind Cooper. "And why didn't you—"

"Not now, Ali!" I scolded, scrolling through Cooper's phone for Sean's number. Once I found it, I hit dial and waited for his rugged voice on the other end.

"Cooper," he drawled as if already put out by the call.

"It's me. There's a problem," I blurted out, my breathing still ragged.

"Where are you?"

"Boston."

"I know that. Where exactly?"

"I have no idea. Some über sketchy part of town. It's all abandoned factories. But listen! You have to get the boys down here. Have Trey trace Janner's phone. There are bodies..."

"Whose?"

"Long story, but none of ours," I said, casting a wary eye toward the rear of the car. "Not yet, at least."

"Are you hurt?" he asked, concern leaking into his voice.

"I'm fine. Coop was torn up, but seems to be fine. Janner and Ali seem to be relatively intact too."

"And Beckett?"

"He's shot up," I said, choking on the words slightly. "He took a bullet for Cooper."

"Silver?"

"I don't know."

"Can you get to him now?"

"Yeah," I said, looking up at Cooper. He nodded once. "Give me a sec," I told him as I scurried into the backseat and over to the trunk area. I didn't know what to expect, but what I saw was grim to say the least.

Beckett lay flat on his back, barely conscious and panting heavily. His hands were draped elegantly across his chest, but even the combined breadth of them couldn't camouflage the gaping hole that lay beneath. My heart sank instantly. I knew that wolves could heal themselves in their coma-esque states, but Beckett didn't appear to be in one.

He also didn't appear to be doing anything other than bleeding.

"Ruby!" Sean snapped into the receiver. "Can you see the wound?"

"Yes," I said softly. "Sean, it's huge. He was shot at point blank range."

"That's inconsequential. You need to figure out if there's silver in it if you want him to live."

"How?"

"What does the wound look like? Is there a shimmer to the blood?"

"It looks wet, Sean. Like normal blood."

He exhaled heavily.

"You're going to have to taste it."

"WHAT? Are you serious?"

"Yes. Do it now. It will taste like metal."

"But blood *does* taste like metal—"

"No, blood has a metallic undertone to it. This will taste like licking your jewelry."

Oddly enough, I'd basically done just that before while working on certain pieces. I never knew it would come in handy.

Gently pushing his hands aside, I looked at the pulsating gristle that was once his beautifully tattooed chest. Embedded in the wound was a pair of dog tags attached to a chain around his neck. I had to fish them out for fear that they would be buried inside him when he healed—if he healed at all. With everything out of the way, I took a deep breath before sticking my finger in the wound. Before I had a chance to chicken out, I shoved it in my mouth and sucked.

Tasted like blood to me.

"It tastes normal," I said, gagging slightly.

"Then tell Cooper to go straight to my place. We have some things to sort out." He paused for a moment before continuing. "Ruby. Try not to get yourself killed before I can see you."

The line went dead.

I threw the phone up to Janner before lying down beside Beckett.

"What did he say?" Cooper called from the front seat. I propped up to find myself being stared down in the rearview mirror.

"He said the wound should be okay and to meet him at his place. He's got the boys on clean up."

"Good."

My mind was still reeling from all that had happened. Things went from mundane to explosive in the bat of an eye, and we'd nearly lost people in the process. I looked down at Beckett, his eyes still closed, his breathing still shallow, and wondered how things got to be so bad with his own pack that they would hunt him and the others down like rabid dogs. Why had they bothered? Cooper seemed to be pondering the same thing because he started in on the two who were conscious at that moment.

Instead of listening, I channeled my energy to Beckett, not knowing if it would make a difference or not. He didn't have a bond with me like Cooper did, and I still didn't know if my outward influencing abilities relied on any of Scarlet's power, but I decided to try anyway. I hoped that it didn't matter how emotionally close I was to the victim; I just wanted it to work. He'd saved Cooper's life and held mine together because of that. I owed him, big time.

We all did.

CHAPTER 25

I don't know how fast Cooper was driving, but it seemed like we were back in Portsmouth in the blink of an eye. All of my energy had been trained on Beckett, hoping to coax him out of his near-death state sooner rather than later. I knew that there wasn't any real danger of losing him, but it was still so hard to wrap my head around his ability to walk away from a wound like that unharmed. It didn't seem to matter how many times I'd seen it done; it was always surreal. Even when it was me.

As we rolled into town, Beckett started to stir slightly. I laid my head on his newly healed chest and tried to keep him still. He may have been doing better, but he wasn't up to snuff just yet. I didn't want him expending any energy that he didn't need to.

"Welcome back," I whispered, my head tucked in tight below his chin. It felt somewhat intimate when he wove his arms around me, hugging me to him, but it made me think of how quickly Cooper and I had bonded during our escape in Utah. Life-threatening situations changed people, bringing them close together in a way that time alone could not. It was just a fact of life—a fact of *my* life, at least.

"You truly are special," he said softly, smoothing my mess of curls away from his face. "We hadn't heard about this *ability* of yours. Just how many tricks do you have up your sleeves, Ruby?"

I laughed, pulling away from him to sit up.

"More than you'll ever know about."

Beckett, like Alistair, was naked, and I suddenly became far too aware of that fact. Needing to maintain some level of modesty, I searched for something to cover him up with. I spotted a duffel bag along the far wheel well and grabbed it, hoping to find what I thought I might. *Bingo!* Inside were spare clothes, and I quickly started doling them out to all in need.

"Here," I said, chucking a t-shirt and jeans at the back of Alistair's head.

"What? You don't like the show?" he asked, his expression and tone cheeky as ever, as though we hadn't all just about died only an hour earlier.

"If *that's* the show," Cooper mocked from the front seat, "then we should get our money back."

Janner laughed. Like *really* laughed. I'd never heard him so jovial or animated. It startled me at first.

"Put you in your place, didn't he, Ali?"

"Rubbish," Alistair grunted, wiggling into the too-big pants I'd given him. "Like yours is any bigger, mate."

Beckett, who had been trying to sit up, crashed back down to the floor in a combination of laughter and wincing while clutching his chest. I reached over to help him up so he could get dressed too. We were almost downtown, and I couldn't afford to have a naked foreigner riding illegally in the back of an SUV, even if the windows were tinted. Portsmouth was small enough that not much ever went on there. If someone spotted us, we'd be the talk of the town for sure, not to mention the precinct.

"You both know that I put you to shame, so I wouldn't start with me, if you know what's good for you."

"I'm quite sure I have you all beat," Cooper warned from the front seat.

I couldn't believe what I was hearing. I had deep concerns that they were all going to start whipping out their wobbly bits in the ultimate man-contest while we parked the car, just to be certain who the winner was. Men—the most ridiculous creatures on earth.

"Could we please just get inside Sean's place?" I whined, wanting to be somewhere that had a feeling of safety attached to it—preferably one that might not be attacked by misguided werewolves. They didn't reply, but all of them departed the car to head into his building without further shenanigans. As we cautiously made our way around the corner, Sean was standing there waiting.

"Glad to see you're in one piece," he said flatly, eyeing the group tightly as he slowly approached us. When he stopped before me, his hand caught my face, and he pinned scrutinizing but concerned eyes on mine. His thumb stroked my cheek gently, and I pressed into his touch slightly before realizing the others were all watching. Maybe they needed a good reminder of who my mate was.

As if that was written on my face, he leaned in and kissed me. Then he stared down at the others before ordering them inside. Shit really was about to get real.

When we arrived at his apartment, a man was waiting inside. Standing military straight with hands pulled behind his back, he watched us all file in with curiosity. I'd never seen him before, but I knew he was a PC brother—his energy carried the same confidence that all the others' did.

"Trey, get their phones and take them downstairs. Work your magic," Sean ordered. "I need to get some answers out of these three in the meantime."

"Wait a second," I blurted out, staring at Trey in disbelief. "How did he get here before us if he was just down in Boston awaiting our panicked arrival?"

Trey and Sean exchanged blank looks before turning their eyes to me. Trey said nothing in response and Sean gave me little more than his trademark ambivalent shrug. Whatever means Trey used to arrive at Sean's before us was clearly going to remain a secret.

Still perplexed, I watched as the tall and almost lanky man approached the boys. The two who still had their phones held them out as was expected. When Trey was finished collecting them, he paused in front of me, looking at me curiously as if I were a puzzle that needed solving. Apparently the phones weren't enough for him to work on.

"She's prettier than they said," he declared with a soft, wistful voice. Then he disappeared through the main door.

I looked to Sean for explanation.

"Trey lacks a filter," he said with a shrug. "I'd think that you of all people could understand that." Suddenly Trey's IT job made far more sense. "Now, what happened out there, and don't skimp on the details. This is important. If they found you, then they've figured out how to trace the phones and are working with technology that few are privy to outside of large government agencies."

"And you," I interjected with a small smile.

"Yes," he replied, the smallest twinkle in his eyes. "And me."

"Well, I was trying to read your directions on my phone, but I just couldn't see them clearly, so I gave the phone to Janner. He made a miscalculation along the way, and we ended up in that neighborhood I told you about with the abandoned factories."

"Yes," he said, his voice dripping with disdain. "I find that very convenient for those trying to hunt you all down. What better place for a massacre?"

"It wasn't an ambush," Cooper said, reading between the lines. "They followed us there."

Sean eyed Cooper in a way that I'd never seen before. He was assessing something about him—*searching*. Without a word of objection, Sean let him continue to explain how the whole scenario played out to the very last detail. When Cooper finished, Sean paused, eyeing him tightly before pressing his lips tightly together and nodding.

I nearly fell over. I think I would have if Sean hadn't turned to me to fill in the blanks of the fight. The battle had seemed to wage on far longer than Cooper had said it did. Apparently it was minutes at best.

It felt like a lifetime.

"Ruby?" Sean called, pulling me from my thoughts. He'd likely repeated himself more than once, given his tone. "What did you see?"

"It all happened really fast," I started, closing my eyes to try and replay the gruesome scene. "There were more of them than us—five to four. Two of them went after Cooper, the others went after the boys."

"Interesting that they doubled up on Cooper right away," he said with growing interest in Janner. "You seem to look unharmed."

"Sean," I said, leaning forward to grab his arm. His eyes were on me in an instant. They didn't look as friendly as I would have liked. "I saw him fighting. He was in trouble for a while. I didn't know it at the time, but the others were too. Ali and Beckett Changed. I didn't know who was who then, but nobody walked away from that fight unharmed. I know that. And the second that the others were free, they went to Coop's aid. Beckett even took a point-blank bullet for him."

"Yes, and I find it highly convenient that it wasn't silver." His voice held a dangerous lack of emotion. Things weren't looking good for the boys.

"If I may," Janner said with hesitation, "I would submit that our former pack is more of the 'wound them and then take care of things manually' kind of family. We rarely if ever had silver ammunition available to us. Even the cleaning crew."

"They would have incapacitated Cooper with the gun, then come after us. They would have disposed of him last," Beckett added, his voice and expression impassive as always.

"And Ruby?" Sean asked, staring the trio down. "What would they have done to her?"

They looked back and forth amongst themselves nervously.

"We don't know," Alistair offered, his sad eyes landing on me. His shielding energy threw up a wall around the three almost instantly.

"She is the most lethal of your kind," Sean said

menacingly as he shook loose from my grasp to approach them. "Surely they would have had a plan to subdue her. It would be suicide to challenge an RB, based on what you yourself said your pack knew her reputation to be."

Again, the trio shared uncomfortable expressions.

"We told you when we arrived that there were rumors of a lethal wolf...a Rouge et Blanc," Janner started, clearing his throat. "There are other rumors—many rumors—some of which are of how they can be controlled. Contained."

Caged...

"How interesting," Sean growled, hovering inches away from Janner's face. "And just what are these rumors?"

Janner swallowed—hard.

"I don't know exactly. We were never high enough up the food chain, but I do know that Tobias knows. And he's ruthless. Who's to say what his orders would have been for Ruby if she had been caught. He could have wanted her dead so that there would be none more powerful than he could ever be. Maybe he would have captured her. I just cannot say. I am sorry."

"Sean," I whispered from behind him. "They *all* risked their lives for Cooper and me today, just as much as we risked ours for them. Please."

"What I want to know," Alistair said, piping up at the worst time possible, just as he always did, "is why you need protecting at all. If you're so lethal, why didn't you just wipe the floor with them so we could be on our way?"

I looked at Cooper, who had been strangely quiet. The look on his face told me why he had been. He knew this question was headed our way. He'd been trying to figure out a viable lie that would be easily believed without exposing any vulnerability in the process.

I prayed he'd come up with one because Sean's look was murderous. He was about to snap, and that was going to come at a high price. He would not allow my weaknesses to be known.

"Because we couldn't risk her exposure," Cooper said with a sigh. "We have to tell them. There's just no way around it now." He looked past Sean to me. I knew that expression. I'd seen it on more than one occasion. It read 'Play along and we'll get out of this without issue'. I hoped Sean would keep it together long enough for Cooper's plan to work.

"Cooper," Sean snarled, a warning. Sean never gave more than one.

"There are many reasons why Ruby doesn't let her wolf out often," he continued, giving Sean the look he'd just given me. "The main reason is that her wolf is far harder to call upon and completely unpredictable once out. There are reasons why they were hunted to extinction—and quickly too. Sean can attest to that."

Sean's eyes narrowed on Cooper.

"He's right," he finally concurred. "That killing ability comes with a complete lack of conscience. Once unleashed, there's no telling what she's capable of. To let the wolf out in a crowded city while under attack would be madness. An RB's bloodlust is unrivaled."

"Ruby has lived this long for two reasons alone," Cooper continued, picking up where Sean had just finished. "She's learned how to cage the beast and she is Sean's mate. But even Sean has said that he will take her down if he has to, and we all know this to be true. It's almost happened. She's on a short leash with both him and the PC."

"And pack or not," Sean added, "she can't be risked for your benefit." He leaned forward into their faces, his eyes black pools of darkness. "I won't allow it."

I stared at Sean, bewildered. *Pack?*

"Understood," Janner said respectfully, with a nod.

"Excellent," Sean purred in response.

A small silence broke out while Sean postured in front of the boys. He wanted to emphasize his point, and he was doing so brilliantly. We all read him loud and clear.

"Sean," Cooper called, breaking the growing tension. "Should we expect others? I'm concerned that if they tracked the phones in Boston then they likely know where the trio had been staying too."

"Agreed. We can't afford to take any chances, so nobody will be returning to the apartment until we know it's safe."

"Um," I started, raising my hand in question. "How will we know when that is?"

Sean cast me his all-knowing glance, and I shut my mouth. It figured that he'd have his tactics all worked out and likely in play. I was always a step or two behind.

"You'll know because I tell you it is," he said coldly, his eyes a deep hunter green. "*You* aren't going back there until Tobias is cold and dead. As for the others: I haven't decided the best plan of action."

"I think the four of us should go back," Cooper offered, stepping toward Sean. "If we suddenly disappear, they'll know something is up. We need to proceed as normal. Lure them in with a false sense of security and then ambush them. If Tobias is as arrogant as these three say he is, there's no way he wouldn't buy it. He'll think we were stupid and complacent, and that's exactly what we want."

Sean looked thoughtful for a moment.

"And what about the store? We can't possibly have Ruby running it until we know who and what is coming, or if they're coming at all. Peyta either. Especially not Peyta."

"I guess I'll have to shut it down in the interim," I said, trying to think on my feet. "A lot of the shops have been doing heavy remodels over the past few months. I don't think it would look strange for me to newspaper over the windows and put up a sign saying 'Closed for renovations'."

"Excellent. I'll have some of the boys get on that immediately." He looked pleased with me, as if I'd come up with the most genius plan ever. It surprised the shit out of me. "Cooper," he continued, "take them back home with you, but I'm going to have Trey and the boys set up a few things. If there's any sort of attack, you'll know before they're inside. And I'll know too."

"And Ruby?" Cooper asked, not looking pleased with me not staying by his side. He was my alpha and it was his job to keep me safe at all costs—at least that's what he thought.

"She stays with me. If harm is headed this way, I want her nowhere near it."

Cooper looked pained but resolved. He knew it was the right play even if it put him on the sideline. "Agreed."

"Glad to see we're on the same page," he said, eyes still pinned on Cooper in what I perceived to be a battle for dominance. It was a pointless one. I may have loved Cooper dearly, but in a fight between him and Sean, the dark-eyed one would win every time, and I knew it. Cooper knew it too. "I'm going to go let Trey know what he needs to do. I'll be right back," he said, coming to my side. "You'll stay here with me. I'll have the boys discreetly bring some things over for you—things I don't already have."

He gracefully took leave of his apartment, heading down to one of the other floors in his place. I'd only ever seen one other than his apartment, and I didn't really want to relive that memory. Wherever Trey was, I didn't want to know the details.

"So," Cooper said, wrapping his arm around my shoulder. I instinctively leaned into his embrace. "You're going to be okay here without me?" He was joking on the outside, but I could feel his unease with the situation, and it called to a part of me that was less than certain that everything was going to work out all right. He and I had been through more than our fair share of close calls. One day, that luck was going to run out.

"I think so," I replied sarcastically. "The question is, are you four going to be okay without *me*. I'm the mindless killing machine, remember?"

He chuckled slightly, giving me a little squeeze.

"You're something, all right."

"She's amazing," Alistair said earnestly, taking a step forward to break away from the other two. "You both were today. I may not have been Changed that long ago, but I knew what having a family was like before that and it was ripped away from me. The London pack was never family to me," he said, looking over his shoulder at his friends, "but these two were. They helped guide and mold me into what I am now."

I heard Cooper mutter some smartass comment

255

under his breath, and I elbowed him in the gut to shut him up. While Cooper exhaled sharply, Alistair reached under the collar of his t-shirt and pulled a pair of dog tags free. Two separate silver-colored chains hung over top of his chest, one significantly shorter than the other; it was much too small for a man to normally wear.

As if he understood what was going on, Janner reached into his shirt and produced two similar dog tags, though his were equal in length.

"Ruby," Alistair said softly, approaching Cooper and me slowly. "I want you to have this." He pulled the smaller stainless steel chain over his head with some effort and presented it to me in his hands. "This was my Jemma's. It's all I have left of her." He was too crippled by emotions to carry on, so Janner stepped in on his behalf.

"They never found the body," he said, placing a hand on Ali's shoulder for comfort. "Tobias gave him those before he tricked us into killing Deacon." He pulled his pair of dog tags up over his head before presenting them to me. "These were Deacon's. At first, I wore them as a trophy of sorts. But now I wear them as a reminder of who I knew him to be, what he stood for, and the alpha he was. The man I knew before we let the chaos and fear take over." He pinned fearsome eyes on Cooper before continuing, and it completely took me aback. Janner had always seemed complacent, almost docile, but in that moment, he was a force to be reckoned with. "I was wrong to let Tobias manipulate us into killing him." His eyes couldn't hold their confident attitude as he uttered those words. His guilt tinged the air around him, and he suddenly looked more tired and sad than normal as he continued. "I let him down," he continued, extending the tags out to Cooper. "I vow tonight, in front of these witnesses, that I will never do the same to you."

"And I," Alistair added, draping the chain over my head to fall lightly against my chest, "vow to protect you better than I was able to protect my Jemma."

Tears sprang forth from my eyes without warning. The weight of their words combined with that of their emotions was more than I could bear. I looked at Cooper, who was staring at the offering Janner held out before him. His energy warred internally—taking *it* meant taking *them*. His animal desire to protect the boys fought with his lingering distrust and his fear of becoming the only other alpha he'd ever known. His eyes met mine, and I saw the fear winning.

"You will never be like him, Coop," I said softly, taking his hand in mine. "You'll be exactly who you've always been—the same amazing man who rescued me back then and has continued to rescue me ever since."

With a squeeze of my hand, his gaze returned to Janner, and he took the token offered to him. Janner's pledge to be one of us. As he slipped it over his head, I could feel something in Cooper's energy shift—a power wash over him and settle deep inside. It made me smile.

Just as Beckett jumped in to try and lighten the mood, a faint ringing sounded in the stairway, growing louder and louder as footsteps ascended. Sean broke through the doorway, storming his apartment with cell phone in hand.

"Answer it," he said, throwing the phone to Janner. "And do not let on that anything has changed. You should sound like you're shaken and on the defensive."

With a nod, Janner hit a button and put the phone

to his ear.

"Tobias," he bit out as though the name was poison on his tongue. It was, as far as I was concerned. "Yes, we did have a run-in with them."

Silence. I watched as Janner's face flinched only slightly on occasion. I felt his energy go increasingly vacant as the one-sided conversation continued. It made me nuts knowing that everyone in that room could hear what was going on except for me, but I knew enough to know that he was being threatened.

My anger grew until a rage boiled just below the surface. I was starting to understand what having family—a pack—was all about. I may not have been crazy about the boys all the time, and God knew Cooper wasn't, but they were *ours*. We could mess with them, but nobody else was going to. Not on my watch.

"I see," Janner said, finally breaking the eerie quiet on our end. "And if we don't...?"

I looked at Cooper as my temper was threatening to spike to epic levels.

"What's going on?" I asked, whispering as loudly as I could.

"Tobias wants them to come back."

"Why?"

"So he can kill them."

"And if they don't?"

Cooper growled.

"He's coming here to kill them."

"So either way, they die?"

"Yes, though allegedly less painfully if they turn themselves in."

I totally flipped my shit.

"Give me that fucking thing," I snapped, lunging for the phone.

I wanted to let Tobias know just what I thought of his offer.

CHAPTER 26

Surprisingly, nobody tried to stop me. I didn't even have to struggle against Janner's grip. He let me have the phone and took a step back as my temper flared along with my use of the f-word. I suppose they knew I could only get into so much trouble over a phone.

"Tobias? Here's the deal. You can't have them. And, if you come here to get them, you'll be getting a world of hurt instead, understood?"

"Well, well, well, what have we here? Have my boys stumbled upon a *female* to ally with? Surely I'm frightened beyond belief." His mocking was duly noted. If he wanted a force to be reckoned with, I could give him that—verbally, anyway.

"Yes, they have, fuckwad. They have a new alpha now too, so I would tread lightly when throwing threats around me or my boys, if you know what's good for you," I spat into the phone as Sean and company looked on. Cooper moved to take the phone away from me, but Sean stopped him with an extended arm. For whatever reason, he wanted to see how the conversation played out. "The problem with that, Tobias, is that you clearly don't know when to walk away. I wouldn't underestimate me or anyone I align with. I have connections you couldn't even begin to comprehend. You fuck with me, you meet your end. Period."

"And who, pray tell, is this who dares to threaten me so brazenly? I'd like to know your name so I can call you by it as I cut out your heart and stuff it down your throat."

"Ruby," I replied with a sadistic grin, "but you'll never get the chance, my friend. Your blood will run free long before I even break a sweat."

"*Ruby...*," he repeated as if rolling the word around in his mouth to see if he liked the taste. "*You* won't kill me, *will* you, Ruby?"

I started to sweat. He was calling my bluff, but how could he have known?

"The hell I won't!" I blustered, hoping that, if I put enough anger behind my words, they would carry more weight.

He laughed.

"Why do you care what happens to them? They're not your wolves—your pack. They are mine to do with as I please."

"Wrong, *Toby*," I mocked, hoping to get under his skin. "It seems they've chosen a different family now, and, having spoken to you, I can sure as hell see why."

"Oh," he said, feigning interest. "Have they now? And how exactly did they do that?"

"They vowed their allegiance to my alpha and me. They are *ours*."

He laughed again.

"Listen," he snapped, his laughter abruptly coming to an end. "You will give them to me or you will die, and if you think for one second that they would protect you from me, you are sorely mistaken."

"They will," I said, glancing over to where the three men stood, their faces solemn but their energies fierce. "And I'm wearing proof of that."

"Oh, that's just darling. Did they buy you a promise ring?"

"No," I replied, calming the rage inside me, "the dog tags of a fallen mate. A female that you undoubtedly killed, either directly or otherwise." Suddenly, Tobias seemed to be at a loss for words. "So you listen to me, you smug, limey bastard. If you so much as set foot on American soil, I will personally see to it that the only time you ever see your homeland again is when you fly over it as dust in the wind. Try me and see if I'm good for it."

After his growling ceased, he managed to compose himself, if only slightly.

"Words, Ruby. They're just words. We both know you're not going to kill me, *don't we*?"

"Actions, Toby. I prefer actions. We both know you don't stand a chance, don't we?" I retorted snottily.

"Say it," he pressed, his voice lower and scarier than before. "Say you won't kill me."

"No," I retorted, trying to keep my heart from jumping out of my throat. "Say *this*: 'I'm a dead man'."

I never got to hear his response. Sean, having had enough of our posturing, grabbed the phone and did what he did best—intimidated the shit out of Tobias.

"I'm going to find you and end you. Keep running," he purred, eyes bleeding to black. "I *love* to chase." He cut the call off and tossed Janner the phone. "The others are ready to go too. He can't trace you now, but we sure as hell can trace him."

"That's why you let me talk," I said, thinking it was strange that nobody had moved to take the phone from me while I blustered my way through the conversation until Sean did. He wanted me to keep him on the line—just long enough to find out where Tobias was.

Before I got my answer, Sean was on his cell, ordering someone on the other end around as he walked out of the room. I presumed he was headed for Trey and the newly acquired coordinates of Tobias' soon-to-be dead ass.

"Well, he sure as hell didn't let you talk because you were helping matters, Ruby," Cooper quipped. "You practically invited him over to start a war."

"He'd lose," I said unconvincingly.

"Hopefully he won't live long enough for us to find out."

Beckett eyed me curiously for a moment until I snapped under the weight of his gaze.

"*What*? Why are you staring at me?"

"You were angry," he said plainly, as if detached from my response. He was so bizarre at times. "Why?"

"*Why*? Because I may not fully get you guys just yet, but I know one thing. You are *so* not being handed over to that twatwaffle. Not on my watch." I was fuming and wasn't certain as to why. The boys were odd and still somewhat unfamiliar, but they belonged to Cooper and me. If we wanted to kill them, fine, but nobody else was going to do it. Not without an epic battle. I may not have had Scarlet's ass-kicking powers, but I could still run my mouth like the best of them. I'd worry about getting Sean to cash that check for me later.

Without another word, Beckett walked over to me cautiously and wrapped his arms around my shoulders. He hugged me—tightly. Then slowly, the others came and did the same. I was in a group lovefest, UK werewolf style.

"Enough," Cooper sighed. "We have things to do. The four of us need to get back and make like things are relatively normal. Ruby, you stay here."

"Be careful," I told him, walking over to wrap my arms around his waist. "I'd be lost without your cooking, your sarcasm..."

"My incredible good looks," he added with flair.

I rolled my eyes even though he couldn't see them.

"Yes, those too."

He pulled away to look me in the eyes with a fierceness I'd not seen for a while.

"You be careful too, Ruby. I don't like not having you near me. Not when trouble is lurking."

"When is it not?" I replied sarcastically. In fairness, I wasn't exactly off base with my question. When he didn't see the humor in my response, I put my serious face on and gave him what he wanted. "I know you don't, but you know that Sean would never let anything happen to me. If you can trust anyone to keep me safe, it's him." His eyes narrowed briefly before he nodded in agreement. He wasn't going to acknowledge that out loud.

After planting a quick kiss on the top of my head, he rounded the boys up and headed out. I walked with them to the doorway and watched as they disappeared down the winding flights of stairs, their footfalls fading before they vanished entirely. It left an eerie feeling in my stomach. Something felt wrong about being away from them—ominous—as if somehow, without my presence, danger was more likely to find them. I was so used to it looking for me that I never realized how terrifying it was to be on the sideline, a spectator of the ultimate game.

Death knew no rules, no timeouts—no substitutions. He kept the score, ran the clock, and called the plays.

The teams were on the field.

The whistle had blown.

Unless Sean could stop Tobias first, all hell was about to rain down on the pitch.

And there wasn't a damn thing I could do about it.

CHAPTER 27

B ut death never came.
Not the first night. Or the second. Or the third. In fact, an entire week went by without contact from Tobias, or even the slightest hint of danger, and we started to wonder if our threats had kept him at bay. Could it really have been that simple?

On the night Tobias had promised us a war, Sean had ordered Jay and the boys to converge upon the location of the traced phone call. They found a newly abandoned warehouse with an underground facility, which was fully equipped with cages—the kind that could house a human. They found no evidence of what had been done there, only stainless steel tables and shelves. Jay described it as an abandoned autopsy room.

Behind the building, they found a mass grave. Fresh body parts had been recently disposed of in it. They'd been crudely dismembered and thrown away like garbage.

They appeared to be human, but the PC boys knew

better.

Tobias was still at large, and though Sean should have gone over to assist with the situation, he refused to leave me. He was torn between love and duty—a more than familiar predicament for him. In retrospect, it was a good decision.

Just as we started to think we were in the clear, Tobias showed up in force, an army of werewolves accompanying him. I watched from the relative safety of Sean's apartment as they converged upon my home, attacking in the dead of night. An alarm had sounded, startling Sean and me out of our slumber. He sprang into action with blistering speed—my vision blurred trying to watch him.

With black eyes blazing, he fled his apartment to aid Cooper and the boys. When I went to yell down the stairwell to him, wanting to tell him I loved him, I couldn't get out. Something was different about the door. I'd been sealed in, either for protection from the attackers or from myself. He knew I'd try to escape. He really did plan for everything.

So there I stood, breathless, clinging to the partially drawn curtains beside me for strength. I never once feared for myself. I didn't have time to. Instead, I stared out into the moonlit night and prayed that they would survive the attack. It was all I could do. Losing any of them was unacceptable, and I did my best to impress that fact upon the powers that be.

Occasionally I would see a flash of light through the bay window of my bedroom, but that was all; I never saw the actual battle. Maybe that was for the best. Some things are impossible to un-see.

What seemed like hours later, Sean reappeared in his living room completely unscathed. I couldn't bring myself to ask verbally, so I let my expressions, which he could so easily read, speak for me. With only a momentary pause, he filled me in.

"They are dead," he said flatly, his eyes as dark as the shadows surrounding him.

My heart sank.

"Dead...?" I whispered as a tear sprang from my eye. My legs disappeared from below me, and I crashed to the floor.

"Ruby, no," he said as he ran to my side. "Not your boys. The others. *They* are dead."

"My guys are all right?" I asked with the hopefulness of a child. "Cooper? Ali? They're all okay?"

"Yes," he said softly, wiping the rogue tears from my face. "I'm sorry. I didn't mean to upset you. I should have worded that better."

I laughed a slightly unstable laugh.

"Yes, well, you are in report mode, so...I guess it's understandable. Frankly, I don't give a shit. I'm just glad they're all intact and breathing," I said, wrapping my arms around him. "Thank you. Thank you for helping them."

"We need to get the PC over there to clean up a bit. Cooper is in your studio bandaging Alistair up, but the others have only minor wounds. Your apartment on the other hand..." he said, trailing off. "Needless to say, it was tight quarters for a battle of that magnitude."

"Aw, man," I sighed, pulling away to see his expression. "Couldn't you guys have taken the battle upstairs to the loft? It already looked like a war zone," I lamented, thinking that it would have been nice for just once not to have my apartment become a battleground.

"Cooper and the boys ambushed them. It was a tactical move that paid off in spades."

"How bad is my place?" I asked, afraid of the answer.

"Decimated might be an understatement."

"Is it something your boys can take care of or am I starting over with a contractor?"

He smiled a devilish grin.

"I've got the *Specialist* coming. It'll be picture-perfect by the time he's through."

"Can I get his number? Maybe I should put him on speed dial."

He laughed.

"I think not. I'm trying to get you out of needing his services, not in need of more. If I have any say in it, this will be the last dramatic event in your lifetime."

"I wouldn't wager much on the bet."

He frowned.

"No, I don't think I will either. You and I don't live in an ideal world, Ruby. This is our reality."

Don't I know it...

I stood up slowly and looked back out the window to my apartment.

"Can I see them?" I asked, looking to Sean, who was leaning against the window beside me.

"Soon."

"So does this mean Tobias is dead? That we don't have to worry about him anymore?"

"He is dead," he replied with a tight expression. "As to whether or not we should still worry, I'm not so certain. I don't like what Jay found over there. Something is off. The boys were telling the truth about pack members disappearing, but we don't know why." He collected my hand in his and pulled me tight against his body. "I need to go over there with Trey. Until we sort out what he was up to, I'm not sure that you or your refugees will be safe." Brushing a curl off of my face, he pulled me up toward him and kissed me softly. "I may not care about their safety, Ruby, but yours is paramount to me. Without Scarlet to protect you..."

"I'm cannon fodder," I lamented. "I know."

He gave me a loving squeeze to acknowledge my frustration. I didn't want to be helpless, but against a werewolf, that's exactly what I was. Even with an Uzi full of silver, I'd likely be mowed down before I could even get a shot off. I needed to hit the firing range. Unfortunately for me, Ronnie was too busy being Veronica to accompany me on that venture.

"I'm going to figure out what's happening to you," he said convincingly. "Scarlet can't be truly gone. It's impossible."

I wasn't so sure.

"How are you going to sort it out?"

His chest rumbled against me.

"There are those who deal in things of this nature. I will have to contact them."

"Who?" I asked, not sure that I wanted the answer. It proved to be a non-issue. He wasn't going to tell me anyway.

"That's unimportant now. First I have to sort out this London situation. After that, we find Scarlet, though I can't say I entirely miss her." Again, his wicked smile stretched wide across his face. "She's a massive pain in my ass."

That logic was hard to argue, though her absence made my ass vulnerable. I greatly preferred having reinforcements.

*   *   *

When we walked into my building, I was immediately struck by a strange vibration, which stopped me dead in my tracks.

"That's the *Specialist*," Sean said, encouraging me up the stairs. "You can relax, but we can't go in there. Not yet."

"Sounds fantastic to me," I replied, walking directly past my apartment door to the third floor. Cooper stepped out onto the landing and looked over the railing at us as we approached.

"I want you to know that I'm not entirely to blame for what happened to your apartment." His grin was wide and warm, and I ran up the final steps, tackling him when I reached the top. He stumbled back against the wall as a result of my flying squirrel attack. I clung to him like falling off meant my death. "Does this mean you're happy to see me?" he asked playfully.

"You could take it that way," I replied, my voice muffled by the chest I'd buried my face in. "Coop..."

"I know, Ruby. I know." He gave me a reassuring squeeze and delicately peeled me off of him. "You should go see the boys—they were worried about you. Ali's banged up pretty badly, but nothing that won't heal up by the end of the night."

Sean lingered behind me not saying a word. If I hadn't known any better, I would have thought that he was becoming more comfortable with the dynamic amongst the three of us. But I did know better, and the second that Cooper leaned down to kiss my cheek, I heard confirmation of it. Sean was not a fan of sharing.

Cooper's grin twisted slightly, making it far more mischievous in nature. He loved getting under Sean's skin. I couldn't blame him; it was really the only weapon he had against him.

"Ruby!" a voice called from my studio. Shortly afterward, Alistair stood in the doorway, bandaged and carrying more weight on one leg than the other. "They didn't come after you then?" he asked, a look of relief washing over his face.

"No, Ali. Nobody got to me."

"We're pleased to hear it," Janner said from behind Alistair. "It was an...*uneasy* feeling, knowing you were left alone."

"They could not have gotten to her," Sean declared from behind me. "I made sure of that."

By the looks of confusion on everyone's faces, it seemed that none of us had any clue what he meant. None of us were about to ask for clarification either. I figured it had something to do with whatever he'd done to the door. Maybe it was werewolf-proof, if there even was such a thing.

I needed him to hook my building up with the same treatment.

As the awkwardness settled in around us, the sound of my apartment door opening echoed through the stairwell. Whoever the Specialist was, he was apparently finished. When I tried to peek over the edge to see the silent wonder who was taking his leave, Sean caught my arm.

"He's shy," he informed me with a wry smile. "If you don't mind..." He pulled me back away from the rail and gently held my arm until he heard the exterior door close. "You may see your home now."

Without pause, I made my way down to the second floor. Sean had described my abode as "decimated." I needed to see just what I was left with.

I should have been shocked to find everything as it was when I'd last been there, but I wasn't. There was more to the PC boys than met the eye, and I was starting to learn that they all seemed to hold special qualities that came in handy. My apartment was a case in point. Not a single detail was out of place.

"How?" I asked, knowing full well Sean was right behind me.

He said nothing in response.

When I turned to look at him, he gave me his most noncommittal shrug that meant both everything and nothing.

"Ruby, I have to leave. Now. Jay needs my help on this one. Trey too."

"I know. It's fine," I said, not really wanting to see him go. On the flip side, it did give me some time with the guys. Time I hadn't had in a week. I needed the normalcy that an evening of popcorn and a movie could provide, even if it was with a few extra bodies.

"I'll text you when I arrive," he said, cupping my face in his hand. "I don't expect this to take long. With Tobias dead, all we have to do is round up the remaining pack members and put the pieces together."

I knew "round up" was a euphemism, but I let it be. Sean's hands would always be dirty in one way or another. It was part of who he was. If I wanted to be with him, it was a part I needed to accept.

"Cooper," he said, turning to find him leaning against the far wall of the landing. "I'm trusting you to keep her safe."

"Always," he drawled, looking bored with Sean's comment.

"I entrust Ruby to no one, but I'm entrusting her to you. Do you understand me?" Sean asked through the doorway. Cooper pushed off of the wall, standing militantly straight. "Do not fail me on this."

The two eyed each other menacingly, but there was something else in their gazes—a respect. They might never like each other, be drinking buddies, or even be remotely cordial to one another, but there was an understanding. Their bond was through me, each knowing that, no matter what, the other would put my life above his. Maybe that was all those two were ever going to need.

Cooper nodded once, and with that, Sean disappeared down the stairs on his mission to kick ass across the pond. I felt bad for those still breathing over there. They were in for an unpleasant encounter very soon.

"So," Cooper said, coming inside the apartment. "I'm not really up for a total rehashing of events, but I am up for a drink. Anyone else interested?"

The UK trio unanimously agreed, so I caved. It had to be close to two in the morning, but we were all so wired that it was clear that nobody would be sleeping.

"Movie?" I asked, arching an eyebrow inquisitively at him.

He grinned in response.

"I'll start the popcorn."

CHAPTER 28

Janner, Cooper, Beckett, and I all scrunched together on the floor in front of the couch, allowing Alistair to stretch his wounded body out on the sofa. He seemed almost back to normal, but I think he was milking it for all it was worth. We indulged him anyway.

Cooper was relatively tight-lipped about what had happened to Alistair during the fight, but I could tell he was proud. All he would tell me was that Ali had made good on his promise to me, attacking Tobias the second he mentioned my name. Outgunned and outclassed, the youngest of the wolves may not have always been the smartest, but he was brave beyond measure.

Forty-five minutes into the movie, my butt was falling asleep. All the toss cushions had already been bogarted, so I got up and climbed over Cooper to head for my bedroom. As I walked past the bathroom, Alistair emerged from what had to have been his third trip. He had the bladder of a five-year-old girl.

"Ruby," he said, catching my arm lightly. His energy was yet again impossible to read.

"Yeah, Ali. What's up?"

"I'm sorry for the pain we've brought you. We really never intended for it to happen."

I smiled and gave him a light kiss on the cheek.

"I know you didn't. I've met enough madmen in my life to know that nobody can plan for what they'll do next. Typically, they'll go to whatever lengths necessary to get what they want. Their egos won't settle for defeat," I told him earnestly. "But dead guys don't usually have big egos." I smiled until I thought about what I'd said, Gregory's image flashing through my mind. "Okay, maybe that's a bad example, but you know what I'm saying."

"In a most disturbing way, I do," he replied, before making his way down the hall. His limp was barely visible, but I'd had a few drinks so it was possible that I wasn't the best judge.

When I reached for the doorknob to my room, I missed entirely. Everything in front of me started to merge together, and I blinked furiously to try and focus. It faded in and out while I carefully walked to my bed. Thankfully, Sean's specialist left my room cleaner than I had so I didn't have to contend with floor snipers along the way.

"Cooper," I called, sitting down on the edge of the bed, "I think I'm going to call it a night. I'm wicked buzzed already, and it's making my head spin. I'll see you guys in the morning."

He walked in through the bedroom door moments later. He looked like a blurry mess.

"You okay?" he asked, standing next to my bed.

"Yep. Just drunk and tired."

"But you only had one beer," he replied questioningly.

"And apparently not enough food or water, but I'm too tired to remedy that. I just want to sleep it off."

"If you say so." He hesitated beside me for a moment before bending over to kiss my forehead. "I'll check on you in the morning before we leave."

"Where are you going?" I asked, feeling totally out of the loop.

"The boys found a place outside of town. We're going to go check it out."

"Really? Even after all of this?"

"They need their own space, Rubes. There's no bathroom up there. No rooms. They can't stay up there forever; besides, it's your studio. You used to love to dance up there."

"Ugh. I so don't want to talk about dance right now," I grumbled. Dance was still a touchy subject for me. Dance equaled Matty, and after killing him, that equation no longer worked.

"Fine, but we're still going. If you're up before we leave, you can come. Otherwise, I'll see you later."

"Sounds good," I replied, closing my eyes to black out my drunken vision. "Love you."

"Love you too, Rubes."

He gently closed the door, leaving me alone to try and get a hold of myself. My physical health had been deteriorating for months due to my neglectful ways, my circumstances never quite lending themselves to excellent self-care. But even taking that into consideration, it seemed to be getting exponentially worse at a far more alarming rate. I needed to get a handle on things before I literally started to fall apart. With my supernatural status in a state of flux, I wondered if that left me more vulnerable to human disease. I didn't have time for migraines, insomnia, or brain tumors, so I hoped that wasn't the case.

While I fretted about the possibilities, I felt an oddly familiar sensation around me. It frightened me at first until I realized what it was—or more specifically, who it was.

"Matty?" I called out.

I received no response. Without Peyta nearby, I couldn't see him or hear him, but I could definitely sense him.

"I miss you...," I whispered, not wanting Cooper to overhear me. "I wish I could talk to you right now. You were always so good to talk to when I needed it."

Silence.

"Ever since that night...the night you died, my life has been a total mess. I feel like everything is falling apart and I have no clue what to do about it. When I used to need to clear my head, I would dance, but now..." I let my words trail off while I stared at the darkness in my room. The truth was I didn't want to dance anymore. Not without him.

"I like knowing that you're here right now. Is that weird? It seems a little creepy but it's true. I like knowing that you're still with me in some way. That you're watching out for me." I paused in an attempt to stifle the emotions that surged at my sentiments. I really did feel better with him around. I always had. "You were always watching out for me, Matty. Don't think that I didn't notice."

Suddenly, I felt his energy fading and I was struck with an instant sense of panic.

"Not yet!" I said more loudly than I should have before lowering my voice to a faint whisper yet again.

"Please. Just stay until I fall asleep...if you can. Please?"

Though his essence never fully regained its previous strength, it didn't disappear. As my mind quieted, I drifted off to peaceful sleep, knowing that I had Matty near me. Peyta had said that she couldn't tell how long he had before he faded, so I selfishly wanted to enjoy those moments while I could.

I knew there would come a time when they too would fade.

*   *   *

The next morning, I flopped over in bed, eyes still closed, luxuriating in the feel of a good night's sleep. It had been eons since I'd had one, and I just wasn't quite ready to give up the welcome sensation it brought with it—the feeling that everything was right as rain. When I opened my eyes, I realized just how cloudy the forecast actually was.

The room looked fuzzy and fragmented, so I rubbed my eyes, thinking that the prior evening's alcohol plus my sleeping overindulgence had led to eye boogers the size of Texas distorting my vision. No such good luck. With several attempts to clear my sight, I was no better off.

I could see light as well as objects, but everything around me had taken on a poorly delineated shape, looking more like amorphous masses than sharply edged furniture. Stunned, I stumbled my way out of bed, tripping on something—most likely my shoes, which I'd kicked off hours earlier—cluttering the floor. I expected Cooper to come running, but he didn't. He and the boys must have already left for the day.

To curb my growing panic, I closed my eyes and

tried to just breathe while I cursed my inability to put things away rather than scatter them around my room. As I did, something tugged at my mind. A memory I'd long ago tried to repress came crashing to my consciousness.

Their voices woke me from my sleep late in the evening. They so rarely fought with one another that I found myself compelled to hear what had caused them to do so.

"It hardly matters now, Robert," my mother sneered, the sound of a glass shattering in the sink punctuating her remark.

"Sheila, please. You know we had little choice in the matter. It's done. There's no sense in dwelling on it years after the fact."

"But I feel so trapped," *she continued, completely ignoring him. "Our lives were so much simpler before..."*

"I know they were, but what else could we have done? We couldn't have given her away. You know *that wasn't an option."*

"We should never have listened to him," my mother lamented quietly as I pressed into the hallway further, unable to ignore what they were saying.

"Listened? That's hardly what we did, and you know it. We had no choice in the matter—he made damn sure of that," my father said with a growl. "He'll answer for his treachery eventually, but for now, we proceed as we have. She'll be out of our hair soon enough. What's another decade or two?"

"An eternity," my mother snapped at him.

"You're being dramatic, Shanley..."

"Do NOT call me by that name. That woman is gone now. He's made certain of that too." She stomped through the kitchen, rifling through cabinets and slamming drawers. I listened intently to the familiar sounds of her frustration—she always cleaned when she was upset.

"A few more years," my father said softly, halting my mother's endeavors. "When Ruby is gone, we can go back to the life we had. We can go wherever you want...do whatever you want

to do. I promise. But for now, she is our charge, and we will respectfully fulfill that duty until it is no longer ours. Do you understand?"

"Yes," she growled quietly, "but keep her away from me until that day is upon us. I never wanted any part in her being here, and nothing you say will ever change that. All she does is drag us down—she's a death sentence."

I retreated back to the safety of my room, tripping on something hard and plastic in my haste. After climbing back into bed, I mulled over what I'd heard, wondering how I could possibly make life easier for them—how to make myself less of a burden. It was painful to hear that your existence was not only problematic for your parents, but also unwanted. In that moment I made a conscious decision to do whatever I could to lessen the offense that my presence   created.

In the wee hours of the morning, long after my parents had gone to sleep, I pulled myself out of bed and crawled methodically around my room, picking up the various items that lay strewn about it. I was far from a neat child. In the darkness of my world, I smiled to myself knowing that surely a tidy room would help my parents see that I was not at all the albatross they thought I was. I would make myself lovable to them.

If only that was all it would have taken. The answers to life were always far simpler the younger I was, and at seven they were positively black and white. No wonder I had forgotten about that day.

It was easy to see why.

I felt around the floor for the rogue shoe that had tripped me and chucked it at the door, letting out a scream as I did. I didn't want to go back to being anyone's burden—never again. Blindness was just another cage.

*　　　*　　　*

Cooper didn't answer any of my calls, which meant he'd left his phone in the car. I chucked mine across the room out of frustration. I was going to have to wait not-so-patiently for him to get it before I'd be hearing back. The situation didn't thrill me, but I lacked options. Sean was gone, and I didn't see the point in calling him in full-on freak-out mode about something he couldn't address from overseas. I decided that I would call him as a last resort.

I was frustrated with my situation, wondering how, once again, I found myself in a vulnerable situation, needing the aid of someone else. Scarlet had seemingly abandoned me, leaving me to fend for myself. Arianna was long gone, which was really for the best. She'd been my constant companion through my life—my human life. As painful as it was to admit to myself, it was likely best that she wasn't around me anymore. She could shelter me from my parents and the harshness of being a disabled person in the real world, but my new reality wasn't well suited to humans. She wouldn't have survived long.

Before I could let my mind wander too far down roads best left untraveled, I started fumbling around my room in an effort to relocate my phone. It took me forever to find it, and even longer to locate the voice command function on it, but I was finally able to call Gavin. I wasn't excited to tell him about my predicament, but there was no avoiding that one. We had scheduled our meeting for that morning, and I couldn't very well make my way through downtown unaided. I had to let him know that our arrangement needed to change.

"Ruby?" he asked, sounding oddly cheerful. "I'm surprised to hear from you now. We're meeting in just a few hours. Is there something that couldn't wait?"

"Um, yep. I think you could say that," I replied, trying to play it cool. "Something has sorta come up, so I can't get down there for our little meeting. We'll have to do it over the phone."

"I'm afraid that won't suffice." His voice had a chill to it that contrasted with his original tone. "I need to see you in person."

"Well, that is no longer an option, so it's phone or nothing," I blustered, hoping he wouldn't see through my bluff. He knew I wanted answers just as badly as he wanted me down at his houseboat in a few hours.

"Does it have to do with what went down at your apartment last night? I'm so glad you weren't there at the time, though not as glad about where you were instead," he growled. "Tell me why we can't meet. I'll decide if it's an acceptable reason or not."

"I'm afraid that's classified, Gavin. You're not the only one with information you'd prefer to keep to yourself."

"Yes, but the difference between you and me, Ruby, is that I actually *have* that sort of information. You don't."

"Oh, I think I do now," I said with a nervous laugh as I panned the room with my newly acquired blur-o-vision.

I could hear him rumble through the phone line. He was clearly displeased with the situation.

"If you won't come to me then I will come to you," he snarled. "I'll be there in a few minutes."

"Nope. Bad idea," I blurted out, moving toward the front door to be certain it was locked. On my way, I crashed into the ottoman that had clearly been moved from its normal position in the room. Its color blended into the floor too easily, and I soon found myself falling awkwardly over top of it.

"What was that?" he asked, his voice alarmed but threatening. "Who is there? What's happening?"

"Calm down," I groaned, retrieving the phone that had fallen away from me. Gavin's menacing voice made it easy to find. "I just tripped on some furniture. Nobody is here."

"You tripped? On furniture?" His voice was dubious to say the least. "How big was this *furniture* that you tripped on?"

"Um...it was an ottoman. Why?"

"Because it's broad daylight outside and you just managed to ambush yourself with a bench the size of a small person. I don't buy it."

"What can I say? I'm really clumsy."

"My ass you are." I could practically hear him thinking through the phone and I didn't like it at all. Gavin quiet was Gavin at his most dangerous—much like someone else I knew. When I heard the sounds of traffic and gusts of wind in the receiver, I knew I was in trouble.

Hanging up the phone, I scrambled most inelegantly to the front door, feeling my way up to the locks. I fastened every one of them before I shuffled my way over to the large armchair and pushed it back to reinforce the door. It was stupid, really, but I wanted to feel like I had something between me and him.

When that was finished, I paced off my steps through the hall, heading for my room while my hand trailed along the wall for comfort. It was a painfully familiar gesture. I wanted to hole up in my bedroom and pray that I could reach someone useful before Gavin arrived. There was only one person left to call.

Remembering the sequence of movements to engage the voice commands, I finally accessed it and spoke as loudly and clearly as I could into the receiver, hoping that my Hail Mary would work.

CHAPTER 29

"*A*lan," I told the phone, hoping it would recognize the name. I couldn't remember if I'd programmed him into it or not. It wasn't the time to find out I hadn't. I needed a distraction in the worst way, and I figured that Alan would do as well as any since Sean was out of town and Cooper was MIA.

The phone rang repeatedly and my heart started to beat faster. After three rings, his voicemail kicked in and I blurted something barely coherent into it before hanging up. I needed him to know that I was distressed. When the phone rang only a few seconds after I hung up, I assumed my tactic had worked—mission accomplished.

I searched for the button to answer the call, then hit it and immediately started talking into it.

"Alan...Alan I need you to come here right away, it's—"

"Not Alan." Gavin's voice was rich and warning—his standard order. "Ruby. You're going to do something for me right now."

I could hear the same blowing distortion in his receiver, so I knew he was still outside. My heart thumped wildly and erratically in my chest. There was no way out.

"Oh yeah?" I snapped, feigning bravery. "What's that?"

"Go to your bedroom window. *Now.*"

Though I didn't enjoy his tone or attitude, I did like that he wasn't trying to order me to open the door downstairs. I didn't know what angle he was trying to work, but my options were limited, so I decided to play along and prayed that I would find a way to bluff through whatever game he wanted to play. I slowly and carefully made my way to the window seat in my bedroom and perched myself on it.

"Good, now I want you to look down at me for a second."

It was an 'oh shit' moment. He could have been anywhere down there, and though I could make out shapes and objects, it was the middle of the day and people were everywhere. My only shot was to try and locate a body that *wasn't* moving. When I found someone that fit the bill, I put all my attention on him, even putting on an annoyed face for good measure.

"Done. You happy now?"

"No," he replied coolly, "I'm not. Tell me something, Ruby, what am I holding in my hand?" *Fuck*...My plan had worked up until that point, but I was sunk, and it seemed like I wasn't the only one who knew it either. "Oh, come on now, it's not like it's not obvious. Do you need glasses or something?"

I panicked.

"Or something. Maybe."

He was silent for a moment and very still, standing under the same street lamp that the Rev had months earlier. It was an unsettling thought.

"So it's happening...," he said cryptically. It wasn't a question.

"What's happening?" I asked, feeling a rolling sensation in my stomach.

"I feared this would come to pass," he continued as if I hadn't said a word.

"What? *What* would come to pass, Gavin? What's going on?"

"I'm coming up," he informed me as he started across the street. "And you *will* let me in."

"No. No, I won't until you tell me what the fuck it is that's going on—right now!"

His blurry silhouette stopped just in front of the parked cars along my side of the road. I knew he was looking up at me, but I still could make out next to nothing.

"You're going blind, Ruby," he replied flatly. "Just like before."

I dropped the phone to the floor.

One sentence confirmed what I feared most: that the sole reason I'd gained my sight was because of Scarlet's presence and that her continued absence may lead to its disappearance, and that Gavin knew far more than I had ever begun to bargain for. I could hear him still talking on the phone, but my mind was numb. All I could manage to do was stare out the window at his blurry silhouette and watch as he closed the last few yards to the exterior door.

He had nearly arrived when a car came flying up the street and screeched into a double-parked position outside my place. Someone jumped out and bolted toward my apartment door. My intercom lit up seconds later.

"Ruby!" Alan shouted into the magical box. "Are you in there?"

More of the most-annoying-sound-in-the-world's buzzing blared through my home.

"Ruby, I'm coming in."

I was half afraid that he was going to bust the glass out in the door to unlock it, so I did my best to hurry down the hall to the apartment door, push the chair back to its original position, and make my way out to the landing. My hope was that he would see me before he did anything too brash. Calling his name several times, I cautiously worked my way over to the long flight of stairs and found my way down them, slowly but safely.

I paced out the four steps necessary to reach the door and fumbled for the handle. Once located, I flipped the lock and pulled the door ajar for Alan, who quickly barged through it like his pants were on fire.

"I just got your message, Ruby. I was on my way over—what in God's name is going on?"

I could hear him moving around behind me. When I turned to face him, it took me a second to locate his outline. I could feel his panic instantly.

"Christ, Ruby," he gasped, most likely staring at me in horror. "Can you—"

"No," I interrupted, cutting his question off. "I can't see. I woke up like this and totally panicked. Cooper's out. Sean is gone. I didn't know who else to call." I started to feel guilty for causing him such alarm, but I had my reasons and he wasn't privy to the why behind them. He was going to want answers though, and I hadn't planned far enough ahead to have some ready.

"I'm taking you to the hospital," he ordered, taking me by my elbow to lead me outside.

"No!" I blurted out, knowing that was the worst idea ever. Unfortunately for me, Alan wasn't going to be easy to convince of that. "You didn't let me finish," I said with a sigh, trying to think fast on my feet. Cooper and Sean had always maintained that I was a horrible liar. I would soon see if Alan agreed. "After I hung up with you, Cooper called me back. I just got off of the phone with him now."

"What's your point?"

"My point is that he knew what was going on. He said something about a side effect of a medication I'm on. Something about visual disturbances. I don't know all the details. I was too busy freaking out to listen."

"Well, you are a shitty listener...," he mumbled, probably not meaning to say it aloud.

"I know I am. Anyway, he said that it was on one of the labels. If anything like this happened, I was supposed to stop the meds immediately and wait twelve hours for the symptoms to dissipate. If they don't, *then* I'm supposed to go to the doctor."

"But why wait?"

"I don't know. It's what Cooper said. I'm sure he'd be happy to explain things to you at great length if you call him. I'm just trusting his judgment."

"Fine. Can you see anything at all? Are you all right to be home alone?" he asked, genuine concern seeping into his tone and energy, "I could bring you over to the house. Kristy just got back last night..."

"I should be okay here. I can see basic shapes and objects, so I'm not totally incapacitated, and Coop said he'd be home soon. Besides, with all those rooms in your house and baby-toy floor snipers, I'm likely to be far more hurt there than in my own space," I argued intelligently. They were valid points. "Can you help me up to the couch though? Maybe turn the TV on for some background noise?"

"Of course," he said, leading me to the steps. He brought me inside and positioned me to his liking on the sofa before announcing his departure. "I'm going to be late for work, but if you need anything else, you call me, understand?"

His voice was kind but firm. He wasn't messing around.

"Yes, sir, officer, *sir!*" I joked, trying to let the smile reach my eyes and set his at ease. I had no way of knowing if my efforts were successful.

"Where's your phone?" he asked, pacing about the room. It took him a minute or so of searching the house to locate it and bring it to me. "Use it if you need to, Ruby. For *anything.* Anything at all."

"Thanks, Alan."

He hovered silently for a moment, his energy tentative and uncertain.

"Ruby," he said softly, hesitation tainting his delivery. "I've got something I've been trying to show you—"

"Ha!" I scoffed, "well that might be a problem..."

"Yes, I see that now—no pun intended."

"What is it?" I asked, propping myself up on the couch.

"It's a letter," he said, sitting down on the coffee table in front of me. "It's from McGurney."

"But he's—"

"Dead. I know. It was sent to me by his daughter," he explained as he worried the paper in his hands. The crinkling sound it made was calming, but his energy was far from that. "She got it in the mail a day or two before he died. It came to her with my name and address on it and instructions to send it to me if anything should happen to him."

"What does it say?" I asked, leaning in close to his face, desperate to glean something from the expression I couldn't see.

"It's crazy talk, Ruby. You'll think I'm nuts for even repeating it," he started, exhaling heavily. "The point is that something pushed him over the edge. Whatever he found out made him crazy, and he died because of it."

"Alan," I said tersely. "What does it say?"

He hesitated before starting to talk.

"He rambles on and on about a conspiracy."

"And?" I prodded, needing to know more than anything exactly what was written in the madman's note.

"And," he sighed. "You won't believe the rest."

"Alan," I said, grabbing at him. "Try me."

Before he could answer, footsteps echoed up the stairwell and Alan quickly shot up to his feet.

"Someone's coming," he said, stuffing the letter into his jacket nervously.

The door swung open. I recognized Cooper's energy straight away, and I sighed with relief.

"I swear on all that's holy, Ruby, there are times when I want to give them back," he barked, before cutting himself short. "Oh, hey, Alan. What's up?"

"Nothing much, Cooper. Ruby called me in a panic about her eye situation, so I came over to make sure she was okay. But I've gotta run. Time for work."

I was willing Cooper to play along. I couldn't tell if

Alan was looking at him or me, but I shot a look in Cooper's general direction that said 'read between the lines please'. He did just that.

"Well, you know Ruby. Drama is her middle name," he joked, headed toward the couch. I could hear the boys upstairs and prayed they were going to stay there. They may have been pack, but they still didn't know all my nuances.

"Exactly," Alan replied with a halfhearted chuckle. "I'll see you two later."

Alan slipped out of the apartment door, shutting Cooper and me in with the CF of the day.

"Eye situation?" Cooper inquired, his tone dubious.

"I'm down to four of my five senses. *That* situation," I delicately told him. "I can't see, Cooper. I'm going blind."

CHAPTER 30

H is emotions assailed me. Before he said another word, he turned the TV up to the loudest possible volume that still allowed me to hear him. He came to kneel before me, his large hands encircling mine delicately, prying my cell phone away. With my hands free, they wandered up to his face, exploring it slowly, working their way across every line and crevice.

"Talk to me, Ruby. What the fuck is going on?"

"I woke up this morning and everything was gone. All I can make out is general outlines," I told him, getting choked up. "I can't see the detail in your face at all."

"So the blurry vision last night...?"

"Was a precursor to this, I imagine. In fact, a lot of things are starting to make sense, actually. Walking into walls. My eyes constantly feeling tired and weak. Something is truly wrong with Scarlet, Cooper. Wherever she is, she's fading away."

Before he could reply, my phone sprang to life,

demanding our collective attention.

"Hello?" Cooper snipped. He didn't love being interrupted. "Who is this? No, not until you tell me who this is."

"Cooper," I called, reaching out for the phone. I had an inkling that I knew just who it was, and with Cooper home, I felt way more confident about getting those answers. Cooper was going to want them too.

He didn't argue, just slipped the Blackberry into my hand.

"Hello? Gavin?"

"He's very testy," Gavin sneered. "If he wants to control a pack, he's going to need to get a hold of those emotions of his."

"Yeah, well, we all have faults. Some of us are hotheads; others are creepy, evasive assholes. I'd call it even at the end of the day."

"I'm disappointed that you trust me so little that you would call in the cavalry, Ruby. I don't know how many times I have to tell you—I'm not the enemy."

"Then start acting like a fucking ally and tell me what you know," I fumed.

Cooper came to sit beside me, wanting to hear all that he could of the conversation. That, or whisk the phone from me once he got pissed off enough to start laying down the law to the old man.

"Ruby, you need to understand that some of what I keep from you is in your best interest. Not everything can come out at once. It would just be too much for you."

"That sounds oddly familiar."

"Do *not* presume to lump me in with *him*. My truths will be revealed in time. His won't. That is the difference between me and him."

"The only difference?" I asked, baiting him.

"Hardly."

"Whatever, Gavin, enough stalling. I want to know how you knew what was going on, and better yet, how you knew I was blind before."

I could hear him take a deep breath in preparation, but nothing came. No explanation followed. Then I heard Ginger in the background, urging him to tell me. *So she knows too...*

"I will answer the latter question first. Probably best to start there," he started, sounding controlled once again. "I knew you were blind before, Ruby, because I've known you since you were a child. Since the day you were born."

I felt the blood drain from my face. It couldn't be true.

"I knew your parents, Ruby. Very well."

My blood ran cold.

"As for why I feared it was happening again, let's just say that I did my best to keep tabs on Scarlet while you were *indisposed*." He paused for a moment before continuing. "She's a very devious creature. You need to get a better handle on that one." Another pause. "If you're ever afforded the opportunity."

I was in shock, and given the lack of commentary from my alpha, he was too. That was a whole lot of shit to absorb in a matter of a few seconds, and it really only begged further questions rather than provide answers.

Gavin knew what had happened during those three weeks, and I could tell he wasn't going to give that up easily. It also meant he lied to me.

"You lying shit!" I spat, wishing I could storm down there and punch him square in his arrogant old face. "You told me you hadn't seen me for a while on the docks that day, but you really knew exactly where I was, or at least where Scarlet was, the whole time!"

"I didn't lie," he replied, sounding truly affronted. "I told you I hadn't seen you around *here* for a while, which I hadn't. That's hardly a lie."

"Splitting hairs much? You should have told me right then and you know it."

"And what would that have accomplished, Ruby? You were already traumatized enough and had plenty on your plate. What I know about Scarlet will keep for now. I promise that when the time is right, I will let you know."

My hands shook with anger, but I knew that there was no way to get him to tell me. I had no leverage in the situation whatsoever, and though it was maddening, that was my reality. I'd have to suck it up and play nice with Gavin until then.

Cooper seemed far less inclined to follow that game plan. He snatched the phone away from me.

"Listen here, you slimy shit! You're going to tell me right now how to fix this fucking mess, understand? If you don't, I'm going to make your life immensely painful. We *all* will."

I heard Cooper's breathing speed up as he listened to whatever Gavin was saying. When my phone crashed into the wall behind me, I could only assume that he wasn't too thrilled with the outcome of his conversation.

"Mother Fucker!" he yelled, pacing away from me toward the kitchen. "Who the fuck was that guy?"

I sighed, not wanting to have to explain to Cooper about the man I had no answers about.

"Remember the old guy who left the note...?"

"Yes," he asked with dubious inflection.

"So, he's not *really* an old guy."

"Am I going to enjoy this story?"

"No. Probably not. I don't love it much myself," I replied nervously. "Here's the short of it. Gavin is the Chameleon."

That didn't ring any supernatural bells for Cooper.

"And...?"

"He's kinda stalking me, but I can't tell if it's a good or bad thing. He knows so much about me, Cooper, even where Scarlet went while she held me captive. The strangest thing about him is that he seems to be on a mission to pry me apart from Sean, though I have no clue why. Those two have a history of some sort. He's constantly feeding me half-facts about Sean and who he really is. I don't know what to make of the whole thing."

"What's his end game?" Cooper asked, anger rolling off of him freely.

"I don't know. That's what I'm trying to figure out."

"Will he try to harm you?"

"That's the thing, Coop. I don't think he wants to...not physically anyway. He's really fucking with my head though."

"I want you to stay away from him."

"And I would love to do that, Cooper, but it's impossible. He pops up everywhere I am when the mood suits him."

"Well then, he and I are going to have a little come-to-Jesus talk."

"I think that's a bad idea. He's the one with the answers that I need. You can't off him. Not yet, anyway."

"I wouldn't count on that if I were you."

"Seriously, Cooper. If you want to try to scare him a bit or intimidate him, that's fine. But I need the truth about Sean and other things. I need him alive."

"What other things?"

I blew out a heavy breath before answering.

"In my purse, there's a picture that he gave me. It's of me and some woman I don't recognize, for obvious reasons. He knows who she is. Apparently, Sean does too. He's trying to force me to show it to Sean for answers, but I don't trust his motives. I haven't done it yet. I'm hoping that if I'm stubborn enough, Gavin will tell me."

"That sounds like a promising plan," he replied sarcastically, getting up from the couch to retrieve the photo in question. "She's beautiful."

"I know."

"And you have no idea who she could be?"

"She could be anyone, Coop. I have no way to narrow it down..."

"I don't know," he said sadly, shaking his head. "I don't like this plan."

"You never like my plans," I chuckled, knowing that perhaps he was right not to.

"After last night, can you blame me?"

Before I could reply, a knock at the door startled us both.

"Everything okay in there?" Alistair called from outside the door.

"We're fine, Ali. You can come in."

"NO!" Cooper roared, moving toward the door.

"Cooper, we're going to have to tell them sooner or later," I said aloud, giving him a wink that I prayed he saw. When he didn't argue any further, I assumed he had.

I heard Alistair enter the room tentatively, coming to sit in the recently repositioned armchair.

"We heard shouting," he said cautiously.

"Cooper was upset with me," I said, looking to the door where Cooper still stood. "I did something stupid as always. He's worried that I may have really done some damage this time."

"What?" Ali asked worriedly.

"I've been taking too much medication, and it seems to have seriously affected my vision. I can't see a thing right now," I told him carefully. "Cooper is worried that I may have done permanent damage."

"But how? Was there silver in it?"

I had planned to let slip that Scarlet and I didn't heal the same way that he or other werewolves did. Cooper and I had agreed to keep as much information regarding my differences away from the boys, but it was all I could think of in the moment. I hadn't even thought of playing the silver card, but thanks to Alistair, I had the perfect out.

"No, not the meds, but the drops I put in my eyes to help the blurriness did. I honestly didn't even think when the lady at the health food store suggested colloidal silver."

"You put bloody silver in your eyes?" he gasped, shooting out of his chair. "Have you gone mad?"

"Ali, I'm still new at all this shit! You've had guidance all along. I didn't get that until recently. You can't plan for every hazard." I could feel his uncertainty with my well-being. It warmed me slightly on a day that not much could. "I'm sure it'll be fine. Please don't worry. I need to talk to Coop about something personal though. Do you mind?"

"'Course not, love," he replied, a sad smile

plaguing his voice. "I'll let the others know, if that's all right?" His question was clearly aimed at Cooper.

"You may. But I don't want them down here fussing over her. She needs to rest and heal. If she can."

"Right. Will do."

Cooper shut the door behind Alistair as he left, then made his way over to me.

"You do need to rest," he ordered, helping me off the couch. "Let's take you to bed." He started leading me down the hall, but I stopped him part way, something eating at me that I couldn't quite work out.

"Cooper, we've thought all along that Scarlet was trapped away in whatever dark corner of my mind she locked me up in, right?"

"Yeah..."

"What if she's not hiding away at all? What if she's disappearing? *Dying?*"

"She can't. That doesn't make any sense. She's part of you."

"I know she is, but I don't feel *anything,* Cooper. Nothing from her, and I haven't since she let me out. I told Sean that maybe since trauma let her out, trauma shut her away again, but I'm starting to wonder if that is even what's going on."

"Explain."

"The mate bond, it's intense, right?"

"Well, I don't know firsthand, but I've seen it. I guess that's a fair estimation"

"Did you ever see that bond broken?" I asked, hoping he would have answers that could shed light on the mystery shrouding Scarlet's disappearance.

"I did. Once." His voice sounded distant and mournful.

"What happened?" I prodded nervously.

He swallowed hard.

"He killed himself afterward. He couldn't handle the loss."

Silence weighed heavily between us.

"What if that's what Scarlet is doing? What if she's slowly fading away? From grief?"

"But that doesn't make any sense. They were *just* newly mated. The wolves I knew had been together for decades. Surely that must factor into things."

"You didn't feel her pain, Cooper. Before she shut me out, it was unbearable. The rage and grief were stifling."

"But it's completely unlike her, Ruby. She's cunning, shrewd, and highly attached to living, if I recall correctly. She wouldn't crawl into a corner and die. No way. That bitch will go down fighting every time."

I wasn't so sure.

"But what if she couldn't fight? What if she had no outlet for it?" I asked, wondering how someone so ill-equipped to deal with emotion of that kind would do without something, or someone, to take it out on. "Alistair killed his alpha because his bond with Jemma had been severed. Once he knew who the guilty party was, he tore him apart without thinking twice. Scarlet couldn't really do that given the circumstances. She had no one to claim her vengeance on."

"Maybe, but I still don't believe she would just walk away into the abyss of your mind. It's just not her nature."

"I don't think she's quite as callous as you make her out to be, Cooper. And it explains everything. My sight repaired the very moment I Changed. Why else would it disappear other than as a direct result of *her* disappearing?"

"Fuck!" he yelled, smashing his fist into the wall beside him. "This just can't be happening. It can't."

"I want to agree with you, Coop, but something Gavin said only further cements my theory," I argued softly, not wanting to upset him any more than I already had. "He said that I needed to get control of her in the future, *if* I was ever afforded the opportunity. I think he means *if* she's still around to get control of at all. That has to be it, Cooper. You know what I'm saying makes sense."

His lack of response was confirmation enough. His crushing embrace was overkill.

"We'll find a way to fix it, Ruby," he whispered into my hair, rustling it softly with his erratic breathing. "I don't want to ask this, but when is Sean home? If anyone can sort this out, it'll be him."

"He said he'd be back later today. He was supposed to be meeting Jay, Trey, and few other brothers in Boston later to regroup and debrief. I can call him."

Cooper made that grimaced sucking sound through clenched teeth. Bad news was headed my way.

"You're gonna need to use my phone for that," he said sheepishly. "Yours may or may not be in pieces on the living room rug."

"Man, I'm going to have to start buying cheaper phones given the rate I go through them," I lamented. "You can get me one tomorrow. Tell Chip, or Tad, or whatever his name is at Radio Shack that I say hi. I swear he knows my name by now."

"I'm sorry. Take mine. Go to your room. Call him. Rest. We'll sort everything else out later."

He placed his cell in my hand after retrieving the number and hitting "call" for me. I reached for his face and pulled him down to me, leaving a whisper of a kiss on his cheek before following the hallway wall down to my bedroom and shutting the door.

I sat on the bed just in time for Sean to pick up.

CHAPTER 31

Cooper was right. I needed to tell Sean what was happening—but not over the phone. Some things need to be done in person, and that was one of them, so I did my best to play it casual and said I was going to stop by his place later that evening. I knew that breaking the news would hurt him terribly—he was a fixer, and as far as I could tell, there wasn't a way to fix my situation. I hoped he would shame me with an easy solution.

Cooper drove me over to Sean's apartment and offered to walk me up, but I declined. I wasn't completely debilitated. Not yet. Taking advantage of the little daylight that was left, I carefully made my way to the entrance of his building. Once inside, I started up the multiple flights of stairs as I counted them off—a habit I never quite lost after I gained my sight. It was just too ingrained in me not to.

Since I had called ahead, he was expecting me and awaited my arrival on the landing outside his apartment door as he often did. The blurry figure could have been anyone, really, but I knew it was him from his energy. It intensified with my every step.

"I was glad you wanted to come over tonight," he announced, sounding every bit as pleased as he proclaimed to be. I loathed that I couldn't see the smile he was likely wearing.

"Yeah, well, my plans fell through so...here I am."

He laughed heartily at my jab. Yet another thing I was sorry I couldn't fully witness.

I knew I was approaching the final step, but as I looked up to smile in his general direction, I caught my toe on the last one, falling toward him. In typical Sean fashion, he caught me without any effort and helped me into the apartment. He had no idea just how much I needed that help.

"Glad to see some things never change," he joked, closing the door behind us. The apartment was dark, which did nothing to help me. What was it with him and lights, anyway?

"It seems like Scarlet was the more coordinated of us two, and, well, she's not really around to help out these days, so..."

"So it's the Ruby that I fell in love with. The one who could find danger in the most innocuous of places."

"Guess so."

"Do you want something to drink?" he asked, walking behind me toward the kitchen. He flipped on the industrial pendant light above the island, which was a godsend for me. The objects in the room were far more easily seen with that little bit of light, but I was still reluctant to move, so I hovered where I was—eight steps into the apartment.

"Um, I don't think I need any further impairment, thanks."

He hesitated for a moment; he was no longer rummaging through the cupboard for his stash. I felt the sweat beading on my back. I did not want to have this conversation with him, but it was coming any way I sliced it.

"Something wrong, Ruby?" His figure approached me slowly. "Why are you just standing there?"

I prayed for a way to tell him delicately.

"I...I can't stay long, Sean. I just came over to tell you something, really."

I could feel his guard go up, and for a moment, I was glad I couldn't see his beautiful but impassive face.

"What is it?" His tone was colder than I'd thought it would be.

"You see, the thing is," I rambled, unable to just blurt out the truth. "Cooper and I were talking and—"

"You and Cooper? I see," he interrupted. "And am I going to like the conversation you had?"

Silence.

"No." I could feel the tears welling up in my failing eyes. They were so not helping.

"No?" he asked, his tone taking that businesslike edge that I dreaded. "Then I suggest you just get it over with and tell me what it is so I can know exactly what it is that I'm not going to like."

He moved closer to me, blocking out the kitchen light. I cracked under the pressure and tried to move away. Stepping to the right of him, I thought I was aiming toward the couch. I should have had a clear path. Apparently, he'd gone shopping since I was last there. In my escape attempt, I caught my toe on the edge of a rug that had never been there before and crashed to the floor.

"Dammit!" I screamed, hating the helpless feeling I had.

"What's wrong with you tonight?" He tried to help me up, but I was too frustrated to accept his help.

"Don't!" I snapped, knocking his hand away. "I can do it myself."

"I'm sure you can, Ruby. That's not the point."

"But it *is* the point, Sean. It's completely the point."

"Are you trying to pick a fight with me to avoid telling me the bad news?"

"No, I'm picking a fight with you *to* tell you the bad news."

"What? You're not making any sense."

"Great! Then I'm acting congruently with everything else that's going on in my life."

"Would you please just tell me what you're talking about?"

It wasn't a request. It was an order wrapped up with a question mark for etiquette. When I didn't reply, he tried another. "Would you at least look at me?"

"I can't," I whispered.

"You mean you won't," he replied, the tension palpable in his voice.

"No! I mean I *can't*, Sean," I snapped. "You want to know why? I'm going blind, Sean. That's why I can't look at you and that's what I came to tell you—what Cooper and I were talking about that you wouldn't like."

I felt the tears overflow and flood down my face. They pissed me off even more.

"What?" he whispered, completely motionless.

"I'm going blind. I didn't realize what was going on

at first. I thought I was just tired and it made things a bit fuzzy, but yesterday...it escalated. I can only make out the general shapes of objects around me," I informed him, slowly feeling my anger drain away to dejection. "I can't even see your face."

I slumped back down to the rug that had exposed me, pulling my knees up into my chest. Growing up blind had never made me feel small and helpless. Losing my sight again did.

"Ruby—" He couldn't even finish his thought. I tried to block his energy, but it was impossible. It coated me, penetrating as he slowly approached. Where I would normally find it comforting, it only served to make me feel worse.

"Please don't," I said, putting my hands up defensively.

I felt the floor give way the slightest amount as he knelt before me, taking my wrists gently in his hands.

"Let me see." His voice was soft and sorrowful, but it was an order nonetheless. Not wanting to fight him, I slowly lifted my head from my knees to face him—eyes closed. He lowered my hands to the floor then cupped my face in his hands so reverently. "Open them. *Please*."

With a deep breath, I did just that. It only saddened me further when, instead of seeing his angelic face in front of me, I saw a blurred mess. It was not how I wanted to remember him.

He ran his palm gently up my face, resting it just over my eyes. He muttered something unintelligible, and I felt his energy shift immediately. It was intense, dark—ancient.

Unfortunately for me, my problem wasn't one that his magic could mend.

I heard the growl growing in his throat as he pulled his hand away.

"I can't do anything to help you," he said. He sounded like he wanted to tear the room apart, his frustration ever-mounting.

"I know," I sniffled. "I didn't come here thinking you could."

He said nothing, only pulled my face towards his slowly. My eyes closed in response. I felt his breath light on my face as he leaned in to gently kiss my eyelids, hovering over each one when he finished. Maybe he thought his love could fix them.

I opened them to see if it had.

"Still nothing," I joked, not feeling especially humorous.

"I'm sorry, Ruby." His voice carried a weight that threatened to break him.

"It's not your fault," I replied, reaching for him. I found his face and did my own exploring, tracing all the glorious angles it held. One last tear escaped as I did.

"We have to get her back—*Scarlet*. We have to find out what's happening to her."

I sighed.

"Sean, I think she's dying, or fading away. Something like that," I said, rehashing the conclusion that Cooper and I had come to. "I'm going to be what I was before she showed up." I choked on the words I spoke, and the ones I needed to say. "Will that...? Will you...?" Another sigh escaped me before I could force the words out. "Will you still be able to love me, if it's just *me*? No Scarlet. No supernatural anything. Just me, blind and everything?"

"Nothing could make me stop, Ruby. *Nothing*."

He said no more, scooping me up silently into his

arms and carrying me off toward his bedroom. Laying me down softly on top of his bed, he slid down beside me, immediately tucking me in close to him. Though his words failed him, his emotions did not. For once, they served him well.

In the darkness, he showed me exactly what I meant to him, and I felt every ounce of it. He tangled his hands in my hair and never let go, kissing me softly and slowly, like nothing else in the world mattered— like the drama could be postponed for another day. But I could feel that he had withdrawn somewhere deep within himself—there, but not—as if his mind had escaped to a place that made him more capable of dealing with the implications of my blindness.

I kissed him back, trying to reach him, to assure him through my touch that everything was going to be all right. Judging by his reaction, he didn't buy my false comforts any more than I did. Our pace started slow, his kisses lingering, but as we proceeded, it hastened, both of us feeling a need to have more, faster. Desperation and fear fed us.

With growing concern, our bodies twisted closer and tighter, clinging to one another like it was pertinent to our survival. Maybe it was. He was so often my lifeline; it made sense that he would be yet again. He whispered soft and foreign words, his breath tickling my lips, causing my body to shudder. They temporarily lulled me, sweetly releasing my fears while I succumbed to the only thing that mattered in that moment—him.

His foreign mutterings picked up intensity and urgency when he finally unlocked his hands from my curls to explore my body, claiming everything he touched. My hands mirrored his, frantically clawing at his clothing, which I suddenly found offensive. Our mouths were still entangled, each trying to consume more of the other with every growing second.

After finagling his shirt off with some effort, I captured the back of his head in my hands, fisting his hair tightly to leverage my body closer to his. The vibration that coursed through me from his chest tightened every part of me in the most glorious of ways. Sean still had, and always would have, an effect on me that was unparalleled.

I scrambled in response, needing to have his bare skin on mine, but he clasped my spastic hands in his, holding them gently down at my sides. With me somewhat immobilized, he continued his mission, unhindered by my rising desire to be whole with him. He pressed down against me, letting me feel the full weight of his body before sliding up along me to put his lips to my ear.

I held my breath, expecting him to say something profound as he always did, but instead he just brushed the lobe ever so lightly with his mouth. Every hair on my body stood at attention. He worked his way down my neck painfully slowly, angering yet pleasuring me the entire way. On occasion he would whisper the same indecipherable phrase over and over against my skin, delighting my nervous system with every melodic syllable.

My shirt strayed upward as his hands traced ghost-like patterns along my sides, my stomach—my chest. I shivered beneath him, willing him to speed up, the wait nearly torturous. When his lips came down upon the hollow of my neck, I heaved up against him, begging him for the contact I wanted—needed—most. To be one with him and him alone.

Sensing my distress, he gently pulled my top over

my head, his body never drifting far. His bare skin on mine felt like heaven, and it was more than enough to keep me focused on the now and block out the uncertainty of tomorrow. Tomorrow could wait.

His fingers continued their balletic dance across my body, memorizing it through touch as I had memorized his face only minutes earlier. I felt as though he was trying to understand how I would live in a world of shadows and unknowns. It was his way of empathizing with what I stood to lose.

Every pass drew the lightest hint of sorrow from him, his foreign words coming more frequently—a confession, a purging of remorse for a loss he couldn't quite understand. I reached for him, trying to pull him back to me, but he evaded me like only he could. I tried to tell him what he needed to hear, but he shushed me quickly, resting his lightly calloused thumb on my mouth. It then brushed a path back and forth across my lips, and they parted with the contact as I inhaled deeply. Instinctively, I took it into my mouth and toyed with it, sucking it slowly until a growl escaped him.

Seconds later, my pants were tossed against the wall, sliding down until they hit the floor with the lightest thud. They were echoed by another pair directly afterward. When Sean returned to me, it was abundantly apparent that the time for tenderness was over.

He slid my underwear down carefully, but with haste. Resting his body, still against me, he spoke the only words I understood during our encounter.

"I will not let you go," he whispered into my mouth as he kissed me.

Then he was inside me, driving himself against my body as though he wanted to thrust my vision back into me—or drive Scarlet out of hiding. With eyes closed, I met his pace, wanting to blend into his rhythm seamlessly. Our timing in life had never been perfect, but that night in his bed, it was.

His repetitive foreign phrase continued throughout, building in volume and cadence to match his power and speed. As we built to climax, he pushed up off of me, grabbing my legs to thrust into me one final time. Energy tore through the room like a crack of lightning in a storm as we came together, both breathing raggedly, bodies tensed and writhing.

He collapsed on top of me gracefully, catching his weight to hover lightly above my heaving chest. I thought I heard the faintest of laughs escape him.

"I wish I could see you right now," I sighed, trailing my fingers around his face for confirmation of my suspicion.

"You will see me soon," he said confidently.

Always so certain...

Deep down though, I could feel he was unsure. His words did not match the dissonance that rolled off of him while I lay in his arms. There was something below his conviction that tipped his hand. He thought that something ominous was at play, causing the disappearance of Scarlet as well as my vision, and in an equally tucked away place, I shared that sentiment. Something was really and truly wrong. But in that moment, I dared to believe that, come what may, he and I could face it and conquer it together—a truly united front, for the very first time.

I fell asleep with Sean curled around me, our limbs entangled, fingers intertwined. Having him near me made it easy to forget. Forget that Scarlet was fading. Forget that I might never see him again. Forget that trouble was almost certainly headed our way, if history was any indication.

He was my balancing force and I was his. The more we gave into it, the stronger it pulled. Something greater than the two of us was at play, placing us in each other's lives. It was a destiny—divine intervention. Troubles would always plague us, but nothing could separate us.

Not anymore.

CHAPTER 32

"So this is the house they found?" I asked incredulously. "This is where you are going to live?"

Even with my failing vision and the scant light of dusk, I could tell the two-story home was dilapidated. The closer we got, the more my suspicions were confirmed. What appeared to be shutters hung askew—where there were still some hanging at all. The front porch sloped so violently that I questioned whether or not it was even still attached to the house. I couldn't fathom why Cooper was taking me to see that tenement.

"It suits me and them just fine," Cooper replied, taking my arm to escort me across the lawn.

"Is it even livable?" I sneered, tripping on something weighty in the tall, unkempt grass. "And why are we checking it out now? It's almost too dark to see anything clearly, not that I could if I wanted to."

"Why do you never stop asking questions?" he

growled, holding me up once again as I stumbled. "This place isn't exactly on the market, Ruby. We were trying to check it out on the down low to see if it was worth taking over. Why are you so high strung about this?"

The truth was I didn't know, but something seemed off in a big way. I'd spent the entire day with Sean until he had to leave for yet another trip to solve the London debacle. Everything was great. But the second he dropped me off at the apartment, I just didn't feel right, and nothing had felt right from that moment on. Not even Cooper resonated with me in the way he always had. Combined with the anxiety I felt as we approached the house, it made me start to question if the problem was me, given that I was the single common denominator in the equation. With my eyesight fading back to the darkness that had once consumed it and Scarlet's continued absence, I had to entertain the notion that maybe *all* of my former abilities were no longer reliable—empath included.

"I'm sorry, Coop. I don't know what's wrong with me."

"Just try to relax a bit. You're making this way more stressful than it needs to be."

I kept my mouth shut the rest of the way to the house and up the five rickety steps on the wooden porch. Cooper continued to usher me, even though I could make things out better once we were inside. The moonlight poured through the vast windows, illuminating a grand staircase—we were in an old Victorian.

"They're here," Ali called from somewhere too deep in the darkness for me to make out, but I could feel him. I could feel *all* of the boys.

Even the ones I didn't know.

"Excellent. I assume everything went according to plan, Cooper?"

I know that voice...

"No issues whatsoever, Tobias. She's all yours."

"Well done," the alpha replied. "And what of Sean? Are you prepared to deal with that too?"

"I'll tell him exactly what you said—that I killed her."

"And when he doesn't believe you—because you know he won't, right?"

"I'll attack him, just as planned."

"And you're prepared to die?"

"Of course."

I couldn't believe my ears. Things were happening so fast that I couldn't process them. I hated how much I had come to rely on my sight, but even without it, I knew I was in trouble. *Big* trouble.

"Cooper?" I asked, attempting unsuccessfully to wriggle out of his hold.

"Do not answer her!" Tobias shouted. Cooper didn't make a peep. That's when I knew the shit I was in ran far deeper than I could have ever imagined. "Is the 'copter ready, Beckett?"

"It is."

"Beckett?" I called out beseechingly. I got nothing in response. "Where am I going?" I looked around frantically to no avail. The room was far too dark for me to make out anything or anyone.

"*We* are going back to London, my dear. You and your DNA are needed there."

"Janner! Janner, help me!" I cried, hoping that he would help me, or at least tell me exactly what was going on.

"They won't help you, Ruby. They answer to *me*,"

Tobias purred.

"But they aren't yours anymore," I said aloud, more a question than statement. None of them seemed to be mine at that moment. Not even Cooper.

"They've always been mine," Tobias continued. "They just didn't know it." I could hear the smile in his voice, and my stomach turned in acknowledgment. "Do you think they would have killed Deacon otherwise? No, I don't think so, Ruby. You see, the truth is that they adored him. Everyone did—except me, of course. He was the quintessential alpha: the one that everyone would kill to have. But I prefer chaos to order and never enjoyed being second fiddle, so with the help of some outsiders, I devised an incredibly elaborate plan to take him down and make a boatload of cash while I did so. There's quite a black market out there for werewolves."

I shuddered as he moved closer to me, prepared to further explain himself before doing what he came to do—take me away.

"Deacon caught wind of what I'd done to the others and was about to make me pay for it, but thankfully for me, I had all the pieces in place to assure that it wouldn't happen."

He stepped into the moonlight, just enough for me to make out his short and stocky silhouette. It was just what I needed: an alpha with a Napoleon complex.

"I'll tell you all about it on the way," he continued. "It seems that you're immune to my little tricks, so I have big plans for you. I'm sure you'll want to know all those details, and if you're like all the others, you'll want to know *why*. *Why me? Why* are you doing this? You know, all of those annoying questions that victims seem to always ask their captors. It really is cliché."

I stared in his general direction while he approached me. I definitely had questions, but most of them didn't revolve around why. That I could grasp, and it had become part of the curse that was being an RB. What I really wanted to know—needed to know—was *how?* How was he making them do what they were doing, manipulating them to do things they didn't want to do?

Or at least I assumed they didn't want to.

Regardless of what was or wasn't in it for the UK trio, I knew without a shadow of a doubt that Cooper would never harm me. The fact that he was all too willing to hand me over to a nefarious lowlife like Tobias was only cause for greater concern, not only for myself but for Cooper too.

I steeled myself, awaiting the transfer to Tobias' custody. It seemed to drag on forever, as though everything around me was moving in slow motion. Shadows milled around in the background—many of them. More than just the boys I had grown to know and care about. *More of his pack...*

Cooper stood beside me, motionless. I couldn't decide if it was because he was awaiting further commands, or if, somewhere deep down inside him, he knew that something was wrong—that something was about to happen to me, and he couldn't let that happen. Not to me.

"How?" I blurted out as Tobias stood before me, coming into as much clarity as he was ever going to. "I don't want to know why. I want to know *how* you made them do this."

He cocked his head to the side, which in my copious experience with unstable people meant he found me either amusing or curious. I was glad I couldn't see either expression on his face. My blood boiled at the thought.

"Fair enough," he said, getting right up in my face. Cooper was still holding my arm, though at that point it was more of a restraint than an aid. "I'm going to keep this as simple as possible because I don't care to waste time; I'm controlling them."

"I can see that," I spat, "but again, what I want to know is how. *How* are you controlling them?"

"It's all very complicated, Ruby. I'm not sure that we have time to go into all the science behind it, but the short of it is that a frequency—an energy of sorts—was discovered. It seems to affect cognitive function, allowing the power of suggestion to reign supreme. We've been testing it for a while now on some of the other pack members. It took a long time to work out all the kinks, and of course we lost most of them along the way, but we've perfected it now. Don't worry, Ruby. If you're as rugged as your reputation leads me to believe you are, you'll endure the experiments just fine."

"A frequency?" I asked, utterly confused.

"Exactly," he replied. "I'm sure you've heard how dogs can hear certain levels of sound that humans cannot. Think of it like that, though for some reason, you seem to be completely immune to it. It didn't affect you in the least when I spoke to you on the phone. My guess is that whatever makes you special is blocking it. We just need to find a way around that."

Or maybe my missing half is why it doesn't work, I thought to myself, not liking the implications at all. Maybe Scarlet's absence was helpful to avoid being controlled, but it was also likely to get me killed. I needed details about what was in store for me and I needed them fast.

"Then what is your grand plan?" I badgered, wanting answers. I was so tired of being used that, for once, I just wanted to be fully in the know.

"I'm not sure just yet," he replied, sounding genuinely uncertain. "But keeping you would give me an incredible boost in power. I'd be virtually unstoppable. Even to the PC."

"Not to Sean," I whispered, wishing I had said goodbye in the way that I'd wanted to the last time I saw him.

"Oh, I think you'd stand a good chance. My boys tell me he fancies you. That you're *mated*. Isn't that really just another way I can control the PC? Through your bond? He won't harm you in retaliation, or let anyone else for that matter, so really I won't have any interference from them at all." He sounded as though some of what he was saying was a revelation to him— like it had just dawned on him, and the awe in his voice was chilling. He would be unstoppable or I'd be dead. Those were the options, and I knew Sean wasn't about to take me down, so it was looking good for Captain Short and Stocky.

"The helicopter will be here in a minute, sir," Janner called out from another room. "We should be outside waiting."

"I couldn't agree more," Tobias replied, wrapping his small, chubby hand around my wrist. "Time to leave now, love."

As he pulled me toward him, I felt the slightest squeeze on my other arm from Cooper, like he was trying to hold onto me tighter or tell me it was going to be okay. It didn't matter either way. I was quickly ripped out of his grasp.

"Let's get you home now. I have big plans for you

and me."

"And I have even bigger plans," a familiar and welcome voice called from just outside the house, "but they're *all* for you." Heavy footfalls tread across the porch and in through the front door—more than one pair. "Let her go and I'll make this painless," Sean growled threateningly. Everything about his voice promised that he would *not* make good on his word.

"And if I don't?" Tobias quipped, feeling far too confident in his situation. He clearly hadn't pissed Sean off before. I had, and the energy coming from his direction had a more menacing feel than even I'd been privy to.

"I won't."

"Well, that's all fine and dandy, but are you willing to let your little lady here get caught in the crossfire?" he asked rhetorically. "No, I don't think you are. You see, what I think you're going to let us do is leave so that nothing happens to her. Well, nothing *yet*, anyway."

I heard the start of Sean's all too familiar battle cry and cringed, fearing what would happen to everyone present if he unleashed the true dark-eyed monster that I both loved and feared. Bodies would drop until he was satisfied, and I wasn't entirely certain that all parties were as guilty as they looked. I feared most for Cooper, who stood just far enough away from me to not look guilty, but surely Sean would question why he was doing nothing.

"Sean!" I cried out. "He's controlling them. It's not—"

A hand clamped down over my mouth, keeping the rest of the secret hidden away. I heard Sean move, but stop almost instantaneously. The blade that I suddenly felt pressed to my throat was the clear reason why.

"I wouldn't press me on this," Tobias threatened. "I can keep you plenty occupied with the others to get her to the 'copter and take off. And if not, well, I'm not above racking up a body count of my own on my way down."

The floor creaked when Sean's shadowy form rolled back on his heels ever so slightly.

"That's better. Now Cooper, do come here for a moment and hold this." In an instant Cooper was behind me, holding that same blade to my throat. "If he moves, I want you to kill her, do you understand me?"

"Absolutely," Cooper growled. It was oddly comforting having him holding me rather than Tobias, but it didn't change the fact that he would kill me just as easily. I tried to thrust my calming energy his way and have the effect that I used to have on him for healing, but it felt blocked, like I couldn't reach him. Instead, I was met with that same guarded energy that the boys had had on occasion.

"Now, Sean, here's what's going to happen. You and your boys are going to let us walk out and head on our way without any objection or Ruby dies, plain and simple."

I couldn't see him, but I knew Sean was struggling to find a solution to the problem and quickly. While he did hostage extraction calculations in his mind, I found myself being dragged backward through the house to what I presumed would be the backdoor. Judging by the thunderous sound and whipping winds that came crashing in through the broken windows, the 'copter was waiting out back for us.

"Ruby," Sean growled, his tone both a question and a warning.

"You can't let them take me," I cried out, but not because I feared for myself. More than that, I feared for what would happen when Tobias succeeded—what would happen if I was under his control.

I started to panic. Visions of dungeons in Utah—bars, cages—ran fiercely through my mind, peppered with labs and white coats, machines and needles. It promised a long and tortuous path to a mass grave somewhere. Without Scarlet, I was certain to die. The boys had not been overly successful tracking Tobias down, and I was under no delusion that I would live long enough for them, or Sean, to find me.

But what if Scarlet wasn't gone? What if she was still a part of me, somewhere deep within like I had been, tucked away and barely living? What if their testing was a success and roused her? What if one day she'd stand toe to toe against Sean in battle? My skin prickled at the thought. He would not kill her if he thought he could save me. Duty or not, I could not take the chance that his love would blind him.

And if it did, what amount of carnage could Scarlet amass while Sean searched for a way to undo what had been done by Tobias? Would she become that which he had hunted so many centuries ago? The mindless killing machine she was labeled to be? There was no easy way out of my predicament. It was a lose-lose either way.

There was only one way to prevent either unthinkable outcome. I would not be caged any more than I would let Scarlet be used as a weapon for a sociopath. For once, I would determine my fate.

With no way of knowing if he could still hear or see me, I looked in the direction I'd last known Sean to be and gave my most pleading face as the tears rolled down my cheeks. I knew what I had to do.

"I'm sorry!" I yelled over top of the helicopter's deafening noise.

Taking a deep breath for courage and clarity, I grabbed hold of Cooper's hand—the one that held the knife to my neck—and with all the force I could put into my body as he hauled me away, I pressed myself against that blade and dragged my throat across it. The world quickly went dark around me as the blood rushed from the gaping wound I had so successfully created. Tobias would not get to keep his prize.

That final thought brought me great comfort.

CHAPTER 33

I heard nothing. I barely even felt the pain. What little I could remember was falling to the ground, unaided and unhindered by Cooper. He dropped me like a sack of potatoes and just hovered above me, unmoving.

Then everything went black.

You would think that, with my numerous near-death experiences, I would have known what to expect, but once again, the universe butted in and changed things up. For once, it was a pleasant twist.

Before I could see anything, a voice—sweeter than any I'd ever heard in life—called to me like an angelic lulling melody. My soul begged to drift toward that voice, aching more and more the longer I didn't.

"Ruby...," she sang. "Open your eyes, Ruby."

Without hesitation, I did.

I was met with the same glowing orb that I'd seen when I saw my parents. But instead of them, the figure of a female floated before me, bathing in the glorious light surrounding her. The sight of her was breathtaking.

"It's not your time yet," she said while her hand lightly caressed my throat. "He's sending you back." Her hand shone with the same white brilliance that permeated whatever realm we were in. The heat it brought to my wound wasn't uncomfortable at all, though I had expected it would be; instead it was warm and comforting. My eyes were having great difficulty adapting to the brightness around me, and I fought hard to see the angel of mercy who sought to heal me.

But I *could* see.

"Sending me back?" I asked, squinting hard.

"Yes. He said it isn't time for you to leave yet," she replied, leaning closer to shelter me from the light.

"He who?"

"Who do you think?" she chuckled with a smile in her voice. "You have a job to do, Ruby. Yours is not yet done."

As my eyes adapted in the shade she provided me with, I tried to absorb what she was saying. *You have a job to do....* Part of me feared as to what exactly that job was. The other half was happy to sign on for whatever task was necessary to let me live.

Sensing my initial unease at her words, she pressed forward further until she blocked out the radiance almost completely. I startled at what I saw. Her beauty was ethereal, but more importantly, it was familiar. The dark hair, olive skin, and perfect face were near enough to confirm my suspicions, but the eyes sealed the deal. They sparkled like fresh spring grass, lightly covered in dew. Like glowing emeralds.

She looked at me knowingly as though she could read my thoughts.

"You're good for Sean. You bring out a side of

him that hasn't been seen before. Not for a long, long time. He *needs* you, Ruby." She wrapped her arms around me, pulling me in tightly against her. The unadulterated love and goodness that resonated from her brought tears to my eyes. Never again would I feel something that pure, that heavenly."And Scarlet needs you too. The burden you carry is for both of you to bear, and bear it you shall. *Together.*" With those words, I felt an absent but familiar stirring in my mind.

The beast had been awakened.

She pulled away from me just enough so that I could see her face.

"I must leave you now," she whispered, her expression forlorn. "I have fixed that which you could not mend. The rest is up to you."

I stared up at her with emotions I could not comprehend. Never in my life had I felt such love and peace. Not even from my parents.

"Are you—"

"Give him your love, Ruby," she said before pulling away again, floating off quickly to whence she came. "Give him mine too."

*   *   *

I shot off the ground, gasping for air like someone long submerged under water had just broken the surface. When I opened my eyes, I could see Sean waiting at my side.

"I couldn't get to you," he said softly, caressing my throat gently. "The light...there was so much light..."

"An angel," I whispered, still stunned. "It was an *angel*. She saved me."

His face went blank.

"An angel?" he asked with the hope and awe of a child. "Are you sure?"

"It was your mother, Sean," I told him, sitting myself up to look him in his eyes. "Your mother sent me back."

CHAPTER 34

He said nothing after that.

After a few moments of staring at me blankly, he helped me stand, moving to scoop me up in his arms, but I refused to let him carry me. Although I was slightly weak from the blood loss, it felt good to be able to walk on my own again, and I relished the opportunity to do so. With my sight returned, that burden was lifted off my shoulders.

But another was put upon them. Sight meant Scarlet, and Scarlet meant trouble with Sean. Trouble I wasn't ready to deal with. His mother may have mended that which was broken between Scarlet and myself physically, but she did nothing to restore the trust that was lost—the communication either. Scarlet, though present, was utterly hidden away, and this time it was of her own volition. The growing sense of unease that I felt was hard to contain.

Scarlet feared nothing—or very little, at least. Whatever she was hiding from, consequences or otherwise, could not have been good. I wanted to find out what she had done before Sean could get to her. If damage control was needed, it was in my best interest to be fully prepared.

As Sean and I made our way to the vehicle, he filled me in on the high points of the battle that I had been too busy dying to be an active part of. He'd apparently made short work of Tobias—the *real* one— once his bargaining chip was taken out of the equation. Toby really had been a clever little bugger, organizing everything that had happened to us, from the planned battle in Boston to the ambush at my apartment that led us to believe that all was safe. Sean didn't say much about how he got that information from Tobias before he died, but I'm sure it was both creative and excruciatingly painful. I was sorry I missed that, though I doubted Sean was. He didn't want me to see him in action. He was still sensitive about me seeing what he was capable of.

Who he was capable of being.

To change the subject, I asked how my boys were doing. Sean became slightly guarded at mere mention of them, informing me that Jay and the brothers had rounded them up and taken them back to the first floor of Sean's building. They had to figure out what needed to be done with them. Having been to only the second and third floors of Sean's place, I was a little concerned about what exactly he had set up on the floor I hadn't yet seen.

I wanted to ask him once we got in the car, but I found myself at a loss for words, and, apparently he was too. Nearly the entire drive home was spent in complete silence with only the hum of the BMW's motor to offer some auditory stimulation. I caught him looking at me twice out of the corner of my eye, but I couldn't read his expression. Disbelief, jealousy, love— they were all in there somewhere, but changed too rapidly to tell for sure which one dominated, or who they applied to.

As we pulled into town, Sean was the first to break the quiet between us.

"Where do you want to go?" he asked, eyes still focused on the road.

I hesitated slightly before answering. It was a terribly loaded question. Turning to face him, I whispered three simple words that told him everything he could have ever wanted to know.

"Wherever you are."

His mouth pressed into a thin line in response.

"Then might I suggest not dragging your throat across a blade like that ever again?" he said, with the slightest edge of hostility. "Because I cannot follow you when you are *dead*." An inky black pervaded his irises, swallowing whatever light was present in the dimly lit vehicle. "Not easily..."

"I'm sorry—"

"I know you are, Ruby," he said, taking my hand in his. "And I know why you did it, so let me make something very clear to you right now. Never, under any circumstances, are you to do *anything* that sacrifices your well-being for mine or anyone else's. Do you hear me?"

I nodded silently.

"Say it. Out loud."

"I won't sacrifice myself for you or anyone else I love," I mumbled, knowing that it wasn't entirely true.

"It will never come to that..." he whispered soberly before quickly composing himself. "Promise me you won't."

"I promise."

His black eyes searched mine until he was satisfied with what he saw, then turned back to watch the road as we neared his apartment.

"I have to deal with the boys when I get home. Are you sure you want to go? You may not like what you see," he said hesitantly. He was inviting me into PC business—something he'd never done before. It was an olive branch of sorts, and I was damn sure I was going to take it. I was worried about what was going to happen to Tobias' pack members—if there were any of them still breathing—especially Janner, Ali, and Becks. I didn't want to believe Cooper was in trouble, but I just couldn't be sure that he was out of harm's way either. I needed to see for myself.

We parked the car around back and took an entirely different route into the building. I'd never known it existed. It led to a narrow, darkened tunnel that ended in a small staircase. At the end of that was a single door made of thick reinforced steel. The implications were not pleasant for what I would find inside.

Without a word, Sean unlocked the door with a security code and swung it open for me. I froze when I looked inside. Rows of cells fully equipped with metal bars—better described as beams due to their extreme thickness—welcomed me into the room. It was a jail for the supernatural, and occupying those cells were all those who remained from the old Victorian outside of town. By the looks of it, not many made it out alive.

That thought rattled me and I quickly searched for the faces I needed to see. In the cell closest to me was Janner, and beside him was Becks. Further down was a man I didn't recognize, then another, then Cooper—they'd chained him to the floor for good measure. I could only imagine the fight he put up once he snapped out of Tobias' hold.

I wrenched my head around, trying to locate any other survivors, but couldn't see anyone else from my vantage point. When I tried to step into the room to look more closely, I was stopped short by a hand around my wrist.

"Not yet," Sean warned. "We're not sure what's truth and what's illusion at this point. We don't know that the effects have worn off yet, or if they'll ever wear off at all. I'm not letting you near them until I know for sure."

"But Alistair. I don't see him. Where is he?"

"He isn't here, Ruby," Janner called out, his voice as saddened as the energy that lazily floated my direction. He was devastated.

"Where? Where is he?" I asked, looking to Sean for the answers I didn't have. I'd missed so much while being healed by his mother. Apparently too much.

"He was really badly hurt," Sean replied, his voice low and controlled. "He isn't here."

"How? Who hurt him?"

Sean's grip flinched ever so slightly at my final question, and my heart sank. If Sean was the one to harm him, then I doubted that there was much left intact when he was through.

"What did you do, Sean?" I asked, looking at him with tear-filled eyes.

"What I had to."

I gulped hard against the sob threatening to escape. Deep down I knew that the boys never meant to harm me. Tobias had been using them as pawns for a long time to do his bidding, and collecting me was just another play in his ultimate quest for power. The energy I felt from them that night was as guarded and walled off as ever. Tobias was working hard to keep them in check. But I had felt them when that energy was down, and in those moments, I knew that they were authentic and genuine. Those were the men I feared for—the men I cared about.

"Sean," I started, trying hard to keep my emotions in check. "Where is Ali now?"

His grim expression did nothing to calm me.

"Upstairs. In my apartment."

Not giving him a chance to say anything else, I bolted for the door, and surprisingly, nobody moved to stop me. Not even Sean.

I flew through the outside door and tore around to the front of the building. Taking three steps at a time, I reached the third floor in seconds and slammed the eight-digit code into the keypad. The second it beeped approval, I faltered. What exactly was I going to walk in on and find? Sean wouldn't have left him there unless there was no threat from him, and my guess was that if he was breathing, he'd have been perceived as a liability.

Ignoring the rising panic I felt, I entered the vast space to an unexpected scene. Jay stood, heavily armed, hovering over the couch—and its barely breathing occupant.

"Ali!" I screamed, diving towards him. "Oh my God, you're alive!"

"Easy, Ruby," Jay said, stopping me just before I could get to Alistair. "Don't touch him. It'll only make it worse."

"But...but why? I can help him heal, Jay. I just need to be close enough."

"Ruby," Jay snapped, spinning me by my shoulders to face him. "He's full of silver. Nothing you can do will stop this. You'll only prolong his suffering."

"Then why don't you just put him out of his misery?" I snapped back, thinking that Jay was doing exactly what he accused me of doing.

"Answers," he replied coolly. "Sean wants answers."

Before I could even begin to share my thoughts on his answer, a voice distracted me.

"Ruby?" Alistair called to me. "I'm so sorry. You have to know that—"

"I know you didn't mean to," I replied, choking back my tears. He didn't need to see me fall apart. He needed me to hold my shit together. "Just lay still, please. I'm going to figure something out. Just rest. Save your energy."

I stared Jay down hard, knowing I was likely about to start a fight.

"Why isn't Peyta here?" I growled.

"Sean won't let her near them." His expression was unfazed by my mention of the sprite-like girl that he'd once loved. Likely still loved.

"We'll see about that," I snarled before storming out of the room.

I was in the basement before I knew it, remembering nothing of my trip there. I was on a mission, and my rage was growing. Alistair wasn't going to die that way. Not if I, or Peyta, could help it.

"Sean!" I screamed down the narrow corridor.

He emerged immediately.

"She can't come here," he started, knowing exactly what I was about to demand.

"I can't let him die like this, Sean."

"I know it's hard, Ruby, but there's nothing to be done."

"Goddammit!" I shouted, slamming my fist into the wall, breaking a few bones against the cinderblock for my efforts.

"I'm sorry," he whispered, moving in on me.

"NO!" I spat. "Not now. I can't deal with this now, Sean. You peppered him full of silver!"

"I did what I had to do to keep Tobias from escaping. He used them like shields, Ruby," he growled, eyes darkening. "It was a choice between taking Ali down or Cooper. Would you have preferred the alternative?" My heart stopped cold. "I didn't think so."

"Let me call her, Sean, please. If she wants to do this, will you let her? Will you let her help him if you're there with her? Jay too? Hell, all of you can be there to keep her safe, I don't care. What will it take?"

At some point in my rant, the tears broke free, and I tasted the salty sadness as they rolled over my lips. His expression grew increasingly pained.

"Call her."

I snatched the phone he offered me out of his hand like a greedy child and dialed her. She answered right away.

"Sean? What's wrong?"

"Peyta, it's me. It's one of the new guys, Alistair. He's dying. They used silver on him. He'll never heal it on his own," I cried, unable to control my overwhelming emotions. "Can you help him?"

She paused for only a brief moment before answering.

"Yes. Of course. I'll be right there."

"I'm at Sean's place."

"Okay. There in five."

It was the longest five minutes of my life.

CHAPTER 35

"He's alive," I yelled out to Janner and the others before pushing past Sean to see them. Disregarding his earlier warning, I walked straight into the prison-like room and over to Cooper. Mind control or not, I had to see him.

When I arrived at his cell, he had his back to me, still sitting on the floor and shackled to it. I sat down next to the bars and tried to reach him through them, but he was too far away. And he wouldn't look at me.

"Coop?" I called softly, letting my voice tell him everything was all right. "Cooper, it's me. I'm fine. Please..."

But he wouldn't respond. I started to get anxious and even backed away from the cell slightly, wondering if maybe Tobias' little experiment had permanently damaged him. Or maybe he hadn't snapped out of it at all.

"Cooper, answer me. *Now*," I ordered, trying to quash the fear threatening to overtake me. "I need to know you're okay. That you're *you* again."

With his head hung low, he turned to me slowly, looking every bit as dejected as he clearly felt. His eyes were so filled with sorrow that I could barely stand to look directly into them. Then the wave of guilt and sadness slammed into me, and I nearly fell over from the assault.

"Cooper," I said, reaching for him once again. "I know it wasn't you back there. You have to know that I know that. You never would hurt me or allow me to be hurt."

"But I did, Ruby," he replied, turning his gaze to the floor. "That's exactly what I did. I failed you..."

"But it wasn't your fault."

He ignored me.

"Sean. Please. Can't we let him out?"

"I still can't risk it, Ruby."

"He's right, Rubes. It's too chancy."

I sighed, knowing that I wasn't going to be able to budge either of them on the issue until we had answers.

"Fine," I snipped, looking back into Cooper's cell. "Then I'm coming in."

I stood and marched toward Sean, hellbent on taking the keys from him, but the sound of the hallway entrance opening waylaid my course of action.

"Peyta!"

I sprinted down the hall to meet her, whisking her back outside and around to the front, then up the stairs to Sean's apartment. Jay heard us coming and opened the door to meet us. I felt Peyta freeze beside me when she saw him. Jay looked impassive, but I felt the surge of emotions that seeing Peyta brought out of him. He really did love her.

"There isn't much time," he told us, leading the

way to the couch.

Jay was right. Ali's breathing was more of a shallow and feeble panting—his color pale and sallow. A light dew covered him and glistened in the moonlight pouring in through the vast wall of windows near the couch. He had minutes left at best.

Without further provocation, Peyta was by Ali's side assessing the situation like a pro. It was a proud and sad moment for me. She was trying to embrace her calling, but I wished she didn't have to. The price she paid was too high.

Sean placed his hand on the back of my neck, scaring the shit out of me. I hadn't heard him come in.

"She's truly amazing," he whispered in my ear. My hair reflexively stood on end.

"I know," I replied as I looked on. Watching Peyta heal was anticlimactic to say the least, which only illustrated further how gifted she was. She was a complete contrast to Sophie, making me wonder if all the Healers had their own methods, or if Peyta was one of a kind.

I guess I already knew the answer to that.

Ali's body slowly repaired itself right before my eyes, lessening the sharp pain in my heart. It was strange to watch the shimmery silver droplets press up out of his wounds and solidify on his chest and abdomen, but with every bit that came up, his complexion rosied, enlivening his appearance.

"Ruby," she called, not turning her focus away from her patient. "Come collect these silver pieces for me, please. And take his shirt off too. I don't want anything residual getting into the wounds that haven't closed yet."

I did as she bade me and picked the fine beads of

metal off of his body, delicately removing his tattered shirt in the process. A flash of light brought my attention up to the dog tags still hanging around his neck—a token of his bond to the London pack. I wanted to tear them off and destroy them. Instead, I reached up and pulled them over his neck as gingerly as possible. He didn't belong to them anymore.

The second I touched them Scarlet growled viciously in my mind.

Get rid of them now...

"Why? What's wrong?" I asked, looking like the crazy girl who talked to herself yet again. I hadn't missed that.

That sound. Can you not hear it? It's maddening. Get rid of them!

"Oh my God...," I whispered, staring down at the seemingly innocuous chain in my hand. "Sean, it's the tags! Take them off of the others. Now!"

I tossed them at him, and for a split second he hesitated, then sent Jay down to remove the items in question from his prisoners. The keys to Tobias' mind control.

You truly couldn't sense that, could you?

"No, I didn't feel—hear—sense anything."

There was a humming...a vibration before, but the second you touched them, it was unbearable.

"I'm going to send them to Trey for analysis," Sean interjected. "He'll find whatever is hidden in those dog tags." His eyes widened and faded to black. "And then I'll find whoever made them."

"Tobias knows," Ali's hoarse voice called from the couch. "Ask him."

"I'm afraid he's a little too dead for that, Alistair," Sean told him grimly. "Time for plan B."

"And what's that?" I asked, feeling a little nervous.

"I think I'll be making a trip across the pond again. Tobias can't be the only one who knew about this. Whoever his second in command was is likely to know as well. He and I are going to have a chat."

Alistair began to push himself up off of the sofa, and Sean quickly scooped Peyta off of the floor and put her down safely behind him. He wasn't going to risk anything happening to her, and rightfully so. She was the best thing to happen to the PC in centuries.

"I've got the dog tags," Jay called from somewhere near the bottom of the stairwell.

"Call Trey. Tell him we have a pickup for him and to get on it now. And tell the boys to let the others out now. The random survivors can be released to Trey when he arrives. As for the others, bring them up here."

"Do you think he can sort it out?" I asked Sean, worried about the implications of Trey failing.

"We shall soon see."

Sean's gaze fell on Alistair, who was rapidly gaining his strength back. He stood before me looking only a little worse for the wear.

"*You*," Sean rumbled, "have some explaining to do."

Much to my surprise, Ali didn't say anything even remotely belligerent. He may have detested Sean, but he knew that he was right. He did have explaining to do, but not to Sean—to me and Cooper. Just as I was thinking that, Ali's submissive eyes took a chance on meeting mine. The sadness in them was painful to see.

"Ruby," he started, quickly averting his gaze. "I don't even know where to start."

"Try from the beginning," Cooper ordered from

deep in the hallway outside. "I wanted them to keep you all alive, but that was only because I wanted to hear the truth, and I'd better get just that. To my *satisfaction*."

Cooper was clearly back to normal.

"Not everything was a lie. The missing wolves part was true. They did kill Jemma too," he said, again looking up at me, this time with tears in his eyes. "They killed her stone cold dead."

"And the rest?" Sean prodded.

Ali sighed.

"The rest was partial truths smattered with lies." His expression was pained but frustrated. "It's hard to discern what's real and what's not anymore. We've had those tags for a long time now. Much has happened since we were given them. I just don't know..."

"He speaks the truth," Janner added, joining the party in the living room. "Truth and fiction were so interwoven that, now, it's hard to tell one from the other. You have to understand that we never consciously knew what Tobias' plans were or that he was even using us at all. He orchestrated this entire thing—let us go on purpose—then strategically guided us along the way." His eyes fell to the floor, ashamed of what had happened. "I'm certain now that our meeting was hardly a chance encounter."

"Did you come here to take her away?" Cooper asked, his eyes harboring the tiniest glint of gold in them. "I would answer that question *very* carefully, friend."

"It is as I said, Cooper. Fact is too hard to filter from falsehood right now. It's as though two separate parts of our brains ran at the same time. We were, for all intents and purposes, our true selves. The moments where we truly felt like we were one of you were genuine. They were our stories, our personalities, our accounts of how events unfolded, at least for the most part. Other times...I just can't explain it. I can't remember saying or doing certain things that led us to this point, but I *know* they happened because I can clearly replay them in my mind. Whatever Tobias stumbled upon is a truly frightening creation. You don't realize what's happening to you even as it's happening. There is no conscious action, even though there is consciousness."

"I don't believe you," Cooper growled. "Part of me knew that what I was doing was wrong, I just couldn't remember why."

"Yes," Beckett said, coming to stand beside Janner. "But you had only just started wearing Deacon's tags and you're Ruby's alpha. Your connection to her is much stronger than ours. We've worn our tags for far longer than I can remember. We've become desensitized to the feeling you speak of, but I know it. I had it too, once. The way he started with us was so slow and subtle that we never really realized what was going on."

While Cooper and Sean grilled the three men, I tried to reach out for what they were feeling, and more importantly, to see if I could detect any of that strange reserved energy that I picked up from them previously. There wasn't an ounce of it left. Whatever hold Tobias had once had on them was gone. For good. The question that plagued my mind was, if they could be controlled once, could they be manipulated again?

I realized that Cooper was asking me something and snapped out of my trance-like state.

"What do you think?" he asked, looking fully annoyed that he'd had to repeat himself. "Should they stay or leave?"

"Stay."

My voice was firm as was my stance on the issue. They were not a threat to me, or anyone else for that matter—not any longer. Furthermore, it wasn't their fault. Would I hold their unconscious actions against them? Would I want whatever mess Scarlet had caused in my absence held against me? I cringed at that thought, thinking that was a conversation I still had to have with her.

Sean inhaled deeply and slowly beside me. He wasn't happy with my plan.

"And do I have a say in this?" he asked, cocking his eyebrow at me. It wasn't in a playful way, though I wished it had been.

"What is your say?" I was avoiding his question with another one, which usually worked about as well as trying to outrun him, but I threw it out there anyway to see what would happen.

"I don't like it," he informed me, "but I suppose if certain ground rules are laid and Cooper agrees, I will allow it."

The Maine boys and I whipped our collective heads toward Cooper to see what his final deciding vote would be. He looked as uneasy as Sean felt. With a loud sigh, he delivered his verdict.

"They can stay." I squealed, then stifled the rest of it to let him finish. The look he flashed me informed me that I was interrupting the rest of his speech. "But on one condition. They answer to *me*. They are mine— part of the pack, and all that that implies." Janner looked relieved. Beckett looked indifferent. Alistair looked sad. "And if any of you fuck up in the slightest, you're dead, understand?"

They all nodded once.

"I'm trusting you to handle this, Cooper," Sean said in tone that let Cooper know who was *really* in charge. "Don't make me live to regret it."

The two formidable men eyed each other tightly, saying nothing. The tension grew by the second, and I just couldn't deal. Something had to give.

"Group hug!" I shouted, diving at the newest pack members. They laughed at me as always, but loosened up enough to let me know that there was genuine affection on their end. "Cooper, get in here," I ordered mockingly. "Come feel the love, big guy. It's a beautiful thing."

"I'm good," he replied, still standing next to Sean. "I'm getting tons of love over here. No need for more."

After getting my squeeze on with the new guys, I turned to address the brooding duo a few feet away from me. A quick scan of the room alerted me to a glaring absence. Two absences, actually.

"Where's Peyta?" I asked, moving toward the door to get a clearer view of the room. "And Jay?"

Just as the others began to look concerned, a voice from the stairwell calmed them all.

"Out here," Jay called, sounding mildly sheepish. He opened the front door and walked in with Peyta trailing behind him, her hand clasping tightly to his. It made me smile.

"So," I started in my most badgering tone. "What have you two been doing? Did you get everything all worked out?"

"We're good, Ruby," Peyta replied, blushing slightly. "We had a little talk."

"Oh, did you? And did you talk about *everything*?" The look I gave her was one of warning—one that said that now was the time to air her dirty laundry to him and not keep it a secret. I knew a lot about how badly that approach ended.

"Yes. *Everything.*"

I smiled and gave her a nod of approval. She blushed slightly and tucked her head in close to Jay's arm, sheltering her emotions from her audience.

"Sean," Jay said, sounding uncharacteristically formal. "I wish to be bound to Peyta. It is your job to pick the Healer for the PC and bind her to us, but we have chosen each other. What is to be done?"

Sean looked pensive for a moment, weighing something heavily in his mind. It was the moment I'd feared and dutifully ignored for months. I'd always hated the thought of Peyta being tethered to our life of violence, but eventually reconciled the fact that it was who she was. It was meant to be. Official or not, she was already surrounded by the chaos that the supernatural world was fraught with. That was a fact I had slowly come to terms with.

What I hadn't come to terms with was knowing that Sean would have to be the one to bind her to the brothers.

"I will find a solution, Jay," he said finally, breaking the silence that had been growing. "For both our sakes, I will find a way." Peyta bolted for Sean and did one of her flying squirrel moves, latching onto him at the last second and hugging him violently. "You're welcome, Peyta," he said, wrapping his arms around her tiny frame, emphasizing their vast size difference.

"Um, P?" Cooper had the most perplexed look on his face. "Isn't your mother going to shit a brick when she hears about this little marriage idea? What exactly are you going to tell her? She doesn't even know what

Jay is, and thinking he's a werewolf isn't any better. And then there's your whole age issue..."

"I'll deal with her," she said, climbing down from Sean. "She's so happy lately that I'm not even sure it'll be a problem."

"Well, either way, I would make sure the firearms aren't loaded first. And make sure Jay isn't with you. It'll be safer for everyone."

Peyta and I gave each other a knowing glance then started to giggle.

"That's a problem for another day," Sean informed us over the laughter. "It's late. Time for everyone to go."

Cooper made his way over to me and scooped me up, lifting me easily off the ground.

"I'm sorry, Rubes," he whispered in my ear.

"Water under the bridge," I whispered back. "I love you, Coop. That guy—he wasn't you. For my sake, please, let it go." He gave me a parting squeeze then set me down on the ground.

"Alice, Jan, Becky: you three ready to head out?"

Their looks were murderous, especially Alistair's, but it was all for show. They were excited to have a new home, a new pack, and maybe, one day, a new family. I knew what it was like to feel that way.

The PC brothers had slowly filed out over the course of the evening, once Sean realized the trio wasn't a threat to anyone without their tags. Peyta and Jay hesitated for a moment at the door, undoubtedly not wanting to have to part from one another. Ronnie wasn't going to be jazzed about Jay sleeping over without the presence of danger, and we all knew it.

"Peyta, do you guys want to go to my place?" I asked the pining pixie.

"Can we? I'll call mom and tell her I'll be crashing with you."

"That's fine. Go ahead."

The two smiled in unison at me before heading out the door together, still hand in hand. As I watched them leave, I realized that everyone was crashing at my house but me, and it made me feel left out. I looked up at Sean with tired but saddened eyes. Instead of being met with the uncertain, closed-off look I expected, I got one of my favorites—the Cheshire cat smile.

"You want to stay at your place, don't you?" His question was a formality; he already knew the answer.

I nodded.

"I want to give you something first," he said, reaching into the neck of his shirt to pull out a chain. A chain with my platinum ring dangling at the end. "It seems like now would be a good time to return this."

"My ring...how long have you had this?" I asked, wondering how I hadn't noticed it before.

"I've worn it since the moment I could retrieve it from the floor the night Scarlet took you from me. I felt closer to you with it on..."

"But you said that you eventually thought I wanted to stay gone, like I wanted to be away from you."

He shrugged in response.

"The heart does not always make sense, Ruby. It wants what it wants, even if what it desires does not want it back. Keeping this with me reminded me that you and I will always be connected—for better or worse."

He unclasped the chain, sliding the ring off of it to hand it to me. I looked at it momentarily before tucking it away safely in my pocket. I had only just gotten Scarlet back. I did not wish to see if placing the ring on my finger would cage her once again.

"Thank you," I whispered, averting my gaze, "for not giving up on me."

"My fear and my ego drove me to believe that you chose to leave me. I could not find you...my failure was more than I could bear, but my heart never believed you would abandon me. You are mine..."

"And you are mine," I countered, a seductive smile playing across my lips.

It pulled the most delightful rumble from deep within his chest, a possessive noise that made my legs weak and my heart race. He would always claim me as his.

And I would always let him.

"Let's go then. I want to make sure none of them crash in your room. I refuse to sleep on the floor."

I cocked my eyebrow at him and threw as much sauciness as I could into my voice. "Who said I'm letting you sleep? I nearly died tonight; I don't want to sleep. I want to feel *alive*." His eyes widened and darkened to alarming levels. It seemed he liked my plan.

"Alive...," he said softly, stroking the side of my face. "Let's keep you that way, shall we? And be sure to tell Scarlet that she and I will still be having that little chat soon. She has some explaining to do."

And boy did she ever. Three weeks was a long time for her to do all sorts of horrific things, including rack up a body count. I hoped she'd be forthcoming with the facts, but knowing her, that was a total pipe dream. She'd been as quiet as a mouse since her return, and I couldn't help but feel that her silence didn't bode well for any of us.

"She does indeed," I agreed before turning the tables on him, "but so do you—like how you knew where I was, or what had happened? I know you know everything, Sean, but that was a stretch, even for you."

"I had a little help," he replied, guiding me out of his apartment.

"Help?"

"Yes. I'd say that your *Boy Scout* earned himself another merit badge tonight."

"Matty?" I blurted out, utterly stunned.

"I'm inclined to say that he and I are even now," he continued while descending the stairs to the second floor. "He was trailing you. He has been for a while. At the first sign of an ambush, he went to Peyta and gave a detailed description of where Cooper had taken you. The rest...well, you know that part."

I felt an overwhelming sense of gratitude and guilt. After all that had happened, Matty still wanted to keep me safe like he always had, and I was immensely thankful for that. My guilt was in knowing that I had no idea how to return the favor.

Matty was on borrowed time, and I knew it.

CHAPTER 36

My promise of not sleeping was a complete farce. We arrived at my apartment to find bodies lying all around the living room—alive, but snoring. Cooper had the couch and the boys peppered the floor around it. I assumed that Peyta and Jay took Cooper's room, unsure as to whether or not Sean and I would be returning.

I fell asleep the second I hit my bed, bloody clothes and all, which surely amused Sean to no end. He knew I'd been full of it back at his place, and I gave him all the ammunition necessary to never let me live it down. My hope was that he crashed just as quickly.

Sleep may have come easily, but it didn't stay long. I woke up with an uneasy feeling in my stomach that I just couldn't stifle. I decided to have a shower and clean off the reminders of what had happened, then try to go to bed again. I was ruining my good sheets.

Five minutes later, I emerged from the bathroom—clean clothes, wet hair, and all. I sneaked down the hall to my room as quietly as the old wooden floor would allow and crept into bed, not wanting to wake Sean, who was sleeping peacefully. I loved seeing him that way.

Just as I was drifting off, I felt him there, hovering over my side of the bed staring down at me. In the light of the moon, I could see through Matty's form to the dresser directly behind him. Given that Peyta was most likely in the room next to us, I knew it wasn't a good sign.

The expression he wore didn't help matters.

He went to speak, but I shushed him quickly with an index finger to my mouth. Sean was still sleeping soundly beside me, and I didn't dare wake him. I signaled for Matty to head out of the room before I precariously wormed my way out from under Sean's arm. My apartment was chilly, but I didn't want to make a ruckus searching my room for something warm to put on, so I slipped out of the room in my tanktop and underwear.

Tiptoeing my way down the hall, I realized it would take a small miracle to not wake anyone else in my quest for privacy. A living room full of werewolves, albeit sleeping ones, was not going to be an easy obstacle to overcome. I managed to make it to the door without incident, but just as I shifted my weight to reach for the knob, the floor let out a groan and Alistair stirred next to the armchair he was passed out beside. I held my breath, waiting to see if my plan was foiled before it was even in play. Luckily, he wriggled around for a moment before settling back down into his deep slumber.

With a silent sigh, I made it out the apartment door and found a very transparent Matty waiting for me on the landing. I carefully walked around him—though I could easily have gone right through him—and continued on toward the studio upstairs, trying desperately to keep the growing concern from my face. The amount his held was more than enough for the both of us.

The instant we entered the third floor space he started in on me.

"Something's wrong, Ruby," he said, his voice weak and distant. My heart sank instantly—he was fading, just as Peyta had warned.

I instinctively reached for him, but was met with nothing but cold air when my hand passed through him effortlessly. My ragged breath caught in my throat as it tightened. I was not ready for this inevitability.

"What do I do?" he asked, eyes pleading. I had nothing helpful to offer.

"Maybe I should get Peyta," I whispered, staring at him blankly while my eyes stung with the welling tears.

"Don't go!" he called out, reaching for me.

"I can't help you." I choked on the words as they left my mouth. Had I ever done anything to help Matty, or did I only cause him greater amounts of pain? "I'm going to go wake her. She'll know what to do."

"I'm fading, aren't I?" he asked, attempting to regain composure.

"We don't know that," I replied. I had to turn away from him so he wouldn't see the tear escape down my cheek.

"You *do* know. Tell me. Now!"

"I can't."

"You *can*," he demanded, flashing in front of me. "Tell me!"

"YES!" I screamed. "You're fading. It's exactly as

Peyta described it. But I'm not ready. I'm not ready to lose you again. I just got you back!"

So much for my attempts to not wake anyone. I was in full-on freak-out mode. I knew it would only be moments before we were joined by everyone downstairs.

"So this is goodbye this time? For real?"

I couldn't force the word 'yes' out of my mouth, even though I knew it was true.

Before I could offer a placating response of any sort, a stampede of supernaturals came barreling through the door, with Sean and Cooper leading the pack. One look at the two of us stopped them all in their tracks, like they'd just walked in on the most intimate of moments.

They sort of had.

"Oh, Matty," Peyta whispered, her eyes full of pity. She couldn't bring herself to say what I chose not to acknowledge. It was the last time we'd ever see him again.

CHAPTER 37

We stood in the room, staring at each other silently. I'd already lost him once—the thought of doing it again was beyond comprehension. I prayed for a way to keep him, but even I, in all my denial, could not ignore the growing white mist that crept toward him from the far mirrors. The pearlescent glow was one I knew well. I'd seen it before.

"It's time," Peyta whispered from somewhere in the room. I was too preoccupied to care.

"It would make this so much easier if you weren't looking at me like this was going to crush you, Ruby," Matty declared with a wan smile.

If only he'd known how true his words were.

He stole a look over his shoulder at the inviting white cloud that beckoned him home. I glared at it with a hatred so cold that my whole body numbed. If I'd known how to fight God himself, I would have challenged him without pause. Matty never deserved the hand he was dealt, and I wanted more than anything to keep him from his fate. He may have believed that heaven was better than anything earth had to offer, but I lacked his faith and was far too selfish to care even if he was right.

He advanced towards his new home, and I reflexively dove after him.

"You can't go, Ruby," he said, holding me at bay with his expression. "It's okay. I'll be all right."

"Matty," I whispered, unable to fight back my tears.

"I'm not leaving you, Ruby. Nobody can. Whenever you dance, I'll be right there with you."

And with that, he was gone.

I stormed the clearing mist, crashing into the mirror, screaming his name repeatedly. For the briefest moment, I saw his image looking back at me from within it, but it faded fast. Much too fast. My fingertips pressed the cold glass, trailing oh-so slowly down, unwillingly giving up their fight to claim him from where he'd gone.

I felt nothing.

I needed to feel *something*.

My fists slammed the reflective surface that had stolen my friend. Over and over again, I pounded it until glass shards and blood rained down around me. Pain shot through my arms, filling the emptiness that Matty's death had left.

It was a start.

As I pummeled the wall before me until my knuckles were broken and mangled, I felt an arm encircle my waist, pulling me away from my therapy.

"NO!" I screamed, flailing against my captor.

"Ruby, stop," Sean whispered, trying to pin my arms down with his.

I struggled against him, my blood boiling with rage. Out—I had to get it out, and he was denying me the only outlet that I'd found comfort in. While he spoke low and soothing words, I thought I would explode, and continued to fight in vain to escape the confines of his grasp.

Finally, with my frustration hitting a fever pitch, I screamed. An unholy sound that threatened to overwhelm the very fiber of my being vibrated out of my body, releasing the evil I felt. I strained hard against Sean, bending away from him, curling over his arms as the sound continued to purge itself. It seemed to last forever.

Once it ended, my legs gave way and I crumpled in Sean's hold. My body was weak—my anger gone. But instead of the emptiness returning, a sadness so penetrating impaled my heart, stopping it short. I didn't care. Caring took energy I no longer had.

He lowered me down carefully, curling his body around mine protectively until we knelt on the floor together. We'd been in a similar situation a year earlier, only that time we were face to face. This time, Sean engulfed me from behind, whispering unintelligible words in my ear soothingly.

"He's gone, Ruby," he said, finally reaching my barely coherent mind. "But I am not. I am here with you now, and I will be with you until the end of time. You may fall apart, but I will *always* pick up the pieces. There is nothing that can keep you from me."

I turned beneath him to see his face. His eyes burned brightly, though framed by a pained expression. "You and I are beyond this world, Ruby. Beyond love."

"Will it stop?" I asked, still barely able to breathe. "The pain? Will it stop?"

He pressed his lips tightly together in a sympathetic gesture, pushing a strand of loose hair out of my face.

"No. It won't," he said softly. "But it will subside. You have to learn to coexist with pain, Ruby. It's not black and white. Not a war you can win. If you keep trying to defeat it, it will erode you inside until you're nothing but a shell of the person you once were. Let me help you."

The stake that impaled me was torn out, releasing my heart—releasing my emotions. I sobbed, unable to contain the sadness, no longer able to control the things I longed to hide away and ignore. I fell forward but Sean was there, catching me before I slammed to the floor, scooping me up in his arms with ease.

He turned to make his way to the exit, and I was reminded that we were not alone. A wall of sad faces met mine, some showing the signs of their own emotional outbursts. I couldn't endure their stares, so I shifted in Sean's arms, clinging to him like a child. With my face buried deep in his neck, I no longer had to face them, but I did have to contend with their sorrowful energies invading mine. Sean whisked me out of there quickly, as if he knew what their pain and sympathy was doing to me. We were downstairs in seconds and tucked away in my bedroom, blocking off the majority of the assault.

He soothed me to sleep, muttering in a language I couldn't understand and didn't need to. His love was apparent regardless. With me clutched in his arms, I eventually fell asleep, and for once, the nightmares stayed away.

CHAPTER 38

I awoke to a cacophony of sound in my living room. When I saw that it was only 7:17 a.m., I sprang out of bed to see what was going on. Alone in my room, I grabbed a bathrobe to cover up with and stormed out into the hallway to find the source of the ruckus. I wasn't at all prepared for what I saw.

The newbies were playing soccer with a tennis ball, banking it off of the walls, the furniture, and any other surface they found beneficial to their game. Peyta sat on the couch, constantly ducking the flying object while Jay hovered by the front door, trying not to laugh and failing miserably at it.

As I moved further down the hall, I saw the most distressing sight of all. Cooper and Sean were in the kitchen—together—attempting to make breakfast, all while having their usual power struggle. They bickered back and forth about who should be doing what and how and where; I never knew there could be so much to debate about frying eggs.

With all the commotion, nobody seemed to notice my presence, so I leaned against the hallway wall and soaked in all the craziness. That was to be my new life, and it strangely made me smile. Perhaps my definition of family wasn't textbook perfect, but as I silently watched them all creating chaos and shenanigans in my apartment, I was glad it wasn't.

Maybe Merriam-Webster didn't know shit.

EPILOGUE

Weeks went by without any drama.

Jay and Sean spent a fair amount of time traveling back and forth to the UK, trying to search for whoever was responsible for the technology that had nearly led to my demise—or did, depending on how you looked at it. Their efforts turned up nothing more than dead ends and missing pack members. Unfortunately, they were dead too.

The boys were acclimating to their new home well, all things considered. After a lot of thought, I decided to remodel my dance loft into an apartment for them, even though they insisted that the accommodations were fine. Cooper had wanted to find them a place in town, but I shut that down. I could feel that, for once, they felt like they truly belonged somewhere, and I just couldn't bring myself to force them out on their own. Cooper got on board with my idea after I pointed out that *he* still lived with me for that very reason. It felt good to be constantly around people who loved you.

The boys may have been settling in well, but Scarlet was not. She and I were left to once again try to navigate our mending relationship, and it was not going smoothly. She rarely spoke to me and wanted nothing to do with coming out. She may have been back, but she wasn't back to normal.

Sean's hostility toward her didn't seem to help matters much. I guess if I had known that his dark-eyed persona was waiting to grill me, I wouldn't have been too excited about showing myself either. I needed to know what happened while she was loose and I was caged, so that if anything required cleaning up, it could be done sooner rather than later. She appeared to prefer the later option—much, much later at the rate we were going.

One relationship that was doing well was Peyta's and Jay's. They were more in love than ever, and I had the distinct pleasure of hearing about it constantly at the shop. If she wasn't gushing about Jay, she was rambling on about how changed her mother was since she and Malcolm had started dating. Ronnie even put her firearms away. As happy as I was that Peyta enjoyed this new side of her mother, I couldn't help but be leery of it. I wanted to check her for dog tags just to be sure her mind wasn't being controlled too. Somehow, I knew the gesture wouldn't have been appreciated.

Peyta did mention that her mother was inquiring a lot more about Jay—his history, his relationship to the others in his pack, and other pointed questions that had me a bit unsettled. Even though Ronnie had softened, I knew she hadn't changed overnight. She was shrewd and mildly paranoid, a deadly combination for sure. I was worried that she was onto something about the PC or had finally seen enough of Peyta in action to truly start to wonder why she'd never heard of something like her before. Ronnie knew more about werewolves and pack life than I did. Happy and in love or not, she wasn't going to keep buying our cover story forever.

From cover stories to cover-ups, the McGurney mystery still remained unsolved. Knowing that something was off about the murder, Alan insisted on investigating, with or without my help, but he started to respect the boundaries that he and I had to operate under. He started treating me more like the days of old, but clearly had reservations, especially when it came to me being around his family. After everything that had happened, it was understandable, but I felt like he knew that, when it was all said and done, I was on his side. I wanted to know what had happened to McGurney too—only for very different reasons.

We never seemed to find a good time to discuss the letter he had attempted to show me at my apartment. Whenever we thought the coast was clear, Kristy would show up and we would be forced to curtail our discussion. It wasn't a matter he wanted to discuss over the phone or at the precinct, and coming to my place was out of the question, so our options were limited. As time went on, she seemed to make it harder and harder for us to be alone, but the bottom line was that I was going to see what was on that paper—before anyone else did.

As much as I wanted my life to stay drama-free, I was a hardcore realist. Knowing that chaos was an inevitability, I nervously waited for the other shoe to drop. Eventually, that drop came in the form of a bizarre dream I had not long after the Tobias showdown. Sean had just come back from the UK for that last time and we'd just spent an amazing night together. Apparently it was a little too amazing for the Universe's liking.

In the middle of the night, I shot up in bed, startling Sean awake beside me. He immediately drilled me with questions while I tried to wrap my head around what I'd just heard in my sleep. I had become accustomed to *seeing* things that jarred me from my slumber. I wasn't used to only hearing them.

Sean's mother sounded positively frightened.

She said only one thing—a warning. "He must find her first—the *Unborn* one. She is safe no longer. If they find her first, she will die." Then she disappeared.

When I told Sean what she said, he seemed just as confused as I did. Who was this mystery *she*, and why did Sean have to find her? I hoped that his mother would return to me again and expand on her enigmatic message, but she never did—I never heard from her again. So Sean and I were left with a sense of urgency for some person whom neither of us knew how to find. Scarlet was no help either. Sean had yet another mystery to solve with no leads, no clues, and a potentially fatal outcome for the one he sought, though for once, that death would not be by his hands.

Then there was Gavin.

It didn't seem to matter how much time I spent around him over those weeks or how many cryptic conversations we had, I just couldn't get a real read on him. I knew he wasn't going to hurt me directly, but something about him was off. I constantly felt that he had an agenda, and that somehow I was an important piece of it.

I wasn't a fan of feeling like a pawn, nor did I like the potential of actually being one, but Gavin had answers—answers I wanted—like who the woman in the photo was and what terrible things Sean had done in the past to make Gavin loathe him like he did. I wondered if those two issues didn't somehow go hand in hand. I wanted the truth at any cost, but I still wasn't willing to risk asking Sean, playing right into Gavin's deviously crafted hand. Instead, I was determined to find a way to drag it out of the Chameleon directly. My biggest fear was that once I got it out, I'd immediately want to put it back in.

I would soon learn that Pandora's box was not so easily shut.

CONNECT WITH AMBER LYNN NATUSCH

I want to hear from you!
Here's your chance to connect with Amber Lynn
Natusch and other readers!
Tweet or Facebook your loves, favorite scenes, crushes,
etc.

Tweet @AmberLNatusch

facebook.com/amberlynnnatusch

Please take a moment to go online (Amazon, B&N,
Goodreads, Kobo, etc.) and leave a review to encourage
others to take a chance on Ruby just like you did!
Your support is greatly appreciated; I couldn't do it
without you!

For more on the Caged Series check out my sites:
amberlynnnatusch.com
facebook.com/amberlynnnatusch

Also By
Amber Lynn Natusch

CAGED Series
CAGED
HAUNTED
FRAMED
SCARRED
FRACTURED
TARNISHED (novella)
STRAYED
CONCEALED (novella)
BETRAYED

UNBORN Series
UNBORN (forthcoming)

Light and Shadow Trilogy
Co-Authored With Shannon Morton:
Tempted By Evil
Tried By Fire
Tested By Faith

About the Author

I'm so over talking about myself and my foibles that I thought I would talk about you, the fans, and how much your quirkiness matters to me (and all the fun little things I've picked up about you all as I've gotten to know you). This should be good...

Amber fans are a rare breed. They're the ones that ignore all important duties when they have a great book in hand. They have a penchant for sarcasm, without which my books would be utterly lost on them. They understand comedic timing, which is sorely underrated these days. Made-up words do not go over their heads. Terms like clusterfuck, creeptastic, and shenaniganery make complete sense to them. They don't shy away from a good bloodbath but can also appreciate a romantic glance, a tender expression, or the fact that love doesn't have to equal sex (though sometimes it's REALLY nice when it does). Lastly, they're just a little off, and I mean that in the best way possible. Who wants streamlined and boring? Not me...give me the crazy, off-color, closet-case-freak-flag-waving kids any day of the week. They never disappoint.

Thanks for being such amazing fans, guys. It does not go unappreciated.